FIRST SHOT

JOHN RYDER

Published by Bookouture in 2020

An imprint of Storyfire Ltd.
Carmelite House
50 Victoria Embankment
London EC4Y 0DZ

www.bookouture.com

ISBN: 978-1-83888-753-7
eBook ISBN: 978-1-83888-752-0

This book is a work of fiction. Names, characters, businesses,
organizations, places and events other than those clearly in the
public domain, are either the product of the author's imagination
or are used fictitiously. Any resemblance to actual persons, living or
dead, events or locales is entirely coincidental.

For my son, a source of constant pride

PROLOGUE

The diner was neither good nor bad. It was a place for humans to refuel, nothing more, nothing less. A server with a life-can't-kick-me-any-further-down attitude was bussing tables and there was an assortment of customers.

Off to one side a large man was munching on a burger and drinking endless cups of coffee. In the booth opposite them a man in a sharp suit was eyeing the menu with suspicion. Over by the door a woman with blonde hair and blue eyes was reaching into her purse.

The only blue-eyed blonde in the diner who mattered to Brad was the one sitting opposite him. Three weeks had passed since Lila had said yes and he was still amazed at his luck. She was beautiful in every way; her inner and outer beauty radiated from her. She was good-looking enough to turn heads, but for Brad, Lila's best quality was her heart. Lila put others first at all times, raised money for charity and never once gave a second thought to herself when others needed her help. She saw the best in people rather than the worst, and even when confronted by the least pleasant examples of the human race, she fought to find a redeeming quality about them.

Lila was beautiful, sexy and caring, but right now none of those qualities were showing because she was pissed. Not at Brad, but at herself for the wistful it'll-be-fun-to-get-off-the-interstate-for-a-few-miles impulse she'd had. Brad had cautioned that, as spontaneous as the idea was, they were traveling through Georgia, so there was a strong possibility that they would see nothing but trees and road.

Six hours of driving had proven him right and Lila wrong. They'd chatted as they'd driven and sung along with the tunes blasting from Lila's iPod, but the long empty roads provided little stimulus and even less entertainment. Even the act of pulling over to refuel both car and passengers had been a non-event.

Daversville was a carbon copy of any small town in the States. The local industry may vary from town to town and the names above the mom-and-pop stores would be different, but essentially these towns were all the same.

A wide main street, often lined by stores, sometimes a police station, a doctor's office or town hall. One or more of the roads intersecting the main street might house services such as attorneys, realtors and dentists. Somewhere in the town would be a school and always a couple of bars.

A lot of the places they had driven through had boasted a gas station or a roadside motel. Daversville had neither; and from what Brad had observed, there was little need for a hotel in the town.

Brad chomped on his burger as Lila used a fork to clear the salad garnish from his plate. She was a fraction his size and had what Brad judged to be a quarter of his appetite. Their friends teased them about their likeness to Beauty and the Beast, due to Lila's good looks and Brad's size.

Back in college Brad had been the football team's wide receiver despite being big enough to play as a linebacker. It wasn't so much that he was fast, he was just so big he took a lot of stopping once he got going.

Lila placed the fork on the table and used a napkin to dab at the corners of her mouth. "Back in a minute."

Brad nodded and reached for another handful of fries. Lila was going outside for a cigarette. Smoking was her one bad habit. But she didn't smoke in the house or the car, so, he reasoned, if she chose to go out and have a cigarette a few times a day that was her business.

The last of the fries were cooling when Brad shoveled them into his mouth and stood ready to follow Lila out. As he dropped a few bills on the table to pay for the meal he noticed the server was watching him. It wasn't just the look of someone calculating the size of the tip, it was deeper than that, almost as if there was a hidden agenda.

He shook the idea off and stretched his frame back and forth until he felt some circulation returning to his muscles.

As he was lifting his phone from the table, the server came over, her eyes looking anywhere but at Brad. Her head was tilted so far forward her chin brushed her collarbone. There was no form to her body; her shoulders slumped with dejection, and her sneaker-clad feet scuffed the tiled floor at every step.

Brad flashed a pleasant look her way as he eased his bulk from where it was wedged between the table and the booth's seats.

"Your girl is in danger. Get out of town right now and don't come back. Don't speak to me, don't ask me no questions. Just go now before it's too late."

To Brad the server's warning was a piece of fantastical nonsense. Being a city boy he passed the server's comment off as nothing more than a closed-off small-town mentality. He nodded a polite thank-you and went outside to join Lila. She'd laugh her head off when he told her what the server said.

Except when he left the diner, Lila wasn't anywhere to be seen…

CHAPTER ONE

Six days later

The area of scorched asphalt was right where Brad had said it would be. In light of this, Fletcher made sure the sedan he'd rented at Hartsfield-Jackson was parked in a spot that would let him leave the parking lot in a hurry should anyone start tossing Molotov cocktails his way.

Fletcher had taken a call from an old forces buddy—Don Ogilvie, ex-US Marine; they met in Helmand Province in Afghanistan. Fletcher was with the Royal Marines. For all the natural inter-service rivalry, Fletcher had become friends with the second-generation Irish-American in a short time, and when Don suffered life-changing injuries saving Fletcher's life, their friendship had been cemented forever.

It had been an average day on patrol. Hot sun, heavy pack and an ever-present threat. Don had been watching the north side of the street and Fletcher the south. Before Fletcher knew what was happening Don tackled him, and they fell into an alleyway. The rocket launcher Don had spotted being shouldered spat forth its deadly load and the shell exploded six feet from their position. Don's legs protruded from the alley, and the blast had peppered them with shrapnel, leaving him wheelchair-bound. Had Don not tackled Fletcher, he would have made it safely into the alley with time to spare, but it wasn't in Don's character to put himself before anyone else. It was an act of selflessness Fletcher could never repay, so when Don had told him about Lila going missing, he'd not hesitated to respond to Don's request that he travel to Daversville to look for Lila. In fact, if Don hadn't asked, he would have offered.

Don's daughter, Lila, and her fiancé, Brad, had been on their way north from Florida when they'd stopped at the diner in Daversville. Lila had gone out for a smoke while Brad paid the check. By the time he'd gone out to join her, she'd vanished. He'd looked around for her and got no help from any of the locals when he asked if they'd seen her. Some twenty minutes after her disappearance, a pickup loaded with young men had turned up. They'd told him they didn't like the questions he was asking or his insistence someone must know something. They'd told him his girl must have left him and he should leave town as none of them could help him. A Molotov cocktail had then arced through the air and landed close enough to Brad for him to leap in his car and flee Daversville.

As soon as he was out of town and could get a reliable cell signal, Brad had called the police and then Don. But when Brad went to the Macon police station, as he'd been requested to, the cops had grilled him for hours before releasing him. Upon his return home, Brad had found himself getting arrested, as the local cop who'd been sent to investigate Lila's disappearance had found no trace of her having ever visited Daversville.

With Don wheelchair-bound and Brad imprisoned on suspicion of killing Lila, or at the very least being involved in her disappearance, there was no way Fletcher was going to turn down his buddy's request that he look into things. As much as he sometimes felt Brad was a useless lump, Don knew that Brad loved Lila and there was no way he'd ever do anything to harm her.

Fletcher's own daughter, Wendy, was only a few years younger than Lila, so he fully understood Don's worries. And after the sacrifice Don had made for him in Afghanistan, he'd agree to anything his friend and savior asked of him. As Fletcher had listened to Don's request, he'd been fingering the locket he always wore. It held pictures of his daughter and murdered wife. After Wendy herself, the locket was the most precious thing in his life.

Rather than stick to the interstates as they traveled through Georgia, Brad and Lila had decided to travel along a series of back roads so they could see more of the country. It was a simple decision, made with good intentions, although it seemed it may have cost Lila dearly.

Don and Fletcher had already shared several theories as to why Lila had disappeared, but, as it appeared the town had closed ranks, none of their ideas had filled either man with hope.

As for why Brad hadn't been taken by whomever had snatched Lila when he'd gone outside to join her, they'd agreed that his size was a factor. At over six and a half feet tall and carrying the best part of four hundred pounds, Brad was a big guy who wouldn't be easy to move somewhere he didn't want to go. Fletcher didn't know him well, but he'd met Brad enough times to know that he wasn't the type of person who'd throw his weight around, regardless of the circumstances. But others wouldn't know Brad was a gentle soul, and being the size he was, he was an unlikely target for abduction.

It was the first time Fletcher had been to any part of Georgia, let alone a backwoods town like Daversville. His first impression was the report from Brad had exaggerated the place's menace.

Fletcher entered the diner and looked for the server Brad had described to Don. According to Brad the girl was in her late teens or early twenties, shy to the point of nervousness and slight of build; but then again, anyone who didn't weigh in excess of two hundred and fifty pounds would be slight in Brad's eyes. A hair color would have been helpful, as would a description of her looks, but Brad hadn't been sure of these things, so Fletcher had ignored his attempts to guess. Better to not know and work from scratch than to go off bad intel. Too many things could go wrong if you based your course of action on wrong information. He'd learned the importance of accurate intelligence in the Royal Marines and he still worked on the same principle.

There was no sign of a young server, so Fletcher ordered a coffee and a burger from the short order cook working behind the diner counter and prepared to wait. Maybe the girl was out back, or not on shift. Time would tell. He needed to speak to her. Had a few questions that needed answering. Number one of these questions was why she'd warned Brad that he and Lila ought to leave town at once because it wasn't safe for Lila.

Fletcher had been in a hundred roadside diners like this one. Like a corporate chain, they all served fried food with a salad garnish and coffee with a refill. This one was better than some and worse than others. The tables were clean and the seats weren't sticky, but the menu had long since had the idea of nutritious meals knocked into submission.

The few patrons in the diner paid him no heed, apart from an old man who sent him toothless grins in between failed attempts to worry at a burger.

When it came Fletcher's coffee was strong without being stewed. Likewise his burger was cooked to his liking and the fries on the side of his plate were crisp and grease-free. Fletcher appreciated the pride the short order cook so obviously took in his work.

With his burger eaten and his coffee on the second refill, Fletcher summoned the elderly server across with a wave and what he hoped was a disarming smile. The girl he was after was neither her nor the short order cook, so he guessed she was off shift.

"How c'n I help you?"

The query was polite enough but something about the way the woman's eyes assessed him told him that she was hoping he didn't want anything more taxing for her than another refill of coffee. A worn name badge bearing the name "Agnes" sat lopsided on her washed-out pinafore dress.

"A colleague's daughter passed through here last week. My colleague said she'd been here and had a great bite to eat, but she'd left her purse and had to come back for it. She said a young server had found it and put it behind the counter for safekeeping. She didn't have any cash on her at the time, so she asked me to drop the girl a thank-you." Fletcher pulled a fifty from his pocket. "I don't suppose she's working today, is she?"

"Just me today." The woman's eyes fixed on the fifty in Fletcher's hand. "If you give it to me, I'll make sure she gets it."

Fletcher could tell the woman's intentions to pass on the tip were as genuine as the garbage he'd just spouted about the lost purse.

"That's very kind of you, but I'm around tomorrow so can come back in if she's on shift then?"

A pause for thought then an eye roll to the left. Whatever came out of Agnes's mouth would be a lie. "She ain't workin' tomorrow. Got herself the whole week off. Best you leave it with me."

"Sure." Fletcher passed across the fifty and then removed a photo from his shirt pocket and gave it to the server facedown. "Give her this as well if you could. It'll remind her who she helped." Fletcher watched with interest as the server turned the picture over and saw Brad and Lila. He saw the fractional narrowing of her eyes and the way her mouth tightened before she recovered her poise. "They never got the girl's name. What is it?"

Agnes left herself a pause for consideration, then gave a short nod to herself. "Mary-Lou Henderson. These look like a nice couple of folks."

"They sure are."

Fletcher turned back to his coffee as Agnes walked away. He didn't fail to notice that by the time she was at the swing door into the kitchen her pace had picked up.

He'd gotten what he wanted from her. The server's name, and most important of all, he'd gotten a reaction when she'd seen the picture of Brad and Lila. This was at odds with what the local cops had reported, as according to what had been fed back to Don, nobody in the diner had admitted to having seen Lila.

It was a shame that Mary-Lou had time off, but he was confident he'd be able to track her down in the small town.

CHAPTER TWO

With his quest in the diner at a temporary standstill, Fletcher took himself outside and waited to see what happened next. As he waited, he walked along the sidewalk and tried to get a feel for Daversville.

The town's main street was wide enough for the lumber trucks that would roll through it with regularity, but short as befitted a town whose population would do well to top six hundred. On his walk he came across two bars, a mom-and-pop store and a tiny police station. Fletcher reckoned that a place the size of Daversville would have a solitary deputy who'd be on permanent call. He also came across a small school and a church large enough to hold the entire town's population. None of his finds surprised him. Like in so many small towns, the locals would all know each other, and when they were as far off the beaten track as Daversville was, they'd be self-sufficient in a lot of ways.

Part of his plan to find Lila was to go into both bars, buy a few beers and flash pictures of her around. Beer and liquor were memory joggers of the highest order, and if the man who was buying them threatened to leave unless he got answers, alcohol-moistened lips were sure to loosen.

But first, he'd set something in motion at the diner and he wanted to see what, if anything, happened before he moved on to the bars.

When he returned to the parking lot, he sat on the hood of his car and pretended to revel in the scenery that lay around him.

The early evening air was cooling to a tolerable level after the day's high temperature, and as such, it carried sound with a clarity that gave him far more warning of possible trouble than he needed. Either someone had a major emergency, or there was a learner driver on the roads who'd never mastered safe cornering speeds.

There was another screech of tires as a second corner was rounded, and then the thumping roar of a V8 being demanded to donate every one of its horses to the driver's cause.

He sent a glance the diner's way. The server was looking out the front window and her gaze was locked on him. Fletcher gave her a subtle wave to let her know he'd seen her watching and resumed his waiting.

The roaring grew louder as a battered pickup shot into the parking lot and squealed to a halt.

Four young men emptied themselves from the pickup and walked towards Fletcher. To him they looked like everyday punks. They had a belligerent swagger and more of a desire to appear tough than an ability to carry out whatever threat they made.

All four were tall and rangy, their bodies hardened as if by physical labor. As a group they'd think someone like Fletcher was little threat. Their clothes were washed-out denims and shirts that had seen better days. No follower of fashion himself, Fletcher still recognized their clothes were nothing like the stylish ones he saw most punks their age wearing.

Fletcher eased himself upward from where he was sitting on the hood of the rental sedan and waited until they approached him.

This was the reaction he'd suspected he'd get when he'd shown the picture to the server in the diner. In every way imaginable, it backed up Brad's story. Now it was a case of seeing how things played out.

The tallest of the young men stepped forward, his whole demeanor filled with the unassailable arrogance of youth. "You're not from round here, sir, and I think you should return to wherever it is you come from."

Even in a potential fight situation, the southern manners of the youth shone through. In these parts anyone conversing with someone older than them by fifteen years or more would always address the person they were speaking to as Sir or Ma'am. It was a respect thing and would be automatic. When the "Sir" was dropped, it wouldn't be bad manners, it would be outright disrespect and a sure sign things were about to get ugly.

Fletcher dropped a lazy smile at Tall Boy, as he thought of him. "Not planning to be here long. Just passing through." Fletcher pulled the picture of Lila from his pocket and showed it to Tall Boy. "Once I find my friend, I'll be gone. Don't suppose you know where she is? She went missing after eating at the diner six days ago."

Tall Boy answered without looking at the picture. "Ain't never seen her."

At Tall Boy's shoulder one of his buddies gave a snort of derision. Fletcher ignored him; he was the thinnest of the four and while he was being cocky, he was also making sure he was behind Tall Boy and his freckle-faced buddy.

To Tall Boy's right was the widest of the four. He was as well-built as Fletcher, but while his body was sculpted, his features had a bovine emptiness to them. Of the gang, he'd be the one who'd be the most dangerous, assuming the coming fight was about brute strength rather than intelligence.

"Are you sure about that? Maybe your buddies would know."

"She ain't anywhere in town, so it's time for you to leave, sir." Tall Boy jerked a thumb in the direction of the road. "Big fat guy was asking the same questions you is. Was accusin' the good people of Daversville of abducting the girl. Folks round here don't like gettin' accused of things they ain't done and if you're fixin' on doing the same, I'd recommend you don't waste no time in leaving town."

Fletcher looked Tall Boy up and down with a deliberate slowness. He wasn't worried about the impending scuffle. These four yokels weren't the kind of people he'd considered a threat since a sergeant major with an inventive repertoire of coarse vocabulary had taught him and a clutch of other recruits to the Royal Marines how to fight.

"And if I'm not ready to leave, what will happen?"

"We'll make you ready. Yeah, boys?"

Tall Boy threw a disdainful look over his shoulder at Cocky for stealing his thunder. As much as the implied threat had now been voiced, Fletcher's attention was on the way the gang's dynamic had been shown. Tall Boy was the top dog, the contrition on Cocky's face had made that clear. Freckles and Muscles had adopted what they must have believed were intimidating stances, but they were keeping silent and taking their lead from Tall Boy.

"As my associate says, we'll persuade you to leave now. Ain't no hospital in Daversville, so it's sure a long walk to the emergency room."

"I like walking. It's good exercise." Fletcher saw the first traces of uncertainty in their faces as he straightened his stance and squared up to Tall Boy. "You're forgetting something, though."

"Yeah?" The solitary word fell from Tall Boy's mouth in a scoffed laugh.

"You never said please."

All four boys laughed at this, and Cocky leaned between Tall Boy and Freckles, his head thrust forward.

"Will you *please* get the hell out of our town?"

"No."

Tall Boy's top lip curled into a mocking sneer. "Kick his ass."

"Wait." Fletcher made a halting gesture. "You're not being very smart about this. You see, I get your thinking, there's four of you. You think you're able to take me down without any trouble. You've all got at least two or three inches on me; you're probably all twenty years or so younger as well. Those will seem like good odds to you. However, have you asked yourselves who I am and why *I'm* the one looking for the girl? Have you also thought about why I'm not backing down?" To further incite their anger, Fletcher wagged his finger like a school principal giving a student a dressing-down. "Here I am confronted by four fit and strong young men, and yet I'm not climbing into my car and hightailing it out of town. Doesn't that tell you that I'm not afraid of you? That, in fact, maybe *I'm* a threat to *you*?"

Fletcher savored the growing uncertainty on their faces until he saw Tall Boy screwing up his courage to strike. He didn't mind having the fight, but he'd rather it was somewhere more private, so that he could persuade one of them to talk once the fighting was done.

"Screw you. You're just some old guy with more balls than brains."

"Thanks, I'll take that as a compliment." Fletcher give a kiss-my-ass grin to Tall Boy. "Let me enlighten you as to how this will go down. You'll move forward, swing a couple of punches that I'll make sure miss me. My first blow will be an elbow to the side of your muscled friend's head. He'll go down hard. You'll follow him when I plant a punch in your gut that will lift you off your feet and land you on your butt. Two blows from me and your numbers will be halved. Your buddy with the freckles will come at me next; he'll be cagier, but my boot will lift his kneecap to a place where it doesn't belong and that'll be the end of him. As for the wiseass who's cowering behind you while trying to act like a tough guy, I'll bet your mama's virtue that he'll have started running away before you've begun gasping for the air my punch is gonna knock clean out of you."

"You're so full of bull you'd call an alligator a lizard." Tall Boy looked as if he was about to launch himself forward, fists clenched and cocked, ready to throw. He didn't, though. Fletcher had put enough doubts into Tall Boy to make him believe things might not go as expected. Tall Boy's uncertainty was mirrored on the faces of Cocky and Freckles. Muscles was the only one to look disappointed the fight hadn't already started.

"You're welcome to try your luck if you that's what you think."

CHAPTER THREE

As Tall Boy glared at him, Fletcher made a point of not getting into a staring contest. One, it would narrow his field of vision, giving Tall Boy's buddies a chance to land a strike of their own, and two, if things weren't to get physical, Tall Boy needed a way out of the conflict that would allow him to save face.

"Forget 'bout him." Tall Boy threw a dismissive gesture in Fletcher's general direction. "Old man like him ain't no threat to us. Be wrong to kick the ass of someone so old."

"So I don't have to leave?" Fletcher made a point of asking his question in a pleasant tone. While he was quite happy to get into it with the four youths, he'd prefer not to until he knew more about them. Specifically, why they'd been appointed as the town's guardians. It's not uncommon for the locals in small towns to protect their town's reputation and stick up for each other, but it's rare that a gang can be hustled together in the space of minutes to run off first Brad and then him. Two separate people, on two different days. While he knew things happened differently in rural areas, the youths' speed in arriving and instant insistence he leave was, at the very minimum, a complete overreaction to his presence and the conversation he'd had with Agnes in the diner.

A parking lot on Main Street wasn't the right location for him to get the answers he needed Tall Boy to supply. A few well-aimed punches or a squeeze on some pressure points would get one of them talking, but across the street a woman was pushing a stroller and looking their way. A gaggle of preteen kids hung on the corner. Their eyes wide with excitement as they watched proceedings.

If these four were an unofficial police force, they'd no doubt have the backing of the locals and, as such, he was in a no-win situation. Fletcher knew how these things went down. If they weren't acting for the townsfolks it would be a different matter, as local punks getting a short, sharp lesson wouldn't bother anyone except the punks' families. However, an out-of-towner using even a mild form of torture on them was another thing altogether. A blind eye might happily be turned to a deserved beating, but anything further than that couldn't not be acted upon for fear of future repercussions.

The whole point of torture was the extraction of information from someone who didn't want to share what they knew. Fletcher could have the answers he wanted from Tall Boy or one of his friends in less than two minutes; however, to break their initial resistance he'd have to hurt them a little. They'd scream before they talked and there were too many witnesses for that to be allowed to happen.

All of this didn't mean he couldn't still put the frighteners on Tall Boy and his buddies. "I've come to the conclusion you're not very bright, so I'm only going to use small words. You do not try and fight me. You'll get hurt. Hurt bad. A friend of mine has gone missing and I am going to find her. You've seen her picture. Her name is Lila: she has blonde shoulder-length hair; she's maybe five three, has a pretty face. If you know where she is, go get her, leave her in this square and hit your horn ten times. I'll come get her; then, and only then, will I leave your town." Fletcher shot a look at Tall Boy's buddies to keep them from getting any silly ideas. "If you don't know where she is, that's cool. But be warned, if I find that you're standing between me and her when I find her, you're going to feel pain like you've never imagined."

Tall Boy eyed him as if he was a circus freak from bygone days. "You's talkin' with the tongue outta your shoe. We don't know where the bitch is, and if you don't leave town, next time we see you, we'll not think kicking your ass is such a wrong thing to do. C'mon, let's get outta here 'fore we catch arthritis from this old coot."

Instead of reacting to the childish and medically inaccurate taunts, Fletcher let Tall Boy have the final word as he turned to head back to the pickup. The lad had come to run him out of town and had failed. Not only that, his failure had been down to a cowardice to engage. Losing a fight hurts your pride as much as your body; chickening out of one means all the hurt is focused on your pride. Tall Boy would regret not having the nerve to take Fletcher on when he had the superior numbers. That regret would niggle at him, make his head and heart fill with a bitter self-loathing.

The worst parts of it all for Tall Boy were that not only had he failed as a fighter, he'd also failed as a leader. His lieutenants were at his shoulder when he'd decided not to lead them into battle. There was no getting away from it, his stock would go down in the eyes of his buddies.

As always, there was a flip side to this. Tall Boy had intimated that he would be happy to have the fight another time. It could be bravado, or it could be the youth's natural cunning that had made him happy to delay the fight until he could get some weapons to make a fight that was four against one the foregone conclusion that it should be. When that happened Tall Boy would be fueled by his own self-loathing, any taunts he'd received from his buddies and the criticisms of the townsfolk for failing to protect their collective reputation.

Next time they met, Tall Boy would be out for blood and would come prepared to spill Fletcher's.

Fletcher had known all of this when he'd squared off against the four youths. On certain levels he welcomed it. The years he'd spent as a single father had been hugely gratifying as he'd watched his daughter morph from a child into an independent young woman. All the same, he missed the adrenaline rush that came whenever he went into combat situations. It had been a long time since he'd felt quite as alive as he felt now, although he knew he'd have to temper his reactions to what was necessary rather than what made him feel good.

One thing was for sure, after the way they'd attempted to run him out of town, Fletcher was looking forward to his next meeting with Tall Boy and his cronies, as he'd make a point of getting some answers from them. There had been a spark of recognition in Tall Boy's eyes when he'd eventually dropped his gaze at the picture of Lila that Fletcher had held against his chest so Tall Boy couldn't help but see it.

Fletcher glanced at his watch as he walked along Main Street and gave a silent curse. It was too late in the day for anywhere with town records to be open, if Daversville had such a place. Had he been able to check the town's records, he could have gotten Mary-Lou Henderson's address. After that he'd have been able to devise a way to talk to her. Once upon a time he'd have gotten her address from a phone book, but the popularity of cell phones had put an end to that.

Brad had described the server as young, so Fletcher figured there was a good chance Mary-Lou still lived in the family home. This meant that even if he found the right house, Mary-Lou's folks could prevent her talking to him anyway. A man his age couldn't just knock on a door and ask to speak to a girl in her late teens without expecting some kind of parental interference.

There was always the option of asking around town, but the longer he was in Daversville, the more he was growing suspicious of the town as a whole. After the appearance of Tall Boy and his cronies, it wouldn't need an MIT graduate to realize it was a bad idea to draw attention to his quest to find Lila.

He could go back into the diner and question Agnes, but he doubted that she'd speak to him. In fact he was convinced it was her who'd sicced the boys on him. A few heavily suggested threats might work on a guy, but he wasn't prepared to threaten an elderly lady, and besides all that, Agnes was in a public place and if he started getting heavy with her in front of witnesses, all it would take for his investigation to grind to a halt would be a call to the town's cop.

If he was to get information from Agnes, it would have to be another way.

CHAPTER FOUR

Special Agent Zoey Quadrado flicked the blinker and made the turn. Daversville was only another five minutes away and she was looking forward to a relaxing shower and a clean bed. The journey from Atlanta after flying down from New York had been uneventful to the point of boring, especially so since she'd left the interstates and started weaving her way through the forests of Georgia. There had been mile after mile of tree-lined roads and little traffic to impede her progress. Apart from the fact she'd had to drive the first fifty miles with the windows open to remove the smells of fried food and body odor from it, the car she'd been loaned from the Atlanta field office was in decent enough condition.

Like the road ahead of her, Quadrado's career was all mapped out in her head. The case she'd been handed was intriguing on one level and insulting on another. Fifteen women passing through the lumber town of Daversville had gone missing over the last four years. They'd travel through, maybe they'd stop for gas or something to eat at the diner, and would never be seen again. Their vehicles would vanish and any triangulation from their cell phones would show the missing women as having left Daversville before their cells hit another one of Georgia's many blackspots.

The sheriff from Douglas had dispatched his detectives to Daversville on three separate occasions but they'd always come up blank. The locals hadn't known anything and the deputy who kept order in the town was as non-plussed as everyone who'd been spoken to.

There were no transactions on the missing women's cards in the town, which meant the only firm clue was that all their cells had shown them as having traveled on the road that passed through the lumber town. The latest to go missing, Lila Ogilvie, was the only person who'd been traveling with a companion. The boyfriend had made up a story about a warning from a server at the diner and about being run out of town. To Quadrado, this sounded too fanciful for her liking and she couldn't help but wonder if he had something to do with Lila going missing. After all, statistics proved that most murders were committed by someone who knew the victim.

But Quadrado knew her initial theory that the area with its cell phone blackspots was a good place for people to drop out of society was sketchy at best, and she also knew that she'd have to uncover any decent leads for herself. While it was the kind of challenge she enjoyed, she'd have preferred a more high-profile case rather than being shunted out to the backwoods of Georgia.

The fact that the fifteen missing women fit a range of demographics left her without any obvious theories. They were a variety of different ages. Some had good looks and, without being cruel or judgmental, others didn't.

No matter how she'd looked at it since she'd been handed the case last night, the only link Quadrado could find between the missing women was the town of Daversville. It may well be that they had joined some new cult or other. Whether it was a religious cult or a band of preppers readying themselves for the end of civilization didn't matter. She'd find them, report back and earn the plaudits of her peers. What she feared most—though if she was honest with herself, made her blood pump that little bit harder—was the idea that the disappearances could be all due to a serial killer picking off lone travelers. If this Lila Ogilvie girl had been taken by this guy, had he made a mistake in selecting his next victim? Or had his confidence grown to the point where he no longer felt it necessary to only target those traveling alone?

The Senior Special Agent may or may not have known about the personal nature of the case for her. As part of her application for the FBI, she'd had to disclose her family history. Her mother's little sister had left the Wisconsin farm that was the family home to go and get some groceries. And Aunt Janet had never returned. Her car was found in a parking lot a block from Medford bus depot and she was never heard of again. Quadrado had been two at the time and while she couldn't remember her aunt, she'd grown up with a family unsure if a loved one had run off from choice or been abducted against her will. Even now, some twenty-plus years later, her family had no more information about where her aunt was than they did the day she vanished. It was this lack of answers for a grieving family that had compelled Quadrado to pursue a career in law enforcement.

It wasn't ideal to arrive at a town late on a Saturday evening and begin an investigation on a Sunday morning, but she was working on the theory that the sooner she cracked this case, the sooner she'd be back in New York and in a position to impress her boss.

As she drew into town and looked for a parking lot, she noticed four youths hanging around a pickup. The look on their faces suggested they were discussing something a lot more serious than the local football team.

CHAPTER FIVE

The room above the bar at Duke's wasn't what anyone would call plush. A threadbare carpet surrounded a bed whose mattress sagged in enough places for it to form a landscape more rugged than the Rockies. The bedcovers were made from materials that had gone out of fashion before Nixon took office. However, when Fletcher gave them a tentative sniff, he wasn't greeted with any scents that turned his stomach.

Fletcher was sure he'd slept in worse rooms, yet try as he might, he couldn't recall when.

He dumped his bag on the nightstand and changed into a clean shirt after washing his face in the closet-sized bathroom. The water from the hot tap was lukewarm at best, but it was clean, so he was grateful for that smallest of mercies.

He guessed the room's usual occupants would be those brought in to repair machinery used in the town's lumber mill or in the woods supplying the lumber mill. Perhaps once in a while a traveling salesperson would need a room, but a lesson would be learned, and the salesperson would arrange accommodation in another town the next time they were in these parts.

While arriving on a Saturday evening was a bad idea in terms of getting access to public records, it was a great time to ask around a bar. It didn't matter where you were in the world—and Fletcher had been to a lot of places—come the weekend, people wanted to socialize, hang out with friends and catch up on what was going on.

Fridays and Saturdays are when bars and restaurants are at their busiest. Duke's was a small hotel with only a couple of rooms above the bar, and there were enough meaty smells filling the air for Fletcher to be confident Duke's doubled as a place to eat.

Fletcher went down the stairs with the picture of Lila tucked in his shirt pocket beside enough dead presidents to loosen the tongue of even the most hardened drinker.

His first order of business was a call to Wendy. He wanted to let her know he'd arrived and that he was getting on with finding out what had happened to Lila. Wendy had been keen for him to find her childhood friend and former sitter, and knowing her, she'd want an update.

With no signal available for his cell, Fletcher had to use the payphone in the lobby. The call lasted a good ten minutes and when he signed off by telling her he loved her, he could hear the affection in her voice as she returned his words.

The bartender who'd gotten Fletcher his room key had been pleasant enough until he'd mentioned he was in town looking for a friend. After that his conversation had been stilted to the point it was forced.

His eyes had held the same look that had been in the server's at the diner when Fletcher had flashed her the picture of Brad and Lila.

When he thought about it, he couldn't help but wonder what the locals made of the disappearances. Before coming to Daversville, he'd scoured the internet and had learned that Lila's disappearance hadn't even been covered in the local newspaper.

Fletcher didn't know circulation figures, but he knew rural towns that were too small to have their own TV news program often still had newspapers. Without a city's worth of news to go online, the papers would focus on all the same news items a national paper did, just on a smaller scale. The president might not get a mention, but the local mayor would have his picture on at least four pages per edition.

For something as newsworthy as a tourist's disappearance not to have been reported was odd. While there was no doubt small-town journalism had a different focus than state or national, it was still unlikely to have been glossed over. Especially as Fletcher knew Don and his wife had offered a reward for information that would help them find their daughter. Though they'd paid for an ad in the paper which covered Daversville, it did seem their appeal hadn't been posted on the online version of the paper.

Come Monday, he planned to visit the library in the nearby town of Douglas, to look through a few back copies to make sure the ad had run in the print version.

Fletcher made his way into the bar and took a look around. What he saw didn't fill him with confidence that he'd get the answers he wanted.

CHAPTER SIX

Duke's was what you'd expect of a small town bar on a Saturday night. Some tables had people tucking into meals and others had groups of men or women surrounding a pitcher of beer. There was a thrum of conversation interspersed with the odd laugh or loud exclamation. The patrons were having a good time and that was fine.

What wasn't fine were the sidelong looks he was getting from them all. As he crossed the room to get to the bar counter, nobody met Fletcher's eyes or returned the nods and smiles he cast their way.

He got that rural life was rife with insular behavior. It was almost as if they were protecting themselves from the interference of outsiders. However, he'd been in a lot of towns small and large, and he knew there was always someone who broke rank and returned a pleasantry that was passed without agenda.

Fletcher was aware that enough time had passed for word of his earlier standoff to have spread throughout the town. He supposed he might be getting ostracized for standing up to the wrong person, or maybe the locals had decided en masse that he was the kind of bad news that was best avoided. He got why they were shunning him. He was a stranger who'd be here today, gone tomorrow. If word got back to Tall Boy and whomever was pulling his strings that they drank and chatted with the guy who'd made a fool of him, they might find themselves facing off against Tall Boy and his cronies next. Either way, his plan to ingratiate himself with the locals by buying a few rounds wasn't looking like such an easy option.

While he waited for the beer he'd ordered, Fletcher took a slow look around the bar and assessed the room as well as the patrons. He kept a friendly look on his face as he took in the bare floorboards and the paneled walls. The beams supporting the floor above were exposed just in case there wasn't enough wood on show. In a lumber-rich area, it made sense that wood had been used wherever possible over other materials, it was just that the amount used was sufficient to create a sensory overload.

The bar counter was a single piece of oak whose edge retained the original contours of the tree's exterior. Polished to a high degree it gleamed beneath the paper coasters. A knot in the oak had the look of a wolf about it and when he squinted its way he saw the animal's head take a more realistic form. Fletcher guessed it would serve as a good barometer of drunkenness. When you saw the wolf without squinting, it'd be time to stop drinking.

As for the bar's patrons, they were a different case altogether. Fletcher tried to assess them without being judgmental. He put aside their lack of reciprocal manners to give them the benefit of the doubt, but there was no escaping the harsh truth: Daversville was a town that time hadn't ever known about, let alone forgot. The clothes worn by the townspeople weren't so much outdated fashion as never having been fashionable. Each item was clean and well presented, but they were clearly worn as an alternative to nudity rather than to make the wearer feel or look good. The men wore jeans and nondescript shirts, sometimes with a vest, while the women were dressed in flowery dresses that mostly covered the ankle and buttoned right up to the chin. None of the women wore cosmetics or jewelry beyond a smear of lipstick or a wedding ring so far as he could see, and their hairstyles were functional rather than fashionable. Most of the men had bushy beards that scraggled down onto their chests. Human nature normally drove people to want to look better than their peers. Whether it was a question of self-worth or for the attraction of a mate, an effort to rise above the pack would be made. Clothes and hairstyles along with cosmetics and jewelry were the foundation stones of this extra effort, and yet, none of the townspeople he'd met or seen had gone down this route in any meaningful fashion. The tables hosting the obvious singletons were surrounded by the same unimaginative styles.

Fletcher knew that a high percentage of Georgians were deeply religious, yet Daversville seemed to be only one step closer to modernization than an Amish settlement. While it was perfectly acceptable to have religious beliefs, it was unusual for an entire town in these parts to forsake modern trends. In any other part of the country, half the people in the room would be fiddling with a cell phone. As he looked around, he didn't see a single person with a cell phone, let alone obsessed by it. His own daughter was more likely to win Mr. Universe than she was to spend more than five minutes without her cell in her hand. While he wasn't keen on a lot of what he'd seen in Daversville, Fletcher could get on board with a world that didn't include cell phones. Whether it was the complete lack of signal in the town or some other reason, he felt it was refreshing to see people actually conversing with those around them instead of someone who might be thousands of miles away.

It may well be the other bar across the street was filled with the people wearing the latest fashions and dancing to the beat of whatever sound was currently popular—Fletcher had little time for modern music and often cringed in horror at the stuff his daughter played. However, the likelihood of that being true wasn't enough to have Fletcher bet more than a nickel.

"You looking for something to eat?"

"No thanks." Fletcher nodded at the bartender as he gestured at the room. "Seems busy."

"Yeah, well, it's Saturday."

"First time I've been to Daversville. Seems like a nice town."

"It's a town. Some parts nice. Some parts not so nice if your face don't fit. Threatening to beat up on the locals for no good reason sure don't make your face fit."

The bartender wandered off to polish glasses where he didn't have to talk to Fletcher. His less than subtle warning wasn't missed, but neither did it trouble Fletcher as it let him know Tall Boy had tried to spin the standoff as locals being threatened by an outsider. It was a clever move and displayed a low cunning in his adversary.

A waitress was carrying a pitcher of beer towards a table where four women who looked to be in their early twenties were sitting. It wasn't much of an opportunity, but the general hostility of the bar was annoying Fletcher and if the buying of beers wasn't going to work, maybe ruffling some feathers would.

"Ma'am, let me get that for you." Fletcher took the tray from the waitress, deposited it on the table and passed a dead president to the waitress. "It's on me, ladies. Getting myself all kinds of lonely over there and you girls are far prettier than the bartender."

Two of the women rolled their eyes and one gave a little sneer, but it was the fourth who gave the reaction he'd been hoping for by snickering at his cheesy comment and returning his smile. He knew that he was neither the handsomest nor the ugliest man to exist, but he also knew that being pleasant, engaging and, most of all, nonthreatening was the best way to instigate a conversation with a woman in a bar.

Fletcher swung a chair round so its back was against the table. No point trapping himself if he had to move in a hurry. For all he was a civilian and had been for a decade, some parts of his Royal Marine training would never leave him. And since arriving in Daversville, he'd been operating on the principle that the more he treated his investigation into Lila's disappearance as a behind-enemy-lines mission, the more likely he'd be to succeed.

"I'm Grant." He held out a hand and did his best to memorize their names as they went through the ritual.

It had been too much to hope that one of them would be called Mary-Lou, but it wasn't beyond the bounds of possibility that he might just get the kind of lucky he was interested in. Rather than the fast-talking and confident manner of many other southern women he'd met, these ladies were reticent, shy almost, when they drawled their words out.

The two eye-rolling women kept tossing glances to the table which held single men of a similar age, while the sneerer did all she could to pretend to be aloof. Fletcher had been in a thousand bars worldwide, but the story was always the same. Single men and women would drink and then a percentage of them would be open to the possibility of hooking up with someone. Whether it was the first or final steps in attracting someone for the night, or for a lifetime partnership, depended on where they were at that moment in time. After a bad break-up, there may be little desire for romance, but they were still there.

The glances at the single men's table told Fletcher lots about the eye-rollers. Since he'd invaded their space uninvited they'd been given a choice. Welcome him, or shun him. While they could have easily moved to an empty table or asked him to move on, they hadn't; instead they'd given him a faux greeting and were now listening to his false tales with an exaggerated zeal, while keeping an eye on the single men. They were using him to make the other guys jealous. It was a test for the men they really fancied. Would they be cool and indifferent, or would they make some kind of move to show the depth of their attraction?

Fletcher saw the setting of jaws and sideways looks at the men's table and saw a familiar pattern. Three of the four seemed unsettled while the other appeared to be preaching calm. They wouldn't be happy about the stranger who'd plonked himself at the girls' table in a poor excuse for an "excuse me" in the middle of their courtship dance. Chairs were fidgeted in and fists clenched and unclenched. Folks from small towns could be very territorial when it came to the town's opposite sex. Outsiders were viewed as threats to the status quo, and when a new face started drawing attention away from the locals, tempers flared.

Several old Royal Marines buddies of Fletcher's had regaled him with tales of the villages they'd grown up in as places where most Saturday nights were spent fighting with guys from neighboring villages. Fletcher had grown up in the suburbs so hadn't experienced the parochial battles. His childhood was all about roaming the edges of the suburbs looking for something more appealing than council-maintained playing fields and the street boasting a half-dozen shops. Until he'd joined the army the day after his sixteenth birthday, his excursions from suburbia had seen him head into the city. Mostly he was looking for girls, but once in a while, he'd feel a more primal itch and would seek out someone else who was looking to pick a fight for no other reason than they too were acting upon ancient instincts.

Life as a soldier had cured Fletcher's need to hunt violent confrontation. It brought him more than enough and, as he aged, he made the kind of lifelong friendships that so many soldiers make. When you've hunkered down beneath strafing machine gunfire with someone, or have put your trust in a person to have your six in a life-or-death situation, you either became friends for life, or one of you didn't come back.

Another standoff so soon after entering town wasn't Fletcher's ambition, but as it felt like a growing possibility, he waved the waitress over and ordered two more pitchers of beer.

With the waitress on her way to the bar, Fletcher rose and crossed to the men's table. "Guys, there's a table full of young women over there who keep looking your way while I'm chatting with them. I know when I'm gonna strike out, so why don't you come join us?"

The invitation had been made, so Fletcher left them to deliberate among themselves and went back to the women.

It took five minutes before the men came over and another four pitchers of beer before they accepted him, but Fletcher got them talking in the end.

One of his key lines of questioning was about the town itself as, regardless of what was online, the locals would give him a clearer picture of life in Daversville than any other source. Daversville was a lumber town and the mill was owned by a family called the Blacketts. Not one of the eight people at the table had a word of criticism for them. They'd eulogized about the Blacketts' generosity in looking after the elderly, providing a school for the kids and for making sure every one of the townsfolk had a job that suited their individual skills.

When Fletcher left Duke's to cross Main Street and try the other bar, he was no wiser about the fate of Lila than he was when he'd arrived in Daversville. The youngsters had opened up as alcohol lowered their inhibitions, but they were more interested in coy flirting with each other than answering questions from a guy nearly twenty years their senior.

All eight of the young men and women had taken a look at the picture of Lila, but none had professed any knowledge about her disappearance.

What he had learned, though, was that while they said they knew nothing, there were enough sideways glances and hesitant answers for him to feel they weren't telling him the whole truth.

At one point he overheard one of the eye-rollers whispering "trench" to one of her girlfriends. The significance of the word was lost on him. He'd been on the point of asking the girl outright, but had dismissed the idea as she'd started talking about something different and she was the least receptive to his attempts to ingratiate himself with the younger crowd.

It was something he could pursue. Maybe Agnes at the diner would be forthcoming if he threw the word at her when she wasn't expecting it.

The more he thought about it, the more he was getting an uneasy feeling about Daversville and its inhabitants. He didn't think they were being deceptive out of spite or malice; rather they were too scared to tell him because of possible future repercussions. The speed with which Tall Boy and the others had turned up after he'd been asking questions in the diner had shown there was someone in town who didn't want those questions asked. The obvious thought that, as the holders of power in the town, the Blackett family might be the ones to exert control, was tempered by the way they were held in high esteem.

Fletcher mentally crossed his fingers that he'd find someone brave enough to give him the truth as he opened the door to the Fellers bar.

CHAPTER SEVEN

The door to Fellers squeaked and squealed its way open, which meant that when Fletcher took his first step inside, all fifteen eyes in the room were looking his way. Each one of them sending suspicion and hostility.

Fletcher got the room's vibe in an instant. The eight men in Fellers all had the same traces of a hard life etched all over them. These were tough men, used to working hard for a living and taking no nonsense from anyone, and he was an outsider who'd breached what they'd think of as their domain.

Fellers wasn't a bar for tourists, it was a spit-and-sawdust kind of place with genuine sawdust and extra spit. Like Duke's the walls were clad with wide timber boards, but where the walls in Duke's had been clean and well maintained, in Fellers they were rough-hewn and untreated. Rorschach-like splotches of spilled beer and bloodstains littered the timber walls, although there were two pictures adding a modicum of decoration behind the bar.

The first picture was of a mighty tree as it fell to earth. The lumberjack scurrying away from possible kickbacks gave enough scale for Fletcher to see the tree's trunk would be at least ten feet in diameter. It was the second picture which made Fletcher lift a figurative eyebrow. It was of a youngster sitting on a swing chair which hung from a porch. The boy's hands held a banjo while his face held a stern and uncompromising look, which still managed to ask a question.

Fletcher recognized the picture as a still from *Deliverance*, and somehow, he knew the actor's name was Billy Redden, but he wasn't sure how the information had popped into his head. That the image hung behind the bar was telling. Redden's character in the film spoke of decades of inbreeding, and the whole of the movie seemed to be a critique of towns like Daversville and the people who lived either in them or on their peripheries. Rural Georgia may not be as sophisticated as New York or LA, but there was nothing to be gloried in a film which stereotyped rural Georgians as simple folk with animalistic appetites for violence and rape.

However, one look at the patrons of Fellers was enough to make Fletcher realize whoever had hung the picture of Redden was either playing to his core demographic or mocking them.

The patrons of Fellers all had the same basic look of dull ignorance about them, and while some of them looked as if they could be brothers, they all looked as if they'd descended from the same shallow end of the gene pool.

One had a missing eye; Fletcher could see at least four had missing fingers and he was prepared to bet a hundred bucks they'd all have missing teeth.

Fletcher had been in enough bars to read a room in seconds and, while he knew he was unwelcome, he was being tolerated. For the time being at least.

He crossed to the bar and ordered a beer.

"We don't serve none to strangers."

"I wasn't asking for a none, just a beer." Fletcher kept his voice even and his face innocent as he looked at the bartender.

A voice boomed out behind Fletcher. "He said, he don't serve strangers. You a stranger in here so you ain't getting served."

Fletcher turned to identify the speaker. A tall man with corded muscles snaking along the arms poking out from his sleeveless shirt was rising to his feet. By the time he'd positioned himself in front of Fletcher, it had been noted the man had seven fingers, two eyes and some teeth.

A wad of notes appeared in Fletcher's right hand. "I came in here for a beer and to ask if any of you have heard about a girl who went missing. I've a hundred bucks I'm happy to put in someone's hand if they can give me the information I'm after."

Some Teeth pulled his mouth into a smile and belched a gutful of beer fumes Fletcher's way.

"How's about you giving me that hundred bucks so you can walk out of here without you gettin' hurt?"

There was the threat Fletcher had been waiting for. The sense of brooding machismo hung in the air of Fellers like the stale sweat and staler beer. From the moment he'd squeaked the door open and recognized the kind of bar he was in, he'd known someone would challenge him. Some Teeth had been the one to do it.

A threat had been made and now it was all about perception. If he gave the money over, there was a fifty-fifty chance Some Teeth would take a swing at him, as the act would have subjugated Fletcher while bigging up Some Teeth.

What Some Teeth didn't realize was that Fletcher had seen the threat coming his way and had pulled out the wad of notes to invite it into his space. Hard men like these didn't respect niceties or decency, only strength. That's what Fletcher needed to show, and Some Teeth had nominated himself for the role of fall guy. Some Teeth wasn't smart enough to realize someone prepared to wave a hundred bucks around in a bar like Fellers would most likely be confident he could defend himself.

This lack of respect and critical thinking was Some Teeth's problem, and if he was dumb enough to challenge Fletcher, then Fletcher had no qualms about whatever may go down. Had Some Teeth shown him some courtesy and not figured him for a soft mark, Fletcher would have chosen a different way to conduct himself. Fletcher had never had time for bullies and therefore considered Some Teeth as the architect of his own downfall.

"The money is for information given, buddy, not for being allowed to leave."

"I'm not your buddy." Some Teeth's voice was a low growl as he glared down at Fletcher. "You either hand over the cash or you don't walk out of here."

"Okay, okay. There's no need for violence." Fletcher made as if to hand Some Teeth the money but kept his left arm back far enough that the man had to stretch to reach the money. When Some Teeth's fingers were two inches from the wad, Fletcher's right hand swung up from his waist and connected with Some Teeth's jaw.

Not only had Fletcher put his shoulder behind the blow, he'd risen onto his toes and swiveled his hips to employ every muscle he could into landing a knockout punch. As his old sergeant had taught him, he'd aimed inches beyond his actual target, so the blow was still gathering momentum when it connected.

When you punch through and beyond a target you multiply the force of the swing on an exponential level. The science is all about momentum and continued drive. The science wasn't important to Fletcher as he'd tested the theory many times and its results were proven to his satisfaction.

Some Teeth's head snapped back as he was lifted off the ground for a moment before slumping to a heap beside a dubious-looking puddle.

Fletcher pocketed the wad, leaned down and rolled Some Teeth onto his side so he'd be able to breathe. Maybe he had fewer teeth now, but along with his newly broken jaw, that was his own fault.

"Out you git."

Fletcher turned to face the barman. An apology was ready on his lips as he spun, but the twin barrels of the shotgun he saw aimed at his belly stilled his tongue. He'd looked down the barrel of several guns over the years, but couldn't pinpoint the last time he'd faced someone so close to pulling the trigger. At the current range of three feet, the shotgun would blow a hole clean through him and the pellets would carry on to maim those behind him.

The bartender's jaw was set, and he'd lined the sights up, not that he needed them. What concerned Fletcher the most was the arthritic finger curled around the shotgun's trigger. The bulbous knuckles would be sore and stiff. They wouldn't have the sensitivity of youth; therefore there was no knowing if the bartender was aware how hard he was squeezing the trigger.

Of course, the shotgun might not be loaded, but Fletcher didn't plan to find out the hard way.

"I hear you." Fletcher's hands came level with his ears as he stepped over Some Teeth's prone body. "I'm leaving."

As he made his way to the door, Fletcher made sure to keep himself between the shotgun and the regular crowd in the hope the chance of a local getting winged would stay the bartender's grip on the trigger.

When he reached the door, he turned and saw the shotgun had been lowered, although it still pointed in his general direction.

He sent an apologetic look at the bartender then faced the rest of the room. "Sorry to have troubled you all, but if any of you want to make yourself some tax-free bucks all you have to do is help me find this girl. Maybe the word 'trench' will jog your memories."

Fletcher's jaw tightened when he saw the six conscious customers and the gun-toting bartender turn their gazes away when he lifted Lila's picture and held it up for them to see.

The barman's shotgun swung his way and the bulbous finger curled towards the trigger again. "Don't you be threatening no one with Trench, boy. That'll get you into all kinds of trouble."

CHAPTER EIGHT

Zoey Quadrado looked at the files arranged on her bed. Each of the names was memorized as were the respective ages, descriptions and dates they'd gone missing. Every one of the fifteen women had been known to travel through Daversville on the day they'd vanished.

The earliest recorded disappearance had happened four years ago. At first the disappearances had been sporadic, but in the last few months they had escalated until a woman was going missing on a bi-monthly basis.

Quadrado hadn't liked the looks she'd got when she entered Duke's. She wasn't so sensitive that she had a thin skin, but the gazes she'd drawn were of distaste rather than indifference. If people didn't like her personality, that was fine by her, but when they chose to look at her as if she was scum just because of the color of her skin, that rankled.

The sensible part of Quadrado recognized the locals were stuck in a time warp, and as such hadn't developed the relative acceptance of other racial backgrounds she was used to from living and working in New York. Other than her own café au lait complexion, every face she'd seen in Daversville had been white or sun-weathered brown. While they might not be outright racists, there was a good chance their shunning of her was born of their lack of understanding and therefore tolerance. Either way, she was tough enough to not let it bother her.

Quadrado's father had been born in a Tijuana *casucha*. A day later his parents had illegally crossed the border into California and claimed he'd been born in the US. It took her grandparents years of legal wrangling to prove their lie, but eventually they managed to get themselves and their son accepted as Americans. Some thirty-one years after that, her father had married a Wisconsin farmer's daughter and started a family.

Her brother worked on the Wisconsin farm her parents now owned and she'd studied hard to get herself the necessary qualifications needed to be accepted into the FBI. Now here she was, four years into her career and sent out on what could either be a waste of time, or a chance to identify a case that would require a full-scale FBI investigation.

This chewed at Quadrado. Part of her didn't want to return to New York to report that the missing women had all happily joined some cult, as it would be an admission her time here was more or less wasted. Yet as much as she loved the thrill of an investigation, she didn't want people to have suffered, and they surely would have if she found the big case she was hoping for. Single by choice right now, Quadrado devoted all her energies into her work. She saw a husband and kids in her future, but she had no intention of seriously dating for at least another five years. And if the husband and kids didn't ever happen, she was okay with that. Her work was her reason for living. The FBI gave her a chance to do good, to make the world a little safer and to bring closure and justice to the victims of crime.

One thing she'd learned early in her career was that a lot of the older agents had developed a thick skin when it came to the victims and their fates. Whether it was compartmentalizing the horrors they'd seen or a sense of indifference created by experience-worn sensibilities, she'd instead vowed early on that she'd always keep the victims front and center of her mind. To Quadrado, each of the victims in her files was someone's Aunt Janet, and having seen firsthand how loss without closure could affect a family, she would do whatever it took to find the missing women.

Quadrado gathered up the files, put them into her briefcase and snapped the locks shut. One name had appeared in the police reports more than others so that's who she'd focus her energies on. An Agnes Jackson had been questioned regarding whether any of the women had visited the diner. Whether she'd be able to help or not remained to be seen, but she was the logical starting point.

CHAPTER NINE

Fletcher loitered outside Fellers for a while, but nobody followed him out. He half expected some of the folks in there would come out to exact a retribution for him knocking Some Teeth out, but not one of them was either bothered or brave enough to do so.

He didn't expect them to come out and give him the information he'd requested, but there was always a slim chance.

Despite his best efforts in Duke's, he'd learned nothing, and while he'd ingratiated himself with the tables of singletons, none of the bar's other customers had taken him on.

He hadn't planned to use violence when he'd walked into Fellers. His plan had been to get talking to folks over a beer and subtly probe them with his questions. He'd recognized Daversville as a hick town before he'd parked the rental car, but he hadn't expected the town to close ranks against him with the same force as a bear trap. Lots of the hick towns he'd visited had been welcoming places, although as a stranger, there had always been a point where the locals had drawn a line on their friendliness.

The bartender's words after Fletcher had mentioned "trench" were informative. He hadn't said "the trench" or "a trench," he'd used trench as a single word. A name.

Therefore Trench wasn't so much a thing, as a person. It wouldn't be a real name, but that wasn't the key point. The patrons of Fellers knew who Trench was and had shown fear when his name had been dropped into the conversation.

Rather than wait around any longer, he set off walking. He wanted to clear his thoughts and the cooling night air coupled with the gentle exercise aided his thought processes. The beers he'd drunk earlier had had little effect on him. While he'd been generous with his dispensing of numerous pitchers, he'd been careful to only make an appearance of drinking from his glass. His Royal Marine days had taught him how to drink, along with a lot of other skills, and while he enjoyed a cold beer as much as any guy, he was in Daversville for a purpose and therefore would always keep a clear head.

With both of the town's bars failing to give him the leads he wanted, Fletcher's mind was focused on what his next step should be. He could canvas the storekeeper and the other staff at the diner tomorrow, but Georgia was deeply religious and he doubted that they'd be open on a Sunday. The other thing he could do was try and track down the server who'd given Brad the warning.

Fletcher had decided against further direct enquiries about the server, and after his experience tonight, he was growing more convinced by the minute that the residents of Daversville were a close-knit community who were hiding behind a veil of feigned ignorance about Lila's disappearance.

In towns such as Daversville, everyone knew everyone's business. Lila and Brad had eaten in the diner on their way north. Brad had said the diner was moderately busy. Brad was a big guy; he'd be memorable to those who'd seen him. So far as Fletcher was concerned, Lila was pretty without being outright beautiful. But as a couple, especially in a town like this, Brad and Lila were as noticeable as Shrek and Princess Fiona.

Daversville wasn't on the way to anywhere of importance, so the likelihood was that a fair proportion of those who'd been in the diner would have been locals.

Human nature made folk inquisitive; people noticed strangers, observed goings-on. They spotted aberrations from the norm and used their knowledge to gain one-upmanship with those they recounted their stories to.

Someone in or around the diner must have seen what happened to Lila. They hadn't stepped in to save the girl and they hadn't called the police to report an abduction. The only reason Fletcher could think of for this abandoning of decent behavior was fear. The unknown witness or witnesses had turned a blind eye to Lila's fate out of fear of reprisal. Fletcher had experienced enough battles to recognize the fear of violence yet to come when he saw it. He'd seen that same fear every time he'd mentioned that he was looking for Lila. It was there in the failure to meet his eye, the ignorant responses when he tried to engage people in conversation and the point-blank refusal to serve him by the bartender in Fellers.

Whatever had happened to Lila had left the town of Daversville gripped by fear. Which in turn begged a single question. *What or who are the townsfolk afraid of?*

Trench was the obvious answer. Before he pursued this lead, Fletcher had to learn a lot more about the mysterious Trench. First, though, he had to find Mary-Lou and see what she had to say.

*

Fletcher's walk took him along Main Street until he reached the edge of town. It was here that he got his answer. When doing his research before heading to Daversville, he'd been surprised to learn ninety-plus percent of Georgia's forests were privately owned. Lumber was huge business in these parts and the young folk he'd spoken to in Duke's had confirmed how the town was reliant on the lumber mill for employment.

He'd arrived from the opposite direction, which meant he hadn't seen the lumber mill. With the night's stillness to aid him, he could hear the whine of saws and the movement of trucks and lumber-handling machines. Figuring the mill must work around the clock, Fletcher leaned against a fence post and kept his gaze pointed towards the mill as his mind started to make sense of the thoughts assailing him.

For someone to hold the town's entire populace in fear, they would have to be powerful. Whether or not they were brutal, the person intimidating the locals would need something more than just the threat of violence to dominate a whole town. The people who wielded power in places like Daversville were the captains of industry.

His research had informed him that Daversville was a relatively new town. It had been built in the early part of the twentieth century and he now realized that it had been constructed for the sole purpose of housing those who worked at the lumber mill. Every house, store and bar would be owned by the lumber company.

The residents of Daversville would rely on the lumber company for their livelihood and their homes. Everything they had would, in some way, be given to them by the lumber company. It was a subservient way of life that had long since been eradicated from the majority of society.

With their outdated perspective of life, the locals were accepting of their lot, and while some might aspire, and actually manage, to leave the town for a life elsewhere, their family would still be in Daversville, under the control of the lumber company. The counterpoint to this idea was the apparent benevolence of the Blackett family and positive things the young people in Duke's had said about them.

Fletcher was aware that his reasoning may be something of a stretch, as a lot of it was based on assumptions, but it all made sense to him. Daversville was gripped by a collective fear. The only one who'd spoken out in any form was the server from the diner who'd warned Brad.

As a way to play devil's advocate with his thinking, Fletcher tried imagining other reasons for the server's warning and the way the locals were all maintaining a veil of silence. He reasoned that they knew something was amiss in the town, and while they knew it had nothing to do with the lumber mill and its owners, maybe Trench was a serial killer who was active in the area and they feared reprisals from him? The more he thought about it, the more he wondered if Tall Boy and his buddies were trying to run him out of town for their own sakes rather than actually having a direct involvement with what had happened to Lila. Another potential idea was that there was something altogether different going on around Daversville, like some religious cult or a group of preppers who had recruited Lila. According to Brad it had been her suggestion they take a back-roads route north, and it could be that she'd engineered the visit to Daversville so she could join up with whichever group it was. That theory didn't sit so well with him though, as it seemed less likely the townsfolk would cover for such a group or that a religious cult would scare the locals sufficiently. The mysterious Trench fit that profile, though.

Conscious Lila had already been missing for six days, Fletcher didn't want to wait until Monday to get Mary-Lou's address, which to his way of thinking left only one course of action. He had to break into the diner and go through their files to learn where Mary-Lou lived. He was aware the longer it took before he found Lila, the lower the odds were that she would be alive and unharmed.

CHAPTER TEN

Fletcher slunk round the back of the diner and kept to the shadows. He would have preferred to have dressed in black, or at least dark blue clothes, but he hadn't wanted to go back to Duke's and change in case he raised anyone's suspicions.

At least he'd been able to grab a pair of nitrile gloves from the trunk of his car when he'd gotten his pen-sized flashlight and lock picks. Picking locks was a skill he'd been taught years before, and although he'd rather not remember the times he'd had to pick a lock, it was something he was competent at.

His instructor had always favored stealth to brute force. He'd been a sneaky man who would rather drop an opponent unawares than risk them getting the first blow or shot off.

It had been the best part of twenty years since Fletcher had first met the instructor, but he still remembered every lesson he'd been taught. The instructor's style was showing rather than telling and he'd demonstrated his combat techniques to a group of increasingly bruised recruits.

Some years after his initial training, Fletcher had been sent back to the instructor to learn a different set of skills, and this was where his instructor had really shone. The instructor had passed on the techniques developed by Fairburn and Sykes, the legendary WWII men who'd trained the men and women who served in the Special Operations Executive. Their teachings were the foundation for special forces training the world over, and the

Sykes-Fairburn knife they'd designed was a lethal weapon in the hands of a trained fighter.

Fletcher gave his head a slow turn, taking in everything around him before approaching the rear door of the diner. He saw no threats and no observers, so he padded the two remaining steps that got him to the door.

The lock picks served their purpose in just under a minute. Fletcher grasped the door handle and got himself ready. This was the crucial moment. He didn't recall seeing any alarm sensors when in the diner earlier, but that didn't mean they weren't there. At that time he hadn't planned to break in, so his attention had been on the staff rather than the security measures.

He tightened his grip and twisted the door handle. His ears alert for the regimented beeps that signaled an alarm requesting a code be entered into a keypad. Hearing nothing he swung the door open, slipped into the back of the diner and snicked the door closed behind him.

Fletcher was in a tiny anteroom which held a desk, file cabinet and a coat rack The desk was laden with papers and there was a safe tucked underneath it. Among many other skills, the instructor had taught Fletcher how to give a room a thorough and efficient search.

The obvious place for staff records was the file cabinet, but when he pulled at the top drawer it refused to open. He glanced around and saw a small box decorating a shelf above the desk. The box was ornamental and had as much place in the functional office space as a penguin might. He popped the box's lid and found a small key inside it.

Fletcher opened the file cabinet's top drawer and leafed through the files. There were guarantees for catering equipment, certificates from the health department and other odds and ends but no staff records.

The next drawer squealed as he pulled it open, which made Fletcher wince. While his eyes were occupied on the search, his ears were on lookout duty. He could hear his own breaths, but he didn't hear anything else as he teased the drawer open.

Its contents were nothing more than a record of the diner's takings. Each month had a separate file and each file had a stack of sheets depicting each day's earnings. The records went back ten years.

The final drawer of the file cabinet was stacked with manuals for catering equipment. The layer of dust on them was enough to have Fletcher pushing the drawer shut without looking beyond the first manual.

The desk drawers were unlocked, and when Fletcher slid them open, he saw nothing more than stationery supplies and a small cashbox.

As each of his searches came up blank for staff records, Fletcher was beginning to suspect that he was right about the lumber company owning all of the town. If that was the case, there would be a central office for the payroll, personnel—if such a thing existed in Daversville—and the accounting staff. It made sense they'd be centralized, but he kept on with his search in the hope he'd find some clue as to where Mary-Lou lived.

There was no computer on the desk, so Fletcher gave the shelves a once-over before patting down the two jackets hanging from the coat rail. He heard the rustle of paper when patting one down and fished an envelope from a pocket.

The envelope was addressed to a Miss M. L. Henderson. It was from the admissions office of Darton College in Albany. Mary-Lou had been offered a place for the next semester. Fletcher smiled in the darkness. The girl had aspirations. She wanted to escape the servility of existence in Daversville. Fletcher memorized her address from the envelope and stepped back to the door.

His fingers were winding their way around the handle when he heard voices outside. They were the quasi-hushed tones of drunken lovers. A male voice was urging a woman to join him, and she was playing at being coy. Fletcher knew that whatever the outcome of the man's intentions, the couple could be outside the door for a considerable time. There was no way he wanted to stay put and listen to them, so he bent over at the waist and crept his way into the diner proper.

The public areas of the room were a riot of light and shade as the street lighting cast a series of shadows from the trees flanking the parking lot. The air smelled of fried food and there was a sense of crushed dreams about the dated interior.

Fletcher kept low as he passed the booths on his way towards the door. Five feet away from the door he stopped and lifted his head just enough so that he could scan the exterior of the diner.

He didn't see anyone moving about, but that didn't mean he was in the clear. He might not have stolen anything from the diner, but he'd still broken in and there was no way he wanted anyone to see him leave.

After the third scan he moved to the door and slid the top and bottom bolts clear of their keeps.

Fletcher teased the door open, his eyes searching for observers as his ears strained for shouts of surprise. Rather than waste time looking and listening for something that he hadn't already spotted, he rose to his feet and slipped out of the door, taking a moment to push it shut.

A minute later he was walking back to Duke's. His gait neither hurried nor slow. Too often people who were up to no good gave themselves away through furtive or hurried movements.

While he was alert to his surroundings, his mind was already working out the best way to win over Mary-Lou so she'd give him the information he needed. As urgent as it was that he spoke to her, he knew that knocking on her door in the middle of the night wouldn't aid his cause, and he firmly believed getting Mary-Lou talking was the key to finding Lila.

There was nothing he could do beyond hope the delay didn't have life-or-death implications for Lila.

CHAPTER ELEVEN

As he made his way to Mary-Lou's home, Fletcher was second-guessing his timing. Eight-thirty was early to knock on someone's door, doubly so on a Sunday, but all his instincts told him that the inhabitants of Daversville would consider seven a late start. His reasoning was backed up by the number of people he could see going about their business. They were mowing lawns, tidying yards and making repairs to their homes.

All the houses were almost exactly the same. Each one a cottage-style cabin with timber sidings. They were all free-standing with a small yard in front and a picket fence surrounding it. Fletcher didn't do the exact math, but he noted that only one in ten had a driveway or cars parked outside them. Those that did had a ramshackle vehicle that looked as if it was one step from a trip to a junkyard.

Fletcher rapped his knuckles on Mary-Lou's door in what he hoped was a respectful fashion. He'd dressed in a smart shirt and clean jeans. His chin was freshly shaven and daubed with cologne. First impressions mattered and he wanted to make a good one with Mary-Lou.

In an ideal world he'd have liked fewer of the woman's neighbors watching him with their suspicious expressions, but there was nothing he could do about that.

There was no response to his knock, so he tried again. It was possible Mary-Lou had gone visiting, but the rest of the neighborhood seemed to be wrapped up in their chores, so he supposed she'd be doing the same.

Another suspicious look came his way from a neighbor, so he tossed her a cheery wave and a broad smile. He knew it wouldn't remove her doubts about him, but as much as he could, he wanted to show her that he wasn't hiding away and that his intentions were to do no harm.

There were no signs of movement in the cabin and the drapes were still drawn which made Fletcher wonder if Mary-Lou was a late riser. For all he knew, maybe she really was on vacation. Perhaps she was away scouting places to live in Albany while attending college.

Rather than wake Mary-Lou with a third, more insistent knock, he decided to scout round the house. Perhaps she was out back hanging washing or busying herself with another chore.

The neighbor's watchful eye followed him as he left the porch and made his way along the dusty sidewalk.

Fletcher cut a left at the end of the street and took the lane between the low-slung cabins. Mary-Lou's was the third on the left.

The back fence was low and in dire need of a good coat of paint, but there was no one in the backyard. The cabin looked deserted, apart from one thing. The back door wasn't closed properly. It hung open an inch or two.

With thoughts of Lila suffering a terrible fate foremost in his mind, Fletcher vaulted the fence and strode towards the door. His eyes were scanning the back windows looking for a woman's face, but they found none.

He rapped on the door and called out Mary-Lou's name. Like the knock on the front door, the impact of his knuckles went unanswered. They did however cause the door to swing inwards.

A familiar smell came his way as the door came to a stop against a wall.

It was the unmistakable coppery tang of blood. The thing about the smell of blood is, it takes more than a few drops to create an identifiable stench.

The pit of Fletcher's stomach coiled into a solid knot as he stepped into the cabin. He paid little heed to his surroundings as he passed through a kitchen then into a hallway.

Fletcher was following the smell as much as anything and a glance into the lounge proved Mary-Lou absent from the room.

He found her in the bedroom. Covers still over the lower half of her body.

The upper half of her body was a different matter. Her throat had been slashed wide and deep. Situated on top of her blood-soaked nightdress was a lump of mangled flesh.

Fletcher was reaching for his cell when he heard the screech of tires outside. A glance out of the window let his eyes rest on the police car. A deputy climbed from the car with his gun drawn and his eyes on Mary-Lou's cabin.

CHAPTER TWELVE

For a brief moment, Fletcher considered dashing through the cabin and out the back door. Being in the vicinity of the body he presumed to be Mary-Lou Henderson was incriminating enough before you added a small-town mentality. He'd been asking about Mary-Lou in the diner just yesterday, and the server was sure to remember him.

He'd also broken into the diner to find Mary-Lou's address. His leaving the front door open might have been passed over as a mistake by a forgetful employee, but when the server heard of Mary-Lou's fate, she'd trot to the local cops with her tale about a stranger asking to meet Mary-Lou and she'd be sure to mention that the diner's door had been found unlocked.

When Fletcher factored in the bygone and secular mentality of Daversville's inhabitants, he didn't so much expect a fair trial, as to be dragged to the nearest tree with a stout branch for a good ol' Georgia hanging.

As much as flight may seem like the best option, a part of Fletcher knew running away would cement his guilt in the eyes of the locals. Therefore he'd have to fight them.

A physical fight was out of the question, as no good ever came from getting rough with a cop, so he'd have to engage another way. He'd have to take the cop and beat him over the head with logic and hard facts until he realized Fletcher wasn't responsible for Mary-Lou's homicide.

Fletcher guessed a neighbor had called the cops about him prowling around the cabin and, while it was unlikely either the caller or the cop knew about Mary-Lou's death, he'd still been found at the site of a brutal killing.

As he took slow careful steps back the way he'd come, Fletcher drank in as many of the details as he could. For all he knew, there could be other cops at the rear of the house and the last thing he wanted to do was walk into an ambush. He was an out-of-towner and it was possible word of his standoff with Tall Boy and what he'd done to Some Teeth had gotten back to the cop.

If that was the case, the cop may well be nervous about approaching him. He'd be keyed up with excess adrenaline coursing through his veins. His thought processes would be dulled by a mixture of excitement and fear. The heightened state he'd be experiencing would sharpen his vision and hearing but dull his wits. He'd act before he thought, and when a man is carrying a gun as he comes your way, you want him to think before he acts.

Fletcher looked out into the back yard. He didn't see anyone, but that didn't mean the cop wasn't crouched behind a fence or had his back pressed against the cabin's rear wall.

With a deep breath hissing out of him, Fletcher grasped the door handle and opened it wide in one steady movement.

CHAPTER THIRTEEN

Quadrado stretched until her muscles felt like they once more belonged to her. The bed at Duke's had been less than comfortable, which meant she'd spent half the night squirming in search of a position that would allow her to get some decent shut-eye.

With the local deputy summoned to a call about a stranger wandering around the town's residential area and breaking into a house, she now had time to properly look around Daversville and begin assessing the small lumber town and its locals.

In an ideal world she'd like to have had the deputy's full attention so she could run through the entire list of people who'd disappeared after passing through Daversville, but things hadn't worked out that way.

Some things couldn't be fixed though, so Quadrado accepted what she couldn't fix and set off along the town's main drag.

As she walked along the sidewalk Quadrado saw several families traveling in the opposite direction. Each member of the family was dressed in smart, if dated, clothes, but obviously their best. The children stared at her in fascination, although one or two of the parents were gracious enough to send a nod her way when she smiled at them.

Quadrado knew it was the color of her skin making the children stare. She couldn't help but wonder if it was simply because she was a different color than them, or if the racist tendencies of their parents had already been passed down to them.

After she passed the third family, Quadrado had reached the point where the main thoroughfare devolved into a mixture of low cabins and a building which she guessed may be a school.

Rather than wander around the cabins as she'd intended, Quadrado decided to forego that idea and do what the locals were doing. Ahead of her were a variety of families, couples and single walkers all heading towards her.

Quadrado turned and followed the families who'd passed her until she arrived at the church whose bells she'd heard ringing since she'd left Duke's.

The church was a Baptist one rather than the Catholic one she attended whenever work allowed, but that didn't matter to Quadrado. In her eyes, the different branches of Christianity were all just various interpretations of a single text. In this church she could worship God and Jesus every bit as much as she could in her regular church.

Quadrado knew how churches worked. There was an unspoken hierarchy. Regular attendees would sit in the same place every week. The more important the worshiper, the closer to the altar their seat. Instead of joining the throng and finding a vacant seat, she hung back and observed the rest of the congregation. Not only would doing so give her a chance to work out who the movers and shakers in the town were, she'd also not cause offense to anyone by taking their seat.

What surprised her more than anything was the number of people filing in. It was as if the whole town was squeezing into the little church. Her own church was lucky if a tenth of its seats were taken on a Sunday, yet by the time the people at the back of the line had entered, there was only standing room left at the back.

From her position at the rear, Quadrado scanned the whole church and saw the front two pews were still empty.

The hushed reverence was broken when the congregation rose and one last family entered. Whomever the family were, it was clear they were respected and admired by the locals. Nodded greetings and wide smiles were given and returned as the family marched down the aisle to fill the two empty pews. Like the other locals, the family wore smart but outdated clothing. Their hairstyles were functional rather than fashionable and their boots carried the same sheen of dust as everyone else's did.

The family's entrance had changed the dynamic in the church. The minister gave them a benevolent smile and he waited until they were seated before beginning his sermon.

Quadrado didn't know who the family were, but the reaction of the townspeople to them was telling. It was obvious the family were powerful, respected and liked. This was a two-way street as the family had shown no falseness in their responses. The younger members had displayed no cockiness or sense of entitlement at being treated better than the rest of the population. She planned to find out about them from the deputy, even if only to sate her own curiosity. The deference shown to the family tugged at Quadrado until she realized they must be the Blackett family who owned the lumber mill.

Once the minister had delivered his service, Quadrado took up a position outside where she could observe the locals as they exited. First out was the family who'd been last to enter. But rather than load themselves into the battered pickups they stood beside, they too waited until the church was empty. A large bag was lifted from a pickup's bed and the town's children all pushed their way to the front of the gathering crowd.

An old woman with a cane waved to the children and they all ran forward and formed a neat line. One by one each of the children received a candy bar and in two instances a box wrapped with brown paper. The boxes were opened with a feverish glee and the basic toys they contained were raised to the skies as if trophies.

More than the generosity in giving out treats to the kids, the way the old woman spoke to each child with a wide smile touched

Quadrado. Every child left the old woman with delight on their faces as they raced back to their parents to show their prize.

For her next move, she planned go to the diner and speak to Agnes Jackson. It had been shut when she'd first looked, but the size of the congregation was enough to suggest the workers from the diner would be at church, as it seemed to Quadrado the whole town had packed themselves into the building.

CHAPTER FOURTEEN

Fletcher looked out the door and saw nobody arrowing his way. Not a cop nor a civilian was in sight. All the same, he kept scanning the area as he exited Mary-Lou's cabin.

What was important now was to engage with the cop in a way that would establish that he wasn't a threat and was a reasonable law-abiding person, instead of a homicidal maniac.

Rather than take the shortest route to the front of the cabin where the cop had parked his car, Fletcher steered himself several feet wide of the corner of the cabin. People who were looking to ambush someone kept close to buildings, those who didn't kept themselves in the open. Taking the route he did would also remove any perceived threat or furtive behavior while also making it harder for anyone to get the jump on him.

To further bolster this thinking, Fletcher had laced his fingers together and placed his hands in front of his stomach, palms upwards. It was a non-threatening gesture. It put both his hands on display and had them in a place where it was hard to strike from.

At least that's what a layman might think. Fletcher knew that the loose grip he was employing wouldn't hinder him from throwing an elbow over either shoulder, and he could scan what was in front of him and disengage his hands long before any assailant could get near him. If the potential assailant had a gun, as this cop did, it didn't matter that his hands were empty, it was more that it was important the person with the gun could see he had no weapon and couldn't suddenly produce one.

Fletcher walked alongside the cabin, calling out as he went. His calls were a mixture of "Hey, is there anybody there?", "Hello, officer" and "Quick, someone help me."

The cop appeared from the front lawn. His still-drawn pistol lifting from where it pointed at the ground until it was aimed at Fletcher.

"Freeze. Who are you?"

Fletcher did as he was told and froze. "My name is Grant Fletcher. I came here to visit Mary-Lou Henderson. I went in," a side nod towards the cabin, "and I found her. She's been killed. Her throat has been slashed."

The cop's gun was raised until it was pointing at Fletcher's face. He could see down its barrel when the cop's hands shook in a certain direction. The shaking hands didn't worry him as much as the way the cop's knuckles were white.

Fletcher couldn't identify the pistol pointing at him, therefore he didn't know how much pressure was needed before the trigger sent the firing pin on its destructive way forward.

"Hands on your head."

"As you say." Fletcher put his fingers on his head and resisted the temptation to make a smart remark about whether the cop wanted him to kneel as well. The cop was nervous, and his features carried the same slightly inbred look that decorated the rest of Daversville's inhabitants. What Fletcher needed the cop to do was listen to reason, not get carried away and make a stupid, and what may be for Fletcher, a potentially deadly mistake. "Did you hear what I said about Mary-Lou? You need to call it in, get some detectives and a forensic team out here. You should cordon off the area to preserve evidence."

The pistol wobbled some more before a determined effort brought it back under a vague semblance of control.

"Turn around. Drop to your knees and keep your hands on your head."

When Fletcher did as instructed, he heard the cop's footsteps approach. It was when he felt his arms being hauled behind his back and handcuffs being snapped around his wrists he regretted not running.

CHAPTER FIFTEEN

Quadrado found a seat in the diner and waited for the server to come her way. She'd already seen the name badge as she'd passed her and knew the server was Agnes Jackson.

A waggle of the coffee pot was used to ask the question as Agnes padded towards her. A nod was returned by way of an answer.

The menu held little appeal to Quadrado; although she recognized that it was laden with typical diner items, it held no consideration for vegetarians beyond a salad which also doubled as its sole healthy option.

Rather than pick her way around a meat-laden dish again, Quadrado chose the salad and hoped for the best.

"Excuse me, do you have a minute to chat?"

"I'm busy right now, maybe in five?"

Quadrado used the wait to ponder on the older woman's expression. As soon as she'd heard the request for a chat, her face had changed from being open, if not quite friendly to a brown face, to a guarded look. It was a familiar transformation to any cop; it was a sign of assumed guilt or worry about false charges that came when a badge was shown to someone.

Except she hadn't shown her badge to the woman. Her badge was in its wallet, where it had been since she'd left Atlanta. Other than the deputy she'd introduced herself to, nobody in Daversville knew she was an FBI agent, which made the worry on Agnes Jackson's face pique Quadrado's interest. If the woman was nervous about talking to a stranger, it made sense the nerves were fueled by some sense of guilt or at least a knowledge of guilt.

"What can I do for you?" Agnes slid herself into the booth opposite Quadrado. "I ain't got long as we'll be busy lunchtime."

Quadrado introduced herself and badged the server. "I'm here looking for some missing women. Do you mind if I call you Agnes?"

"That's what it says on here." A tap of the badge. "You ain't the first to be in here askin' 'bout missing women, had us some cops from Douglas and of course, Deputy White."

"I've met the deputy." Quadrado kept her opinions of the brief impression Deputy White had made upon her to herself for the moment. "These women who've gone missing, I read the statements you gave to the officers from Douglas. Is there anything you can add to them?"

"I'm sorry, I see so many new faces in here they all kinda blur." A rueful smile that was as false as a liar's promise. "I ain't so young as I was and my memory ain't too hot. Can remember me what happened forty years ago and then forget what'n I ate for dinner last night."

"Fair enough. Just thought I'd ask."

Agnes had a relieved look in her eyes and there was something of a tremor in her fingertips that wasn't there before. Maybe her tale about her memory was true, but Quadrado was tempted to think it might be a convenient smokescreen she was hiding behind. Time for her to put some pressure on Agnes.

Quadrado dropped a photo of Lila Ogilvie on the table between them. "This woman was in here with her boyfriend a week ago. She vanished while he was paying the bill. According to Deputy White's investigation, you swore you'd never seen her. She was with her boyfriend, he's a real big guy so I'm not sure you'd forget them."

"I don't remember them being in here, but after Deputy White asked me, I did hear someone saying something 'bout a young couple going at it out on the street. 'Parently she was pitchin' a hissy fit with a tail on it, an' he was giving back good as he was getting. Can't remember who told me 'bout it, but they said he was real tall and fat as a tick." A pause to scratch at the side of her nose. "Big guy like him all riled up don't make for a happy ending if he got any mean in him. Ask me, never a bad idea to put some gone between you an' a man like that."

"Can you remember who told you this?"

Agnes looked at every part of the diner as she trawled her memory before shaking her head. "Nope, can't remember who said it. Sure I told 'em they should tell Deputy White, but I don't know if'n they did."

This new development put a different slant on whether Lila Ogilvie was connected to the other missing women in Quadrado's mind. If she'd had a fight with her boyfriend, there was a chance he'd gotten physical with her. Considering the size of him compared to Lila, he was more than powerful enough to kill her and dump her body somewhere in the woods. The report from the cops who'd grilled Brad had made no mention of the two of them falling out. Either Brad was lying to those who'd interviewed him, or Agnes was.

Her next move was to get back to Deputy White's small station and see if he'd been approached by the witness.

CHAPTER SIXTEEN

Fletcher sat on the cell's bed and put his mind to not just proving his innocence, but trying to work out what effect what had happened to Mary-Lou might have on his quest to find Lila. At the very least, his search would be held back by however long it took him to get the cop to believe him.

Once again he cursed his decision not to run. The arrest was an inconvenience, but he believed that he'd be freed. Other than the delay it'd cause, that wasn't the problem. The greater effect his arrest would have was that the townsfolk would all believe he was responsible for Mary-Lou's homicide. Before he faced that hurdle, he had to persuade the town's cop of his innocence.

That would be easier said than done. A dull wit had shown itself to be swimming beneath the uniform. Rather than investigate Mary-Lou's homicide in the proper way, the cop had arrested Fletcher and locked him in the back of his squad car. With that done he'd disappeared into the cabin for a total of five minutes before emerging and driving Fletcher to the small building which acted as Daversville's police department.

The police building was small enough for Fletcher to observe the cop as he sat in his cell. The cop did nothing he should and everything he shouldn't. There was no call for detectives or crime scene investigators to attend Mary-Lou's homicide. Nor had he sealed off the crime scene.

What he did do was taunt Fletcher about the trouble he was in. Not by way of an official interview, instead he made snide comments. It was as if he'd appointed himself both judge and jury.

As much as he believed in the due process of law, Fletcher was regretting the honesty which had made him stay at the crime scene instead of slipping out of the back door. He'd known it was a calculated gamble when he'd made the decision, but he hadn't expected things to go so bad so quickly. But had he escaped the crime scene, he wouldn't have been able to stick around and investigate Lila's disappearance, which was the primary reason he hadn't run.

The cop took a call.

Fletcher could only hear one side of it, but the number of times the cop said "yes, ma'am" told him that he was speaking to a superior. What was more concerning to Fletcher were the nervous looks the cop kept sliding his way.

CHAPTER SEVENTEEN

A Hispanic woman entered the police building and Fletcher saw the cop stiffen as soon as he saw her. The woman pointed his way and the cop took her outside.

It was the first piece of discretion the cop had shown, although Fletcher hadn't failed to notice that the cop hadn't been pleased to see her. She must be the person he was calling "ma'am." While she was half the cop's age, it was clear she held authority over him.

After a few minutes, both the cop and the woman came back in. There was a look of disgusted anger on the woman's face, and the cop's hands shook as he got a chair for the woman to sit on.

Once she'd spun the chair around and was sitting with one arm along its slatted back she reached for the phone on the desk and typed a number from memory. The way she kept her voice low made Fletcher think the call was about him.

Once the call was over, she wheeled her chair to where she could look straight at Fletcher as she flashed him a badge. "Special Agent Quadrado. FBI. And you are?"

"Grant Fletcher." The FBI getting involved so soon could either bode really well or really badly for him, so Fletcher planned to say as little as possible until he could assess this new development.

"Apologies for the lack of a real interview room. Before I have you transported to Milledgeville PD for a formal interview, I'd like to establish a few basic facts."

A formal interview sounded good to Fletcher. The more he'd thought about the cop's actions since he'd been arrested the more he'd grown to distrust the man. It wasn't so much that he wasn't close to doing his job right, it was the fact he seemed to be doing everything wrong on purpose. Whether she liked it or not, Agent Quadrado was cast in the role of savior so far as he was concerned.

What stake the FBI had in the murder was as yet unknown, but if it got him out of the cop's care he was willing to answer any questions Quadrado had for him. He took a closer look at her now he'd learned who she was. She was late twenties. Slight but with a wiriness that spoke of exercise rather than malnourishment. Her clothes were the traditional FBI uniform of a dark suit and a white shirt. A crucifix hung from her neck, and while her face was set in a neutral pose, there was a fierce intelligence shining from her brown eyes.

"That's what I'd like too. The first and most important fact is that I'm innocent. I didn't kill Mary-Lou Henderson." Fletcher knew that as much as he wanted to give a long protestation of his innocence, Quadrado would mistrust ramblings. Her training would have taught her guilty people ramble on. Therefore he planned to give her the bare minimum until some kind of rapport had been established. There was also his judgment of her to factor in. She'd want to earn his story, to draw his truth out with her questions rather than be handed it on a plate.

"According to Deputy White, you were arrested at Miss Henderson's house after neighbors saw you banging on her door and then going round back and letting yourself in."

"I wasn't banging. I was knocking. I saw the neighbors and went round back because it was important I speak to her as soon as possible. If her door hadn't been open I would have asked the neighbors if they'd seen her or knew where she was."

Quadrado's face never changed, but Fletcher could see her gaze hardening. He needed to answer better.

"Do you know Miss Henderson?"

"No."

"So, let me get this straight. You visited a stranger's home and when you found an open door, you entered her house? Why? What was so important that you felt you had to enter her house? Because from where I'm sitting, it looks like you went in, murdered her and you're gambling on being able to talk your way out of her homicide."

"I admit it was foolish of me to go into the house, but it was imperative I speak to her as soon as possible. I thought she may know something about a friend of mine who's gone missing."

There was no mistaking the look that flashed in Quadrado's eyes. It was one of surprise, shock almost. She gave an instinctive flick of her eyes towards the cop that was filled with disdain. Fletcher knew he'd wrong-footed her and was keen to press home his advantage, but the look she'd given the cop had warned him that she too had no faith in the man.

"We'll come back to your missing friend in a moment. All the evidence points to you as her killer. There's also the information Deputy White has shared with me. Since you arrived in Daversville yesterday, you were on the verge of getting yourself into a fight in the parking lot outside the diner. From what I've heard, it was only the fact those boys walked away that prevented you from attacking them. Then there's the assault you committed in front of several witnesses in Fellers bar. All in all, it would seem like you've quite the taste for violence. I don't think it'd take a lot of imagining for anyone to put you in the role of murderer." Quadrado sent another look White's way. "Once I had your social security number, I put a call in to the Atlanta office who ran you through a few databases. You're a mysterious man. Cashiered out of the British Royal Marines ten years ago, you wound up living in Vernal, Utah. You apparently now work construction and have a daughter, Wendy, approaching college age. Your wife is listed as deceased. But there's no escaping the fact that you're a former soldier—a trained killer—with a penchant for violence, who happened to be present at the scene of an unprovoked homicide. I have to say, all the evidence is pointing at you being Mary-Lou's killer."

Fletcher let a soft smile caress his mouth. He'd expected Quadrado to dig out his past career. Granted, he'd thought it might have reared its head later in the day once he'd gotten a chance to get his side of the story across. This was a complication, but not one he couldn't deal with.

"You might think all the evidence is pointing that way. I'd disagree. In fact I'd go so far as to guess that you haven't visited the crime scene."

A sculpted eyebrow arced upwards. "What makes you say that?"

"Several things. You're an FBI agent so it's unlikely you're in town to deal with a homicide that's only been discovered in the last few hours. It may be that Mary-Lou Henderson is someone you've been keeping a watch on as part of an investigation, but I just don't think that is the case. Your eyes are clear and bright, there's no horror at a repulsive sight in them. Add all that together, and you're only questioning me out of your own curiosity rather than a professional interest in the homicide. If you had visited the crime scene, you'd have noticed the blood. Miss Henderson's throat was cut. I'm sure Deputy White will back me up and agree there was a lot of blood on her chest and on top of the covers. However, where it had soaked into the covers it had dried and hardened. That's right, isn't it, Deputy?" A nod of confirmation came from White and it was all Fletcher could do to keep the smile off his face. If what he suspected about the deputy was correct, the affirmation of this point may well come back to haunt him. 'I don't know the exact timescales it takes for blood to dry, but Deputy White went in there no more than ten minutes after I did." Another look. Another nod. "And I'm confident that fresh blood takes a lot more than ten minutes to dry. Therefore I couldn't have killed Miss Henderson just before Deputy White arrested me as there wasn't time for her blood to dry."

"It was you. I know it was you, you goddamn liar. Stop with your lies and twisting of things."

"Thank you, Deputy, I'll take it from here. You can carry on with your duties now."

White stood and glowered, clearly unsure whether to fight back against Quadrado dismissing him from his own office. The FBI agent outranked him, so after a full minute of impotent staring at her waiting for her to change her mind, he stomped out of the door.

"All right, I haven't visited the crime scene, but what's to say you didn't kill her and then went back there this morning to establish this messed-up reasoning?"

Fletcher gave Quadrado a look. "You don't believe that anymore than you think Deputy White is a competent law enforcement officer. Doing what you say would put me at a greater risk of detection if I was her killer, therefore it makes no sense that I would do it. Another thing, what do you know about the victim? Do you know where she lives? That she lives alone at a young age? That she had plans to go to college in Albany? Also, I'm still wearing the clothes I was arrested in. Do you see even the tiniest speck of blood on me?"

"No."

'When you go to the crime scene you'll see that Miss Henderson's blood sprayed out in a wide arc. There was a gap in the spray where her killer must have stood. Ergo, it couldn't have been me this morning, and I've already established that for me to return to the scene would be ridiculous. Therefore I'm not your killer."

"You may well be innocent of her homicide, but that doesn't explain how you got into two fight situations in your first few hours in town. Nor does it explain your interest in Mary-Lou Henderson."

Fletcher spread his hands wide in a supplicating gesture. "I came to Daversville to try and find out what had happened to a girl called Lila Ogilvie. She's a friend's daughter who went missing after stopping at the diner. Her boyfriend was warned to leave town by Mary-Lou. When he went outside to meet with Lila, he couldn't find her. He went to the police. Deputy White told him she must have dumped him and moved on. My friend asked me to come and look into it. I came and made the diner my first stop. I hoped to speak to Mary-Lou. She wasn't there, but when I asked after her, the other server told me she was on vacation. I left the diner and four punks came at me. They tried to run me out of town; I refused to let them and explained what I'd do to them if they tried to get physical with me. They then *chose* not to get physical. As for the fight in the bar, I was asking if anyone had seen Lila and this bonehead decided to take issue with me. He fronted me up, so I dropped him. I only hit him the once and in my mind it was self-defense."

"I know about Lila's disappearance." A hand lifted. "Not where she is, just that she's missing. Again, we'll come back to that. You are a Brit by birth, but you speak like an American. Why is that?"

"I married an American woman and settled in Utah. I've always been adaptable to wherever I've been stationed or lived, so I guess that my speech patterns and so on subconsciously became Americanized as I tried to fit in."

Fletcher didn't bother telling Quadrado about the three years he spent swapping between foster homes until he was formally adopted at the age of eight. Those years had been when he'd learned to fit in, to do as he was told and to keep his feelings and emotions to himself. His adoptive parents were good people, and he still valued having them in his life despite not having seen them since what had happened with his wife. It wasn't that he didn't want to see them, more that the distance between Manchester in the UK and Utah was a good excuse for not getting close enough to them for either parent to sense his guilt regarding her death.

"True." Quadrado looked pensive. "I guess a psychologist would suggest that after being cashiered out of the Royal Marines, you felt a certain level of anger towards the UK and rather than cling onto your heritage as most ex-pats do, you cleansed it by Americanizing yourself, as you say it."

"You say potato, I say potahto."

Quadrado didn't give any hint of amusement at his quip. "Very droll. The fact remains, you're a trained killer who, within twelve hours of arriving in town, got into two fights and was then found on the scene of a homicide."

"You make a good argument, Agent Quadrado, apart from one or two salient points. First, you haven't visited the crime scene yourself, so you're not in possession of all the facts. Second, it was one fight and one standoff. Third, you showed surprise when I told you why I was in Daversville, but you keep shying away from discussing Lila's disappearance. You said you knew she'd gone missing before I told you. There's also your presence in Daversville. To be frank, I'm surprised a town this size has a cop, let alone an FBI agent. Therefore you need a reason to be in town. My guess would be that you've been sent here on a case. Not Mary-Lou Henderson's homicide as your accent isn't Georgian, and there was no time between my arrest and your arrival for you to travel from either Quantico or wherever it is you're based, which means it's something else. Would I be right in saying that Lila isn't the only person to have gone missing in these parts?"

"I am not here to answer your questions, Mr. Fletcher. I am here to ask my own. Your first point about me not knowing all the facts, what else was there at the crime scene?"

Fletcher wasn't bothered about the deflection of his question. It was an answer in itself. The bigger issue was that he was right and that it meant a number of people had gone missing. In turn, this reduced the chances of ever finding Lila alive and unharmed.

"Mary-Lou's tongue had been removed and left on her chest." Fletcher took a deep breath. "I maybe didn't kill her myself, but I think I may have caused her death. The fact I was asking questions about her highlighted that she'd tried to help Brad and Lila. Whoever took Lila and the others I suspect you're here to look for must have heard about my enquiries. And I think they chose to use Mary-Lou to send a message."

CHAPTER EIGHTEEN

Quadrado tried not to let her surprise at Mary-Lou's tongue being removed show on her face, but she could tell by Fletcher's reaction that she'd failed. As she cursed herself, she threw a few extra curses towards Deputy White. Not only had he totally screwed up the crime scene, but he'd failed to inform her about this gruesome detail.

The removal of a tongue was a less than subtle message and what Fletcher had said about Mary-Lou having warned his friend to leave town gave a potential reason for her mutilation.

The other side of the coin was that while Fletcher was making a lot of sense with what he was saying, she only had his side of the story to go on.

A CSI team had been summoned to the scene, but until they'd completed their results, there was nothing that could be done with regards to the investigation.

The telephone on the desk rang so she got up and answered it.

The caller was the coroner who'd attended the crime scene. Quadrado asked him a number of questions, got her answers and ended the call.

Fletcher was where she'd left him. She gave him a good look over to see what kind of man he was. He was average in build and height, yet there was a rugged handsomeness to his features that many would find attractive. His eyes were bright and full of not just intelligence, but also wisdom. His face was implacable, but she'd already figured he was smart enough to have worked out from hearing her side of the conversation who she'd been speaking to. Throughout her questioning, he'd been calm, never angry at his arrest, and both his words and manner were that of a man who was at peace with what was happening to him. She'd interviewed many people as an FBI agent and never had she come across someone who could be so emotionless about their predicament. Guilty people tried for Fletcher's level of composure without ever quite achieving it, while the innocent suspects were obviously terrified of wrongful imprisonment. The only sign of humanity he'd shown was when his stomach had rumbled. Wrong, she corrected herself; around his neck was a gold locket hanging from a corded chain. Lockets were more often worn by women than men, yet in front of her was a former elite soldier with a locket. She guessed it must hold a deep meaning for him, otherwise she couldn't picture a man like him wearing such an effeminate piece of jewelry.

"What did the coroner say about the time of death?"

Quadrado crinkled her nose at Fletcher's directness. "Between ten last night and two this morning."

"I guessed as much." A shrug. "So, Agent Quadrado, how do you think that affects Deputy White's case against me? Let's be honest here, if I was the one to kill Mary-Lou, and it's already been established I didn't do it in the minutes before my arrest, we've discussed how stupid it would be of me to have returned to the scene of the crime. I'm guessing the coroner confirmed it was Mary-Lou's tongue on her chest. We both know that removing her tongue was a warning to others not to talk. I can easily produce witnesses who'll corroborate that I was here looking for Lila. A subject you have yet to address. You have also shied away from my suggestion that Lila isn't the only person to go missing. There are larger forces at work here than either of us imagine and I'll bet that you've already recognized that."

Quadrado kept her mouth shut, but she couldn't help the corners of her mouth turning upwards. Fletcher was smart, he'd pegged her from the start and his story made perfect sense. There were a few details she needed to clarify before she had to make a decision on whether or not to release Fletcher from his cell.

"Why are you looking into Lila's disappearance rather than her father himself or a private investigator?"

"I owe her father a favor. Don would have been here himself, except he's confined to a wheelchair. Besides, he's two steps past being your typical overprotective father. His way of looking into what happened to Lila would end up with you putting Don on death row or in a jail cell for life."

"As opposed to your gentle methods?"

Fletcher gave an easy shrug. "They picked a fight with me. I warned the four punks what'd happen. They weren't dumb enough to try their luck. The guy in the bar was. Him getting his ass kicked is his fault, not mine. He thought he was tough enough to rob me. All I did was prove him wrong."

"Coming to look for a friend's missing daughter is a big favor, what did he do for you to earn such a debt?"

"He saved my life in Afghanistan. Me finding Lila won't square my debt, but he won't see it that way."

Rather than continue fencing for a straight answer, Quadrado decided to try a different question. "You're obviously an intelligent man, yet a lot of the things you're saying hint at some law enforcement background, or at least investigative training, and that doesn't fit with your military background. Do you want to tell me about your training?"

Fletcher gave that nonchalant shrug of his again. The way Fletcher kept doing that shrug was starting to irritate Quadrado. It was as if he had all the time in the world and was convinced of not just his innocence, but his righteousness. It was one thing to be self-confident, but Fletcher's self-belief was bordering on arrogance, a trait Quadrado hated, although she was too much of a professional to let her feelings show.

"I have no training at all. However, my adoptive parents being a cop and an investigative journalist made for interesting conversations at the dinner table. I guess I picked up a few things from them."

"Hah! So you're an amateur sleuth, are you? That doesn't ring true at all." Quadrado cursed herself for the scoffing in her words and voice.

"You're forgetting something. You've looked into me. You said as much yourself. Ask yourself where on my file it said that I had been trained as an investigator. At the risk of sounding arrogant, I'm not an idiot and I can use my common sense. I'm entertained by investigations and since I got to Daversville, I have been putting myself in the shoes of an investigator. Trying to work out what a real cop would be looking for and then looking for it myself. I'm sorry if that annoys you, but it's the truth."

Quadrado fell silent as she mentally recapped Fletcher's file. He hadn't had any formal training, but she was still skeptical that he'd learned so much about investigative techniques from listening to his parents. Rather than pursue the point, she tried another angle. "So you're here trying to find out what happened to Lila. Want to catch me up on what you've discovered so far?"

"I got nothing. Mary-Lou Henderson was my one good lead and you know what happened to her." Fletcher leaned back, a pensive look on his face. "You know, it's odd that you're not pressing me for more details about Lila. You've never asked when she actually passed through Daversville. That means one of three things: you're a shoddy investigator—which I highly doubt; you don't care—which seems preposterous; or you already know all the details about Lila's disappearance. When I suggested earlier that she wasn't the only person to go missing in Daversville you were quick to change the subject. That explains why you're in town. You've been sent to investigate the disappearances."

"You're too smart for your own good, Fletcher."

"I'll take that as a compliment. Tell me, Special Agent Quadrado, have you come across the name Trench in your investigation?"

"No. Should I have?" The name meant nothing to her, but it'd be easy enough to find out about it. "Who is it?"

"Someone the locals seem to be afraid of." Another one of his shrugs. "That's all I know."

A banging at the door interrupted their conversation. Quadrado rose to answer it.

A man was standing outside. His eyes full of fury and unshed tears. "Where's Deputy White? I need him to tell me what's going on. They won't let me see my daughter."

Quadrado closed the door behind her. If, as she suspected, this was Mary-Lou Henderson's father, she didn't want him seeing Fletcher, in case he jumped to conclusions or tried to assault him. She introduced herself.

"Please. Tell me you've caught the man who killed my Mary-Lou."

There are plenty of stock phrases cops use when dealing with distraught relatives. There're ones that are designed to pacify and inform without giving away any details, or offering a false hope. Quadrado knew lots of such phrases. Had used them on many occasions, yet with the proud man in front of her fighting to maintain a semblance of composure, she heard the trite messages for what they were, useless entreaties designed to free up the cop rather than help the relative.

"Sir, I'm sure that you'll be able to see your daughter soon. Right now it's important that Deputy White does everything he can to preserve the crime scene, so we have the best chance of catching your daughter's killer." She laid a gentle hand on his shoulder. "Why don't you go home and look after your wife. I'll have Deputy White contact you as soon as he's free."

"Ain't got no wife. Lost her to cancer last year."

"I'm sorry." Quadrado paused a beat then took a gamble. "Tell me, sir, does the name Trench mean anything to you?"

Henderson's mouth hardened as he crossed himself. "Is that who you think killed her? Lord have mercy on her soul."

Quadrado watched as Mary-Lou's father shuffled off, broken by the grief of losing his daughter. She wanted to run after the man. Envelop him in a hug that would take his pain away, salve his breaking heart and give him a reason to get up in the morning.

She didn't move. It wasn't her place to fix him and he wouldn't want a stranger's interference, although she hoped for his sake Mary-Lou's killer was found.

When she entered the tiny police station, Fletcher was looking at her with his usual directness. "So where do we go from here?"

"*I* am going to continue my investigation. *You* are going to be on the next plane back to Utah."

CHAPTER NINETEEN

The bar at Duke's wasn't as busy as the previous evening, but that didn't mean Fletcher was any more welcome. The town's jungle drums must have been beating loud as every local he saw eyed him with disdain or open hostility.

Public opinion of him was the least of Fletcher's worries. Since being released by Special Agent Quadrado and a resentful Deputy White, he'd become hung up on what the next step to finding Lila should be. On top of that was the guilt he felt for making the indiscreet enquiries that had led to Mary-Lou's homicide.

On a logical level he was aware that he was nowhere near as guilty as the person who'd killed her, but he knew his questions had painted a target on her back.

Since Quadrado had confirmed there were more disappearances, Fletcher's thoughts had turned darker. If a number of people—Quadrado hadn't given him an exact figure—had vanished after visiting the town, it spoke of organization rather than opportunism. Before she'd released him, Quadrado had shared her theories that it could be a cult brainwashing the women or a network that was designed to help people escape their current life and start over somewhere else.

While both were credible theories, they both seemed improbable to Fletcher. Doubly so when you added in the numerous ways Daversville's residents all seemed to live in a bygone era. The starting over idea made the most sense, but Lila doted on her father and Fletcher couldn't imagine her doing anything that would upset him. He was the one she turned to when she had problems, so for Lila to drop out and leave him behind was unthinkable.

So far as Fletcher was concerned, the reason for the disappearances were more nefarious. He just couldn't work out what it was beyond a serial killer selecting innocent women as his victims.

The Brunswick stew he'd ordered was tasty, although he would have preferred it to have been a good few degrees warmer. He'd half expected to have been refused service at Duke's, but he supposed that his money was as good as anyone else's. With so much to think about, he'd foregone a beer in favor of an overly brewed coffee. The caffeine hit was needed, but more than anything else, Fletcher's concentration was on working out what he should do next.

A team of detectives would be assigned to Mary-Lou's homicide, but he doubted they'd learn much about her death. None of Mary-Lou's neighbors was likely to come forward with information about her killer after what had happened to her. As one they'd all play dumb and pray they weren't next. Whether it was the mysterious Trench or someone else who was holding Daversville in a grip of fear was unknown, but someone was, and Fletcher reckoned it would be the same person responsible for the disappearances. What was most remarkable was the way the locals were so afraid they didn't dare to speak out. Logical thinking would suggest it was better to help the police catch the killer and thereby remove the threat, but such was the level of terror, none of the locals had chosen this option.

Quadrado would do her thing, but she was looking for missing women in general, whereas he was only really concerned with a specific individual.

As for Deputy White, Fletcher had no faith in the man whatsoever. Apart from a catalog of mistakes, plus his taunts and threats before Quadrado had shown up, there was that call he'd taken. The look he'd given Fletcher afterwards was one few people outside of combat situations and doctor's surgeries ever used. He'd looked at Fletcher in the way that people do when they know the person they're looking at is sure to die.

That in turn begged the question: who was Deputy White speaking to? A woman because he'd called her ma'am, beyond that, there was no way to guess.

It was as he was chewing on the Brunswick stew that the answer came. Daversville was a lumber town, the lumber mill provided all the employment save a few service jobs. The town was steeped in an outdated ideology, and when he'd researched Daversville online before coming here, he'd noticed that none of the real estate was for sale. He'd seen only TV antennas on houses, and Mary-Lou's home had had a TV that looked to be as old as he was. He got that youngsters had to use hand-me-downs when starting out, but he couldn't picture Mary-Lou being content with the aged set. The appliances in the kitchen were basic staples such as kettle, stove and toaster, yet there wasn't a coffee maker, microwave or any of the other electrical goods found in most kitchens. Her house had also been devoid of the charging cables which littered his own house.

If he was right in his thinking, the whole town was controlled by the people who owned the lumber mill. Therefore the townsfolk were afraid to speak out as they could lose their homes and jobs. There was also the ripple effect that family members may also suffer.

When Fletcher added Mary-Lou's fate to the equation, it became clear to him that the townsfolk were afraid of losing more than just their homes and jobs. Try as he might, he couldn't work out if the lumber mill owners were keeping a lid on things because the serial killer was a member of their family, or because they were being threatened or coerced in some way.

He was finishing off his stew when Quadrado walked in, the heels of her boots pocking on the wooden floor. She scanned the room and scowled when she spotted him.

After releasing Fletcher, she'd reiterated her desire for him to leave town post-haste, so it was no surprise that she was sending angry looks his way. He'd seen worse. When it came to fierce looks, Quadrado's features were nowhere near battered nor mobile enough to contort into a fearsome grimace.

She got herself a soda from the bartender and strode his way.

"I thought I told you to leave town."

There was anger in her voice, but no real hostility. Fletcher suspected there may be a sliver of respect, but he was self-aware enough to know that might well be wishful thinking.

"You did tell me. But you're forgetting that I came to Daversville for a specific reason. I haven't achieved my goal, so it's not time for me to leave yet." Fletcher kept his tone and face neutral, as pissing off FBI agents was never a good idea. "However, you needn't worry about me interfering in your investigation, and, you have my word that once I have found out what's happened to Lila, I'll be gone before you can say goodbye."

He meant it. Behind the tough FBI agent exterior she was presenting, Quadrado seemed to be a decent person. He knew that her dislike of him was a combination of his wiseass comments and her own frustrations at the case she was working. The distasteful looks she was getting from the locals wouldn't help. Fletcher had been fortunate to never have been racially abused or slighted for the color of his skin, but he'd enough friends who'd been on the receiving end of both casual and direct racism to know how much it could infuriate those who suffered at the hands of bigoted fools. The fact she was a young woman would also go against her in these parts. All in all, he didn't envy her the task of finding the trail of the women who'd gone missing in the town and he wanted to help her although he knew any offer of assistance would be refused. If him finding Lila did that, then all the better.

"That's not good enough." Quadrado leaned across the table, her voice lowered until it was just above a whisper. "What if the guy whose ass you kicked decides to get some retribution? What if Mary-Lou's family decide they are going to avenge her?

This isn't the kind of town that'd think a lynch mob is a bad idea. I can only protect you so much. You can't stay here, for your own safety. Don't you see that?"

"I've been in more dangerous places."

"Don't be a wiseass, Fletcher."

Fletcher didn't allow his gaze to reflect Quadrado's venom back at her. She was in an impossible situation and he knew that while she couldn't run him out of town, she wouldn't want to have her own investigation impeded. "Okay, I take back the last comment, but you needn't worry about me, I can take care of myself and I don't think the locals will dare do anything with an FBI agent in town."

Quadrado's expression told him that she didn't believe him. That was okay. Fletcher didn't believe himself either. He expected that since he'd been fortunate enough to escape Deputy White's attempt to frame him for Mary-Lou's homicide, another course of action would be taken against him. Sometimes when hunting you had to force your prey to attack you so they'd reveal their whereabouts; that's what he was doing now, laying himself out as bait in the hope that whomever was behind Lila's disappearance and Mary-Lou's death would do something to remove him as a threat.

CHAPTER TWENTY

As a precaution against uninvited guests entering his room, Fletcher had left the key part-turned in the lock. It wasn't a foolproof method of preventing entry, especially with both the key and lock being as worn as they were, but it was a start.

Fletcher's next measure to deter intruders was just as lacking in advancement as the first, but it was every bit as effective. With the room's chair not being tall enough to jam under the door handle, he'd placed it tight against the door and balanced the ornamental wash basin and water jug on top of the seat. The slightest nudge of door against chair would topple the porcelain tower onto the floor and create a racket that would be sure to wake him.

Although he was in a strange town and half-expecting a nocturnal visit from aggressors, Fletcher went through his regular nightly routine. First he kissed one side of his locket. "Mom is watching you from heaven. She's so incredibly proud of you." Then he kissed the other side. "Goodnight, beautiful. Love you loads." These were the last words he said to his girls every night when he was with them, and to the locket once he'd entered his own bedroom. It may have been fourteen years since Rachel's murder, but he still loved her as much today as he had the day she'd died.

The luminous hands of Fletcher's watch had just passed 2:00 a.m. when a scratching at the door was enough to bring him from his slumber. With eyes open and ears straining, he struggled to hear the faint scratching, but he knew to trust his instincts.

Humans may have evolved over the millennia, but at heart they are still hunter-gatherers able to detect a threat before rational thoughts could formally identify one. During his years in the Royal Marines, Fletcher had been trained to recognize out-of-place sounds, smells, and a thousand and one other indicators of danger. During covert ops, his life had depended, not just on his training, but on the animal instincts that were as much a part of him as his hair, teeth and eyes.

Someone was trying to enter the room. That was okay. He'd not expected to get a full night's sleep. In a lot of ways he'd prepared for it. His key was turned in the lock just enough to make it awkward to push out. It would deter an opportunist thief, but not someone who had a greater reason to get into the room.

To Fletcher's way of thinking, it was a good thing someone was trying to break in. It meant that he'd done enough to worry whoever had killed Mary-Lou Henderson.

Because he'd anticipated this intrusion, Fletcher had slept fully clothed on top of the bed, boots on. His steps to the position behind the door were soundless as he waited.

The end of the key vibrated and quivered as it was gently rattled back to the vertical. As it was eased out of the lock towards the interior of the room, Fletcher tossed the basin onto the bed and removed the chair. As weapons went, the chair would do more damage than the water jug in his left hand, but the chair was large and heavy which made it cumbersome. If the boot was on the other foot, Fletcher would much rather face someone swinging a heavy chair than a light jug. There would be ample time to dodge the chair whereas the jug would be a quick weapon that would shatter and create the potential for leaving him holding a makeshift dagger.

The key dropped to the floor with a dull thud.

Everything fell silent for a moment. Fletcher assumed the person on the other side of the door was listening for movement, ears alert for the sounds of him waking or other hotel guests stirring at the thud of the fallen key.

A hissing scoosh whispered in the lock and the smell of released oil wafted up Fletcher's nose. It was a clever touch, oiling the lock so it wouldn't squeak or clunk when the new key was turned.

There was another moment of near silence, then Fletcher saw the door handle begin to turn.

This was the crucial point. The next second would determine who won the confrontation that was about to ensue.

How they came through the door would tell Fletcher everything he needed to know about the threat his opponents carried.

He'd been trained in shock-and-awe tactics for moments like this. Bursting into a room brandishing weapons, shouting and shining the barrel-mounted torch on his assault rifle into the eyes of the target.

Fletcher had also been taught about stealth. Before his instructor had given Fletcher his seal of approval, Fletcher had had to break into the man's sleeping quarters and put a plastic knife on his pillow without the instructor being woken. It had taken Fletcher thirty-two attempts to get the knife onto the pillow and his instructor hadn't held back with his defensive retaliations. Every one of those thirty-one painful lessons was etched in his mind, and when he saw the tip of a knife appearing as the door teased open, he could picture his old instructor's head shaking and hear his favorite saying, "If you want to get yourself killed, go jump in front of a bus instead of wasting my time."

Another inch of the knife appeared, so Fletcher tensed himself ready to spring into action.

CHAPTER TWENTY-ONE

As soon as the hand holding the knife came into view, Fletcher took two steps forward and grabbed the hand's wrist. A sharp twist and a vicious yank later and the knife fell to the threadbare carpet as Fletcher hauled his attacker into the bedroom and twisted the knife arm up his back.

Fletcher released a hand from the attacker's wrist and snaked an arm around his throat ready to apply a chokehold. It was then he noticed the attacker wasn't alone. Two men stood in the doorway. One freckled, the other muscly. Both with a hunting knife grasped in their right hands. It was the youths from the parking lot. The one he held in the armlock was Tall Boy.

Taking down one knifeman was child's play to someone with Fletcher's training, two could be done with relative ease, but three, three was a different matter. In a wide-open space, Fletcher could bob and weave, deliver blows and then retreat to a point of safety before striking again. In that scenario, he'd be able to take his opponents down one by one. However, the bedroom was too small to allow him the room he needed to move.

He might have disarmed one of his opponents, but in a space as small as the bedroom, there was no room to maneuver.

Tall Boy was now a vital tool in Fletcher's armory. Where Fletcher had planned to apply enough of a chokehold to see the man slump in an unconscious heap, now he knew the number of opponents he was facing; he'd adapted his initial plan and was using Tall Boy as a shield. Neither of the other two attackers were able to slash or stab at him without first striking their buddy.

As they fanned into the room, Fletcher stood his ground. To retreat until his back was against a wall would be foolish. While having a wall at your back was normally a good thing in a fight against multiple opponents, Fletcher's current position meant the way he held Tall Boy kept him standing in a bottleneck between the bed and the door. Therefore to properly flank him, one of the other two would have to climb over the bed. The ceiling was too low for them to stand upright on the bed, so they'd be in either a crouch or they'd have to cross the bed on hands and knees. Whichever way they crossed the bed, there would be a minimum of two seconds where Fletcher would be able to face off one-on-one against the other knifeman.

The two knifemen slashed their knives in front of them as if they thought doing so would intimidate Fletcher. With Tall Boy as a shield, Fletcher felt no threat, but he felt Tall Boy stiffen. It was a bad sign. Either he knew his buddies didn't care about friendly fire, or he was tensing himself ready to try and escape Fletcher's hold.

To discourage him from any heroics, Fletcher gave his arm an extra twist. He hadn't yet broken any of Tall Boy's bones or torn his ligaments, but he knew it would feel like he had to Tall Boy. The armlock he had him in was tight enough that there was no way to escape without risking greater pain and damage.

Freckles lunged forward and slashed his knife right to left at shoulder height. It was the smartest thing any of the attackers had done so far. Fletcher leaned back, but he wasn't quick enough to avoid injury. Freckles's knife found the arm he had around Tall Boy's neck and he felt its kiss.

Fletcher knew from the amount of pain coursing through his arm that the cut was little more than a superficial one at the elbow. While it was good he wasn't badly slashed, the fact contact had been made was enough to prove to Freckles that his tactics were good. Fletcher could open his mouth and yell for Quadrado, who was bound to be staying here, as it was the only place in town that rented rooms, but it wasn't his way to call for help.

It was time for Fletcher to go on the offensive. He pivoted his shoulders and hips so Tall Boy was moving side to side in front of him. Freckles slashed again; his attack thwarted by the way Fletcher was manhandling Tall Boy. At Freckles's side, Muscles was licking his lips and making feinted thrusts as if he was waiting for the moment when Fletcher twisted Tall Boy enough that he could get a clear opportunity to stab him.

In this situation the odds were against Fletcher and he knew it. He had to change the narrative in the next few seconds, or it would be too late.

Fletcher increased the pressure on Tall Boy's throat. He wasn't choking him so much as cutting off the blood flow to his brain. Fletcher could feel Tall Boy slipping into unconsciousness, so on his next twist left, he released his chokehold and thrust him into Freckles once the knife had flashed past on a wild swing.

While Freckles was grappling with a semi-conscious Tall Boy, Fletcher stepped forward, blocked the thrusting stab Muscles swung upwards at his gut and dropped him with the same brutal uppercut that had felled Some Teeth.

When Fletcher turned to face Freckles, he found the man taller than he'd previously thought. That wasn't a worry. While a taller opponent might have a longer reach in a boxing match, when it came to close range fighting, the smaller opponent had more room to maneuver and could land more potent blows because of it.

Freckles made a couple of wild slashes that drove Fletcher backwards, then he made the mistake Fletcher was waiting for. Instead of continuing with the slashes until Fletcher had nowhere to go, he reversed his grip on the knife and aimed a downward stab at Fletcher's head.

The downward stab was such an amateurish move that Fletcher didn't have to think about how to deal with it. Muscle memory took care of the problem as his training kicked in. Fletcher's hands grasped Freckles's wrist and rotated his arm through ninety degrees until it was locked into an armbar. By the time he'd done that, Fletcher had spun himself round so his back was facing Freckles. A yank down on Freckles's arm drove the man's already hyperextended elbow onto Fletcher's shoulder which acted as a fulcrum. Freckles's elbow didn't stand a chance and snapped with an audible crack.

Before Freckles could bellow in pain, Fletcher was throwing powerful elbows towards his chin. The second backwards elbow caught him on the sweet spot and he collapsed into a heap of untidy limbs.

Tall Boy was climbing to his feet, so Fletcher reapplied the chokehold until all three knifemen were unconscious on the bedroom floor. With his assailants out of action, Fletcher crossed to where his bag was and removed a roll of duct tape and his emergency medical kit.

When he'd gotten the three men restrained, he'd able to start getting some answers from them.

CHAPTER TWENTY-TWO

Fletcher sat and watched Tall Boy as he came back to conscious-ness. Like his two buddies, his arms were secured behind his back with duct tape. Unlike them, he was sitting on the heavy chair and held in place with wraps of tape around his ankles and chest. Freckles and Muscles lay back to back on the floor, their arms secured together with more tape. All three had a strip of tape gagging them.

Tall Boy had been chosen as their spokesperson for two reasons. The primary one was that, as he was the one who'd done the speak-ing in the parking lot and had been first through the door, it made sense to consider him the leader of the group. The second reason was more practical: both Freckles and Muscles were still out cold.

Tall Boy's head shook as he tried to clear the fog of unconscious-ness from his mind. Fletcher stood in a relaxed pose above him. Toe to toe so he was towering over Tall Boy. His arms folded and face hard.

This was a crucial point in his plan. He had no desire to torture Tall Boy into giving him information. A hotel room in the middle of the night was no place to coerce someone into talking. It was a miracle the fight hadn't roused any other residents as it was. Fletcher replayed the events of the last few minutes in his mind. None of the attackers had spoken and neither had he. There'd been the odd grunt, some thumps from boots and the noise of fists on flesh, but he figured his attackers had also been trying to limit the noise.

Regardless of the location, Fletcher needed answers and Tall Boy was the person he'd chosen to supply them. Real torture might be out so far as Fletcher was concerned, but that didn't mean Tall Boy had to know that. To this end, Fletcher had to make him believe that he was prepared to do whatever it took to get answers. The next few minutes were about dominating and intimidating Tall Boy until he spoke without coercion.

Tall Boy tried to move and when he couldn't, he writhed and struggled with no effect. When he realized he was trapped, his head bent back so he could look up at Fletcher. His eyes were a mix of fear and fury and there were stifled grunts fighting to pass the duct tape covering his mouth.

Fletcher squatted down until he was at eye level with Tall Boy. "You're an amateur. You and your buddies are amateurs. Three of you came for me with knives. I took you all down and all you managed to do was give me a scratch. The moment I saw your knife come past the door, I knew I would win. In a couple of minutes, I'm going to ask you some questions, I'd suggest you answer them."

Fletcher stopped talking to let his words sink into Tall Boy's brain. He wasn't lying. He *had* known he'd win as soon as he'd seen the knife appear. When making a stealthy entrance, a professional doesn't let their weapon enter a room first unless they know where the threat in the room is. Nobody with the slightest bit of military training would do that, much less present the weapon at a nice attackable waist height. Trained knife fighters grip their weapon in a way that sees the knife held parallel with their forearm, blade outwards. The only time Tall Boy or his buddies had adapted this grip was when Freckles had tried his *Psycho*-style stab.

Hatred burned from Tall Boy's eyes for a moment before fear quenched its fire. Fletcher could see the internal debate on his face. It didn't say much, but it didn't need to. Tall Boy would be worrying about what Fletcher would do to him, whether the cops would be called, and how much trouble he'd be in if he gave Fletcher the information he was after.

Fletcher leaned forward and picked up two of the three knives that he collected and set on the floor. Without speaking he laid them gently on Tall Boy's thighs, their tips pointing at the top of his groin.

After a few minutes letting Tall Boy stew in his own worry, Fletcher deemed it was time to tighten the screw again.

"Your buddies and you kinda look alike. I'm guessing that you're all brothers or cousins. Something like that." Tall Boy didn't let his face react, but his eyes confirmed the truth in what Fletcher was saying. "I'd also say that while you're a rank amateur, you're probably tough enough to make me really hurt you before you give me my answers." Again, Tall Boy's eyes validated Fletcher's words. "You are probably wondering what I'm going to do. How I am going to make you talk. I'm sure you've already realized that I'm not going to kill you because you can't give me the answers I want if you're dead." A flash of triumph crossed Tall Boy's eyes and his jaw set beneath the duct tape covering his mouth.

Fletcher kept the smile off his face. Tall Boy had made the mistake of allowing himself to feel that most destructive of emotions: hope. Rather than disabuse him of the notion, Fletcher let him bask in his moment of glory, allowing the hope to build.

When he judged that Tall Boy was as confident as he could be of his survival, Fletcher retrieved the third knife from the floor, straightened up and lifted a foot. He took care to make sure the heel of his boot was butted against the handle of the knife he'd laid on Tall Boy's thigh as he rested his foot on his leg.

The fear was back in Tall Boy's eyes, but there were still traces of hope and defiance. Time for them to be dashed.

Fletcher used the tip of the knife in his hand as a pointer and indicated the back of his ankle, inside of his knee and several other points on his body. "Do you know what can be found at all the body parts I've just pointed at?"

Tall Boy's head shook, confusion filled his eyes.

"Tendons. They're the cords which attach muscles to bone. Tendons are the support ropes of the human body. Without them, our muscles can't control our limbs." Fletcher thumbed the knife's blade. "This is very sharp, and as strong as a tendon is, I reckon this knife will slice right through them. Except I won't just cut your tendons, I'll shred them. A cut tendon can be repaired by a doctor and will heal in a matter of weeks. A shredded one will be a lot slower process provided there's enough left for a doctor to work with. We're talking extensive surgeries, a lot of bucks' worth. How's your health insurance? You paid up to date?" The look on Tall Boy's face said he wasn't. "You could spend months relying on other people to feed you, wash you and, yeah, wipe your ass."

Sweat covered Tall Boy's brow as Fletcher talked. His head sawed side to side and his lean muscles strained to be free of his bindings. Fletcher had achieved his aim. Tall Boy was now petrified of what he'd do to him.

One last crank of the handle to apply a final piece of pressure and then he'd trust Tall Boy would tell him what he wanted to know.

"For every question you don't answer, I'll shred one of your tendons, and one on each of your buddies. Do you understand me?" A nod that sent droplets of sweat down onto Fletcher's boot. "Good. I'm going to take the tape from your mouth. If you say anything that's not an answer to one of my questions, one of your tendons will be shredded. If I think you're lying to me, well…"

Fletcher started off with a few simple questions. He asked what town they were in, the name of the bar and one or two other meaningless questions, to establish a baseline so he could tell when Tall Boy was trying to lie to him, and because he wanted Tall Boy to get into the habit of answering him.

"Why did you come to my room?"

"What do you think?"

"Three of you with knives? I'd say you were going to cut my throat and leave me with my tongue on my chest."

"That would be homicide. Ain't no way I was gonna be killing no one." Tall Boy's head shook as he spoke.

Fletcher didn't believe him, but the question could be revisited later.

"What's your name?"

No answer.

"Who sent you?"

Again Tall Boy didn't answer. Didn't look at Fletcher. In fact, his eyes closed and he started mumbling a prayer.

"I asked you a question. You know what the consequences of not answering are."

When Tall Boy opened his eyes Fletcher saw they were filled with resignation. Neither spoke until Fletcher slid his knife behind Tall Boy's ankle and laid the blade against his Achilles tendon.

Tall Boy's voice was tight with the fear of anticipated pain, but his tone was resolute. "Do what you gotta do. I ain't answering no more of your questions."

CHAPTER TWENTY-THREE

Quadrado was sipping orange juice and buttering a slice of toast when Fletcher walked into the bar-cum-dining room of Duke's. There were bags under his eyes and a concerned expression on his face, although his chin was clean shaven and there was something of a spring in his step.

The night had been a long one for her. She'd finished looking at her notes around midnight and had struggled to sleep as her mind chewed over the events of the day.

Fletcher piled a plate high with scrambled eggs and ham, filled a cup with coffee and wandered over to her table.

"I take it you're having a hearty breakfast before the long trip home."

Her sarcasm bounced off him without a flicker of acknowledgment.

"Actually I'm refueling after rather a fraught night. I had a visitor or three come to my room."

"Your sexual adventures are neither my business nor my interest." Quadrado curled her lip into a sneer. "Look, Fletcher. You need to eat your breakfast, leave town and drop the macho bull, okay?"

"First, three men with knives don't count as a sexual adventure so far as I'm concerned. Second, although I hardly know you, I can tell you're being uncharacteristically sarcastic. I've had less than two hours' sleep. I chose not to bother you with stories of my nocturnal escapades until this morning so your rest wasn't interrupted, and third, if my suspicions are correct, instead of running me out of town, you ought to be thinking of your own exit strategy."

Quadrado wasn't sure what Fletcher was getting at, but she was intrigued enough to give him five minutes. Her butter-smeared knife pointed at the chair opposite her. "Sit. You have until I've finished my breakfast."

"Why thank you, Special Agent Quadrado. You really are a terribly accommodating officer of the law." Fletcher's eyes were hard. "You might have a fancy-ass badge, but you don't have a monopoly on sarcasm."

Rather than answer him with words, Quadrado took a large bite of toast and shot him a glare. As much as she was angry with him, she was also annoyed at herself for being caustic. She put it down to the combined lack of sleep and leads on her case. All the same, she wasn't proud of the way she'd lashed out at him.

"Like I said, three men with knives decided they wanted to come into my room last night. Something told me they weren't coming for a whittling contest, so I explained the folly of their ways to them."

Quadrado scanned Fletcher's face and hands, saw no obvious defensive injuries. "And what? They left after a chat?"

"Actually, I invited them to stay. They're still up there now."

The first thought in Quadrado's mind was that Fletcher had killed them. She could feel her blood chilling at the prospect and, if he had killed them, the fact she'd let him go yesterday would be a stain that would blot her career for years.

"And?" She didn't dare ask more. The toast in her mouth felt as dry as an unsalted cracker.

"They tried to do their thing. I did mine. I'm here in front of you. They're not."

"Do you know who they are?"

"They're three of the four who squared up to me outside the diner." Fletcher did another one of his annoying shrugs. "They didn't tell me their names."

Quadrado fought to keep her anger at Fletcher in check. She could tell he knew what she was thinking and was playing with her. Making her ask the question she didn't want to. Damn him. Another thought struck her: if Fletcher was telling the truth, he must be a formidable fighter to have taken on three knife-wielding opponents and remained unscathed.

"So." She kept her tone dry and laced with disbelief. "You fought three guys with knives. Where are they now? Who should I call, the coroner or an ambulance?"

"They're upstairs in my room. No need for a coroner, but at least one of them may be glad to see an ambulance.'

Quadrado pushed her chair back and winced at the squeak it made on the floorboards. "Come on then, let's go see them."

CHAPTER TWENTY-FOUR

Fletcher wasn't happy at having to leave his breakfast uneaten, but in the greater scheme of things, it was a small price to pay. He was certain the three men who'd paid him a visit were responsible for Mary-Lou's death and confident Quadrado would hand them over to proper cops rather than the corrupt Deputy White.

As a way to at least get some food inside him, Fletcher had scooped the ham from his plate and was feeding it into his mouth as he led Quadrado to his room.

He fed his key into the lock and resisted the temptation to say "ta-da" or any other such exclamation.

When he saw the room was empty, it was all he could do not to throw a punch into the wall. The fact the men had vanished spoke volumes about the amount of collusion going on in Daversville. He'd already worked out that the men had obtained their key to his room from a member of the bar staff. Therefore someone who'd seen him this morning hadn't expected to and had taken it upon themselves to check his room while he was at breakfast. Whether they were looking for the three intruders or just signs of a fight wasn't important. Someone had known what was going down and when he'd shown up for breakfast, had had enough initiative to go to his room. They would be the one who'd released the trio of knifemen. Fletcher was convinced the men were too securely bound to free themselves. He'd gone so far as to add a few extra loops of tape to their bindings before he'd gone downstairs in search of food and FBI agents.

"Where are they, in the bathroom or the closet?"

Fletcher didn't like the layer of derision in Quadrado's voice, but he couldn't blame her for being skeptical. In her shoes he'd have felt the same way.

"They've gone. Someone must have come and released them."

"Yeah, of course they have." Quadrado took a step backwards so she was in the doorway.

Fletcher could see how his story looked, but the apprehension in Quadrado's eyes pushed a button in his brain. "What? You think I've made this up as a way to get you alone in my room?"

"I didn't say that." Quadrado took another step backwards.

Rather than make any attempt to close the gap with her, Fletcher sat down on the bed. "You didn't say it. But you're thinking it. I swear to you, on my daughter's life, I haven't told you a single lie. Three men let themselves in here last night. I subdued them and left them bound and gagged when I came down to find you and get something to eat."

Quadrado pulled a disbelieving face. "So you say."

"I do say, because it's the truth. I'm not some predator who lures innocents to his room. You're an FBI agent, for God's sake. I'm hardly likely to start getting fresh with you against your wishes. Unless I murdered you afterward, there's no way I'd get away with whatever it is you think I had planned." Quadrado's face softened a fraction, but only the smallest amount. "Besides, I'm not interested in you or anyone else. There's only ever been one woman for me, and I've already lost her."

"Say you're telling me the truth—"

"I am."

"Don't interrupt me again, I'm finding it hard enough not to arrest you as it is. Say you're telling the truth, what you said about someone coming to release them speaks of help from an as yet unknown source. That suggests a larger scale than three men. Would it be the fourth?"

Fletcher didn't speak, but he was giving Quadrado a mental high five. She'd gotten to the same conclusion he had, and that meant not only was she smart, she was also able to think rationally despite her instincts setting her against him.

Quadrado remained where she was as Fletcher eased himself from the bed. He'd had an idea about how to prove his story was true.

He crossed to the chair he'd tied Tall Boy to, kneeled beside it and ran a finger up the inside of one of the chair's front legs. As he'd hoped, it was sticky. Not the unclean kind of sticky, but the coated-with-a-layer-of-adhesive sticky.

Fletcher made a play of squeezing his fingers together and letting Quadrado see the skin pulling as he went to separate them. "I taped one of them to this chair. The leg still has traces of the tape's glue on it."

"You could have easily done that yourself."

Despite the accusation of her words, Quadrado's tone told Fletcher that she didn't believe her own theory.

"I could have. But you're already here so what have I to gain from doing that?" Rather than argue further, he rolled his sleeve up and showed her the fresh cut that Freckles's knife had made to his arm. "Do you think I did this myself as well?"

He carried the chair to the doorway, making a point of keeping it as a barrier between them. Quadrado was suspicious of him and he needed to get her onside before things got further out of hand. It wasn't so much that he needed or wanted her help, more that if he was going to find Lila, he didn't need to be getting arrested all the time. He had to be free and able to pursue his enquiries, follow the leads as they presented themselves and ask the right questions of the right people.

"It's possible, although I doubt it as I don't see what you have to gain."

"Thank you." Fletcher offered Quadrado the chair and sat on the bed again. "Shall we work on the theory I'm telling you the truth? The four punks seem to be trying to keep outsiders from asking questions. This makes me want to know why they're doing that, who's paying them to do it, and what the person pulling their strings has to gain from doing so." He leaned back, resting his hands on the bedspread. "The why is obvious: they're covering for someone. The who isn't so obvious, but my money is on the Blackett family who own the lumber mill. They're the ones with the power in these parts. As for the gain, all I can think of is that they're trying to prevent a shitstorm from hitting Daversville and the cops costing them money by disrupting the work at the mill."

Quadrado's raised hand caused Fletcher to stop talking.

"Want to slow it down there? Those punks, as you call them, maybe they're self-appointed, so don't go jumping to conclusions. As for your idea the Blacketts are mixed up in this, that's preposterous. Have you seen them at all? Do you know anything about them?"

Fletcher spread his hands wide. "Other than a couple of the townsfolk putting them on pedestals, I know nothing about them. Let's face it though, this place is held in a time warp and the only ones who can do that are the ones with the power. The Blacketts."

"I saw them at the church yesterday. They're good people. They are liked and respected. There was this sweet old woman—the grandmother, I guess. She was giving out candy to the kids, and there wasn't one person there whose face showed anything other than warmth, trust and Christian kindness. Trust me, Fletcher, it's not the Blacketts who are the problem. Well, not directly."

"What do you mean by that?" Fletcher couldn't help but pounce on that last sentence.

"Rather than waltz into town with a head full of assumptions and start picking fights, I did what detectives do and spoke to the cops. Specifically Deputy White." Fletcher harrumphed at the mention of White. Quadrado ignored him and carried on. "According to him, this Trench character you asked me about yesterday lives in the woods and survives on what he can kill or forage. Maybe, just maybe, it's this Trench acting alone who's behind the disappearances?"

There was a lot to consider in what Quadrado had just said. One guy acting alone might well be responsible. His reason for snatching women would then be obvious, although Fletcher was loath to jump to another conclusion.

"Say it was him who took Lila. How did he get in and out of town without being seen, especially with a hostage? If he took other women, what became of their cars? And why are the townsfolk covering this up?"

Quadrado shifted in her chair. Not a lot, not enough to suggest she wasn't comfortable, but enough to intimate her unease. "From what Deputy White said, most folks know who this guy is. He's ex-army. He served in Vietnam."

"So who is he?"

"He's a cousin of Constance Blackett. It's her sons who own and run the lumber mill."

"Hah. I knew it." Fletcher couldn't prevent the triumph in his tone. "A Blackett."

"There's no proof. Only rumor. The deputy said nobody has seen Trench for years. We don't even know if he's in the woods. For all we know, he could have died years ago."

Fletcher considered her points. If this mystery Blackett guy had lived off the land in the woods for years he'd have skills as a hunter. As a Vietnam vet, he'd be trained in camouflage and weapons handling. There were hundreds of square miles of woods around Daversville. Each one imbued with valleys, streams, mountains and thick undergrowth. To find one man in such an area would be nigh on impossible without a full-scale military presence. He didn't envy Quadrado the task.

"Everything you've just said may be true, but he's your chief suspect right now, isn't he? I'll bet you're thinking he somehow found out about me asking questions about Mary-Lou Henderson and killed her to ensure her silence and to issue a warning to others in town who may speak out."

Quadrado didn't say a word and her face gave nothing away.

To Fletcher's mind, this mystery Blackett soldier adrift in the woods was a weak suspect at best. If he was behind things, it begged the question of how he was getting information about goings on in the town. The timeline was also too short. He'd arrived in town late on Saturday afternoon. By Sunday morning Mary-Lou Henderson was dead. The posse to run him out of town was assembled and outside the diner fifteen minutes after he'd shown the photo of Lila and Brad to the server. Cell phones made communication easy, but a man living rough in the woods wouldn't be able to charge his, and Fletcher's own cell had lost signal before he'd arrived and never reconnected, so he doubted that would happen. It also spoke of collusion from the inhabitants of Daversville and he doubted one man could hold an entire town in a grip of fear.

More than anything, though, Fletcher knew he'd have to change his tactics. Asking questions outright and throwing his weight around had gotten Mary-Lou Henderson murdered and prompted an assassination attempt on him.

Once he was done here with Quadrado, it was time for him to leave town. Before he joined Mary-Lou on the coroner's table.

CHAPTER TWENTY-FIVE

Fletcher drove north out of Daversville and contemplated his next move. Quadrado had seemed pleased he was leaving, and there had been a relieved look on the face of the guy behind the counter of Duke's when he'd handed his key in and said he was heading home. In an ideal world, he'd have dropped a couple of threats on the guy and got him talking. However, he'd realized the locals were more afraid of the person or persons behind Lila's disappearance than they were of him.

That point had been proven when he'd put the knife against Tall Boy's Achilles tendon. The guy was willing to potentially face life as a cripple rather than give up the information Fletcher was after. Although it left him floundering without a decent lead to follow, Fletcher couldn't help but admire the guts Tall Boy had displayed to call his bluff.

As much as anything else, it had been galling to Fletcher to have his bluff called. Next time he encountered Tall Boy or someone who knew about what happened in the bedroom at Duke's, his threats wouldn't carry any weight because they'd know that he would stop shy of actually torturing them.

Fletcher had no qualms whatsoever about hurting people who tried to hurt him or those he cared about, but when it came to torturing someone, there was a line he wouldn't cross. A few punches or a hard squeeze on a pressure point was one thing; to start using weapons on someone was a different level of cruel he wasn't prepared to sink to. In his mind, it was a line that once crossed could not be returned from. Resorting to torture would also lower him to the level of those he was up against and he was damned if he was degrading himself that way.

He'd heard tales of things that had gone down in Afghanistan. Things that had been done by both sides. From the US and British side, it had been desperate men needing information in a hurry. That didn't excuse it, didn't make it acceptable, but it did at least make it understandable. The worst sight he'd seen out there was a local woman who'd been tortured by the Taliban. Death would have been a kindness, but even that consolation had been denied her. Fletcher had shot the man who wielded the knife on her and seriously considered ending the woman's pain once and for all. Along with three others, Fletcher stretchered the screaming woman out under heavy gunfire and did what he could to treat her wounds. She'd died four days later.

The rental car ate the miles west across Washington County without complaint; Fletcher's destination was Macon. He'd never been to the city before and he didn't know what to expect when he got there. Whatever he found wouldn't matter; he'd be able to buy the provisions he needed without having to worry about prying eyes. He'd also be able to swap the rental car for another model in a different color. He might be leaving Daversville, but that didn't mean he wasn't coming back.

As soon as his cell picked up a signal he was confident it would keep, he put a call in to Don to update him and then called Rachel's parents to see how Wendy was.

*

By mid-afternoon, Fletcher had achieved all his aims save one. His rental car was now a dark SUV; he'd bought a large-scale map of Washington County, and he'd done some research on the owners of the lumber mill at a public library. He'd also bought himself a few items of outdoor equipment and a hunting knife.

The one thing he hadn't gotten was a gun. If this was a proper military operation, he'd have had an SA80 machine gun and a good quality pistol; a Sig Sauer or Glock, something along those lines. However, with the gun laws what they were in Georgia, there was no way he could get his hands on a legal gun without waiting until he got the necessary permit to buy one from a gun store. He could buy one from a private seller without needing a permit, but that would take time, and time wasn't something he had a lot of as there was no telling what Lila was going through. Therefore he would have to go the quick route and get an illegal one.

Fletcher was convinced a lot of time had been wasted already in his quest to find Lila—having to leave town like this just added to the delay—and he wanted to get back onto her trail at once.

There are always ways to get an illegal gun in any city. He could find the right bar and speak to the right people. Give it a few hours and he'd be faced with one of two situations; either he'd be shaken down and then beaten up, or he'd be thought of as an undercover cop and given the run-around. Neither of these scenarios would see a gun placed in his hands.

It may just be that he could strike it lucky and find someone willing to sell him a gun. It would come with a premium price and there would be no way of knowing its history. It may well have been used in multiple homicides, a robbery or some other crime. There was also no guarantee the seller wouldn't frame him to get rid of the weapon and their association with it.

Fletcher had worked all this out during the drive from Daversville and had included the solution to the various issues in his research at the library. Rather than try and navigate his way around the strange city, Fletcher stashed all his purchases in the rental SUV and hailed a cab.

CHAPTER TWENTY-SIX

Quadrado arced her spine in a forlorn attempt to get the cricks out of her back and neck. After a poor night's sleep, being hunched over a laptop for most of the morning hadn't helped.

Not being able to get online had been a real nuisance. Instead of doing her own research, she'd had to call back to New York and get a colleague to run the searches she needed done. This had meant she'd had to wait by the phone in White's little station instead of going out and conducting interviews. According to Deputy White the phone lines were awaiting renewal so they could get internet, but he'd not sounded sure of himself when tackled on the subject.

She'd gotten another salad at the diner and had tried to get information about Trench Blackett from the server Agnes. The woman hadn't known much, but she'd mentioned he had gone off the grid after a scandal with a former teacher at the school. Agnes's recollection was sketchy at best, but she'd recalled a budding romance had turned sour and had ended up with the teacher being discovered with her throat cut. Trench had never been seen since that day, but from time to time, local hunters had come across signs of someone living wild in the surrounding woods.

Nothing she'd learned had brightened her mood. Fletcher's tales of nocturnal intruders kept distracting her and, while she'd come to believe some of what he said, she couldn't see how he could be telling her the full truth. If he was on the level, he was talking about town-wide collusion. From the woman at the diner to a staff member at Duke's to all the locals who kept their mouths shut and their eyes unseeing, there wasn't anyone in Daversville who didn't know what was happening in this hick town. The locals' obvious affection for the Blacketts made them less likely suspects, which left Trench as the best lead she had. It may be that there was someone else prowling the area, yet that was too much of an unknown and she had a firm belief a town as secular as Daversville would know about such a person.

She wished that Fletcher's intruders, if there had indeed been any, hadn't gotten away. She would have liked to question them in the nearest field office. Maybe sitting in an interview suite with recording equipment and bright lights would get some truth out of them.

As the alleged knifemen had refused to give Fletcher their names, she didn't know which door to knock on to find them. Agnes Jackson at the diner was an obvious starting point, yet Quadrado knew that if the woman was mixed up in something with the youths, she'd only deny calling them after Fletcher had started asking his questions about Mary-Lou Henderson.

Another grave concern was Deputy White. As the town's lawman, he was either dumb on a biblical scale, or he too was mixed up in covering up what was going on. She'd like to spend some time in an interview suite with him, too. However, she was of the opinion that if Deputy White was as rotten as she thought, his sheriff must also be culpable, either through collusion or their failure to properly oversee an ineffective officer. At the back of her mind was the fear she may be wrong about White; therefore she was reluctant to make career-staining accusations until she had proof.

What Quadrado couldn't get her head around was that which-ever way she looked at her own case, and the situation that had arisen with Fletcher, something was very rotten in Daversville, and while there were a lot of indicators pointing at the town, the only real evidence of wrongdoing was the homicide of Mary-Lou Henderson. Everything else was circumstantial at best.

Maybe the detectives on the case would identify Mary-Lou's killer. That would give Quadrado someone to offer a plea bargain to. Someone she could work at, secure in the knowledge that a link in the chain had been forged. Quadrado's first impression was Trench had killed Mary-Lou and kept the locals compliant by threats of reprisals. Maybe he was only known to them by reputation, but if he'd paid someone a visit and threatened them or their family, it was conceivable the townsfolk were covering for him as he left them alone and took outsiders. It was a stretch to think one person could do that, but not beyond the bounds of possibility. Quadrado was certain that within five minutes of a threat to Daversville's people being identified as coming from a specific person or persons, a posse would be heading out to remove that threat. It was possible they'd tried to find him themselves, and Trench had eluded their efforts or picked off one or two of his hunters as a warning.

Quadrado would be the first to admit that she hadn't looked at the Blackett family too hard, but from what she had seen of them, they were much the same as the rest of the townsfolk. Their styling hadn't been any more modern than anyone else's, and while the lumber mill would be a business that was sure to be turning over a lot of money, the family hadn't displayed any obvious sign of wealth or betterment.

Try as she might, Quadrado couldn't think of a credible reason for the people of Daversville to abduct the diverse group of missing women whose disappearance she was investigating. The same applied to the owners of the lumber mill. Round here they might be big shots, but in the greater scheme of things, they were yet another small family business providing employment to a rural community.

To Quadrado's mind, the people of Daversville, including the owners of the lumber mill, were being terrorized by a third party responsible for the missing women. Fletcher had been right,

Mary-Lou's homicide had sent a message. All she had to do was find Trench, a man used to living wild and with a far greater knowledge of the woods surrounding Daversville than anyone she could bring in.

CHAPTER TWENTY-SEVEN

There was never a good time to be mugged, but, if there could be such a thing, the middle of the afternoon was possibly the best. The afternoon sun streamed between the buildings and lit up the dark spaces where muggers hung out. At this time of day, the junkie muggers would be strung out, desperate for their fix, yet still together enough to know that they had nothing to gain by hurting their chosen victim. The counterpoint to this was that those who mugged as a career choice rather than through a desire to fuel a habit weren't likely to be on the streets yet.

Darkness was their friend as they preyed on the vulnerable, the naïve and the drunk. It was this group Fletcher was looking for. Junkie muggers would carry a knife of some sorts as their weapon, whereas the others may carry a gun. The gun's history could well be dubious, but Fletcher planned to dispose of any weapon he got, so he'd decided not to worry about that side of things.

When he exited the cab, Fletcher cast his eyes around the area and liked what he saw. The area was down at heel. Thrift shops lined the streets and there was a palpable sense of despair that the heat of the afternoon sun couldn't burn away. The people on these streets didn't move in a business-like march, theirs was the slow, shuffling gait of those whom life had beaten and left for dead.

The suit Fletcher had bought in a midtown thrift store was tighter than he would have liked, but it helped him play the role he needed to play to flush out the muggers. He walked along the sidewalk, weaving between the overflowing trashcans and a young mother pushing a stroller with one hand while focusing all her attention on the cell in her other hand.

Fletcher had his own cell in his hand, but unlike the young mother, he was only pretending to be focused on it. His eyes were flicking right and left, as he navigated the sidewalk. He spotted a battered sign for Bridge Avenue and felt his tense muscles relax.

Bridge Avenue was Macon's mugging hotspot. In the newspapers he'd scoured in the library, it was mentioned with increasing frequency. As he approached the junction, Fletcher noticed that, unlike the other streets, nobody was hanging on Bridge Avenue. There were no gangs of youths, no panhandlers and no hookers waiting for a john.

So far as Fletcher was concerned this was a good thing. A street the locals feared was exactly what he was looking for. He continued doing the looking at the cell in his hand act, and turned onto Bridge Avenue.

To further play his part of the lost businessman, Fletcher made sure his stride wasn't a march, that his shoulders were slumped and that his natural athleticism was hidden as much as possible. Maybe he should have bought the other suit in the thrift store; it had been a size too big, and made him look as if he'd recently lost a lot of weight, whereas the one he'd bought outlined his biceps and powerful thighs.

Twenty paces along Bridge Avenue, Fletcher saw the first signs of would-be aggressors. It was nothing concrete, and he couldn't begin to identify the person he'd seen in the alleyway as they'd ducked out of sight, but the fact they'd tried to stay hidden was enough.

Back in Afghanistan, such a movement would have seen him swing his weapon that way and then investigate along with some of his unit. In Macon, it was all he could do to keep the smile off his face.

Come into my parlor, said the spider to the fly.

Fletcher counted forty-five paces before his eyes picked out another human being. This time it was a hooker who lurked in an alleyway. Her gargoyle-hard face sat above a body that was emaciated. When she saw Fletcher, she asked if he was looking for some company.

"No thank you, ma'am." Fletcher's response was automatic in his politeness. Good manners cost nothing and the hooker's life had quite obviously not gone to plan. If she was plying her trade in a place like Bridge Avenue, a polite turndown might be the best thing that happened in her day.

Thirty paces later, Fletcher heard the scuff of footsteps behind him. He didn't look back, didn't react in any way. He just kept walking along the street, cell in hand. Ahead of him another alleyway lay between a pair of boarded-up houses that looked old enough to have had their foundation stones laid by Abraham Lincoln. Once upon a time they would have been grand houses, homes to wealthy, privileged people. Now they were decrepit shells, full of loom and menace.

The alley was narrow between the tall houses. Its recesses filled with dark spots.

The footsteps behind him were closer now. With his cell set to take a selfie, Fletcher could use it to look over his shoulder. There was a tall rangy youth wearing a basketball shirt, baseball cap and a cocksure expression. Beside him was a shorter version. Fletcher guessed it'd be a younger brother.

He was five paces from the alley when two youths came running out. Like the two behind him, they both wore sports clothing and were filled with the confidence that comes with experience.

A hard shove in Fletcher's back propelled him forward towards the alleyway.

Fletcher let himself be driven there; these boys were about to learn a hard lesson, but before he could begin educating them, he wanted to be away from witnesses. This wasn't the kind of neighborhood where the cops would be called, but it was the kind where other hoods would be more than happy to join in a fracas.

A kick on Fletcher's butt sent him staggering into the alleyway. The kick wasn't too painful; all the same, it was all Fletcher could do not to react with violence.

That may well be a mistake. There were four of them and Fletcher hadn't yet had chance to assess their varying threat levels. Too often people got themselves hurt or killed by letting emotion rather than logic decide their actions.

Fletcher exaggerated his stagger, so he was deeper in the alley when he turned round to face the four youths.

Big and Little Brother were on the left side of the alley with Big Brother a half step in front of his sibling. On the other side were a pudgy youth and one who had a knife scar widening his mouth.

None of this mattered to Fletcher. What they looked like was immaterial. Scar and Big Brother both held guns, while the other two held long kitchen knives.

For the first time since setting out to get a gun, Fletcher felt that he'd made an error. Taking down a solo mugger with a gun was child's play for him. Taking out two when they were backed up with a pair of knifemen was a whole different matter.

If he was going to walk out of this alley alive, he needed a rapid change of plan.

CHAPTER TWENTY-EIGHT

As the individual whose name appeared in every one of the files of the missing women, Deputy White was the logical person for Quadrado to speak to. Being the cop who'd been asked to look into their disappearances, he ought to have his own theories. The problem was, he was at best incompetent. The more Quadrado thought about his part in Fletcher's arrest for Mary-Lou Henderson, the less she trusted him.

That she had to mistrust another cop was something that didn't sit well with her. To protect and to serve were ideals all cops should adopt. As for the FBI's own motto of Fidelity, Bravery, Integrity, she tried to live her life by those values. She knew that in every section of society, there was always a percentage of drunks, abusers and other unsavory types. It stood to reason that some people in law enforcement would be corrupt or malleable to blackmailers. The thing was, she'd never encountered any of these officers. But she knew some cops got a kick from the power their badge gave them and the fact that power corrupts was well-known.

For Zoey Quadrado, catching criminals was a calling rather than just an occupation. From the age of eight when she'd begun to understand about her Aunt Janet never being traced she'd wanted to be a cop, and if Deputy White was proven to be corrupt, she knew that as the person to expose him, she'd take his corruption as a personal betrayal.

"Okay, so tell me again about your investigations into the women who are alleged to have disappeared after passing through Daversville."

Deputy White shrugged and pulled a noncommittal face. "Like I told you when you turned up yesterday morning, I asked around, spoke to Agnes in the diner, Duke and his staff, but got the same answers every time. They either didn't remember them, hadn't seen any strangers, or said they'd seen them the same way they see all folks who pass through."

Quadrado understood what White was getting at with the last part of his statement. To the local businesses, folk passing through were a source of income rather than interest. Duke's and the diner may see hundreds of new faces in a year, but they'd serve them, maybe engage in a little polite conversation and then forget them. In a town as closed as Daversville, strangers weren't to be trusted.

"You've said that. What about Mary-Lou Henderson? She is alleged to have given a warning to the boyfriend of the last woman who went missing. Did you speak to her at all?"

"No, why would I? She was just a daft girl with a head full of silly ideas."

"Really?" Quadrado lifted an eyebrow in response to Deputy White's bullish tone and damning assessment.

"Yeah, really. She wasn't a bad kid, but she wasn't liked none."

"Why wasn't she liked?" *Finally* Quadrado had a thread she could pull at. "Was it because she planned to go to college?"

"Exactly. She had a head full of dreams. Ain't got no place for dreams in Daversville. We work hard, go to church on Sunday and look out for each other. She wanted to go off'n learn. The Lord himself alone knows what kind of people she'd get mixed up with down in Albany. Saw enough myself when I went through my training. That's a weird old world out there."

The way he wouldn't meet her eye told Quadrado what kind of people Deputy White meant. Different races and religions, not to mention liberals, intellectuals and anyone else who wasn't exactly like them. Like the rest of the Daversville population, Deputy White's mind was as modern as cave drawings.

"All the same, you never spoke to her? A person who was likely to remember strangers. You say she had a head full of dreams, lots of young people do, it's what fuels people to learn a new language, explore the world and absorb other cultures. Did you not think, when looking into the movements of the women who went missing, that a young woman with aspirations to better herself, and a fair chance of encountering the missing women, might be a good person to speak to?"

Deputy White's eyes narrowed. "Are you questioning my methods?"

The affront in his tone was a natural reaction to criticism and Quadrado could see the shake in his hands, and the nervous way he kept licking his lips. He was rattled. Scared at the idea of being caught out. The trap had been laid and he was about to step into it. All she had to do was nudge him forward a little and see if he had the wit to avoid it.

"No, but it's interesting that you ask if I am. Should I be? Or should I just continue finding out what you've done so I don't waste my time repeating your work?"

Quadrado had purposefully given him a way to escape the trap. For the time being she wanted him to think he'd outsmarted her before she truly caught him.

"You shouldn't be questioning me like this none. I done everything by the book. I spoke to those I thought could help and kept my eyes and ears open. Not my fault I didn't see nor hear nothing."

Deputy White's poor attempt at self-justification didn't wash with Quadrado. His use of a double negative irked the grammar pedant her mother had made her.

"Tell me, when the number of missing persons' enquiries coming your way kept increasing, did you think it was strange? More than one hundred sixty thousand people over the age of twenty-one went missing in the United States last year. Divide that by fifty states for easy counting and you get three point two thousand per state. Georgia is in the top ten of the most populous states, so it'd be fair to say that is a good number to work off. Now, as an FBI agent, I can tell you that the majority of adults who tend to go missing do so from their homes or their jobs. One day they're there, and the next they aren't. Whatever their reason for leaving might be, they generally don't want to be found. Sure, some people will disappear when away from home due to an auto accident or some other mishap, but from the research I've done, those numbers are minimal. You said yesterday that none of the locals had gone missing. That's fair enough for a town the size of Daversville. However, the number of people who've been reported missing after passing through here in the last four years has been well above what could be expected."

"I'm sorry, ma'am. I'm a deputy in a backwoods town, I don't know nothing about what goes on elsewhere. I deal with what comes my way and don't worry none about nowhere else."

"How long have you been a deputy in Daversville?"

"Twenty-two years."

"So tell me, in your twenty-plus years of experience, has there always been an average of one missing person's report every other month as there has been in the last few months? I have fifteen missing persons' cases all taking place in Daversville in the last four years. Six of those cases have happened within the last twelve months. As an officer of the law, what do you think about that, Deputy?"

Deputy White licked his lips. Looked over Quadrado's shoulder. At the floor. Anywhere but her eyes.

She knew she'd got him now. If the stats were consistent, there was no way the beads of sweat on Deputy White's forehead would be so pronounced. He'd been aware of the escalation in missing persons' cases connected to Daversville, had done perfunctory investigations but had dismissed all the cases as nothing to do with the town. His next words were sure to damn him by their admission or fabrication.

"Come on now, Deputy. It's a simple question."

"Well, you see, it's different here. Missing persons' cases aren't something I keep detailed records on. I'm only a deputy. I keep the peace in Daversville and that's about all I have to do. There's not a lot of crime here."

"Enough." Quadrado had little time for Deputy White's attempts at obfuscation. "It's a simple yes or no answer to my question. In your experience as the lawman responsible for the safety of Daversville's inhabitants and those passing through, have you averaged one missing person's report every second month for all of the twenty-two years you've served? I'll repeat myself: I am looking for either yes or no as your answer. If you choose not to answer me, that's fine. I'll make a couple of calls and you'll be taken to an FBI field office and you'll be asked the same question in a more formal setting. You know, with recording devices, two agents and a lawyer. I'd guess you'd want a lawyer. From where I'm sitting, it very much looks like you're going to need one. Naturally, before your formal interview, all of your records would be examined to give us an insight into which other questions we should be asking you. I'm sure that once you've helped us, Internal Affairs will probably want to speak with you as well."

The look of hatred in Deputy White's eyes was enough to give Quadrado the answer she wanted.

"No."

"I see." Tempting as it was to gloat, Quadrado didn't want to give the forlorn deputy a reason to find the courage to start resisting her now he'd made his first damning admission. "So, I'm assuming you're smart enough to have recognized that there was a serious surge in a particular crime. Can you tell me what steps you took to prevent anyone else going missing after coming to Daversville?"

Deputy White replaced the look of hatred with one tinged with despair and fury. "What do you mean?"

"Surely after noticing a pattern emerging, you passed word onto your sheriff? Personally I would have run a poster campaign warning visitors to the town that women had been known to vanish. I would also have made a much greater effort to find out what had happened to the people who disappeared."

"You've got it all wrong. They ain't disappearing 'cause they came through Daversville."

"Aren't they? Then why are they going missing?"

"I don't know. Could be lots of reasons. Maybe they were abducted by aliens or they just got tired of their lives and dropped out. Perhaps they joined the Moonies. I don't know what happened to them, and I don't much care… for the way you're suggesting I haven't been able to find them."

The way that Deputy White looked sheepish was almost enough to bring a smile to Quadrado's lips. He'd almost admitted he didn't care about the missing women, but had tagged a few more words onto his sentence to try and cover up his mistake. Until that point his anger had been building and he'd been getting to the point of having a full-on rant.

Regardless of how sheepish he looked, or however much he tried to wheedle out of responsibility for the disappearances not being properly looked into, there was no doubt that he was either incompetent or he was covering up the disappearances for someone.

Whichever it was didn't matter to Quadrado. Deputy White was finished as a cop in her opinion, and she'd make sure that he and every report he'd ever filed would be scrutinized in every possible way. The question now was what should she do about it: give him a chance to come clean to her, or arrest him and hope he'd share what he knew in the interview room?

"You haven't left me with much of a choice, Deputy. I have to believe that you're either the most useless cop who ever wore a badge, or you're covering up the disappearances. Which is it?"

"Neither. I'm a deputy in a small town doing my best to keep the peace. You're wrong saying I'm useless. Wrong, I tell you; I do the job I'm paid to do, and I did what I could looking for them gals, but I ain't covering nothing up."

As much as she wasn't convinced by the deputy's protestations, there was enough doubt in Quadrado's mind to not arrest him on the spot and throw him into his own jail cell.

"Okay then. Now we've established there are women going missing, who do you think is behind it? You know the local folks, know who has an eye for the ladies. Who do you think is snatching the women who've gone missing?"

White looked at every part of the little police station except where Quadrado sat. "Only one person it can be. If he's out there, Trench is who we'd be looking for."

"Do you know where he camps? Holes up when there's bad weather?"

"Nope. Don't know nothing about him. Folks reckon they see his trails from time to time, but ain't nobody claimed to have seen him for years."

"I see. Get me your reports on each of the missing women, please, and then you can go."

Quadrado got a murderous look and a sharp nod, but she held the power in the room and they both knew it.

Deputy White passed her a report within seconds; it was for Lila Ogilvie. The most recent victim and the one Fletcher was looking into. Quadrado knew the name and the circumstances by heart, but rather than the overview reports she'd read, she wanted to read what the deputy had put into his reports. So often there were snippets of information hidden in a cop's notes on how they felt about the person being interviewed, and, as poor a cop as White was, he might still have jotted down something she could use.

The connection between Fletcher and Lila made her think of Fletcher again. She'd watched him leave town, but there was something about the passive way he'd left that had made her doubt he'd stay away. She hoped he would. Although she was sure that wherever he was, trouble wouldn't need a GPS to find him.

CHAPTER TWENTY-NINE

As he assessed the four youths, Fletcher was calculating his moves like a chess grandmaster. The most disconcerting thing about the guns in the hands of Big Brother and Scar was they weren't shaking, and they were held in the correct upright style. The whole gangster thing of holding a pistol horizontal had either passed them by or they'd learned how to properly shoot a pistol.

"Put your cell, your wallet, watch and any jewelry you have on the ground and we'll let you walk away."

Scar's tone was level with no inflection. It was as if he was ordering a takeout coffee rather than instructing Fletcher to hand over his possessions.

Rather than obey, Fletcher did nothing.

Fletcher knew the mechanics of distance. They'd long been burned into him. In a one-on-one situation against an opponent with a holstered gun, twenty-one feet was the accepted distance an average person could expect to be able to attack the gunman from with a high level of success before the gun could be drawn, aimed and fired.

However, that was for one-on-one situations, not one against four when two guns were already drawn and aimed. The fact the two guns were backed up with a pair of knives just added to the danger Fletcher was in.

The four youths were ten feet away from Fletcher. Too far to mount an attack, yet too close for him to gamble on the guns missing him. He had to close the gap by at least half. If he could get within reach of the guns, he'd stand a chance. With close fighting against multiple opponents, the lone fighter could strike without fear, whereas those he was fighting against would have to avoid hurting their buddies.

Fletcher took a pace forward, his billfold extended before him. Scar's gun lifted so he was sighting it as if at a shooting range. "I said on the ground. One more step and I shoot."

Not good.

Eight feet between them now.

The next step would be crucial. While Scar's threat to shoot was delivered in a confident tone, it was the middle of the afternoon and even in a neighborhood like Bridge Avenue, a gunshot would be bound to elicit a reaction from someone.

Fletcher drew himself to his full height. Scar's aim followed.

With a hand moving slowly into his jacket, Fletcher produced his cell and offered it forward as he took a half-step towards Scar.

Seven feet.

Scar's gun never wavered.

"Here. Please. Just take what you want and let me go." Fletcher wasn't looking at Scar as he spoke. He was making it look as if his entire attention was on Pudgy. Doing this served a dual purpose: first it set Scar at ease as he was not the focus of attention, and second, he was able to shift his position to one side of the alley instead of the center.

Pudgy made a mistake. He stepped forward until he was at Scar's shoulder.

Fletcher took it as a cue and took a step himself.

Five feet.

"Here. Take my money. And my cell." Fletcher again proffered his phone and billfold forward. Before embarking on this mission he'd emptied his pockets of all valuable possessions. He had maybe forty bucks and a cheap cell to lose. "Please, just take them and let me go."

Not being an actor, Fletcher couldn't inject any fear into his tone, but adrenaline was coursing through his body fast enough to give his voice a different edge.

From the corner of his eye, he saw Scar's gun twitch in a threatening manner as Pudgy moved forward until his outstretched hand was a foot away from Fletcher's billfold.

"Please. Don't shoot me." As he spoke Fletcher backed away from Scar, but rather than making a retreat, he was maneuvering himself sideways. The four youths were now in a line and Fletcher's back was against the alley wall.

Rather than delay and give them time to fan out, Fletcher planted his right foot on the wall behind him and launched himself forward. The billfold and cell dropped from his hands as he shoved Pudgy backwards and grabbed Scar's pistol.

Instead of wrestling for control of the weapon, Fletcher simply twisted the weapon away from Scar's body, breaking the finger Scar had looped through the trigger guard. His knee drove upwards into Scar's groin, and as the youth doubled over, Fletcher thrust him into Little Brother.

Big Brother was next. He might be experienced at muggings, but he lacked the sense to know to reposition himself when his target was shielded by a buddy. His gun was coming up, but he was a half second too slow and in a fight, microseconds count big.

Fletcher grabbed Big Brother's gun arm by the wrist and twisted it into an armbar. A downward strike on Big Brother's elbow bent his arm the wrong way. His gun clattered to the ground and, as the youth fell after it, Fletcher whipped round ready to see what Pudgy was up to.

As expected, he'd recovered his poise and was advancing knife first.

To counteract his threat, Fletcher drew his own knife and faced him down. With the most dangerous half of the four already taken out, there was uncertainty in his eyes.

Fletcher was aware that Little Brother may soon be joining the fray, so he stepped forward, his knife flashing in a series of feints that drove Pudgy back without actually harming him.

When Fletcher paused, Pudgy went for a counterstrike. His knife thrusting towards Fletcher's gut. It was the foolish move of an amateur. Fletcher side-stepped the thrust and, dropping his own knife, collected Pudgy's wrist with both hands and twisted.

Pudgy's arm went straight, locked in an armbar, but rather than striking down on the elbow as he'd done with Big Brother, Fletcher hauled Pudgy round so he could keep an eye on Little Brother.

Little Brother was in front of him, his knife held high ready for a downward slash.

"Drop your knife. Now." Fletcher put authority into his voice and saw the fear on Little Brother's face.

The knife lowered but didn't drop, so Fletcher added a few more degrees to the twist he had on Pudgy's arm. Cartilage and bone strained against Fletcher's pressure until the ligaments ruptured and his arm broke in a spiral fracture.

Pudgy screamed in agony as he fell to the ground where Scar and Big Brother already lay.

Fletcher watched as Little Brother did the math. He could risk getting hurt sticking up for the rest of the gang, or he could run and save himself.

For a moment, Fletcher thought bravery would win, so he bent down and lifted one of the fallen pistols. Little Brother's thudding footsteps echoed in the alleyway as he beat his retreat.

A minute later Fletcher had Scar's pistol in his waistband and Big Brother's pressed against Scar's kneecap.

"Do you have any spare ammo?"

Scar's head sawed from side to side, but Fletcher caught the way his eyes never left Big Brother and pushed the gun against his kneecap a little harder while fixing Big Brother with a stare.

A magazine was fished from Big Brother's pocket.

When Fletcher left the alley, he had two loaded pistols and a spare magazine. It was more than he'd hoped to get, but he wasn't sure it'd be enough for what he had planned.

CHAPTER THIRTY

The door opened to reveal a frail man who eyed Fletcher with suspicion. With a gray beard and thinning hair, he looked as if every one of his years alive had extracted a brutal toll on his health and well-being. It hadn't been hard to find the guy's address. Once he'd seen his name on a public list of the Blacketts' accounts, it had been easy to find where their attorney lived.

"Are you Norm Sipowich?"

"I am. And you are?"

"Grant Fletcher. I want to ask you a few questions about former clients of yours up in Daversville."

"Come in." Sipowich turned and led Fletcher into his home. "I expect it's the Blacketts you want to discuss."

Fletcher took the seat that was offered on one side of the kitchen table. Sipowich's house stank of cigarettes and there was a full ashtray in the middle of the table. The old man lit one, went into a series of wracking coughs and eased himself into a chair opposite Fletcher.

"How did you know I wanted to talk about the Blacketts?"

"I been an attorney in these parts best chunk of fifty years and never had me a client quite like the Blacketts. Always guessed that one day there'd be a knock on my door. Figured it'd be the cops or some government department." A keen look escaped Sipowich's rheumy eyes. "I know your name, son, but I don't know who you are or why you're here."

Fletcher explained who he was and why he'd chosen to visit, including mentioning the cousin who supposedly lived in the woods.

"That figures. What do you want from me?" A liver-spotted hand lifted from the table. "Mind, I was their lawyer for more years than I care to remember. Ain't going to spill anything against them that will do them harm. They put a lot of work my way and that put my kids through college and that's long before I mention client privilege."

"Are you saying there's a different side to them? That they're not the benevolent people they appear to be?"

"I ain't saying that at all. So far as the folks of Daversville are concerned, the Blackett family have taken care of them as if they were their own kin." Sipowich blew a stream of smoke over Fletcher's head. "You did ask about Tom, though. I never represented him, so you can ask what you like there."

Fletcher worked out Tom must be the proper name of Miss Constance's cousin. "Is it true he dropped off the grid to live off the land? Why did he do that?"

"It's true. Against the family's wishes, he joined up and went to Vietnam as a nineteen-year-old back in seventy-three. Was there 'til they pulled out. You look like a fighting man. You'll know how war changes folks. Well, Tom came back from 'Nam a different man. He was always a serious type, never one to hoot nor holler. After 'Nam he lost interest in the lumber business. All the Blacketts were given jobs in the mill and they all worked themselves up to where their daddies were. Tom wanted no part of it. Started insisting folks call him Trench, cause that's how he was known in 'Nam."

"What did he do then if he wasn't in the family business?"

"Oh, he still worked there. You don't escape family that easy, son. He did what was asked of him and not a spit more. There was a lotta fights about it and I don't mean shouting matches." Another cigarette got lit and it hung from Sipowich's mouth as he talked. "Tom was sweet on a teacher at the school and by all accounts she was sweet right back. His poppa said no, and while I didn't hear them, I understand there were a lot of harsh words spoken on all sides. The kinda harsh that can't be taken back." Ash dropped to the table as Sipowich adopted a faraway look. "Next thing you know, the teacher gets herself found with her throat cut and Tom ain't around no more. It was a bad business. Folks said he'd cut her throat in anger when she wouldn't run off with him. That would be around seventy-nine or eighty. He always did have a temper on him, and the army taught him the skills to harness it."

The old attorney's story was making Fletcher suspect Tom, or Trench as he was now known, more than he ever had before. All the same, it was a stretch to think that someone who'd lived wild for nigh on forty years could influence a whole town.

"I heard rumors he's living in the woods round Daversville. Do you think that's possible?"

"Damn straight I do. You ain't from these parts so you won't know. Those woods have a pull on those who grow up around 'em. Ain't many leave and most of those who do come back before long. Them woods got a real hold on folks and there ain't never been no more heard about Tom. He never turned up nowhere else, not dead nor alive. I know because his family had me look."

All of this made sense to Fletcher. Back in the seventies PTSD wasn't diagnosed, and he knew from his own experiences how much fighting a war could change a person. Many veterans struggled to adjust to a civilian life and there was a high percentage of former soldiers among the ranks of the homeless. Maybe in his own mind, this Trench was still fighting a war against the Vietcong.

"What about the missing women? Do you think he'd have had anything to do with that?"

Sipowich washed a hand over his left cheek. "Way I remember him, he was always a gentleman towards the ladies, but forty years of living in the woods thinking about war and a woman he loved can change a man. Can't say if it's him or not. Would surprise me if it was and yet, wouldn't surprise me if it wasn't."

Fletcher dug into Sipowich's memories a while longer and then left. He had woods to hike through and wanted to make a start before nightfall.

CHAPTER THIRTY-ONE

The hike through the woods of Washington County was similar to a thousand other treks Fletcher had been on. As part of his research before leaving home he'd boned up on the wildlife he might encounter should he find himself in the woods. Georgia played home to rattlesnakes, cottonmouths and copperheads, plus brown bears and coyotes.

Snakes could be avoided with vigilance, and, unless there was a full-on pack, coyotes could be scared away with a few shots from one of the Glocks he'd liberated from the muggers in Macon. Brown bears, however, were a different matter. They wouldn't be scared off with a gunshot and while a .380 round would deliver a fatal wound to a human, unless he landed a brain or heart shot, it wouldn't do a lot to stop a bear. Always at the back of his mind was the idea Trench might be watching him, or that he might come across him by accident.

As he trudged through the woods, his eyes switching between the ground and the GPS he held, Fletcher's mind was on the Blackett family. Sipowich had answered most of his questions about the whole family as well as his ones on Trench. Blackett Holdings owned not just the mill, but, as Fletcher had suspected, also had the entire town of Daversville listed among its assets. Three people were named as directors: Constance, Jimmy and Chuck Blackett. According to Sipowich they were a mother and her sons. The company had a website which advertised its wares. The site had a few pictures of various woodcutting machinery and trucks hauling loads of cut and uncut lumber. There was an eco-friendly mission statement about replanting the trees they felled, but that didn't surprise Fletcher. Not only was it probable there would be a government mandate stating felled trees must be replanted, it made sense the Blacketts would plant trees for future generations to harvest so the family business would never run dry of potential income.

Fletcher had scoured the website for pictures of the Blacketts but found none. A Google search of their names returned a few newspaper articles, but like the company website, the articles displayed no photos of the owners. Each of the articles had focused upon charitable deeds. Money given to a local hospital, sponsorship of a high school football team and other minor acts of generosity.

The pack on Fletcher's back was heavy, but nowhere near as heavy as the one he'd carried while in the Royal Marines. The problem with this one was that it wasn't as well put together as a military backpack and he'd further exacerbated its discomfort by packing it with his purchases from Macon. He'd bought a hammock, first aid kit and plenty of fruit as well as a snakebite kit. The suit he'd worn was replaced with combat fatigues bearing a woodland pattern, and he'd picked up a pair of infra-red binoculars. Should the weather turn nasty, he'd bought a thin waterproof smock. His last purchases had been a water bottle, a handheld GPS and an old-fashioned compass. The water bottle could be refilled at any of the streams he encountered, and the compass was a backup should the GPS fail in any way.

His primary destination was the Blacketts' home. For all Trench was the obvious suspect, he couldn't align a loner hiding out in the woods as someone who was able to gather intel and react as swiftly as a family who controlled a whole town. Therefore he wanted to check out the family, and the best way he could think of doing so was to observe them in their home. If he was right about his suspicions, he'd see some of the youths he'd tangled with since arriving in Daversville.

If he saw anyone he recognized, his plan was to get into the house and start asking questions.

A check of the GPS told Fletcher he was within a half mile of the house.

This was where he cut out the long strides and took a more measured approach. He doubted that any of the family would be out walking in the woods, but he wasn't taking any chances.

When he was a quarter mile from the house, and by his reckoning at least a mile and a half from Daversville, Fletcher could see where the treeline began. Slowing his pace further, he crept forward until he was able to see the house with clarity while also being shrouded in the foliage of a bush.

The Blacketts' house wasn't anything like he'd expected. He'd been prepared for a colonial style building or an elaborate log cabin. What he saw instead was the polar opposite.

He fished his binoculars from his pack and put them to his eyes. When he had them focused, he scanned the house from left to right, his mouth falling further and further open the more his eyes drank in the details of the house.

CHAPTER THIRTY-TWO

As Fletcher made his way from the Blackett household to their lumber mill, his body was operating on autopilot as his mind chewed over what he'd seen. Branches were moved so they didn't scratch his face or head, his eyes scanned the ground for snakes and ears listened for woodland predators as his legs drove him forward, yet he was only aware of such things on a subconscious level. His every shred of mental energy was focused on the house he'd just observed. The light might be fading, but he was acting on instinct and the GPS would keep him right if he veered off course. Not once on his journey through the woods had he seen a sign of the mysterious Trench. The more he thought about it, the less inclined he was to believe Tom Blackett had decided to live in the wilderness around Daversville. Fletcher's best guess was that Trench had met up with former army buddies and had started his life over again. It was possible he'd become a mercenary somewhere to escape his past and the ghost of the woman he'd killed.

Fletcher got that some people were paranoid about home security, understood that people feared home invasion, and that a house in the middle of nowhere was more vulnerable than most.

It made a certain amount of sense the Blacketts had taken precautions to protect themselves as they lived in such rural isolation. Yet the level of security on the Blacketts' house wasn't akin with deterring burglars. It was more in line with a high security prison.

Fletcher had seen the wall around the house that was topped with broken glass. The ornamental wrought iron gate matched the wall's twelve feet in height. To further increase the deterrent for would-be burglars, three Doberman Pinschers ran loose, patrolling the garden areas in a languid style that Fletcher was sure would devolve into attack mode should the wrong person crest the wall or breach the gate.

While the level of security was way over the top for a house few people would know about, it also reassured Fletcher that he was right to point a finger of suspicion at the Blackett family. It was obvious to him the Blacketts had something to not only hide, but they were afraid of something too. His first guess was a rebellion by the people of Daversville. Downtrodden and held in a time warp by the all-powerful Blacketts, there was every chance the people would one day rise against the family which controlled their lives and seek a backwoods vengeance for one piece of oppression or another. The second guess he made was that it was Trench they were afraid of.

The house itself had been something else; it carried itself three stories high, with the first floor raised so the downstairs windows were a minimum of nine feet from the ground. Each of these windows were covered by ornamental frames that were little more than glorified portcullises. Fletcher had examined the lower areas without finding any windows that would let light flood into a basement. The upper two floors had little obvious protection other than their height from the ground, but when Fletcher had zeroed in on one, he'd seen sturdy window locks and the rectangular blocks of alarm sensors.

The construction of the Blackett house was brick rather than the timber the rest of Daversville was built with. Solid and fore-boding, its very demeanor was hostile and it was more likely to have a machine gun tower than a welcome mat on the front step.

As a former soldier, Fletcher welcomed the challenge of breaching all the levels of security. The problem he had was that it was a tough ask for one man. There was also no telling what further anti-intruder alarms would feature inside the house. With so much security adorning the exterior, Fletcher figured there would be motion-sensors, pressure pads and possibly some CCTV cameras. Fletcher knew that CCTV cameras could relay images to cell phones, but he'd never seen any of the locals with a cell, and whenever he'd tried to use his in the town, there had been a profound lack of signal.

Another concerning issue was the number of antennas and dishes adorning the roof of the house. Fletcher had checked his cell signal and found it missing, so the antennas had nothing to do with cell phones. Instead they were there to communicate other things. The dishes may well be for TV channels, as the house was a long way from anywhere that would offer a cable connection, but Fletcher doubted all the dishes were for TV subscriptions.

At the rear of the house, a wide parking garage had sat with its doors open. Fletcher hadn't gotten a look far inside, but he'd managed to see a dirt bike and a dark green quad bike. What other vehicles the garage held was unknown.

The dogs and the off-road vehicles added a further complication to Fletcher's planned assault on the house. His plan had always hinged on him slinking back into the woods, but with dogs who could track him and ATVs that could outpace him, he'd have to either leave no one in a fit state to follow him or steal one of the ATVs for himself, although that wasn't without its own set of issues. The Blacketts and their minions would know the woods way better than he did.

There was every chance he'd run himself into a dead end, or over the edge of one of the steep bluffs which littered the woods.

With every step Fletcher took in his two-mile hike to the lumber mill, the more his plan for the assault on the house began to take a shape he was happy with. As a soldier he knew that plans only lasted until the first contact with the enemy, but he was also experienced enough to know that once he'd embarked on his quest to gain entry to the house, the longer he could delay contact with any family member, the better his chances of finding Lila if, as he suspected, she was being held in the house. He knew he was basing his suspicions on instinct rather than anything tangible, but the whole set-up of the town bothered him, and while he hadn't met the Blackett family, as the people with the power in the area, he couldn't see how they weren't mixed up with the disappearances, even if it was hushing them up to protect Trench.

Ahead of him, his eyes could pick out floodlighting and his ears detected the whine of high-powered saws and the thrum of heavy machinery.

Fletcher wasn't surprised the lumber mill operated around the clock. The lumber-cutting machinery would be expensive to buy, and if the volume of lumber coming in was sufficient to require round-the-clock working, the sooner the machines would pay for themselves and the greater the profits from the mill would be. It being located a half mile north of the town would allow the workers silence to sleep in their homes.

As he crept to a point where he could watch over the lumber mill, Fletcher couldn't help but marvel at the size of the operation. Front loaders with grabbers rather than shovels were feeding lengths of tree trunks onto conveyors which disappeared into large sheds. At the other end of the sheds, stackers were exiting with loads of sawn lumber they were loading straight onto trucks. In other areas there was what Fletcher presumed were kilns for drying the lumber; a series of huge submarine-style cylinders he guessed were tanks for pressure treating the lumber; and at the far end of the sprawling site there were stacks that, when Fletcher zoomed in on them, he found were a series of manufactured timber products such as fence panels, timber decking and pre-made structures such as gazebos and children's playground sets.

All in all, there was a lot of industry going on, and there was no denying that the whole set-up appeared to be working better than a Swiss watch. There was a balletic grace to the choreography employed by the various machines as each operator ran back and forth through the same path. As hypnotizing as it was to watch the loaders and stackers, Fletcher's mind was fixed on the scale of the operation he was observing.

This was no backwoods lumber mill that employed three guys to operate an ancient machine, this was a slick modern site that utilized heavy equipment and ran with a smoothness that spoke of intelligent planning and execution.

Along with the heavily secured house located in a secluded area out of town, the lumber mill indicated that the Blackett family had a serious amount of money behind them, and if, as Fletcher suspected, they weren't paying the wages other lumber mills were, they would be making a lot of money.

All of these new facts pointed towards the Blackett family being smart, wealthy and, judging from the design of their home, paranoid.

Fletcher made his way through the tree line until he was nearer the one brick building in the lumber mill. It would be the office. The place where he'd be able to get confirmation of the scale of the Blacketts' reach and finances. It might not be the nerve center of their business, but at the very least it would be a key hub. Fletcher didn't believe for one second that he'd get any incriminating evidence from the office, but that didn't mean he wouldn't learn something that would either confirm or eradicate the Blacketts as suspects. The top floor of the office building was flanked by windows on all four sides like an airport's control tower. It would allow the mill's foreman a view of the entire site so he could assess every aspect of his domain.

Rather than cross the lumber mill's sprawl, Fletcher kept skirting through the woods until he was at the nearest point to the office before he stepped from the darkness of the woods into the artificial light that bathed the lumber mill.

Fletcher waited until the nearest front loader was traveling away from him and dashed towards the office.

CHAPTER THIRTY-THREE

Fletcher got to the office door without incident, but it was predictably locked when he tried the handle.

The office door was in an exposed position and, while the workers were all busy at their tasks, all it would take for him to be spotted was one of the front loader operators looking over their shoulder when reversing. Clad as he was in camouflage clothing, there would be immediate suspicion about his reasons for being at the office door.

While the door was sturdy, Fletcher reckoned he could be through it with a single well-placed kick. That however would leave evidence of his presence. He would have to pick the lock to get in without leaving a trail. He could pick most locks in less than two minutes, but the front loaders were moving back and forth in ninety-second cycles, which meant he'd have at best forty-five seconds before the hulking machines started backing up to grab their next load.

Forty-five seconds was nowhere near long enough for him to pick the lock. It wasn't as if he could do it in thirty second instalments while returning to cover, as once he released his grip on the lock picks, there was little chance of them staying in place until he resumed his attempt to get through the door.

He needed another solution. He could hope that there would be a break where the machines would all pause while the workers grabbed a coffee and a sandwich, but when that break would be was anyone's guess. If the shifts were eight to eight, the odds were that the first break would be around midnight. Two hours' time.

Fletcher didn't want to wait around for two hours. Sure he could skulk back into the woods until there was a break, but he'd still have to get back in and there was no telling where the workers would assemble for their break. Maybe a foreman or team leader would use the break to check something in the office.

To stand the best chance of getting in and out undetected, Fletcher had to find another way to gain access to the office without waiting around half the night.

Using the building to shield him from the workers, Fletcher backed off a little and looked for another way in. As he examined the office's walls he noticed that one of the windows flanking the office's top story was open. Not wide, but enough that he'd be able to clamber through it if he could get up there.

Slinking back to the office wall for cover, he scanned his eyes around looking for a ladder or something he could use to boost him up towards the open window.

He found a ladder. It lay alongside a stack of lumber whose every row was on narrow slats to allow air through and banded into bundles. Around him machines roared and whined as he picked his moment to grab the ladder and carry it to the office wall.

The ladder was around eight feet in length causing Fletcher to grunt in dismay when it fell short of the window by a good five. There was nothing he could use to stand the ladder on to give it an extra couple of feet in height, so Fletcher shucked his backpack onto the ground and started climbing.

As he neared the top of the ladder he found himself coming into contact with the office's wall, the rough brick scratching at his face.

Fletcher hugged the wall, his fingertips grasping at the joints between the bricks when they ran out of ladder to hold. He wasn't overweight by anyone's standards, but he still felt as though his stomach was pushing him backwards away from the wall as each new step on a rung forced him forwards against the wall.

He sent the fingers of his right hand clawing upwards, but they found only rough brick. A glance down informed him that he still had another rung left to step on. It would give him the extra inches he needed to allow him to grasp the window frame and haul himself upwards.

A deep breath. A rapid count to three and he put his foot on the next rung. His knee was bent outwards and yet it still pressed against the wall.

Fletcher gave a thrusting heave upwards, driving with his leg and grabbed for the window frame with brick-scuffed fingertips. His right hand caught but his left fell short, leaving him half dangling, half braced. He found the top of one of the ladder's runners with his right foot and pushed upwards enough to allow his left hand to join his right on the window frame.

He took a deep breath and pulled himself upwards, biceps straining until he could hook an elbow onto the window's sill. A second later his other elbow joined it.

Now for the tricky part.

The window was on a restrainer to stop it opening far enough for someone to easily fall out of it. There was enough room for Fletcher to burrow his way through it, but it would be tight, and he knew from bitter experience both parts of the window's locking mechanism were likely to leave gouges in his flesh as he squirmed over them.

An added complication was the control tower design of the office. Anyone looking his way would see his body silhouetted against the illumination created by the floodlights bathing the entire lumber mill in near-daylight brightness.

Still, there was nothing for it but to proceed.

Fletcher teased his head up until he could look over the windowsill. He saw nobody looking his way, and when the nearest front loader trundled forward with its mouthful of trunks, he hauled upwards, squirming his body through the narrow opening as he heaved.

His shoulders passed through the window and his chest and back were scoured by the catches, but he just gritted his teeth and ignored the pain. Fletcher's stomach burned as he teased himself over the catch, but worse was ahead. As the weight of his body pulled him towards the office's floor, his legs couldn't help but lift until they caught on the half-open window.

He was prepared for this, and as he was pulled down by gravity, he was twisting his body so that he landed on his back, his head colliding with a stack of lumber samples hard enough for him to allow a brief yelp to escape his lips.

Fletcher kept low as he cast his eyes around the room while rubbing at what was already a growing bruise.

The office was pretty standard. A couple of desks topped by computer monitors and phones, a wall of file cabinets and various heaps of paperwork.

What wasn't normal was the temperature. Despite the cool evening air, the office felt like a blast furnace. There was a desk fan, but no sign of any air-con system nor a portable store-bought unit. During the day the heat would be intolerable in here. The heavy machinery of the lumber mill would mean the workers wouldn't hear a thing if the windows were open during the day, and that was before you considered the dust the machines would kick up.

Fletcher lifted one of the monitors from the desk, placed it on the floor and tweaked its brightness settings, before powering up the computer it was connected to. His thinking was to do everything he could to lessen the glare from the screen.

The screen came to life and displayed a dull gray background. Worst of all, it asked for a password. Fletcher had expected this, but he was still disappointed to find it. Working on his knees, he scoured the drawers of the desk he'd lifted the monitor from but didn't find anything which contained the password for the computer or anything else.

He tried a few obvious ones to see if they'd work, but the screen never showed anything other than an error message.

Fletcher placed the monitor back on the desk and turned his attention to the file cabinets. Four of the five were unlocked and held nothing more than billing and shipping lines going back three years.

It took Fletcher thirty-eight seconds to pick the lock of the fifth file cabinet. He drew its bottom door open and found a pistol, manuals for various saws and lumber machinery, and a small metal box with a handle and a slot for a key. Fletcher surmised the box would hold maybe a couple hundred bucks of cash in various bills and change. Most offices had a petty cash tin for minor purchases, and he didn't expect this one to be any different. It was tempting to add the pistol to his own armory, but he left it where it was as taking it would indicate that someone had been in here.

The next two drawers upheld a plethora of hanging files. Each file was narrow and bore a name, date of birth and what Fletcher presumed was a start date. It was your typical employee file and while it may prove useful if he knew the names of individuals, collectively it told him little other than the fact that the majority of people employed by the lumber mill all came from the same few families.

As he ran his eyes over the names he noticed that, while they weren't arranged in a complete alphabetical order, they seemed to be collected into groups which in turn were alphabetized. He scoured the files for a group with female names and when he found it, he picked out Mary-Lou Henderson's file.

So far as he could tell, Mary-Lou's employment started on her fifteenth birthday. She'd worked the diner and nowhere else. There was a sheet marking down sick days, and time she'd taken off to care for her father. Included in the file were details of Mary-

Lou's home and how much of her salary was deducted to pay the company rent for the cabin she lived in.

Mary-Lou had dreams and aspirations she was working towards realizing. She had the college place ready and Fletcher would have bet a good amount that she'd already secured herself a part-time job to subsidize her college education. Mary-Lou's college adventure made him think of his daughter. Wendy would be going to college in a couple of years and he was already dreading the financial implications her going would bring for him. In an ideal world, she'd be able to take as many subjects as she liked, and he'd be able to support her. Problem was, there was no way he could afford to do that. Wendy would have to get a part-time job to supplement what he could give her. Her college experience would be dominated by work of one kind or another and she'd have to forego a subject or two so she could work. She was a worker and would accept these circumstances, but Fletcher wanted her to enjoy her time in college, as life soon kicked in once you embarked on a career.

Fletcher slid the file back into the cabinet and opened the final drawer. It was the most telling of all. It held the files which detailed the company's accounts. There were bank statements showing the various transactions. Fletcher saw that once a week, thousands of dollars in cash would be withdrawn; he guessed that would be for the payroll. On the credit side, there were regular payments from a number of companies. From what he could tell the lumber mill was making good money. As he flicked through the statements, he saw that every time the account reached more than two hundred and fifty thousand in credit, fifty thousand would be transferred to a different account. A high interest account was his first guess, but from everything he'd seen of the Blacketts' stranglehold on Daversville and its people, he wouldn't be surprised to learn the money was being squirreled away where the IRS couldn't find it.

Fletcher spent another five minutes searching the office, but he found nothing else of note.

Rather than squirm his way back out of the open window, he crept downstairs and found himself in a room full of chainsaws and the protective clothing worn by their users. The sharp tang of petrol filled the air, and while the equipment appeared to have been well used, it was all in good condition and arranged in neat rows, rather than dropped in an untidy heap.

When he'd picked the mortise lock on the door which led outside, Fletcher tuned his ears into the sounds of the front loader's engine. At first its roar was accompanied by beeps and then both fell silent for a couple of seconds before the deep rumble began again.

Fletcher worked out it had been reversing and was now going forwards. The question was, was the loader going on the short run to the woodpile, or the long one to where it dropped the trees onto the conveyor?

As he counted the seconds off in his head, he realized it was doing the longer leg of its route.

He listened for the beeps indicating it was coming back. They came, faint at first, but they got stronger as the machine neared the office. The warning beeps stopped. In his mind's eye, Fletcher could see it scooping up tree trunks in its pincered grab. The beeps started to come through the engine noise again.

Fletcher's hand grasped the door handle. Two seconds after the beeping stopped and the front loader roared off, he swung the door open, slipped out and made his way to the rear of the office where he'd left his backpack.

As Fletcher was feeding his arms through the backpack's straps, he heard a strong voice call out.

"Hey. You there. Whatcha bin doin' in the office?"

CHAPTER THIRTY-FOUR

The aged springs of the mattress dug into Quadrado's hip and shoulder whichever way she squirmed in her quest for comfort. No matter which portion of the bed she lay on, the springs were either crushed flat or forming stalagmites of resistance.

She was aware that most of the issue with the mattress was borne from the whirring of her mind. After the conversation with Deputy White, she'd gone over his notes on the missing women and had tried to interview as many of the Daversville residents who may have had contact with the women as she could.

The sum total of people she'd spoken to was four. Agnes Jackson at the diner, an ornery woman who manned the Daversville general store, plus Duke and the girl who helped him out.

None had been forthcoming with information. Least of all the storekeeper. She'd been contrary to the point of insolence. She'd not met Quadrado's eyes once, and as she left the store, Quadrado had heard the woman mutter "damn uppity spics" to a customer.

It had taken all of Quadrado's self-control not to turn and confront the woman. The only thing that had stopped Quadrado was the knowledge that by challenging her, she would harden the shopkeeper's beliefs. Hearts and minds were the way to win people over, although some people were so set in their outdated views they'd never change.

Duke and his helper were the most forthcoming, but like the two old women, they had nothing of note to say. Though, unlike Agnes and the storekeeper, they at least were pleasant to Quadrado.

Given a chance, Quadrado would have liked to grill Duke's helper on a one-to-one basis. The girl looked around the same age as Mary-Lou Henderson and there was a good chance she'd know something about Mary-Lou the older members of the community didn't. Whether she could pry that information from the girl remained to be seen, but Quadrado felt she was her best lead.

Quadrado had crossed paths with the pair of detectives investigating Mary-Lou Henderson's murder, and while they had been guarded when she'd asked them about their case, they'd told her that they'd been met with a virtual wall of silence. Not one of Mary-Lou's neighbors had seen anyone apart from Fletcher near the cabin and there was a growing sense within Quadrado that the townsfolk were all covering something up. The pathology report on Mary-Lou had come through and, while the cause of death was obvious, for the girl's sake, Quadrado was pleased to learn that she hadn't been sexually assaulted before her throat was slit. It was a small mercy, but a mercy nonetheless.

She'd swapped cards with the detectives along with promises to keep each other informed of developments in their respective cases.

That both detectives had picked up on the town's wall of silence hadn't surprised Quadrado. Daversville was time warp central, and as far as strangers were concerned, its residents lived lives of fear and mistrust. It was a trait Quadrado had encountered before. In the cities, gangs ruled the roost in certain areas, and none of the residents unfortunate enough to live in their territory would dare speak out lest the bullet of reprisal have their name etched into its casing. Daversville was the same, just with a styling and mentality that was a hundred years out of date.

Her mind whipped back and forth on the idea Trench had evolved into a serial killer and the missing women were his victims. To a point, it was a credible theory, but she couldn't get her head around the way the townsfolk were complicit by their silence. For a whole town to support a killer, even if their silence was bought with fear for their own lives, was remarkable. That fear was palpable. It hung in the air like a ghost observing all conversations she had with the locals. It was there in the meek way Mary-Lou's father had obeyed her and returned home. She'd checked with Deputy White that he'd spoken to the father, and had learned that while Mr Henderson was grief-stricken, he had no idea who'd killed his daughter and had implored Deputy White to find the killer.

What also grated at her was the complete lack of evidence. No possessions of the missing women had been found. From the cars they drove right down to inconsequential items like an earring, not one trace of them could be found. It was possible they were being spirited away to restart a new life elsewhere, but as four of the missing women had young children waiting for them at home, Quadrado didn't believe that was the case. All the same, she planned to request that the missing women's computers and phones were given a forensic examination in case there was a link between websites they'd visited.

The most pressing issue on Quadrado's mind was the location of Deputy White, as she hadn't seen him since their conversation.

Now Quadrado had spoken to the various townsfolk, she had several follow-up questions for the deputy, but he hadn't been at his desk, nor his home. She'd checked both the town's bars without success.

In her mind he could be in a number of places: his squad car, desperately leaving Daversville and his deceit behind to start over someplace else; or, and this was the option Quadrado thought most probable, he was sitting with a bottle of bourbon trying to work out a way to extricate himself from the trouble he was in.

As Quadrado's brain finally slowed enough to allow her eyes to weigh heavy, she was puzzling on the whereabouts of the mysterious Trench and wondering if Deputy White was about to join the ranks of the missing or if he'd stay around to face the music.

CHAPTER THIRTY-FIVE

Fletcher didn't bother answering the challenge. Instead he set off for the tree line as fast as he could. Within two paces he was building speed, after five, momentum. Someone rounded a building and made as if to grapple him, but Fletcher had played enough rugby for the Royal Marines to know how to deal with his would-be tackler.

First he ducked left. Saw his tackler mimic the action from twenty yards away.

Again he ducked left. The tackler once again aped his move. Shouts of encouragement from the person who'd spotted him flew past Fletcher's shoulder, but his focus was on the tackler. He was a big man with gorilla arms and a determined expression.

Fletcher must get past the tackler before the spotter joined the fray. Yes, he could take both men down, but in the greater scheme of things, they were innocents protecting their workplace and as such he didn't believe they deserved to be hurt.

Fletcher juked left a third time and as soon as his left foot hit the ground he drove his already-tilted body off to the right so he effected the same quick-footed sidestep that had fooled so many of the fullbacks he'd faced on a rugby pitch. Tackler was quicker than his size suggested, and he'd corrected his momentum and moved himself left towards Fletcher's new path.

Tackler was off-balance though, and Fletcher had enough experience and time to take another sidestep left. A heavy boot swung his way, but the tackler was falling as he kicked out, so Fletcher was able to hurdle the outstretched leg.

"Stop, you sumbitch."

The shout was easy to ignore. Fletcher knew things wouldn't go well for him when the Blacketts found out that he'd been snooping around their office. If the workers called the cops, Deputy White would be more than happy to pin a breaking-and-entering charge on him, and there was no telling how pissed Special Agent Quadrado would be. Whatever happened, he had to keep her onside, as her presence was all that was stopping Deputy White from fitting him up for one crime or another.

What wasn't so easy to ignore was the proximity the shout had come from. When he'd heard the first shout, Fletcher had cast a glance around and saw one of the workers twenty-five yards away. The spotter must be able to at least match Fletcher's pace as he now sounded a lot closer than twenty-five yards.

Fletcher was aware the weaving sidesteps had slowed him down, as did hurdling the boot that had been swung in what he assumed was an attempt to trip him up. What he hadn't counted on was the spotter being so quick on his feet.

Rather than risk looking back and stumbling as his body twisted, Fletcher concentrated on pumping his legs and arms in a powerful beat as he dashed for the tree line.

The thud of his boots and the roar of the front loader's engine were all Fletcher could hear as he ducked beneath the branches of the trees flanking the lumber mill.

Now he was in the woods he faced a different set of problems. Night had arrived and brought with it a stygian blackness. With the spotter on his tail, there was no time for careful monitoring of where his feet were placed. He was in a headlong dash and didn't want to give the spotter chance to catch him up.

As he covered the first few yards into the woods, Fletcher's brain was alive to the problems he faced and the solutions to them.

First was the darkness. His pupils would be narrow from the floodlights of the lumber mill and he needed them wide to cope with the inky blackness that would afford him a chance to escape his pursuer. In another ten seconds or so, he'd lose all vision as the darkness of the woods blinded him. The only solution to this was to cut left or right and skirt the floodlit areas until his eyes adjusted. This in itself wasn't a long-term solution because if either the spotter or tackler had properly raised the alarm, other workers may be tracking him as he ran around the lumber mill's perimeter. Sooner or later one of them would set an ambush and then he'd have to fight Lord knows how many workers.

The second issue on his mind was how to throw off his pursuer. The man's speed was evident due to the way he'd closed the gap while Fletcher was dodging the tackler. He might well be gaining on Fletcher now. It would be simple enough for Fletcher to stop, turn round and incapacitate the man. As much as he had no qualms about hurting those who moved against him, this man hadn't done anything wrong. Fletcher knew that in the guy's mind, he was doing the right thing by protecting his place of work. It was a laudable thing to do and, for that, the guy didn't deserve to face the kind of hurt Fletcher would have to inflict to make sure the man stopped coming after him. A solid gut punch would afford him a strong advantage but there was no guarantee it'd be enough. A knockout blow to the jaw or the temple would be better, as would dislocating a knee or stomping down on a twisted ankle, but no matter which way he tried, Fletcher couldn't see past the fact the guy chasing him was the one who was morally in the right, as it was Fletcher who'd broken into the office.

Fletcher could pull one of the guns from his backpack and send the guy on his way back to the lumber mill. That would be an easy solution. It'd solve all his current problems in one fell swoop. However, doing this would be detrimental to his main goal. Whichever way he escaped his pursuer, the man was sure to be quizzed by his bosses about the intruder he'd chased off. It was bad enough he'd shown his hand and the Blacketts would find out that he'd snooped about in their offices, but it would also inform them he was armed. They might not know who he was at first, but with the whole town on their side, they'd soon find out.

The third problem Fletcher was chewing on was the fact that very soon he'd have to run through the woods with only poorly developed night vision to guide him. Nocturnal predators, animal burrows that could turn an ankle if his foot slipped into one, steep bluffs and fallen branches lying in wait to send him sprawling headlong to the ground were just some of the hazards he wouldn't be able to spot until he was upon them.

Whichever way he tried to talk himself out of it, Fletcher knew that sooner or later he'd have to submit himself to the dark.

Later was what his heart desired, but his head was telling him sooner. He still hadn't looked back to see how close the spotter was, but he'd strained his ears and recognized there was only one set of boots crunching twigs behind him. That meant the would-be tackler was either far back, or he'd never entered the foot race. This in turn meant he'd be busy raising the alarm.

This would lead to several possibilities, all of which were complications he'd rather not face. More men would come after him. They'd carry flashlights and weapons. Shooting a person running through a wooded area is never easy, but it wasn't impossible either. The biggest worry Fletcher had was that there would be dogs sent to track him. He already knew the Blacketts had three dogs guarding their house, so there was a good chance they'd either have others or, with all the woods around them, one of the mill workers would have a dog or two that was trained as a tracker.

With every twenty yards he was progressing forward, Fletcher was making sure that he was slipping further and further to his left, away from the glare of the lights. The trees he was running past nothing more than black pillars that offered obstacle rather than support.

His night vision was only good enough to see the dished ravine as he came upon it. He had two choices: go left and enter the ravine, thereby losing what light was bleeding from the lumber mill and trust he'd be able to see enough not to run himself into danger, or veer right and emerge into the floodlit areas once more.

There wasn't really a choice at all, so he leapt into the dished ravine and tried not to let his forward momentum send him tumbling forwards as he barreled down the slope.

CHAPTER THIRTY-SIX

It was all Fletcher could do to stay upright as he ran down the side of the ravine. Gravity was pulling his torso forwards, trying to topple him into a headlong plunge, but the more he tried to lean back to stay balanced, the more his feet slid on the soft pine needles carpeting the ground.

The trees were far more formidable obstacles in the ravine as his ability to dodge and weave was curtailed by the slope. Behind him he heard a wet thud followed by a grunt that brought a satisfied smirk to his face as he imagined the body of his pursuer slamming into one of the mighty trees. The smirk disappeared from his mouth when he failed to avoid a tree himself.

Fletcher's shoulder bashed into the trunk of the tree hard enough to rattle his teeth. Had he been running on level ground, he might have been able to counteract the sudden impediment to his progress by spinning and carrying on. The slope of the ravine and the tree he hit had different ideas.

Rather than spin and continue, Fletcher was pirouetted by the impact, his feet unable to move fast enough to maintain his balance. He went down still spinning, his arms flailing until he pulled them into his body. As he rolled downwards, he was doing everything he could to turn his movement into a slide rather than a spin.

His calves thumped into a tree which stopping him spinning but also sent him sliding towards the bottom of the ravine headfirst. Fletcher dug the toe of his right boot into the slope and used his hands to help twist his body until his feet were leading his downhill slalom.

Fletcher could feel himself slowing and when the next tree came into view, rather than trying to steer round it, he simply lifted his legs and braced himself ready for the impact.

When it came it jarred his legs and left the soles of his feet feeling as if he'd jumped from a ten-foot wall onto a concrete pad.

The pain didn't matter. The fact he was bashed and bruised didn't matter. He was alive, and while the fall had knocked out what little wind was left in him after the sprint from the office, he was still in a good enough condition to keep running.

He pushed himself to his feet and set off downhill. He was ten yards from the bottom of the ravine when he saw the stream in its basin. Fletcher paused for a brief second to judge the direction of the stream's flow.

It was running left to right. This meant the higher ground was to the left and the stream would go on to form or join a river if he followed it to the right.

Fletcher turned right. Instinct made a lot of people think higher ground was safer. Instincts were often wrong. Running uphill was a sapping experience. People who tried to evade aggressors by seeking high ground often found themselves trapped at their supposed place of safety. While he might be able to crest the mountain where the stream originated from, there was no guarantee of that. Also, by running downhill he'd have much more places to go. At some point, uphill was sure to run out; until he got to the Atlantic, downstream would always offer an escape route.

As he ran along the bank of the stream, Fletcher heard fewer of the grunts and curses that had come from his pursuer.

Confident he was opening up a lead, Fletcher settled into a fast run and concentrated on nothing more than picking a route and keeping his breathing at a steady pace. He'd run enough miles in the Royal Marines to know his body's limits and recognize how far he could push it.

The backpack chafed at his shoulders as it shifted back and forth, yet it was only a discomfort rather than anything else. To offset the irritation caused by the backpack, his locket bumped against his chest giving him a reassurance that he was always connected to his girls.

After covering what he estimated was a mile, Fletcher ducked behind a tree, held his breath and strained his ears. He heard nothing. No thudding footsteps. No grunts or pants for breath. No shouts of rage.

He was clear of human pursuit, now he had to make sure that any tracker dogs they sent after him would lose his scent. Fletcher trotted out from behind the tree and plunged his booted feet back into the stream and set off downstream, his every step sending splashes wide as he ran along the bed of the stream.

The stream's bed was a mixture of smooth, slippery stones and boggy areas that tried to grasp his boots and hold onto them. Fletcher didn't allow either the stones or the soft bogs to impede his progress as he trotted forward.

After another mile or so the stream merged with a narrow river when it entered a new ravine. Fletcher turned and followed the river upstream. For the time being he'd lost his tail, so higher ground wasn't such a bad option. A quarter of a mile from where he'd joined it, the river split into two.

Fletcher followed the right fork until he came across a stream that was one of the river's tributaries. He stepped from the river and trotted up the stream's bed until he was confident he'd covered at least a half mile.

When the stream's bed ran through a stony section, Fletcher stepped out and ran across the stones. His boots squelched and his feet were chilled from running through cool mountain water for miles, but that was the least of his worries. Top of his to-do list was working out where he was in relation to the lumber mill and putting some distance between himself and the point where he'd left the water, on the off chance anyone who came after him with dogs was determined enough to scour every possible route he could have taken when in the stream.

The thing bothering him most was a realization about what he'd seen in the office. Like it or not, he needed to speak to Quadrado, and not having her card or number, the only way he could do that was to go back into Daversville and seek her out.

CHAPTER THIRTY-SEVEN

The drive to Macon was uneventful for Fletcher apart from all the yawning and the desperate need to get a strong coffee into his stomach at the first opportunity. After he'd left the stream, he'd retrieved his GPS from the backpack and had set off on a wide looping circuit in the general direction of the rental SUV.

He'd traveled for two hours and had then slung his hammock between two trees and collapsed into a fitful sleep. His primitive senses were alert for predators as he slept, and as such, they kept waking him when they heard a noise they didn't like. The grumbling growl of a bear had seen him clutch in panic at the pistol he'd rested on his belly, but the animal had too little interest in him to show itself.

Now he was heading towards the town with a couple of items on his agenda. The first was to get to somewhere he had a cell signal so he could try calling Quadrado. He might not have her number, but he knew she would most likely be found at either Duke's or the little police station Deputy White worked out of. The numbers for both of those could be found online. He also wanted to reply to the messages Wendy had sent him. Even though there was no real importance attached to her messages, they were from her. And his daughter was always a priority.

He was ashamed that he didn't think of this last night, but he put it down to being focused on escaping his pursuers and anyone who may track him. All the same, with the way things were going, he was going to have to be a lot sharper than he had been so far.

Lila's life depended upon him, and as the only avenue he had yet to fully explore, he would have to check out the Blacketts' house and if that was a bust, convince one of the Blacketts to tell him where Trench was likely to be holed up. As the owners of these woods, they'd know more about them and the various structures hidden in their valleys than anyone else. If Trench was abducting the women, he'd need somewhere to keep them or least somewhere he could have his way with them before killing them. As much as he didn't like this line of thinking, he knew he had to be realistic in his expectations.

To extract this information from a Blackett he needed the element of surprise and a time and place where he could grip their pressure points. To do that, he had to breach the security at their house in a way that would allow him to ambush one or two members of the family. Hence his trip to Macon to get some treats for the dogs.

As soon as his cell showed three bars of signal, Fletcher pulled over and googled the two numbers he needed. Getting the number for Duke's was easy, but he had to dig into the Washington County Sheriff's Office's website to get the number for Deputy White's mini-station.

Fletcher tried Duke's first of all. The voice that answered was strong and manly, so figuring Duke himself had answered the phone and might recognize his accent, Fletcher faked a lisp as he asked for Quadrado.

"She ain't here. Left after breakfast."

Fletcher left his number and suggested that Quadrado would tip Duke when he delivered the message that she was to call the number at once. It was a cheap trick, but if it worked, Fletcher was more than happy to reimburse Quadrado for any cash she gave Duke.

Next he tried the police station. The phone rang in his ear for a solid five minutes before he gave up. Neither Quadrado nor the hapless detective were there to answer the phone which made him wonder what developments had taken place that he didn't know about.

As he entered Macon, Fletcher felt the cold shiver of premonition when he realized the reason Deputy White and Quadrado weren't picking up the phone may well be that they were looking at the bodies of the two men he'd encountered last night. One had failed to tackle him and the other hadn't been able to catch him. He suspected Mary-Lou Henderson had been executed because he'd made it known that he wanted to speak to her. If that was the case, how the two men's failure to capture him might be received wasn't something he wanted to think about.

He knew that if he wasn't able to get through to Quadrado on the phone by the time he returned to Daversville, he'd have to go into the town to seek her out. While he wasn't too worried about a public confrontation, he didn't want to get into any more fights than were necessary. His aim was to find Lila, and the quickest way to do that was to go to the head of the snake. Lila had been missing for days now, and he was worried that she was already dead.

However much he thought the Blackett house might look like a fortress from the outside, from the inside it would feel like a prison.

CHAPTER THIRTY-EIGHT

Fletcher eased himself down to the ground and wriggled his way through the bush. He still hadn't been able to contact Quadrado, so whether he liked it or not, when he left the Blackett house, he'd have to go into Daversville and find her.

The trip to Macon had eaten up a large portion of the morning but it had been a necessary evil. He needed a way to get past the dogs. To do this, he'd have to silence them, as while they patrolled the grounds, they did so without barking. As soon as they picked up his scent they'd bark. This in turn would warn the householders that he was approaching.

What he had to do was get past the dogs and then find a way into the house. There were no trellises he could scale to get to an upstairs window. Likewise there were no drainpipes located near windows and there were sure to be sturdy locks on the doors.

Fletcher had known all of this before he started back towards the house, and while it would make entering the property tougher for him, he'd come prepared. He was also expecting a higher level of security than he'd seen yesterday. Once they'd heard about the events at the lumber mill, the Blacketts were sure to have taken extra precautions with their home.

He saw movement at the house and focused his binoculars on the three figures walking to the garage. One was an elderly lady, and the two others were men of around sixty. They must be Constance Blackett and her sons Jimmy and Chuck.

Fletcher refocused his binoculars and zoomed in to get a better look at them. All three were wearing modern clothing that was stylish and looked to have been tailored to fit. Their hair was cut neat and while one of the men had a bookish air about him, the other looked as if he wrestled bears for fun.

The bookish son entered the garage and a moment later drove out in a top-class Mercedes which glinted sunbeams from its every polished surface. The bear wrestler tapped his foot as he waited for Constance to climb into the back of the car and then joined his brother up front.

Fletcher was pleased to see the gates open by themselves. It spoke of a remote device controlling them rather than a security guard at the gate opening them manually.

The Blacketts leaving was a boon and a drawback. On the one hand, he'd stand a far better chance of getting into the house if they weren't there, but the whole purpose of getting into the house was to question them.

From their clothes and choice of vehicle, Fletcher was certain they weren't going anywhere near the lumber mill or Daversville. Whether it was a business meeting somewhere, or a family lunch date, they would be gone for a few hours.

The only reason Fletcher could think of for them not being at the lumber mill was the family knew nothing of his nocturnal visit. It made sense for the workers not to risk the family's wrath. Better to cover up the fact they'd let an intruder get away, than admit it and risk losing the family's goodwill.

Fletcher knew he couldn't look a gift horse in the mouth. This was his best chance to get into the house unnoticed.

CHAPTER THIRTY-NINE

The first piece of meat laced with a strong animal tranquilizer arced through the air and hit into the wall surrounding the Blacketts' house. Fletcher reached down and fed another piece into the catapult he'd picked up in Macon.

Given a sniper's rifle he could have shot the dogs with ease, but apart from the noise the gun made, Fletcher saw no reason to harm the dogs. They would have been trained to be vicious attack dogs, that much he was certain of, but all the same, the dogs weren't guilty of anything other than obeying their masters and, as such, killing them didn't seem right. Apart from any of this, he'd always been a dog lover and could no more harm a dog than hurt his daughter.

The second piece of meat cleared the wall and dropped in the corner where Fletcher had aimed it. His thinking was that if the meat landed in the corners of the garden, it would be a lot less visible to anyone in the house.

Five minutes later, ten of the twenty pieces of meat he'd bought had been fired into the corner of the garden.

Fletcher gave it five minutes and then started making his way to the gate. He left the backpack under the bush from where he'd surveilled the house, although he had both pistols tucked into the waistband of his combat fatigues.

As he approached the gate, Fletcher made sure to keep his ears pricked for any noise the dogs might make. He hadn't seen them emerge from the corner, but that didn't mean they were fully in the grip of the tranquilizers.

When he got to the gate he took a peek and saw nothing except the house standing alone in a sea of perfectly mown grass. There were no bushes, flowerbeds or yard ornaments where an intruder could hide, just an open space devoid of cover for anything larger than an ant.

He took another look and saw the three Dobermans. They were all laid on the grass in what would be a drunken collapse if they were human.

Score one for his plan.

He checked the gates for wires. They could be fitted with sensors, or worse, have an electrical charge pulsing through them.

The gates had neither, so he grabbed the rails of the one closest to him and started climbing. With the empty yard offering no cover from the morning light, he was now in a race against time. He had to scale the gates and get to the house wall in the least time possible, lest there be someone in the house looking out of a window. Depending on who it was, he'd either find himself facing a frightened wife or a gun-toting Blackett imbued with a sense of superiority and the law behind him when it came to shooting intruders. He was breaking into their house and he had two guns on him. The Blackett in question was unlikely to be arrested, let alone charged for killing him.

It took little more than a few seconds for Fletcher to cross the gates and another ten for him to sprint across the lawn and press his back against the house's brick wall.

He could feel the adrenaline coursing through his veins as he made his way to the door. The height of the windows meant he didn't have to duck down, although he did keep close to the wall, lest someone inside glance out and down.

Upon reaching the door he stretched an arm out and tried the handle. It was locked. That was no surprise.

He could try skirting the house and seeing if the rear door was unlocked but it didn't make sense that it would be. The Blacketts had clearly gone out for the day, and the level of security at the house would mean there was no way they'd leave it unlocked. All the same, before he retrieved his lock picks from his pocket, he pressed an ear to the door and listened for movement inside the house.

With the house apparently empty, Fletcher didn't delay any longer. He set to work picking the lock. As expected, it was better than the average lock, but it still wasn't good enough to resist his picks.

The door swung open with a soundless grace. Its path followed by the foresight on one of Fletcher's pistols. Neither his eyes nor the pistol's sights picked up a threat.

Everywhere he looked there was opulence on a scale Fletcher had seldom seen. The hallway was laden with gilt-framed pictures and the furniture was in a style favored by European royalty. There were solid oak doors bearing heavy brass handles leading off the hallway. A staircase curled upwards towards the second floor. It had marble steps and an oak handrail supported by wrought iron spindles.

Fletcher padded across the floor, the parquet tiles silent beneath the press of his rubber soled boots.

With no open doors inviting him forward, there was no obvious way to go first, so Fletcher went left through the nearest door.

As a precaution against unknown threats, and due to years of training, he went in hard and fast, throwing the door open and scanning the room over pistol sights until he was convinced there was no threat.

The room was filled with more period furniture. Couches and chairs were arranged in a semi-circle so they were all pointed towards a huge TV screen that wouldn't have looked out of place in a movie theater.

There were no doors leading from the room, so Fletcher returned to the hall and checked the next door. It was a dining room with a grand table bearing six places along each side and a sole place at its head.

A door from the dining room led to a kitchen that was industrial in its capacity. There were cooking ranges, a central island and a worktop bearing culinary gadgets whose purpose Fletcher could only guess at. The kitchen had three doors. One led outside while another led to a utility room bedecked with laundry machines and cleaning products. A washer whirled as it went through its routine.

The final door led back to the hall where there were four doors yet to be explored. The first led to a home office that resembled the study of an English country house, all dark wood panels and leather wingback chairs. There were computers on the two desks, but neither was on and Fletcher didn't want to waste time on them until he was sure he was alone in the house. The second door was to a library that was styled in the same way as the study.

The third door Fletcher opened revealed a home gym complete with treadmills, rowing machines and a complicated contraption with sets of weights on various pulleys.

It was what he found behind the final door that made Fletcher's pulse rise.

There was a staircase leading to a basement. He flicked the switch by the door and descended the stairs with hope in his heart. After there being no outward sign of a basement, he hadn't expected to find one. If it was the Blacketts behind the disappearances, a basement would be an ideal place for them to keep those they'd abducted.

A second door was at the bottom of the stairs. He tried its handle expecting it would be locked. It wasn't. It swung open with the faintest of creaks. The basement was in darkness, so he groped for a switch wondering what he'd find. His nose picked out the smell of cigars, but there was also a hint of damp, which wasn't so unusual for a basement.

The lights came on and flooded the basement with artificial illumination. Fletcher couldn't help but curse when his eyes took in the vista before him.

CHAPTER FORTY

The detective lifted the crime scene tape fluttering between two trees so Quadrado could join him and his partner. Both wore grave expressions and the younger male detective looked queasier than his older female partner.

"Thanks for coming out here." The words from the female detective were polite, but there was no mistaking the hostility in her voice.

Quadrado hadn't had a choice, at least on a moral basis, when the detectives had called to request her presence out here. Deputy White had been found hanged, and as the detectives working the Mary-Lou Henderson case, they'd been assigned this one too.

Her instincts about his suicide were jangling to say the least. She'd expected him to run, or mount a preposterous attempt to bluff his way out of the trouble he was in. What she hadn't anticipated was that he'd take his own life.

The younger detective, Palmer, and his partner, Anderson, watched as Quadrado pulled on a protective suit lest she contaminate the crime scene.

They were in the woods, ten miles south of Daversville and a quarter mile from the road. Some hunters from a nearby town had been out there and had found White's body.

With the forensic suit rustling at her every step, Quadrado let Palmer and Anderson lead her to White. None of the three spoke and Quadrado was happy to keep silent as she was still trying to assess the situation from her own perspective. She and White had

had that big conversation yesterday, and she'd more or less told him that she knew he was corrupt and that she'd bring him to justice.

The idea that she'd driven White to his suicide was one which was unbearable to Quadrado. Her Catholic faith had taught her to think of suicide as a sin, and while she couldn't assume responsibility for the actions of another person, she knew that she was culpable to at least some degree. If she had arrested him yesterday, he'd still be alive. This meant that she too had sinned by her actions in driving White to this desperate measure.

It was his boots she saw first. Then his legs, still clad in his deputy's uniform. His police shirt looked immaculate, but it was his face and head that would stay with her.

His head was twisted off to one side where the noose's knot pressed against his ear. White's tongue lolled from the corner of his mouth and there was a desperation to his face that remained in death. His eyes were hollow sockets, but that didn't surprise Quadrado; birds were quick to devour such easy meals and it was around eighteen hours since she'd last seen Deputy White.

Quadrado let out a relieved sigh as her eyes traced the rope upwards. It was looped over the bough of a large tree above White's head, oak or ash she guessed, and then it ran down to where it was tied off against the bole of another tree.

"Well, Agent Quadrado, what do you think?" Once again there was hostility in Anderson's tone.

Quadrado didn't know what the woman's problem with her was, but she was sure she'd find out soon enough. As for White's suicide, it was clear to Quadrado what had happened, which meant that either the two detectives had the investigative powers of the nearest tree, or they were looking to her to confirm their theory.

"I think you have another homicide case on your hands." Anderson rolled a hand to indicate Quadrado should elaborate. "Look at the drop from the branch to where Deputy White is. It's at least fifteen feet. While he's not a large man, he must be what, two-twenty, two-thirty pounds. The branch he's slung the rope over is at least eighteen inches in diameter, so there's no way he could hold onto it and let himself drop; he had to have been standing or sitting on it before he dropped. Two-twenty pounds falling a minimum of fifteen feet plus at least three from where he was sat on the bough with the rope around his neck." Quadrado pulled a face at the distasteful images her words were conjuring. "That is a lot of weight falling a long way. The impact of the rope when it tightened would be severe, violent even. His neck would be broken, that's a given, but that weight falling that far, I'm pretty sure that would have decapitated him. Unless there was some kind of stepladder beneath him that you've already removed, you have another homicide case." Quadrado looked at Palmer then Anderson. 'Need I go on?"

The rest of Deputy White's story needed no explaining. Rather than take his own life, someone had put the rope around White's neck, hoisted him until his feet were six feet from the ground and then tied the rope off leaving White to suffocate.

Anderson dipped her nose to look over the thin spectacles she wore. "You needn't."

"In that case, I appreciate you letting me know about his death, but as you're the local cops, this will be your case and not mine." Quadrado went to leave.

Palmer took a half step to one side blocking her path with his body. Quadrado detected no threat in his body language, but she would have preferred a verbal request that she not yet leave to his physical one.

"We agree." Palmer's voice was soft without inflection. "However, you told us that you're in Daversville investigating a number of women who've gone missing when passing through the area. The Fletcher guy White arrested for the Henderson homicide, his story was that he was looking for the most recent woman to vanish and the Henderson girl had warned the woman's boyfriend to leave the town. Then she turns up with her throat slashed and her tongue on her chest. As clear a warning as you're ever likely to see. Her father is distraught, as you'd expect, but he's not blaming anyone in particular, which is unusual. Next up we find the deputy from the town where all this has been going on is the latest victim. Something is rotten in Daversville, and while I don't want to speak ill of the dead, it very much seems as if Deputy White was mixed up in it all. We think that everything is connected to all the missing women, which is your case. What we're proposing is that we work together, share information and forget all the departmental BS. What do you say?"

The animosity from Anderson now made sense. She was stumped and her younger partner had persuaded her to seek the help of a visiting FBI agent. Anderson wouldn't like that and would resent Quadrado on principle. Yet she'd still been a big enough person to swallow her pride and go along with Palmer's idea for the good of the case. That's why he'd been the one to make the offer. The trek up to see White's body had been Anderson's way of testing her investigative skills.

"Sure, I'm up for that." Quadrado had made all the same reasonings the two detectives had about the connections between the victims and the people she was trying to find. If they hadn't made the offer to cooperate on their cases, she would have. "Where do we start? Do you want to bring me up to speed from your end, and then I'll do the same from mine?"

CHAPTER FORTY-ONE

Fletcher had been hoping to find Lila in the basement, but what he found was a man cave. There was a full-size billiard table, pool table and a pair of large screen TVs with games consoles resting on their stands and La-Z-Boys facing them. Off to one side a bar had been fitted and there were several retro arcade machines, such as Pac-Man and Donkey Kong, adorning the walls.

Fletcher slammed the heel of his hand against a wall as he checked to see if there were any doors leading from the man cave. There weren't, so he turned back towards the stairs leading to the hallway. As he ascended the stairs he had to fight his growing frustration. He'd been sure the basement was his best bet and now that was dashed, he had to regroup himself and search the rest of the house. He should have known it was unreasonable to expect to waltz into the house, find a basement and the target of his search so easily. It was amateurish thinking at best and he knew he'd have to be more realistic with his expectations.

With the first floor and basement searched, he made his way up to the second floor. The staircase opened onto a landing where a corridor bisected the house. There were two rooms to his left, one either side of the corridor, and the same on his right. As with downstairs, the doors were all solid oak with brass door furniture.

He went left and tried the first door he came to. It revealed a large and sumptuous bedroom. Fletcher knew little about interior design, but he could tell cheap furnishings from expensive ones, and those he was looking at appeared to be top quality. A door from the bedroom revealed a bathroom complete with a large ornamental bathtub and a shower. The handrails around the bathroom told him this was most likely the old woman's room.

The other three bedrooms on the floor all bore the same lavish styling, although they all had their individual traits as each room's occupant personalized their space.

Now the second floor was checked, Fletcher set off up the stairs towards the third and final floor. Could Lila be imprisoned in one of the bedrooms up here or the attic?

The upper floor had four rooms per side rather than two. The door across from the stairs was ajar and when Fletcher crept towards it, gun extended in front of him, it opened to reveal a woman carrying a hamper overflowing with dirty laundry.

When her eyes met Fletcher's pistol, she screamed and dropped the hamper.

"Please. No shoot."

Fletcher eased his finger off the trigger a fraction and looked over the woman's shoulder. He saw no one else, so he whirled to check the corridor in case the woman's scream brought someone running from one of the other rooms. Nobody came. Nobody shouted asking if the woman was okay.

Fletcher didn't think that anyone in the Blackett family would care about the woman. She wore the outfit of a housemaid and a look of desperate fear etched on her face.

Yes, she would be afraid of him, the stranger with the gun, but that was a new fear, which hadn't yet had time to ingrain itself on her face. As well as the uniform and the look of terror, the woman's skin was a different shade to anyone else he'd seen in Daversville, with the exception of Agent Quadrado.

He turned to the woman, making a show of putting the gun away. She'd retreated into the room and was pressing herself against the far wall. Fletcher kept his voice low, his tone soft and non-threatening as he walked into the bedroom. "Hey there. It's okay. I'm not going to shoot you. I just want to ask you some questions."

The woman paused her attempts to hide and turned to face him. She kept her head down allowing her hair to shroud the most of her face, but beneath her forehead, brown terror-filled eyes assessed him as he sat in a chair by the bed.

"Who are you? What you want? When she find out, Miss Constance not happy at you coming here." The brown eyes widened. "Are you here to take me back?"

"I am…" Fletcher paused. He couldn't say he was a friend as friends didn't tote guns in their buddy's house. Nor could he say that he was any kind of salesperson. That line may have worked at the front door, but it would be exposed for the lie it was by the very fact they were on the third floor and he'd just pointed a gun at her. All he could do was tell the truth. "I'm looking for a friend. A girl I think may be held here against her will."

"Your friend not here. Please, go before Mr. Chuck or Mr. Jimmy come back. They very mad if they know you here talking to me."

"Don't worry, I won't tell them." Fletcher gestured for the maid to sit on the bed. "My name is Grant, what's yours?"

A glance from under her fringe. "Elena. You go now please?"

"Not yet. You asked if I was going to take you back. That makes me think you aren't in America legally. Don't worry, I could care less about your immigration status. I would like to know where you're from, though." Fletcher saw tears fall from Elena's downturned face and land on the hands she was wringing. The girl was petrified, and as much as his heart was going out to her, he needed her to talk. As easy as it would be to pull his gun on her or threaten her with deportation back to wherever she came from, there was no way he could be that cruel. "It's okay, Elena. I want to help you if I can."

"Guatemala." The word was uttered alongside a noise that was half sniff and half sob.

"I've heard it's a lovely country."

"Is not lovely. Too many drugs. Too many gangs."

Fletcher couldn't argue with Elena's assessment of her home nation. Like so many of the countries sandwiched between North and South America, Guatemala was a place where gangs of drug traffickers often ruled the roost. Poverty was an ever-present issue, which meant that young people were easily recruited by the gangs.

Now that he knew where she came from, he could almost trace her journey from Guatemala to Georgia. She'd have left home with the few possessions she held dear. Her passage into America purchased by her meager savings being placed in the pockets of human smugglers. She would either have traveled overland and been snuck across the border between Mexico and the US, or she'd have joined other people desperate to escape impoverished upbringings in a small boat that would land somewhere on the coast of one of the southern states. From there she'd have either been left to find her own way in life or shipped to a place where unscrupulous employers would purchase new staff from the human smugglers.

"Tell me, Elena," Fletcher produced the picture of Lila, "have you seen this girl in the house?"

"No. No girls in this house like that. Only Blacketts in house." She gave a tragic smile. "Blacketts and Elena."

Fletcher had to fight to keep the disappointment from his voice. Things would have been much simpler for him if he was right and it was the Blackett family rather than Trench behind the abductions. "Okay. So there's just you and the Blacketts. Do you like it here? Are they nice people?"

"They give me job and place to sleep."

The answer was a sidestep if ever Fletcher had heard one.

"Are they good people? It's okay, Elena, I am only asking because you seem very scared of Mr. Chuck and Mr. Jimmy."

Elena's head sawed from side to side. "You wrong. Blacketts are nice. Miss Constance a good person. She kind to Elena."

Fletcher might have believed Elena were it not for the quavering desperation to convince that layered her voice.

Her presence changed everything about his plan to lie in wait for the Blacketts to return. It was one thing extracting information on Lila from the family, but to do so when there was a witness present, however cowed she might be, was something else.

Elena being an illegal immigrant working in the house did give him another thought.

"Tell me, Elena. Do you get paid for working for the Blacketts?"

"Mr. Jimmy says I have food in my gut and a roof over my head so I not need money. I clean and cook to pay for food and roof."

It was as Fletcher had suspected; Elena was a slave. Kept captive in the house and made to serve the Blackett family. Whether she had to serve the male Blacketts in another way was unknown. If he could persuade her to come with him and tell her story to Quadrado, the FBI agent would have grounds to come and pick the place apart. If that happened and Lila was being held captive by the Blacketts, they'd find where Lila was.

"I'm going to go now. Why don't you come with me? I can help you become naturalized, then you can attain citizenship and stay in America."

"No." Elena shrank away from him. "Mr. Chuck tell me every day bad men will come. Make promises. Tell lies. I stay here. Miss Constance keep me away from bad men."

Fletcher spent ten minutes trying to reassure Elena that he was one of the good guys, but it was to no avail. The Blackett men had done a thorough job of brainwashing their slave. and although he was offering Elena what she'd traveled to America for, she'd been told so many lies she didn't recognize the truth when she heard it. The one spark of hope for her was that Miss Constance seemed to be doing what she could to look out for Elena in spite of her sons enlisting the girl into slavery.

"Okay. I'm going to go now. You can come with me if you want, or you can stay. Either is fine with me. But before I go, I have to tell you something, Elena. Mr. Jimmy will be very angry if you tell him I was here. Very angry. He will be angry with you because I won't be here for him to be angry at. You are welcome to come with me, and I promise on my daughter's life that I will help you in any way I can."

"Please. I stay."

Fletcher left the house and Elena behind. As much as he didn't want the Blacketts to find out he'd been in their house, he didn't want Elena to suffer any retribution for his actions. Mary-Lou Henderson had tried to help Brad and Lila and had paid a terrible price once he'd shown up in town and started asking questions. And if the Blacketts were responsible, the last thing he wanted was for another innocent to suffer because of his actions.

CHAPTER FORTY-TWO

Fletcher crested the top of a small rise and set off down the other side. The GPS in his hand was taking him on a straight line from the Blacketts' house to Daversville. He could have gone back to the rental SUV and driven to Daversville, but the town was closer than the SUV and he was sure that when she heard what he had to say, Quadrado would take him back for it. Not only did he have the news of what he'd learned in the mill's office, he also had Elena's story to share.

After leaving Elena and the house behind, he'd been going over things in his mind. He was trying to comprehend the audacity of the Blacketts. They lived a life of luxury in that house with all its modern devices and poor Elena to look after them. Not only had they enslaved her, they also controlled the entire town of Daversville.

What the deal was with Lila, and the other women Quadrado had said were missing, was currently beyond him, but he was starting to believe that he was going to be too late to save Lila. Too much time had passed since she'd gone missing for there to be much chance of her still being alive when none of the other girls who'd gone missing had ever surfaced. He didn't want to be right, in fact he hoped he was wrong about this, but the more he thought about it, the more he was convinced Lila was already dead.

The Blacketts weren't as cotton-white as the image they portrayed to the townsfolk, and the further he got from the house, the more he was concentrating on the puzzle elements as a way to distract himself from his rising anger at the way the Blacketts dominated so many lives. Fletcher's feet were stomping as he marched towards Daversville, and there was a fierce throb in his temples as he worked out what he wanted to say to Quadrado. She might be glad to hear the information he was bringing to her, but there was no way in hell that she would approve of his methods.

Fletcher froze. He'd seen something move. It was ahead of him and a little off to his right-hand side.

CHAPTER FORTY-THREE

There was a second movement. Nothing defined, just a shifting of light and the grasses that littered the woodland floor moving in an unnatural way. There were no sounds beyond the whispering of the wind through leaves.

Fletcher drew one of his pistols and aimed it in front of him. Every sense he possessed was on high alert as he waited for the next movement. It may well be a wild animal he'd seen, although his sixth sense was saying otherwise.

One careful step at a time he advanced, his pistol leading the way as he scanned the undergrowth for movement. An arm shot out from a tree, forty yards in front of him. It was bent at the elbow with a clenched fist pointing to the sky: the military "halt" signal.

Instinct and years of training made Fletcher halt. The signal could be for him or against him. If it was against, then he was facing at least two people who possibly had military training. They could be kids playing at soldiers, members of the Blackett family who'd observed him entering their home, or members of the National Guard summoned by Quadrado to search for Trench.

When in doubt assume the worst and you won't be surprised was a maxim that Fletcher believed in. So far as he was concerned, the arm he'd seen belonged to an elite soldier, someone the government had invested in and had trained to kill in hundreds of ways.

He had two options. Proceed and take them on, or retreat and hope to lose them in the woods.

Fletcher chose neither. The signal irritated him. Whomever had given the signal was something of a wraith. He'd not picked up anything other than a shifting of grasses and, until the signal, hadn't been one hundred percent certain it wasn't an animal, and that he was overreacting. All the same, his heart thumped harder as he twisted his body left then right in a vain attempt to find other threats.

A twang was followed by a whoosh. In the distance a thwack was followed by the sound of something tumbling to the ground.

A man stepped out from a different tree than the one where the signal had come from. At least Fletcher assumed it was a man. He was short in stature and clad in an eclectic mixture of animal skins that were layered with ferns and grasses. His face was covered with a dense white beard and a bow hung from his hand.

"Got him." Then, without another word, the man turned and wandered off into the distance, ignoring the fact that Fletcher had a pistol pointed at him.

Fletcher went after him. The man was walking towards Daversville, so it made sense to keep going after the woodland hunter. After following the guy for seventy yards, Fletcher saw a deer lying on the ground.

The deer had an impressive pair of antlers and an arrow protruding from its chest. While Fletcher understood the urge to hunt, it always saddened him when a magnificent animal was killed in the name of sport.

The hunter was bent over the deer, a large hunting knife in his hand. From what Fletcher could tell he was getting ready to gut the animal, removing its stomach and entrails. If he was doing that, it stood to reason that he planned to eat it, which made the animal's death a fraction easier to stomach.

As he neared the hunter and his quarry, Fletcher noticed the animal had a nasty wound on its hindquarters and graying whiskers around its head. The hunter may have killed an animal for his pot, but he'd chosen an old and injured deer as his target.

As much as he was desperate to get to Daversville, the hunter intrigued him, so he stopped, although he kept a few feet away from the man. The gun in his hand was trained on the man's back as he suspected this was the mysterious Trench. As much as he had his suspicions, he couldn't work out why the man had shown himself to an outsider when he'd avoided the locals. Adrenaline coursed through Fletcher's veins at the thought he might have his gun aimed at a serial killer.

"That was an impressive shot." They were empty words serving no purpose other than an opening of dialogue.

"Done better. Been hunting him since coyotes ripped his flank."

Fletcher hadn't been expecting the Gettysburg Address from the hunter, but the offhand way his compliment had been answered irked him.

"You hunt these woods often?"

"Don't hunt 'em. Live in 'em." The hunter used the tip of his knife to slice into the deer's chest so he could pull the arrow out. "You been spendin' some time in 'em too. Followed you last night. Did a good job of not leaving an easy trail."

"You followed me?" Fletcher hadn't been aware of the hunter's presence. Fair enough, he had been focused on getting away from the guy chasing him, but even so, he was perturbed to learn that he'd been followed by someone who he hadn't once detected.

"Yep." The hunter looked at Fletcher for the first time. His eyes were deep pools of crystalline blue. They didn't so much sparkle as shine with a fierce intensity. "You didn't need to run so far. Guy after you got himself persuaded to stop."

It took a second for Fletcher to realize what the hunter was intimating. "You did that? Why? Did you hurt him?"

"Yep. I don't like Miss Constance none." A shrug that rustled the foliage decorating his animal skins. "No more'n he would hurt me."

Fletcher felt his pulse begin to race. The hunter hadn't just expressed a dislike for the Blackett family, he'd gone so far as to actively get involved by helping out a stranger.

"Who are you?"

"Folks call me Trench."

There it was, confirmation the man before him was the mystery figure no one had seen for forty years. Or at least it would be confirmation if there was a way to verify the man's words.

Fletcher had picked up on the way Trench had said Miss Constance rather than Constance Blackett. Elena had used the same words which made him think that was the way she was known.

"You don't care for Miss Constance. I get and appreciate that. I'm no fan of her family myself. Why don't you like her?"

"My business. Not yours. You been snooping her and hers. Twice at house and once at mill." Trench slid his knife along the deer's underbelly and started pulling at the entrails as they spilled out. "Why you doin' that?"

Fletcher gave Trench the basic facts and watched the old man's reaction as he absorbed what he was saying. There was no obvious sign of surprise or anger, but Trench's face was so covered with beard it was hard to assess, although his eyes hardened when he heard about Mary-Lou's fate and Elena's enslavement.

"Them's good reasons." The last of the entrails were scooped from the deer and deposited in the same heap as the others Trench had removed. "Generally keep myself away from their place. Was only there after following you. Ain't seen no goings on, but me not seeing 'em, don't mean they didn't happen."

Fletcher nodded. This wasn't the information he'd been hoping for, but it wasn't Trench's fault he hadn't seen anything. As the man in front of him was a suspect in Lila's disappearance, Fletcher was fighting the urge to put his gun to Trench's temple and demand the old man take him to her. For the time being, though, he was content to keep looking at Trench over the sights of his gun.

"The missing girl I told you about. Would you care to tell me who you think is top of the suspect list?"

"That'd be Trench. Not be the first time he'd been blamed for something he didn't do."

The bitterness in Trench's voice was enough to override Fletcher's surprise at the words he'd spoken, or the fact Trench was referring to himself in the third person.

A new picture became clear to Fletcher. It was one of someone who'd lost a lover to family strife. Of someone who'd been forced to live in the wilds to escape prosecution for a murder he didn't commit.

If his thinking was right, Trench hadn't killed the teacher; another member of the Blackett family had slit her throat to end a romance they didn't approve of. Afraid he'd be blamed for her murder Trench had spent the rest of his life hiding out in the woods because of this.

"You didn't kill her, did you?"

"Nope. I was sired by the man who did, though."

Fletcher didn't speak. There wasn't an answer to what Trench was saying.

The woodsman looked over his shoulder at him. "That gun you're pointing at me better be loaded if'n you're planning on taking me in."

Using slow movements lest Trench decide to throw the knife at him, Fletcher let the man see him as he returned the gun to the small of his back.

Trench carried on skinning the deer's hindquarters.

"That locket round your neck, does it hold a picture of your girl?"

"It does."

"You're a lucky man. All's I got is memories. Old, old memories."

"So far as I'm aware, you've not shown yourself to anyone for years. Why show yourself to me today?"

Trench's knife tapped the deer's rump. "This old girl was lame. She was hurting and sooner or later the wolves would have ripped her apart. I've known her family for years and wanted to make sure she didn't suffer none."

The man's reasoning made sense to Fletcher. Every word Trench said was spoken with a quiet conviction that added believability to his statements. After having met Trench, Fletcher could no more suspect him than he could believe Quadrado was behind the disappearances.

Not having been seen in society went a long way to explaining Trench's lack of knowledge regarding the abductions and discounted his involvement, as the people of Daversville were certainly covering something up, and he couldn't have been involved without making his presence known to them.

The one thing Trench would know about, though, was the woods and what was in them. If there were any abandoned military bunkers, mines or old houses where the missing women could be held, he'd be the one to know where they were.

He asked the question.

Trench cocked his head to one side as he began skinning the deer. His knife moving in fast, accurate strokes that spoke of long practice.

"Ain't no bunkers on my patch. Two mines, one all caved in, other is where I sleep. No houses that ain't lived in. C'n only speak 'bout my area. Don't wander the whole woods. Goes where I needs and no place else. Ain't seen no one bringing no ladies out into the woods."

Fletcher was running out of questions to ask. Although Trench wasn't what anyone would call talkative, he was giving the answers Fletcher needed, if not wanted.

"If the Blacketts are behind the women going missing, where would you suggest they're keeping them?"

"Somewhere close they own. A wise Blackett trusts nobody. Not even they own kin."

The mention of kin sparked a whole raft of ideas in Fletcher's mind that he knew should have been there anyway.

"They're *your* family. Who are they all? What are they like?"

"I've not considered them as family for a lot of years." Trench's knife kept working at the deer. "Startin' at the top, there's Miss Constance. Her boys Chuck and Jimmy. Chuck got brains and Jimmy got muscle. The girl Agnes married Duke Jackson. Three of 'em all got a clutch o' kids, but don't know much about 'em 'ceptin' they's prob'ly trouble."

Fletcher was joining the dots as Trench spoke. Chuck would be the one with the glasses; he'd already fingered him as the brains. It was interesting to hear Agnes was married to Duke. With Agnes running the diner and Duke the hotel, between them, they'd meet most of the people who stopped in Daversville on their way through. It also explained how the four youths who'd fronted him in the carpark had been summoned so quickly when he'd been asking questions in the diner.

"What else can you tell me about the Blacketts?"

Trench spoke for another minute, but a minute of his staccato bullet points was worth an hour of other people's ramblings. All the same, beyond where each of them fit within the family business, Fletcher didn't learn anything.

When Fletcher bade his goodbye to Trench, the hunter stopped working on the deer and locked eyes with him. The old man's eyes shining with a fervent intensity. "Your name's Fletcher. Prob'ly think yo'self a straight arrow. Let me tell you. You ain't gonna beat 'em playin' fair. You gotta shoot round corners, 'less'n you gonna get yo'self killed dead."

As he continued on towards Daversville, Fletcher couldn't get Trench's warning from his mind. He wasn't averse to the rough stuff and had no issue cracking skulls where necessary, but he had a moral line he wouldn't cross. Yet from what Trench had intimated, he might have to get a lot closer to the line than he wanted to.

CHAPTER FORTY-FOUR

The GPS brought Fletcher to the edge of Daversville. He was a hundred yards from Mary-Lou Henderson's house and a quarter mile from the tiny police station.

There was no getting away from it, he was going to have to walk through the town in broad daylight. If any of the Blackett minions came his way, he'd just have to deal with them in the most efficient way he could.

Before leaving the tree line, he'd swapped one of the pistols from the small of his back to the point of his waistband where the button was. It went against all his training, but the backpack hindered him from drawing the gun as quickly as he might need to.

Without the shade from the trees, the sun was a lot hotter, but as it was still in the early reaches of summer, the stifling humidity of the summer months hadn't yet kicked in. All the same, compared to the temperatures at his home in Utah, the heat was oppressive.

As he walked through the town, Fletcher saw two women collecting laundry from lines hung across their yards. The women glanced his way then averted their eyes. He saw no one else until he turned the corner onto the lane where the tiny police station was.

He recognized Quadrado's back as she slid herself into her car. By the time he'd run across the road and caught up with the car, she'd gunned the engine and was starting to move forward.

Fletcher banged on the car's trunk and the brake lights came on. He ran to the driver's window and showed himself to Quadrado.

Exasperated fury decorated her face, but that didn't worry him. She'd soon change her opinion when she heard what he had to say.

The window lowered with a soft whirr.

"I thought I told you to leave town."

"You did. I'm only back because I need to speak to you."

Quadrado lifted a manicured eyebrow. "Then you best start speaking."

Fletcher did as he was told; he'd known Quadrado would be haughty and a bit offhand at first, but he could see her digesting his tale. As expected she pulled a face when he detailed breaking into the office at the lumber mill and the Blacketts' house, but her features softened when she heard what he'd found.

When he recounted his conversation with Trench and his thoughts after having digested what Trench had said, her eyes widened at the possibilities he'd uncovered.

She waited until he was finished and cut the engine. The window going back up automatically. Quadrado climbed from the car and walked back towards the police station.

"Come with me, I have some questions for you."

CHAPTER FORTY-FIVE

Quadrado eased herself into Deputy White's chair. She would have foregone it out of decency for his memory, but there were only two chairs in the station and the bed in the cell. Better that a law enforcement officer take the deputy's seat than someone who'd just admitted two counts of breaking and entering.

"So, you ignored my advice to get out of town and came back, broke into two separate properties and now you're here feeding me stories of illegal immigrants being held as slaves. Why should I take a single word you say seriously?"

"Because of what I found." Fletcher's voice was level and he was relaxed. His body language was open, and he was meeting her eye. "You said you were in town looking into a lot of women going missing. I'm looking for one of the same women you are, Lila Ogilvie. You've been here a couple days, you'll have seen how the town is. The whole place is beholden to the lumber mill and the family who control it. Either that or that *and* a serial killer is terrorizing the locals to keep his presence secret. Think about this, what about the cars the women you're looking for were driving? Have they vanished too? My guess is that if their cars are missing too, more than one person is involved. My dime to your dollar says that if you can find the cars, you'll find the women. You think Trench is behind it, but I've met him. He's not a killer. He's an old man who's still hurting about a girl he lost forty years ago. For God's sake, Quadrado, he thinks his father was the one to kill her."

"I get what you're saying about Daversville. The town is a one-trick pony, but they all rely on that pony's trick, so it gets well looked after. What you're suggesting is town-wide collusion behind the disappearances, or at the very least, they're turning a blind eye through fear of reprisals." Quadrado had formed her own conclusions about the town, but she wanted to press Fletcher, to get him speaking without thinking. She didn't believe he was holding anything back, but she wanted to test him and his theories to breaking point. People trying to win a heated argument were less guarded than those offering up information. "Have you any idea how preposterous that is? Plus this talk about an illegal immigrant, has it ever occurred to you that she was a genuine maid who was scared witless? Tell me, when you went into the Blacketts' house, were you armed? Put yourself in the maid's position. Rather than looking like the loyal family servant she really is, maybe she fed you a line so you wouldn't hurt her."

Fletcher shifted in his seat. Not far, but enough to tell her that she was right about him being armed.

"I hear you, but I don't for one minute think she was spinning me a line. She was petrified. The house is her prison, and her guards are three big Dobermans. However, it's nice and easy for you to prove me wrong. Just go out there and speak to Elena yourself. Proving me wrong won't change the other facts though. The Blacketts control this town and they have people in place to spot potential abductees. Their home is as modern as any I've seen, yet they have the town held in a virtual time warp. They have computers in their office and home. Tell me, have you even once seen a local with a cell phone? Or a car? How many cable dishes or TV antennas have you seen on the houses round here? Mary-Lou Henderson, a young woman with dreams of going to college, didn't have a cell and her TV is damn near as old as I am. Does that sound right to you? I haven't seen so much as one basketball hoop. I'm telling you, there's something rotten going on in this town and the Blackett family are behind it. Not Trench, the Blacketts who own the lumber mill."

The quiet conviction in Fletcher's voice was strong enough to make Quadrado think he may be right about the Blacketts and their grip on the town. He made logical sense and she'd pretty much arrived at the same conclusion herself. However, what he'd said about the mysterious Trench wasn't enough to make her think of the reclusive woodsman as anything other than the prime suspect for the abduction of the missing women.

The thing was, what to do next? She could easily take a drive up there and try to gain entry to the house, but she was sure that if they were involved, the Blacketts would have a hidey-hole where they could stash the girl if they were afraid of her being discovered. On the other hand, she didn't have enough evidence to warrant a full-blown search. Fletcher's tale might be God's honest truth, but so far as her bosses were concerned, his story was compromised by his actions and the methods he'd used to get the information he'd just given her. By rights she could and should arrest him; however, his unconventional methods had given her far better leads than her own investigating had.

Fletcher was right in what he was saying about the town being a closed book. Nobody would talk to her about anything of note, and it was intriguing to learn Agnes Jackson from the diner was a member of the Blackett family. Fletcher's insistence Agnes and her husband were well-placed when it came to the selection of people to abduct made more sense than she cared for, but the elusive Trench was still a better suspect in her mind.

"Okay, supposing you're right. What do you expect me to do now, ride into the Blackett house at the forefront of an FBI posse? Everything you've told me is compromised."

"So what are you going to do then, nothing?"

Quadrado let Fletcher's sarcasm bounce off her. She knew his anger was mainly at himself, rather than at her.

"No, I'm going to duplicate your information by going about things the proper way. I'm going to visit the lumber mill and the Blackett household myself. When I'm at the house, I'll make sure that I look for Elena."

"What about the file cabinets and the employment records? The Blacketts are breaking all kinds of employment laws and you're saying you're going to ask to see all their sensitive information. Will you have a warrant with you? Because if you don't, you'll not get anything of value and by the time you come back, all the papers in those file cabinets will be ash and Elena could be lying in a shallow grave with her throat slit. You can't pussyfoot around these sorts of people. You need to go in hard and strike fast instead of prancing around giving them time to cover their tracks."

"I get your frustration, but we can't go around kicking down doors after what you've done."

"So it's my fault then, is it? I'm the one to blame for the FBI's inability to act."

"Yes, you are, but in the greater scheme of things, you've also given me solid leads. What I have to do now is make sure that I follow the correct procedure and find enough evidence to justify a search warrant. Believe me, when I get one of those, I'll tear their place apart looking for evidence."

"Good luck with that. They've got the whole place sewn up. I'm sure Deputy White is in their pocket." Quadrado saw Fletcher cast his eyes around the room. "Where is he, anyway?"

"He's dead. He was found hanged in the woods a few miles south of here."

Fletcher's face clouded in thought. "Suicide… or something else?"

Quadrado didn't answer; she didn't feel comfortable sharing any more FBI business with a civilian, but she also wanted Fletcher to know as he had a unique way of looking at things. One thing was certain, he was smart enough to work it out for himself.

He stood, walked over to where she was sitting at White's desk and pulled open the drawer.

"What you looking for?"

"Dirt. Specifically, the kind of dirt a corrupt cop might be trying to amass on the people who'd corrupted him. Not leverage as such, more protection in case he became expendable. If none of that can be found, there may well be something that explains how the Blacketts are controlling him."

Quadrado joined the search and together they checked everywhere that White may have hidden something they could use. It was only when Fletcher picked up the photo frame on the desk that they saw how White was connected to the Blacketts. It was a picture of White on his wedding day. White's wife was at least ten years younger than him and looked to be no more than her late teens at the time the photo was taken. His wife was with him and so were members of both their families. Right at the bride's elbow, a woman with a cane beamed a wide ugly smile that spoke of contentment.

'That's Miss Constance. What's the betting the bride is one of her granddaughters?'

Quadrado didn't respond. Fletcher must be right. With his wife a member of the Blackett family, Deputy White would be easily manipulated. He wasn't a smart man and his backbone was missing in action. He'd made a mistake in marrying into that family, but his wife was prettier than a man like him might expect to find in a town like Daversville. Looking at the picture, Deputy White's betrayal of his sworn oath seemed inevitable with an attractive wife pulling his strings to the tune a domineering father dictated.

The further implication of his death was something that cut deep into Quadrado's values. If Fletcher was right and the Blacketts were behind everything, as seemed likely, then by killing Deputy White, they'd effectively sacrificed one of their own to ensure his silence. Whomever replaced White as the local deputy would have to be ensnared in the same way or they'd push forward their own candidate so their misdeeds could be covered up. Either way, if they were behind it, then their ruthlessness appeared to have no bounds, and the fact they'd killed a lawman and one of their own spoke heavily of their self-confidence.

"So, Special Agent Quadrado." Fletcher had a way of addressing her that made her name and rank seem like a burden on his tongue. "What's our next move?"

"Yours is to leave town and stay gone. Mine is to follow the lines of enquiry you've opened up."

"I disagree. Killing White was bold, but it won't be without consequences. They'll know you're sniffing around and will be ready for you. My guess is they have a spotter watching the trail that leads to their house. Soon as you get anywhere near, the spotter will alert the others and they'll spirit Elena away and invite you into their home with a look of aggrieved innocence on their faces. You'll ask to see round, and they'll let you see whatever you want. You'll end up leaving with no evidence, which will make it all the harder for you to return with a warrant. Before you ask, there's an area near the house where the spotter could hide and watch the trail that's far enough away for me to have got in and out without being seen."

"You're so clever, what would you do?" Quadrado hated the snarl that had crept into her voice. Not only did it show her mounting frustration, but it made her seem less professional.

"You don't want to know what I'd do. In fact, if you ask me again, I'm going to plead the fifth."

Quadrado couldn't help but throw her hands up. "I might have known. You'd play the white knight and storm the castle to save the pretty lady. Get this straight, Fletcher, if you start any more of your vigilante stuff, I won't hesitate to throw your butt into jail. And for the record, I meant what would you suggest *I* do?"

"Storm the castle. SWAT team, hostage negotiators, whatever it takes. I'd throw the entire weight of the FBI at the Blacketts and keep throwing until I found out where the missing women are."

"Haven't we already gone over this? Thanks to your blatant disregard for law-abiding behavior, that's not an option."

The devil-may-care look in Fletcher's eyes was troubling to say the least. "In that case, we throw what FBI we can at the Blacketts. Namely, you. I'll take you up to a place where we can observe the house. I'll get you in so you can speak to Elena yourself if the opportunity arises."

"How are you going to do that?"

"Some smoke, a few mirrors and a whole lot of trouble making."

Quadrado shook her head. "No way am I getting mixed up in anything like that."

"You got a better way of getting proof? Besides, you'll be nowhere near where the trouble is, so you'll have complete deniability. Hell, if the manure hits the air-con, we can deny this conversation ever happened. What's your other options? Are you going to call out the entire US Army to search the woods for Trench, because you better believe that's what it'll take to find him and even then, I'd back Trench to slip through their search lines."

Quadrado knew Fletcher was right and as she didn't have any better ideas, she listened as Fletcher outlined his smoke-and-mirrors plan. If nothing else, it would let her strike the Blacketts' names from her list of suspects.

Fletcher's idea was pretty basic as plans went, but that was all the better. Complicated plans had more room for failure. However, she recognized that what he was suggesting was more than a little dangerous for both of them.

When he was finished speaking she was left with a choice. Admit to her bosses that since she'd arrived in town, two people had been killed and she was certain one of them was because of her asking questions, she was still no closer to finding any of the missing women, and the best chance they had of rounding up her chief suspect was to instigate a manhunt that would require hundreds of bodies to march through wooded areas looking for someone at home in that environment. The second option was she go along with Fletcher's madcap plan and potentially risk her career.

After a few minutes of thought, she made her decision.

"We go with the smoke and mirrors, but I have a few things of my own I want to add."

She didn't give voice to it, but Fletcher's plan gave her the opportunity to lay herself out as bait to the person she most suspected of taking the missing women: Trench.

CHAPTER FORTY-SIX

As he led Quadrado to the Blackett household, Fletcher was mindful of the guard he expected would be watching the trail to their house. The last thing he wanted to do was run into him unannounced, so he skirted a wide path. Quadrado was matching the pace he set, and while there was only a thin sheen of sweat on her forehead as a sign of her exertion, the way she was clomping through the undergrowth would alert the guard long before they got near enough to confront him.

The plan was that he would deposit Quadrado near the Blackett house with the catapult and the last of the drugged meat. Once she was in place, they'd wait until the Blacketts returned home before they moved onto step two.

Fletcher kept his eyes alert for any sign Trench was following them, but he wasn't sure the old man would show himself unless he had a good reason. Everything about Quadrado, from her scraped ponytail to her off-the-rack business suit, screamed cop. Trench had spent most of his life on the run, so he doubted that he'd see him again today, if ever. The fact he was leaving a woman alone in what was Trench's domain also played on his mind. He'd discussed it with Quadrado, and she'd waved away his fears. She'd argued she was an FBI agent and would have her gun in her hand at all times. All the same, he had his reservations about her safety.

The closer he got to the Blackett house, the more he eased back from the rapid pace he was setting. If the Blacketts were already back, they might now have heard about last night's escapade, or

Elena could have told them about his earlier visit. If that were the case, he'd be naïve not to expect them to have taken extra precautions with their security. For all he knew, the dogs could still be tranquilized, which in itself would have them quizzing Elena.

When he reckoned he was within a half mile of the house, he turned to Quadrado. "Right. You stay here until I come back for you."

"Why?"

Fletcher picked his words with care. He was pushing his luck as it was, roping an FBI agent into this madcap scheme. To make her pissed at him would be foolish in the extreme. Instead of the accurate, but insulting, "noisier than an explosion at a fireworks factory," he suggested military levels of stealth might be beyond her and it'd be safer for everyone concerned if he went ahead to scout the house out first.

Quadrado pursed her lips and looked as if she might protest, but she relented and sat on the trunk of a fallen tree.

With the FBI agent seated, Fletcher slid off into the trees, eyes and ears set on high alert. His nose primed as he tried to detect an out-of-place smell such as body odor, cigarette smoke or cologne.

He saw, heard and smelled no threats, but that didn't mean he got cocky. As soon as he was within sight of the clearing where the house was, he cut to one side and circled the clearing looking for threats.

Twice he went round the house. The second time at the halfway point between his first circuit and the edge of the clearing, no guards were present, so he set off back for Quadrado. A marker set on the GPS made sure he knew where she was.

When he got within a couple hundred yards of her he slowed to a virtual halt.

He wasn't the only one approaching her. A figure off to the right was heading on a course which would converge with his at the point where the FBI agent was sitting.

Worst of all, the figure wasn't moving at pace. He was creeping as if stalking an unseen animal. A shotgun was held at high port—close into the body with the barrel pointing upwards.

Had the figure been traveling in any other direction, Fletcher would have dismissed him as a hunter who just happened to be in their vicinity. That wasn't what he was to Fletcher, though, he was an enemy hostile closing in on a comrade.

The question now was what to do.

Had Quadrado been a greater distance away, it would have been easy to loop in behind the figure and approach from his six before he got within striking distance. With the figure being a hundred and fifty yards from his target, there wasn't time to go down that route without rushing and running the risk of alerting the unknown hunter. While the shotgun wasn't much of a distance weapon, its effective range would be at least twice that of the pistols Fletcher carried. Therefore he'd have to get close enough to remove the shotgun from the man's grasp.

With no time to consider other plans, Fletcher began apprehending the guy, taking a less circuitous route than he would have if time had been on his side.

Off to Fletcher's left he could see Quadrado sitting on the fallen tree, oblivious to the approaching threat as her entire focus was on a part of the woods straight in front of her. Twice she leaned to the side as if trying to peer round a tree. He got within a hundred yards of the figure at the same time as the guy closed within seventy of Quadrado.

Fletcher cursed Quadrado out in his mind. Here she was, alone in the woods, while they were hunting a person or persons for abducting lone women and she wasn't taking even the most basic precaution of looking around her every few seconds. So help him, if he rescued her unscathed from the person stalking her like a game animal, FBI agent or not, he was going to give her a piece of his mind.

He needed to speed up, but it was a dangerous thing to rush through a wooded area when sneaking up on someone. A branch snapping underfoot would sound as loud as a thunderclap to someone with the heightened senses that were nature's way of equipping humans and animals for the hunt.

Fletcher's eyes flicked between his quarry and the ground. He was picking each step with care while also trying to make sure the target of his ambush didn't check his rear.

By the time the guy was within fifty yards of Quadrado, Fletcher had made up enough ground that he was within sixty yards of the guy. It boded well the guy was trying to sneak up on Quadrado rather than just walking up to her with a cock-and-bull story and then pulling the gun on her. To Fletcher it suggested the guy wasn't intent on killing her, but by the same token, Fletcher was convinced he wasn't sneaking up on the FBI agent so he could surprise her with a huge check.

Shotguns loaded with birdshot were an effective weapon at anywhere up to forty-five yards. Less than thirty-five they were deadly if they hit center mass. At under twenty they could shred flesh from bone, and at under ten they would remove a limb or blow a hole clean through someone. If the shotgun the man held had been loaded with a slug instead of bird or buckshot, its range would be increased but conversely it would become more like a rifle and need greater aim to guarantee a hit.

While great for close range jobs like clearing houses due to the spread of their pellets, shotguns made for poor distance weapons. Fletcher was well inside the kill zone as he approached the back of the man. Quadrado was fifty yards ahead of him and the man twenty. In another few yards, the man would be close enough to make his move on Quadrado.

By the time the man had crept forward another five yards, Fletcher was within ten. Now came the thorny issue of how to take the guy down. At this distance, pulling a pistol and shouting freeze might work in the movies, but if the guy whirled and leveled the shotgun, the advantage would be all his. The optimum way would be to get close enough to grab the back of the man's collar and grind a pistol into his ear. This worked best if an arm could be looped around a shoulder, but with the shotgun at high port, there was a fair chance it'd go off if he startled the guy holding it. At the range involved, Fletcher would be lucky to get any other outcome than having his arm blown off at the elbow.

There was also how the guy would react. He would have to assess Fletcher's intent and gauge whether or not he dare try to fight back. The answer would lie in the guy's own psyche. If he was a coward at heart, the shotgun might get dropped. On the other hand, he might expect to die anyway and go for broke by fighting back.

Another scenario was that he'd lower the shotgun until it was pointing at Quadrado and create a standoff neither could retreat from.

Fletcher got within five yards of the guy as he started to lower the shotgun.

There was no more time available for planning, so Fletcher went with his gut and slipped his finger out of the pistol's trigger guard as he took three brisk paces forward.

The guy with the shotgun had instincts and they were good ones. The branch Fletcher's right foot trod on snapped, causing the guy to half turn to his right, as he cast an instinctive look behind him at the noise. The shotgun followed the movement of his body.

With the momentum of the brisk paces adding to Fletcher's weight and the thrusting motion of his upper body, the collision between the flat side of the pistol and the guy's face was a brutal one. His head jerked back as blood exploded from his ruined nose and mouth.

Fletcher's hands grasped the shotgun and drove it downwards, away from fingers that might instinctively curl around the trigger, while also making sure to keep its barrel pointed away from his body.

Two seconds after the pistol strike, Fletcher had the shotgun in one hand and a pistol aimed at the guy's eyes.

"You don't move, you don't speak. You just stay where you are until I say otherwise. Understand?"

The guy gave a jerking nod that sent droplets of blood cascading down his grubby shirt.

CHAPTER FORTY-SEVEN

The guy whose arms were handcuffed around the tree had freckles covering the areas of his face that weren't blood spattered. Quadrado could feel the thump of her heart beating, although it was nowhere near as loud and fast as it had been a few moments ago.

Half of the reason for the racing of her heart was the shock she'd just had, while the other half was due to the anger and shame she felt. Instead of being alert to her surroundings, she'd allowed herself to drift away, locked in her thoughts about the case and the shadows she'd seen flitting across the woods in front of her. As she'd trekked through the woods, she'd begun to doubt the impulsive way she'd agreed to Fletcher's plan.

While he'd gone off to look for further threats, she'd let herself become unaware of her surroundings, and it was all she could do to control the shaking in her body when she thought of what might have been.

Fletcher's intervention had been so sudden and brutal, the first she'd known of the two men's battle was the thwack as Fletcher had struck the hunter. When she'd caught the look Fletcher had sent her way, she'd seen the anger in him and known it wasn't just aimed at her, but deserved. If she was to carry out her plan and capture this Trench if he tried to abduct her, she'd have to be a damn sight more aware of what was going on around her.

With the guy out of action, it had been a moment's job for Fletcher to use the handcuffs she'd fished from her pocket to fasten the guy's arms behind the thin but sturdy tree he'd slumped against.

Fletcher pointed at the guy with a pistol—the less she knew about him being armed the better. "I know who this bozo might be. He's the double of one of the four clowns who attacked me outside the diner. His brother's arm might have got bent the wrong way when he and his buddies came into my room." He gave the guy's boot enough of a kick to get him to shift his gaze from the ground. "So, Double. Want to tell us your real name and why you were stalking this young lady?"

Double's answer was to turn his head away, so he was looking away from Fletcher.

Before Quadrado had time to react, Fletcher leaned forward, grabbed Double's shattered nose between thumb and forefinger, and gave it a violent twist.

There was a yelp and a few curses, but neither name nor reason were forthcoming.

Quadrado planted a hand on Fletcher's chest to stop him torturing Double any further. Twisting a nose was one thing; however, she suspected that Fletcher was prepared to go a lot further and there was no way she could let that happen.

There was enough adrenaline coursing through her veins that her own emotions were heightened, and the scare had awoken parts of her psyche that she didn't like. If she allowed Fletcher to torture Double, there was every chance that if the guy didn't talk, she'd give in to her primal instincts and join in.

To counteract the threat from Fletcher and her own desire to exact some form of revenge, Quadrado squatted down so she was in Double's eyeline and showed him her badge.

"I'm Special Agent Quadrado of the Federal Bureau of Intelligence. You were sneaking up on me in an isolated area carrying a firearm. You do realize you're in deep trouble for that, don't you?"

Again, Double turned his head away.

This time Fletcher was ready and waiting. He flicked the tip of Double's shattered nose. "The lady asked you a question. I'd suggest you reply."

Double turned his head back to Quadrado and gave a slight nod.

Quadrado hardened her gaze. "Your name."

"Hank."

Quadrado sighed. So this was how Hank was going to play it, holding onto every piece of information as if it were a family heirloom. "Hank what?"

Hank's eyes flicked from Quadrado to Fletcher and back again. "Ain't saying no more 'til I got a lawyer representin' me."

"You'll talk if I say you'll talk." Quadrado caught Fletcher's arm as he drew it back, fist bunched.

Even with a ruined mouth, Hank was able to send Quadrado an infuriating smirk. "You're FBI, you're not gonna let him beat up on me. Maybe a little, but nuthin' I can't take. Do what you have to do, but I tell you now, I ain't talkin' no more until I got me a lawyer."

Quadrado looked at Fletcher, saw the bunched fist and the fire in his eyes. As she watched him the fire was doused until there was nothing left but smoldering impotence.

She knew she'd made a mistake pulling her badge and letting Hank know who they were. With her identified, he'd done his reasoning and had come to the same conclusion she had. Fletcher wasn't going to be allowed to really hurt Hank.

Quadrado watched as Fletcher gave a terse nod, pulled a knife from his belt and cut away the left sleeve of Hank's denim shirt, the knife sharp enough to slice through the material as if it were silk. With the knife back in its sheath, Fletcher wound the sleeve into a braid and used it to gag Hank.

It made sense; Hank being able to shout his mouth off would aid those who'd eventually come looking for him. The gag was tight and with broken teeth and split lips it'd be painful as well as uncomfortable. Quadrado could live with that; it'd soften Hank up for when she got him to an interview suite.

Quadrado caught Fletcher's eye. "Are we still doing this?"

Fletcher's answer was to set off walking.

CHAPTER FORTY-EIGHT

The diner was quiet when Fletcher walked in. A couple were trying to round up their children ready to leave—Fletcher could tell they were passing through from the modernity of their clothes—but apart from the family, the only other person around was Agnes Jackson.

Fletcher had guided Quadrado to the Blackett house and waited with her until the family had returned. Luck had been on his side as the Blacketts' Mercedes had driven through the gates a quarter hour after he'd gotten Quadrado a good vantage point and disguised the shape of her body with a few well-placed ferns and a leafy branch.

The hike back to town had been far quicker than the journey out, but he'd had to temper his pace as he didn't want to reek of perspiration when he arrived in Daversville.

Agnes Jackson gave him a furious look as she crossed to the booth where he'd stationed himself. There was no doubting her enmity, but that didn't worry Fletcher in the slightest. If anything, it gave him the advantage. He knew more about her than she him.

"What c'n I get you?"

"Coffee, the Special Burger with fries, and can I get extra bacon on the burger, please?" Fletcher hadn't planned to eat in the diner, but on the way back from the Blacketts' his stomach had rumbled and after two days of eating little but fruit and energy bars, he was ready for the "heap of meat" the Special Burger promised.

Agnes wheeled away and made for the kitchen. Her shoes scuffing the floor with every step.

When the burger came it was everything the menu had promised and more. Fletcher left most of the fries and focused on the meat. Succulent and well-cooked, it was delicious, and he could feel its restorative effect as he ate. Not eating the fries irked him as he hated to waste food, but he expected punches would be thrown before the evening ended, and the last thing he wanted was to feel bloated and stuffed. A gut punch would leave him vomiting, which in turn would end the fight there and then.

He finished the meat and left some money on the table. Rather than leave a few bills, he scattered most every coin from his pocket all over the table, as he wanted Agnes to be there for more than a couple of seconds.

He'd selected this booth on purpose. It was right beside the payphone fixed to the wall.

Fletcher dialed his home number and waited until the answering machine kicked in. After the beep, he began talking.

From the corner of his eye, he could see Agnes coming to collect his dirty plate.

With his smile kept internal, he continued with his one-way conversation. "Yeah, that's right, buddy. It's the Blacketts behind everything… Nah, I'm certain. I've got the proof on me. All I gotta do is find the FBI agent who's in town. If I don't find her soon, I'll take it to the cops in Macon tomorrow morning." Fletcher gave a lengthy pause as if listening to the other person before picking up his story. "Don't worry about me. This bunch of rednecks couldn't organize a bun fight in a bakery."

While he was speaking, Fletcher was observing Agnes's reaction as she cleared the table in the booth. Her body was stiffening with each new utterance he made. If he'd talked much longer, he suspected she'd have ended up with rigor mortis.

This was just what he wanted. As soon as she could, Agnes would be sending word back to the Blacketts.

Fletcher hung up the phone and left the diner to set phase two of his plan into action. As he made his way along to Duke's, he removed the locket from his neck, and slid it and its chain into his pocket lest he lose it in the fight he expected to be coming his way.

CHAPTER FORTY-NINE

Quadrado's muscles were stiff and sore as she watched the house through Fletcher's binoculars. It had been an hour since he'd left her and not one thing of interest had happened. There had been various animal noises and she'd heard many birds squawking above her, but there hadn't been any great sign of activity until a gang of four young men had exited the house and made their way to the garage. They piled into the truck beds of a pair of aged pickup trucks, two apiece and waited. Their bodies were hardened with youth and physical labor and their hands held a variety of weapons. The one bonus was that none of them appeared to be carrying a firearm. All the same, she spotted two hunting knives, a baseball bat and what appeared to be the chain from a motorcycle.

As much as Quadrado was pleased Fletcher's plan was working, she couldn't help but wonder if he'd find himself outmatched by the four young men, armed as they were.

The house's front door opened again, two men and the benevolent woman Quadrado had seen handing out candy at the church came out, the men flanking the woman on the way to the garage, neither stepping in front of her slow pace as she leaned heavily on her cane.

With everyone loaded into the two pickups, the vehicles started moving forward, not with a steady pace, but a fast one that left the four in the truck beds holding on lest they be bounced overboard.

As soon as they were out of sight Quadrado rose to her feet, ignoring the protest of muscles that hadn't moved for too long.

She wanted to grimace and groan at the discomfort, but she didn't have the luxury of time on her side, so she gritted her teeth and made her way to the gate.

The drugged meat Fletcher had left with her sailed over the gate piece by piece, landing in an area the size of a dinner table. One by one, three huge Dobermans galloped into view, and started chomping on the meat.

Quadrado watched as the dogs wolfed down the meat. Once it was all gone they looked at her with puzzled, glassy eyes. One opened its mouth as if to bark, thought better of it and lay down, a huge head resting on black paws. Within seconds it was joined by the other two.

A minute after she'd seen their eyelids slip down over their eyes, Quadrado began to scale the gate. Its thin railings didn't make for an easy climb, but she managed to get herself up high enough that she could clamber over the top and drop down the other side.

One of the dogs snored, another broke wind as Quadrado stepped past them. Her entire focus was on getting from the gate into the house.

To get into the house she'd have to get Elena to open the door, but that shouldn't be too hard. She had been trained in negotiation; so long as she could enter a dialogue with the Guatemalan, she was confident she could persuade the maid to let her in.

After that, she'd have to find a way to get Elena's story. If Fletcher had told the truth, her plan was she and Elena would hike alongside the road the Blacketts used to access the house until they made it to where she and Fletcher had agreed to rendezvous. If she got a different story from Elena than Fletcher had, she'd have to report back and pass the decision to call out a search party for Trench to someone with the clout to make it happen.

For some reason the door had a mail slot, so Quadrado pressed it open and put her lips to it. "Elena. Are you there? My name is Zoey and I'm here to help you."

There was no answer from inside the house, so Quadrado tried calling out again, only louder.

"Don't even think about moving."

The hissed words were accompanied by the ratcheting sound of a pistol's hammer being drawn back.

CHAPTER FIFTY

Fletcher ordered a bottle of beer and surveyed the clientele of Duke's. There were eight other patrons. Two couples wearing the bemused looks of those who'd stepped through a time portal and three guys and a girl, all early twenties.

The couples were obviously not locals, so Fletcher paid them no heed. It was the younger crowd who, along with Duke, would have loyalty to the Blackett family.

Fletcher walked over to them, hands loose by his sides in case one of the guys thought about being a hero. "Let me buy you a beer." Fletcher waved a hand at Duke. "Set these guys up, will ya?"

"Thanks, buddy, but we'll buy our own." The nearest one turned his head to look at him.

The response was pretty much what Fletcher expected. None of the four looked to have had more than one beer, and unlike the other night when he'd offered beer to guys halfway in their cups, these four were still sober enough to maintain their natural distrust of strangers bearing gifts.

"I insist. After tomorrow, this town is gonna be a whole lot different and the least I can do is buy a couple drinks for the folks who'll suffer."

The nearest one turned round to snap at the bait Fletcher had laid with his words. "Whaddya mean?"

"What I mean is that the folks who own the lumber mill are gonna get what's coming to them. I'm guessing the mill will end up shutting down and you'll all lose your jobs."

The crowd of four all exchanged glances and nervous laughs. There was uncertainty on their faces and no small amount of fear at the thought of not having the mill to support their lives.

The girl stepped forward, her face a mixture of anger and derision. "So, what's gonna happen tomorrow? You gonna prove that instead of creating jobs 'n' homes for the people of Daversville, the Blacketts are bad people? You don't know nothing, mister. The Blacketts take care of us. They've given us a school to get educated and there's always food in the store for us to buy. If'n one of us gets sick, it's them who brings a doctor. They even got a house where the old folk get looked after till they pass."

"No, I'm going to prove that as well as creating the jobs and homes, they've been oppressing you and using you like slaves. Not only that, I'm going to prove that they are evil."

As he spoke, Fletcher was beginning to think he'd made a huge mistake. He'd never thought of finding out how the sick and the elderly were cared for. As much as the Blacketts might oppress those who could work, he'd never once entertained the idea they'd look after those who couldn't. He couldn't decide if it was a communist or socialist model, until he recalled the opulence of the Blacketts' own home. As much as they might take care of certain folks, he didn't believe they had a genuine desire to put anyone else's best interests before their own comfort. The way he saw it, they were giving a little and taking a lot.

"That's enough from you, buddy. I knew you was trouble minute I clapped eyes on you." Duke moved from behind the bar and pointed at the door. "It's time you either stop your mouthing off or get out."

"Fair enough." Fletcher took his bottle of beer to a table and sat with his back to a wall so he could survey the room.

To the server's bemusement, Duke lifted the empty plates from the nearest couple's table and returned them to the kitchen.

Fletcher bit down on the smile he could feel forming. This was Duke's way of leaving the room so he could get in touch with the

Blacketts. With a second source relaying bad news, the Blacketts were sure to react.

In essence his plan was a simple one. He was the distracting smoke, drawing attention and a response that would afford access to Elena for Quadrado. In turn, Quadrado would be able to reflect on what she found and take the appropriate action. If needs be, she could lead Elena from the house at gunpoint, but when all was said and done, every part of their plan hinged on Quadrado being able to open up a dialogue with Elena.

Now that Duke had left the room, Fletcher checked his watch and did the same. It was eighteen minutes since he'd left the diner.

He'd worked out the numbers in his head on a best-case scenario basis. Five minutes for Agnes to convince the Blacketts of the conversation he'd staged for her benefit. A minimum of another five minutes for the family to mobilize themselves. Ten for the drive from their house to Daversville, which meant the earliest he could expect the Blacketts was in a couple minutes. It could be they wouldn't react until Duke also messaged them, which meant they'd be another fifteen to twenty minutes.

That was fine, he was in no hurry. They'd arrive with a superior force and would be intent on battle. It was a fight he wasn't expecting to win, but having it was a necessity, as the only other way he could think of drawing them all out was to set fire to the lumber mill.

For all his words in Duke's, he didn't for one minute think there would be any job losses in Daversville or, at least, not in the long term. Either another member of the family would continue running the mill or it would be sold, and the folks of Daversville would be introduced to the twenty-first century. This reasoning was what compelled him to take the beating that was coming his way rather than ruin the town's only industry.

Fletcher had left both pistols in his backpack on purpose. Other than Hank with his shotgun, the Blacketts had never used firearms on their victims, and there was something final about shooting someone. A bullet in the arm or leg would slow or stop any opponent, but that required precise shooting, and having never fired either of his new pistols, he had no idea of their accuracy. He could live with putting a bullet in a limb, but with a moving target and an unfamiliar weapon, the odds were that he'd miss, or, in the heat of battle, his training would kick in and he'd automatically aim for center mass. He wasn't here to kill the Blacketts. Maybe if the fight took place in a less public arena he'd have to kill them if it became a kill-or-be-killed situation. That was another reason he'd chosen to have the fight in a place where there would be onlookers. The Blacketts might well control the town and its people, but the two couples in Dukes would be witnesses who'd call the cops. Fletcher's knife was with the pistols on the premise that if he arrived without obvious weapons and lost the fight, the beating he'd suffer wouldn't be as bad as the one he'd get if he left the Blacketts and their cronies with any life-changing injuries.

Once outside Duke's, Fletcher found a spot halfway along a wall where he could wait for the arrival of the Blacketts.

He didn't have to wait long: two pickups came into view, all racing engines and furious intent.

CHAPTER FIFTY-ONE

Both pickups looked the same to Fletcher. Wide-bodied and hunkered down on suspension no longer fit to suspend anything heavier than a flea. It made them look squat and menacing.

The first shot five yards past him and screeched to a halt, its resting place at right angles to the road. The second did the same thing on the other side of him.

Two youths approached Fletcher from either side. From Trench's descriptions of Miss Constance's sons, Fletcher could see they were backed by Chuck on his left side and Jimmy on the right. Miss Constance sat immobile in the truck, her wattle-laden arm resting on the ledge created by the pickup's open window.

Fletcher pushed himself off the wall and walked until he was in the middle of the road. He recognized Tall Boy, Cocky and Muscles. The fourth youth he didn't know, but he was the spitting image of Cocky, so Fletcher thought of him as Twin. From seeing Jimmy Blackett's physique behind Muscles and Tall Boy, Fletcher figured he was father to at least Muscles.

On his right, Chuck was behind Cocky and Twin. With both Cocky and Freckles having a doppelganger, it was obvious there was a genetic trait in the Blackett family for identical twins.

The four youths had weapons, but it was the greater numbers that worried Fletcher most. Jimmy looked as if he was a handful in himself, and if he joined the fray alongside the youths, things may go a lot worse than he'd anticipated.

He was glad he had moved the fight from the bar to the middle of the road. Out here he had room to move and could fight without having to worry that he'd harm an innocent.

All four of the youths were trash-talking. It wasn't a surprise to Fletcher. Lots of guys made smart-assed comments about the enemy on their way into battle. It was a way of bolstering courage, not just in yourself, but in those at your side. If the enemy was belittled and made to seem weak, they were less of a threat. There was also the possibility an insult would hit home and cause an opponent to react in anger. Losing your cool in a fight resulted in a one-way trip to Silver Medal Land on more occasions than not.

Fletcher ignored the jibes and focused on the task at hand. The most important thing he had to do was find a way to try and even the odds.

Cocky had already proven himself to be a coward, and he was backed by the tall, intelligent-looking Chuck rather than the powerful Jimmy.

Both Cocky and Twin held a weapon. Cocky had a knife he was flashing in front of him as if it was a sword, while Twin held a baseball bat. He reasoned they'd make the easier targets to tackle first so he could deplete the Blackett numbers.

By the time Fletcher arrived at Cocky and Twin, he'd built up speed from the five dashed paces he'd covered. Now to use that momentum and the increased force it would give his attack.

Fletcher ducked beneath Twin's attempt to hit his head for a home run, his right arm flashing out; bent at the elbow, it careened into the side of Twin's head, sending him reeling backwards as the concussive effect of a hard blow shook his brain around the inside of his skull. With his left hand, Fletcher had grabbed the back of Cocky's shirt as the youth turned away from his attack and pirouetted, his momentum far outweighing the lad's attempts to run away.

Cocky's head collided with the pickup's fender, adding another dent before he slumped to the ground. Twin was already on his ass, shaking his head to clear the elbow-induced brain clouds.

Chuck had his hands raised in a boxing stance, but that was far too long a process for Fletcher's liking; Jimmy and the other two would soon join the fray, so he charged at Chuck, intent on ducking below his punches and propelling him into the pickup's door.

It didn't work like that.

By the time he reached Chuck, the man had already danced sideways, his right cross ringing Fletcher's ear.

Someone said something, but it was white noise to Fletcher. They could say what they liked, he planned to make his actions speak louder than any of their words.

The adrenaline was coursing through Fletcher's veins as he flicked a glance to his left. Muscles and Tall Boy were advancing on him, but Jimmy had stayed where he was, his massive arms folded and a look of wry amusement on his face. Muscles held a knife, but unlike Cocky, he wasn't flashing it around and he held it the same way Fletcher would have. Tall Boy had a chain of some sort hanging from his right hand.

The decision Fletcher now had to make was whether or not he should pick up one of the dropped weapons.

He chose not to for two reasons: the first being that he still felt that he could win the fight without disrupting his original plan, and the second was that a crowd were gathering. If this went as pear-shaped as it might, the crowd would be his witnesses. It would also be a huge step towards showing the folks of Daversville that the Blacketts weren't as powerful as they appeared to be.

Fletcher leaned back to evade a jab from Chuck, then danced forward to feint a couple of blows of his own. Chuck stepped back, bobbing and weaving, his hands lifted high to protect his head.

"C'mon, Champ. Put 'em up and let's see what you've got."

This was a bad sign. It was obvious Chuck had not only been trained how to box, but that he had the smarts to keep his cool and maintain his composure. There was no way Fletcher was going to fight Chuck on the guy's own terms. He would have to wait. Even so, Fletcher took another step forward pushing Chuck back and then propelled himself towards Tall Boy.

The thing about a chain as a weapon that people always overlook is its lack of structure. The impact of a chain can be devastating as it will mold itself to its target and land with increasing force as its entire length assaults its victim. On the downside, the longer a weapon is, the more time it takes to bring it into action due to simple physics. With a chain, the tip—which inflicts the greatest damage—will always be behind the rest of the chain until its whip effect has it colliding with its target.

Tall Boy wound up to swing the chain for all he was worth, but it was a heavy chain and it lagged behind his body, meaning his arm was behind him as he twisted to apply maximum force. His kidneys were wide open, and Fletcher wasn't going to pass up such a glorious chance.

He buried his left hand into the side of Tall Boy's torso, driving the lad sideways. As Tall Boy started to fall, Fletcher snatched the chain from his hand and wound it around his left arm.

A glance over his shoulder was a mistake as Chuck nailed him with a straight jab that filled his mouth with the iron taste of blood. Even so, Fletcher had learned enough from the single blow to not repeat the mistake. Chuck had been waiting for the right time to snap the punch away and he'd failed to follow it up with a flurry of blows to the back of his head or to his kidneys. Chuck was playing by the rules, even if the four youths weren't.

Fletcher took a step left so he could see past the bulk of Muscles. Jimmy was still playing the part of spectator rather than participant. The grin on his face suggested that he was enjoying the show and wasn't worried by Fletcher's relative success.

That didn't bode well.

Muscles feinted with the knife, threw a punch and then followed with a slashing move that would have opened up Fletcher's forearm had the chain around it not been there.

Fletcher threw a hard right to Muscles's gut that had the same effect as punching a cliff and expecting the mountain behind it to move.

Another feint from Muscles was followed up by a series of flashing swipes. Muscles was a quick learner. He'd altered the angles of his attack so the knife could slip between the gaps where Fletcher had wrapped the chain around his forearm.

Blood dripped from Fletcher's arm, yet he paid it no heed; to start worrying about a cut that hadn't gone deep or severed anything vital would be foolish. Instead he gave a couple of telegraphed feints of his own before striking out at Muscles for a second time.

Muscles went to block the blow with his knife arm, as Fletcher had expected. The knife's blade caromed off the chains and did no damage, but it went upwards, exposing Muscles's torso.

Fletcher had already learned the futility of gut punching Muscles, so he aimed his next blow at the youth's face. When forehead and nose collide, nose never wins. Muscles's nose lost big time. It lost structure, rigidity and more than a little blood. Muscles might well have a washboard stomach, but there was a softer area a little further south and that's what Fletcher's knee was aimed at. If the bellowed howl that erupted from Muscles was any indication, Fletcher's aim was true.

With the four youths taken out of action, Fletcher could focus on Chuck and Jimmy. He took three dancing steps off to one side and threw a quick look at the brothers.

Jimmy's arms were unfolded, but he was still a good ten feet away and showing no indication of moving forward. Chuck on the other hand was coming at him, fists raised. There was a look of determination about him that suggested he was done landing odd blows, and was ready to finish the fight.

Chuck had several inches of reach on him and appeared to have enough technical skill to keep his distance and pick Fletcher off at will. In a ring, Fletcher could weather a few blows, push Chuck back against the ropes and unload his own punches. Out here there was too much room to move, so he needed a different tactic if he wasn't going to fall victim to the bony knuckles Chuck kept thrusting his way.

Fletcher took a step forward then danced sideways away from the jab arrowing at his chin, threw a low blow towards Chuck's stomach. Chuck instinctively dropped the hand he'd retained to defend against such counterpunches.

That was what Fletcher had intended. He grabbed Chuck's wrist, and yanked his arm straight as he moved outside Chuck's body.

With his arm twisted the way it was, Chuck's body had to obey the force Fletcher was applying or risk having his arm broken.

He obeyed when Fletcher raised his arm high enough to allow a thunderous left uppercut to nail him sweetly on the chin.

Chuck wobbled but he didn't go down. He was shaking his head to disperse the uppercut-induced grogginess as Fletcher wound up a second blow.

Fletcher never got to throw that punch. He felt his own left arm being pulled round and then a fist the size of a baseball mitt was arrowing towards his face. Fletcher didn't have time to try and roll with the punch. He went down hard.

The last thing he felt before passing out was heavy boots thudding into his defenseless body.

CHAPTER FIFTY-TWO

The guy with the pistol was calm. He'd always been calm. From the moment he'd ambushed her at the door of the Blacketts' house, to the time he'd spent watching over her, he'd been at peace with what he was doing.

Quadrado had told him who she was. That she'd left word with other FBI agents as to where she was going. That very soon a tactical team would be arriving at the house and it'd go better for him if he lay down his weapon and set her free.

The guy hadn't reacted to any of this. He'd kept silent, his only words instructions as to where she should go and promises to shoot her if she didn't comply.

He was in his early twenties and wore the same hillbilly clothes as the rest of the Daversville locals, but there was a spark of keen intelligence in his eyes. His face was the double of Hank, who they'd caught in the woods, and his right arm was in a cast that ran downwards from the top of his bicep until it covered all save his thumb and fingers.

Quadrado had long ago given up trying to get through to the guy. The more time that passed, the emptier her threats of an FBI tactical team arriving at any minute became.

The chair she was handcuffed to was a folding wooden garden one. If she'd been alone, she might have been able to topple it and land hard enough for parts of the chair to snap under the force of the impact. Then she'd be able to effect some form of escape.

Had she been tied to the chair with ropes, she might have been able to wriggle a hand from her bindings then unpick the other knots. With handcuffs cinched tight against her flesh, there was no chance of freeing herself.

The fact the guy who'd caught her had taken a seat six feet away and sat watching her made all the other points moot. The pistol sat on his thigh in the same way her father rested the TV remote, and there was nothing but calmness about him.

Quadrado's thoughts were on how she'd messed up. She'd known she needed more proof, but instead of going along with Fletcher's madcap scheme, she ought to have called the Atlanta office and requested a surveillance team.

Had she not been bound to the chair so tightly, she knew she'd be shaking. Whichever way she looked at it, there was no escaping the fact she'd been captured by the people who were the prime suspects in her missing persons' case. While she expected to find out what had happened to the abducted people, she didn't think she'd live long enough to share the knowledge of what she'd learned.

The sound of approaching engines cut through the near silence of the woods.

Quadrado steeled herself. This would either be the moment of truth, or the end of her life. Whichever it was, she planned to face it with fidelity, bravery and intelligence.

The two ancient pickups pottered into view. Her guard stood and waited until the pickups halted outside the garage and disgorged their passengers.

All four of the younger Blacketts looked in worse shape than the aged pickups, but there wasn't a mark on Jimmy and Chuck's face bore only the slightest bruising.

"In you go, boys." Miss Constance pointed at the house. Her voice thick with backwoods upbringing and tinged with triumph.

The boys high-fived each other and made off for the house with a series of half-hearted whoops and hollers.

The look Miss Constance sent after them was not one of fond exasperation.

"You were right, Miss Constance." The freckled guy who'd captured Quadrado handed his pistol over to Jimmy and told them about her.

Miss Constance looked at her sons. "Well, what are you pair reckoning?"

Quadrado watched as they shrugged. Chuck was the one who spoke first. "She's FBI. Whether she's left a trail or not, we need to get rid of her. I say we slit her throat and put her with the others."

"No." Jimmy's voice was forceful but higher than a man of his bulk suggested it should be. "We make sure there's no trace. We take her body down the swamps and let the gators eat her."

"Good point." Chuck nodded to emphasize his agreement. "The farther away the better."

Miss Constance spat a globule of spittle the size of an oyster onto the ground. "You pair are nuthin' but chickenshit pussies who couldn't pour piss from a boot if the instructions were on the heel. You're talkin' 'bout driving her hundreds of miles just to feed her to some gators. Look at her." The old woman's cane became a pointer. "Yes, she's a spic, but she's pretty. Prettier 'n any gal you pair ever brought home. Killing her, putting her in the pen, ain't gonna matter which we do cause she's been here and willa left that trace evidence you see on the TV. She's FBI, young and pretty. She'll fetch a penny that'll be even prettier than she is. Put her in the pen and treat her like the others. When you done that, go rub some manure on your balls and see if that'll make 'em grow."

Quadrado said nothing. She couldn't speak. Could hardly think. The three Blacketts had discussed her fate in front of her as if they were choosing a restaurant. Jimmy and Chuck had wanted her dead. Miss Constance wanted to make money from her. How the Blacketts would make money from her remained to be seen.

No matter how many other things she had to think about, the point that was foremost in Quadrado's mind was that she'd been wrong about the Blacketts involvement in the disappearances, wrong to believe Miss Constance was nothing more than a kindly grandmother who doled out candy and presents to the local kids, and wrong to have come here without backup.

All she could hope for now was that Fletcher could somehow find a way to rescue her.

CHAPTER FIFTY-THREE

Fletcher came to in increments. Each one discovering a new level of agony. He'd taken a beating before; you don't make the grade in the Royal Marines without pitting yourself against other testosterone-fueled young men and women who were intent on proving they were every bit as good, if not better, than you were.

All the same, there wasn't a part of his body that was free from pain when he moved. The first thing he did was send a prayer of thanks to whomever might be listening. He wasn't dead. He was alive and, if not exactly well, he was still able to function.

When he teased his eyes open, he found that he was in some kind of lumber store illuminated by a pair of bare bulbs hanging from cables. Surrounding him were piles of lumber, each layer separated by narrow slats. It was hot in here, but that was the last thing on his mind. He was strapped to a central pole that ran up and disappeared into the ceiling.

The bindings holding him to the pole were duct tape. There were wide bands above and below his knees and another across his chest. His hands were bound at the wrist by tape. Why he was locked in here was beyond him, but the first item on his agenda was escape.

There are ways to escape most restraints if you have the right training. Fletcher had that training and now it was time to put it into use.

He lifted his arms above his head until they were as high as he could lift them. His muscles protested, but he ignored them. He'd treat his muscles to a week's rest if he got out of this alive.

In a mighty movement he drove his arms downwards, until his elbows passed by the sides of his body and carried on until his hands collided with his stomach. As much as he was trying to be silent, he couldn't help but let out a low moan of pain.

The pain didn't matter; the way he'd driven his arms past his sides had applied a lateral pressure on the tape binding his wrists that was far greater than any he could have applied using his strength alone. The duct tape had all but parted, so ignoring the pain, he gave it a wrench that was enough to finish the job.

For some reason, he was bathed in sweat. There wasn't a single pore on his body that wasn't leaking perspiration.

Fletcher's next move was to find the end of the tape binding his chest. It took a bit of searching, but he eventually found it behind his right armpit.

It was a stretch to reach it, but by gritting his teeth and twisting his body as far as was possible, he was able to pick at it and grasp the triangular tab between his fingers. It slipped a few times from his sweat-greased fingers, but he managed to get a good enough hold to start unpeeling the tape. Thankfully the duct tape peeled forwards towards his chest rather than round his back.

By passing the end of the tape from hand to hand behind his back, Fletcher was able to remove all seven of the wraps it had made around his body.

Freeing his legs was an exercise in masochism, as the last thing his bruised body wanted to do was bend over and strain forward. Sweat was pouring from his body and dripping from his face by the time he'd dropped the last of the tape onto the ground.

With the pace of an arthritic sloth, Fletcher took a few gentle steps forward. The agonized movements made his legs feel weak at the knees as every part of him protested. Again he ignored them. Pain was good. It told you that you were still alive.

Fletcher made his way around the perimeter of the building until he found wide double doors. He pushed one.

It didn't move so he tried the second. It didn't move either.

Fletcher leaned his back against the point where the doors met, braced his feet against the rough concrete floor and pushed on the doors. There wasn't a hint of give.

Whether he liked it or not he was trapped in this store until someone rescued him.

He wiped the sweat from his brow and realized it was getting hotter in here. His throat was parched, and although they were in rural Georgia, the air felt dry and arid, as if he was in a desert.

Fletcher retraced his steps around the lumber store's perimeter. He wasn't so much looking for a way to escape as assessing the area he was imprisoned in. At one side of the store he could hear an engine running. The walls and door weren't typical materials used for a lumber store. They were faced with Formica and when Fletcher found an area where the Formica was damaged, he saw that there was heavy grade insulation.

That's when he realized where he'd been imprisoned. This wasn't an ordinary storage space at the lumber mill. It was a kiln built to dry out lumber.

For the first time since coming to Georgia, Fletcher began to doubt he'd survive the experience. Each breath was that little bit harder to take than the last one.

The Blacketts didn't just want to kill him, they wanted him to suffer. To die slowly and in agony as the kiln's increasing heat cooked his internal organs and scorched his skin.

CHAPTER FIFTY-FOUR

The bag over Quadrado's head smelled of death. She was sure some piece of roadkill or another had been transported in the bag. The smell was gamey, yet there was the unmistakable tang of blood.

Had she been vain, she might have worried about particles of the bag's former occupant getting into her hair, but in the greater scheme of things, that was the least of her worries.

More than once she felt the barrel of a pistol touching her back as she was led by the wrist towards her fate.

Quadrado tried to measure the distance and direction she was taken, but soon lost track. The Blackett brothers would periodically stop and spin her around. She felt the ground steepen as she went uphill and then before she knew it, it would level off and she'd be digging her heels in and trying not to slip as she was led back downhill. On two occasions, she was taken through a stream. The burbling water cool against her feet and lower legs.

Eventually, she felt level ground beneath her feet. The ground was harder here, like a sidewalk or tiled floor. She could hear the pocking sounds the heels of her boots made as rough hands gripped her upper arms and guided her in a specific direction.

"There are steps in front of you. They go down."

The voice was Chuck's, Quadrado was sure of it. She'd only heard Jimmy speak once and his voice was several octaves higher than his brother's. Where the steps led was something she didn't want to think about. She guessed it would be a former military bunker or maybe the basement of an abandoned house. Wherever the steps led, it was probable it would be the end of the line for her.

The warning about the steps puzzled her. As did the way that she'd been led through the woods. She'd expected to bump into trees and be laughed at, that branches would be pulled back and left to twang in her face and that she'd trip over a dozen unseen objects. None of that had happened and the only reason she could think of for the Blacketts to take care of her this way was that they didn't want to harm her, or damage her looks before they made their money from her.

Miss Constance's comments about her prettiness might have been flattering in a different circumstance, but Quadrado didn't want the compliments of an evil woman like Miss Constance.

Quadrado's nose crinkled beneath the foul bag. The place she was being taken smelled like a sewer.

The hands on her arms guided her, turning her one way and then the other before they released her and whipped the bag from her head with a theatrical flourish. The handcuffs binding her hands were released and Quadrado felt a push in her back and heard the metallic clang of steel on steel.

She was oblivious to the push. All her focus was on what her eyes were seeing. After the time hooded by the bag, the dim light of the basement made her pupils contract as she blinked until her eyes adjusted enough to show her that she was in a cell constructed of steel mesh that formed eight-by-eight-inch squares.

In between the blinks Quadrado saw five shadowy figures looking at her from other cells. All five had fear and pity etched on to their faces. Fear for themselves and pity for her as she would now endure the same fate as had befallen them.

Worst of all about the people she could see, was the fact that she not just recognized them, but knew about their lives right up until the point they'd traveled through Daversville. Through a metal mesh, Quadrado could see Lila Ogilvie, who Fletcher had come looking for; she'd been missing for over ten days now.

Beyond Lila was a trim woman in her forties. She was Frances East, an air-con saleswoman from Jackson, Florida. It would be four weeks tomorrow since she'd last been heard from. In the cell opposite East's was a man. Quadrado knew nothing about him, but she could tell he was every bit as much a captive as everyone else in the room.

In the cells either side of East, two women looked at Quadrado. She recognized the woman on the left as Kiera Vincent, a student from Greensboro, North Carolina. On the right was Melissa Gilpin, an accountant from Knoxville in Tennessee. They'd been reported as missing three and five months ago respectively.

The reasons for their abductions was making little sense to Quadrado. While public perception is that rapists fantasized about beautiful victims, the reality is that the vast majority of rapists are opportunists who select their victims by their availability and vulnerability. She knew from many hours of classroom training that rape is far more to do with control and domination than sexual fantasy.

Quadrado herself had ended up here because she'd been ambushed and so had become both available and vulnerable. In her file photo, Lila had a beautiful face, but now it was covered with grime and her hair was unwashed and lank; she didn't look anything like her usual self. Kiera looked the most scared of all the other captives and had only moved from where she'd pressed herself against the back wall once the door to the room had slammed shut. Melissa was an older woman and there was no disguising the hardness in her eyes.

While all the women had a certain level of desirability, the fact a man had been abducted as well didn't make sense if the Blacketts were selecting people to rape. For all his gym-honed physique, the man had the looks of a bulldog that constantly ran into walls.

More than any other, the questions that Quadrado couldn't shake from her mind were: what had happened to the other eleven women who'd disappeared from Daversville? Would it happen to her in time? And had her Aunt Janet ended up in a place like this?

Now she was trapped in the cell, she knew her hopes of rescue were slimmer than ever as Fletcher had to not only have survived his confrontation with the Blacketts, but also find the cellar where she was now kept. All she knew about her current location was that it was within walking distance of the Blackett house.

CHAPTER FIFTY-FIVE

Industrial kilns are made up of several parts that work in tandem to dry lumber from its natural state to one where it could be used for construction projects or furniture making without the lumber splitting or warping. There's the storage area, a heating system, dehumidifiers and fans to circulate the warm air around all the lumber in the kiln. The kilns achieve temperatures of over two hundred degrees for softwood and one seventy for hardwood.

They're designed to heat the air, circulate it and then remove the moisture content until the drying lumber is suitable for its desired purpose.

Fletcher didn't know any of this, and if he had, he wouldn't have cared. All that mattered to him was escaping the kiln before he started to cook. As it was, he could feel the increasing heat as a physical thing pushing against his exposed skin.

He'd scoured the whole store and had found the places where the fans were located behind grills.

The angry part of his psyche wanted to jam some of the lumber into the fans, not because it would prevent the heat increasing, but because it would do damage that would cost the Blacketts time and money to repair. The wiser, more rational part of his brain had told him not to waste his energy on a petty and pointless revenge. There was little to be gained by being destructive for the sake of it.

Fletcher's body was soaked in perspiration, his clothes sticking to him as if he'd just fallen into a river. Breaths were getting progressively harder to take as the heated air seemed to have less and less oxygen content. The heat itself was making him pant like an overweight dog on a summer's day.

Despite the rising temperature and the increasing difficulty in drawing a decent breath, Fletcher made himself sit down and focus. Striding around, reexamining the same walls and floors several times wasn't going to get him anywhere.

There were two ways out of the store. He'd learned that much from his searches. The first was a hatch in the ceiling which would lead to the loft space. If he could get in there, he'd have the insulated panels below him and corrugated tin above him. With heat always looking for a way to rise, going through the hatch would be a frying pan to fire situation if ever there was one.

All the same, he clambered onto a stack of lumber and forced the hatch open. The air smelled dusty and dry.

Fletcher dropped back to the ground exhausted at the effort it had taken him to perform this simple task. The injuries from the fight coupled with the temperature were crippling him in a war of attrition.

The result was worth the effort though. Down at floor level, the temperature was lower. Only two or three degrees, but every last degree mattered to Fletcher.

His hand drew the locket from the pocket where he'd stashed it and he slid the chain around his neck. Now he had his girls back in their rightful place, he could set his brain working on a way to get out of the kiln.

The lumber on the stacks was of varying lengths. As he looked at them the beginnings of an idea started to form in Fletcher's brain. He wasn't sure it'd work, but it was the best idea he'd come up with, so he picked himself up and got ready to put it into action.

First he selected a length of lumber from the nearest stack and laid it on the ground between the door and the pole he'd been taped to.

It was about four inches short, but that wasn't a problem. He found a stack of lumber that was six feet in length and selected four pieces that were two inch by nine.

He carried the four pieces of lumber to the doors and stood them against the left-hand door at the point where the doors met. This would be the weakest point. Although he hadn't been able to budge the doors using his own strength, the lumber he'd collected would provide a far stronger option.

With the four two-inch timbers against the door the original length Fletcher had collected was too long to fit in the gap. He made sure that one end was planted firmly against the pole, and lowered the other end until it was resting on the four timbers against the door. The door end was at eye level for Fletcher, which meant it was a little over five feet from the ground.

He gasped and panted as he placed a second piece of the same length on top of the first and then walked to the pole.

Fletcher used the stacks of lumber to help him maintain his balance as he walked up the sloping timbers. As he neared the door, he pulled a four-foot length that was six inches square from the nearest stack and carried it up the slope with him. The lumber he was carrying was slickened by the sweat pouring from his hands and dripping off his face, but he managed to get a good enough grip of it to drive it downwards onto the timbers he was standing on.

Inch by inch, they went down. Each thud from the four-foot length was interspersed by a rasping breath and perspiration that was falling off Fletcher like sprinkles from a donut.

The doors creaked and groaned as the lumber pressed them outwards. The pole was an immovable object as it was set into the concrete floor. Therefore by creating this massive wedge, the only thing which could give was the doors.

When he'd beaten the timbers to a near horizontal position, Fletcher got three more six-foot lengths and placed them in front of the original four. Another two longer timbers were braced against the pole ready for the cumulative effect of Fletcher's weight and the blows from the four-foot length to drive them downwards.

Fletcher couldn't resist putting his face to the crack that had opened between the doors. Sweet cool air was blowing in, refreshing his face and lungs in equal measure.

He didn't enjoy it for long, though. While his face may be getting cooled, the rest of his body was still exposed to the insidiously rising temperature.

With the four-foot length back in his hands, Fletcher set off up the sloping timbers a second time.

It was harder to knock the second pair of timbers down than the first two. After six hefty blows had failed to move the timbers an inch, Fletcher had to resort to a more drastic measure.

The six blows had cost him dear as he'd put everything he had into the last five. Sweat ran from his head into his eyes, the salt content stinging, but it was bearable. Fletcher reached down into the pit of his last reserves, braced himself for the inevitable fall and the pain it would bring and jumped upwards.

When he landed he drove his legs down, adding the power of his quadriceps to the weight of two hundred pounds being dragged down by gravity. He'd set his feet at angles to cope with the sloping timbers and he felt his ankles jar as he made contact.

Loud cracks and splintering filled Fletcher's ears as he tumbled to the ground. The impact with the concrete floor squeezed out what little good air there was in Fletcher's lungs and left him gasping.

After the fourth or fifth gasp, Fletcher noticed the air he was sucking in was sweeter and less arid than it had been a minute ago.

He looked towards the doors. Pieces of lumber lay strewn in front of them, but it was loose, lying in a haphazard way when he'd expected it to be jammed tight between door and pole.

The door on the left was open. Not far, but enough for Fletcher to get through.

He crawled to the door, peeped around the corner and made sure no one was coming his way. There wasn't, so he clambered to his feet, staggered out of the kiln and slid off into the night, the pre-arranged rendezvous with Quadrado his only focus.

CHAPTER FIFTY-SIX

Quadrado shivered and wrapped her arms around her body. There was no heat to be had in this prison and she'd taken only the slightest sips of water from the bottle which had been awaiting her in the cell. It wasn't that she wasn't thirsty, more that she'd noticed the way all the other prisoners had lacked any spark of personality when she'd tried speaking to them.

She'd learned the man was Pierre Lautrec, a construction engineer from New York but nothing more. The obvious answer to the prisoners' stupefaction was drugs, and she didn't think for one second the bottle of water was there for altruistic reasons. It would contain roofies, GHB or some other date rape drug. Hence the fact she'd taken only the merest sips and had then spat out the water into a bucket, which, she presumed due to the smell from other cells, was the sanitation facilities.

Her leg still twitched from its contact with the cattle prod. She'd only been in her cell for a short time when they'd come for her.

The four young Blacketts had opened her cell; the tallest of the four had held the dual prongs of a cattle prod an inch from her nose, while the other three picked her up. She'd considered fighting back, but the four were too many for her to stand a chance against, even had the cattle prod not been a factor.

As much as she knew that she was being taken somewhere where she expected bad things to happen to her, the investigator in Quadrado had to know the answer to why all the people were being abducted. She didn't fight them as logic had given her two good reasons to believe she'd be returned to the cell unharmed.

First. Miss Constance had intimated that the Blacketts would get a good price for her, which suggested that she'd be sold at some point. As terrible as that thought would be, she'd been confident that she wouldn't be harmed as that would affect her sale price. The cattle prod would hurt like hell, but other than a couple of scorch marks, she knew it wouldn't leave any lasting damage that couldn't be covered up with clothing.

Second. Some of the other prisoners had been missing for months and, while they might have been incarcerated in horrible conditions, they were still alive.

The youths had led her to a room that was decked out like a bedroom. There was a large bed made up with nice furnishings and a dresser where there were hairbrushes, straighteners and various beauty products.

Compared to the dim and dirty cells, this room was palatial. Quadrado had turned to her captors when they'd put her down. None of them had met her eye, but in the better light she'd seen the fresh battle scars on their faces.

The tall one with the cattle prod had been the one to speak. He told her to remove her clothes until she had nothing on but her underwear.

Quadrado had feared she was going to be raped and had refused to undress.

The cattle prodder had stepped forward and sparked his weapon against the outside of her left calf. A second later she was writhing on the floor as she tried to simultaneously scream and not bite her tongue off.

Strong hands had removed her clothes for her as she twitched the last of the shock away. Even as she regained control of her muscles, her first instinct was to cover her chest and groin.

When she was strong enough she had pushed herself across the floor until she was huddled in the corner where the bed met the wall. She'd known that she couldn't shrink away from the men with any level of success, but some things were instinctive and couldn't be rationalized away.

Two of the four had picked up digital cameras and a third a video camera that was attached to a one-legged stand which had half a rubber ball as a base.

The tall one with the cattle prod stepped forward, the prod aiming towards the bare flesh of her lower legs. He'd told her to lie on the bed and put her hands by her sides.

Quadrado hadn't known what was coming next, but she'd already worked out they'd stripped her for a reason. The fact she was to be sold was bad enough, but them taking pictures and videos of her in her underwear had suggested she would be sold as a sex object rather than a human being.

Rather than wait for another jab from the cattle prod, Quadrado had clambered to her feet, doing her best to cover herself as she did so. When she was about to climb onto the bed she'd sprang into a sudden movement, catapulting herself across the bed until she was at the dresser.

Quadrado's next move was to grab the largest bottle of perfume she could see and bash it against the side of her nose. She'd heard the cartilage crumple as her nose broke and she had managed to split one eyebrow before the cattle prod did its thing on the back of her right calf.

She'd fallen to the ground and had been left to writhe and twitch until she was showing signs of recovery. Three more times the cattle prod had kissed her calves until she was left without the energy to offer further resistance.

They'd lifted her onto the bed and positioned her as the tall one had instructed. They'd taken various photos and videos as

Quadrado had fought her immobility and tears of frustration with equal strength.

When the ordeal was over, she'd been carried back here and dumped in her underwear, with her pants and the torn remnants of her blouse tossed in after her.

She'd gotten her answer, but it had cost her more than expected and she was sure there was still a debt owed.

Quadrado knew as she tried to rub warmth into her limbs that Fletcher was her only hope of escape. Even so, he'd need hours to get to the next town and summon help. Hours she could tolerate, but worst of all, was the realization that no matter what happened when the FBI were notified of her disappearance, there was no chance of her ever being found unless one of the Blacketts talked.

CHAPTER FIFTY-SEVEN

Fletcher eased his battered and bruised body into a slow jog. After the heat of the kiln, the night air was cool enough to raise gooseflesh on his arms, but since nearly being cooked to death, he wasn't about to start complaining about the cold.

The one tiny benefit of his experience in the kiln was the heat had eased his muscles a little after the beating he'd taken.

There was also the ripple effect of the Blacketts thinking him dead to consider. Unless he wasn't the first person they'd locked in the kiln, there was no way that they could know how long it'd take him to die. His best guess was that they'd check in the early hours of the morning.

That gave him a few hours leeway to meet with Quadrado, and for her to whistle up a SWAT team before the Blacketts had time to learn of his escape and prepare their defenses by destroying any evidence which may incriminate them.

To keep himself out of sight and maintain the illusion of his death, Fletcher stuck to the woods, although he made sure he kept the tree line in sight. Woods were an easy place to get lost at the best of times if you were unfamiliar with them, and Fletcher had left his backpack, all his weapons and the GPS stashed near the sign where he was due to meet Quadrado.

On and on he jogged, the initial rasping breaths giving way to quietly taken lungfuls of the sweetest oxygen he'd ever tasted. Now that he was into his stride and his breathing was normal, he could focus on what his conversation with Quadrado might entail.

If she'd managed to speak to Elena, Quadrado would be sure to share his thoughts on the Blacketts and would be only too keen to call in a SWAT team. Perhaps learning of how they'd left him in the kiln would be enough to convince her to take action. He got why she didn't want to make the request until she had the evidence to back up her claims. In any hierarchal organization, there were people who strived to reach the top and those who were happy to cling on to whatever plateau they'd reached. He figured Quadrado was on an upward trajectory, but the fact she'd been sent alone to look into the missing women was never far from the back of his mind. Perhaps her partner was on vacation, or tied up giving evidence in a courtroom somewhere. It could be that her boss was a fool and had only sent one agent to look into the missing women because they didn't believe that anything untoward was happening.

All of the people above Quadrado would assess her request for a SWAT team with two questions in the back of their minds. Can I defend my decision if the shit hits the fan? And, who can I blame if it all goes wrong?

His biggest fears were Quadrado wouldn't have the courage of her convictions to make the request and the person who received it wouldn't action it.

As he skirted past the woods at the edge of Daversville, Fletcher cast looks into the town. He was looking for signs of the Blackett family. For all he knew they were still in the town rallying the locals to some task that would cover their tracks, or they could be searching for Quadrado. None of the things he was imagining were evident in the deserted streets. There were no people gathering with flaming torches, nor were there pickup truck beds of men scouring the streets.

All the same, Fletcher knew it would only be a matter of time before his escape from the kiln was discovered. When that happened, the search parties would come out in force. There was little doubt in his mind that when that happened, he'd need to have gotten away from Daversville, with Quadrado too. He was trained in concealment and had undergone enough missions to have used the skill in life-or-death situations. As good an FBI agent as Quadrado might be, she wouldn't be trained in camouflage and the art of staying still for hours.

There were also dogs to consider. Fletcher knew for a fact the Blacketts had three of their own and he'd be amazed if there weren't also huntsmen in Daversville.

With nothing worth observing in the town, Fletcher picked up his pace again and made for the rendezvous point.

A quarter mile out of town he saw the back of the sign for Duke's. Once he drew level with it, he edged into the woods until he could only just see the road. From there it took him a mere few seconds to spot the tree that was the meeting point.

The tree was a mighty American oak that was out of place in all the pines. It was far larger in girth than any of the pines, and although they were the same height, the oak would be many years older than the trees surrounding it.

Fletcher had stuck his knife into the oak's side and hung one of his backpack's straps over the knife.

There was no sign of Quadrado, but they'd agreed upon 2:00 a.m. as a deadline, so Fletcher retrieved his weapons from the backpack, sat down to wait and peeled himself an orange. He'd drunk a few cupped handfuls of water from a stream on his way from the lumber mill, but he was still parched and the moisture content of the orange, along with its vitamin C and its natural sugars, would give him a much-needed boost.

As he ate, he listened for movement from Quadrado and kept his eyes open for pinpricks of light from the flashlight he'd left with her. He'd wanted to leave his GPS with her, but had needed it to get back himself, plus the plan was for Quadrado to make her way back by following the path of the road.

The longer Fletcher waited, the more he was thinking about what Quadrado may or may not have found at the Blackett house. The fact she hadn't yet returned had Fletcher oscillating between hope at what she'd found and fear at the thought she'd gotten herself into trouble. Before leaving her in the vantage point, he'd impressed on her the need to keep her wits about her and how important it was that she wasn't ambushed for a second time.

At ten past two, Fletcher rose to his feet. Quadrado was late, which meant that it was time for plan B.

Quadrado had been insistent that if she didn't return at the allotted time he was to take her car and drive to the next town and raise the alarm. He'd agreed with the instruction to her face despite never having any intention of doing what she said. By the time he'd gotten to the next town, convinced a cop or deputy of the urgency of the situation and they'd mustered a posse, the Blacketts would have had more than enough time to do whatever they needed to do to cover their tracks and disappear Quadrado.

Fletcher had been trained by the British Army and there was no way he was going to leave a soldier in the field.

With the backpack on and a gun in his hand, Fletcher set off towards the Blacketts' house. Part of him wanted to go direct as it was the quickest route, yet the less impulsive part of his psyche had him following the path Quadrado would have returned by in case she'd been held up. It would add a half hour to his journey time, but it would also allow him to find her if she was still navigating her way to the rendezvous point.

CHAPTER FIFTY-EIGHT

Fletcher eased himself into a crouch and surveyed the Blackett house through the trees. Dawn's first rays of light were casting enough of a glow for Fletcher to see the house in all its prison-esque glory.

The rooms on the second floor had their drapes pulled open and he could see the silhouettes of bodies moving around. The upstairs floor still had all their drapes closed. This was no surprise as that was the floor where he remembered from his recon of the house the younger members of the family seemed to live and there was the fact that older people generally needed less sleep than young ones.

A look to the gardens told Fletcher the dogs weren't visible in any area, which meant one of two things. Either the dogs were suffering from a second dose of the tranquilizers, or the Blacketts had discovered them knocked out and had moved them inside and were relying on electronic methods of defense.

As he'd jogged up here, his mind had been working as fast as his legs. Before he tried to access the house, a task that was already hard enough without a well-equipped platoon to aid him, uppermost in his mind was the need to look for Quadrado and determine if she was safe.

His primary port of call was the vantage point where he'd left Quadrado. It was two hundred yards from where he'd set himself the previous day and he moved in full stealth mode as he made his way there. Every sense he possessed was alert to threat, yet other than a raccoon scampering off when it smelled him coming, there was no sign of anyone.

When he got there, the first thing he did was check Quadrado's hiding spot in the bush. It was devoid of blood and there was none of the broken branches indicative of a fight. Most telling of all was the shotgun that was stashed under the bush. It was the one they'd taken from the guard called Hank. The plan had been for Quadrado to leave it here and then return for it on her way to meet with Fletcher.

The shotgun's presence gave two pieces of intel to Fletcher. First, the fact it was still there confirmed that Quadrado had left the bush of her own volition, as if she'd been spotted and moved out at gunpoint, whomever had taken her would have picked up the shotgun. It also told Fletcher that Quadrado hadn't been able to return here; therefore she'd had a chance to visit the house and the reason for her lack of return lay within the house's walls.

With this intelligence fueling nightmarish outcomes for Quadrado in his brain, Fletcher wasted no time in getting himself to the point where they'd left the hapless Hank.

As Fletcher approached the area where Hank was bound to the tree he could tell something was badly wrong. A pair of raccoons were snarling and hissing at each other by the man's feet. Fletcher gave up stealth and hurled a stick in the direction of the raccoons; he wasn't trying to hit them, just scare them away. Both raccoons sent a series of snarls his way, but they retreated as he stepped forward.

Hank was right where they'd left him. He'd be going nowhere. His neck and chest was a mess of blood and his eyes would never again open. As much as there were toothmarks from where the raccoons had been feasting, there was an unmistakable slash across the man's throat. Like Mary-Lou Henderson, his throat had been slit wide.

The most terrible thing about Hank's murder was the callousness with which it must have been inflicted. Hank was a member of the Blackett family, trusted enough to have been given the task of lookout. To Fletcher's mind there were only two suspects for the homicide: the Blackett family and Trench.

No matter which way up he stood things, he couldn't see what Trench had to gain by killing Hank. If he was taking a swipe at family members, he was starting at the bottom of the pyramid rather than the top.

Another factor which went against Trench as a suspect was the clean way he'd taken out the deer. That kill had seen him down an animal which was failing and was likely to die of natural causes soon; to assume he'd kill a bound and helpless human, even if they were a Blackett, was a leap. It was also the wrong thing to do if he was looking to engage the Blacketts. With Trench's stalking skills, he'd be able to get himself within range of the Blacketts with ease and then it would be a case of him loosing some of his arrows their way. Fletcher had already seen the old man's accuracy and he was sure Trench could take down any target he wanted to.

However much Fletcher didn't like his line of thinking about Trench's possible guilt for Hank's death, he liked the other options less. If he was right about Trench, the Blacketts were the frontrunners for the homicide. This in turn meant they had turned on one of their own without mercy. Fletcher knew from bitter experience what it was like to take the life of another human being. He'd not racked up as many kills as some of his comrades, but he'd taken lives both at a distance and in close quarters.

As much as he could understand the brutal killing of Mary-Lou Henderson being used as a warning for the other townsfolk, Hank's death served no purpose other than the punishment of failure. In a lot of ways the move would be counterproductive as, if more than one member of the family had been involved, word would spread, and rather than pulling together as a family, the Blacketts would begin to become uneasy around each other as they all started to suspect their relatives of plotting to draw a knife across their throats. Following this logic gave Fletcher the confidence to assume that either Chuck or Jimmy had acted alone. Hank may well turn out to be the son of the other brother, yet Fletcher was sure the blame for Hank's death would be laid at either his or Quadrado's feet. That Hank's throat had been cut rather than him being shot was another way to muddy the timeline's waters. A slash to the throat was a silent kill whereas gunshots could be heard from a distance. Therefore no one except Hank's killer would know when he'd actually died.

The final reason for Hank's death was one Fletcher hated to think about, but there was no escaping the thought. It was him who'd made Hank bleed. Him who tied the man up and left him alone in the woods. He'd been the one who argued with Quadrado that leading Hank back to Daversville would be a long slow process that could see them ambushed by the Blacketts. Whichever way Fletcher looked at it, he'd been the one to spill Hank's blood and leave him in the wilds like a ready meal. It was entirely possible that Trench or a Blackett had discovered Hank having his throat and face feasted upon by raccoons and had drawn their knife to put an end to Hank's agony.

The only counterpoint to this was that if a Blackett had committed the act of mercy, they would have removed Hank's body and returned it to the house. For all Fletcher had fought with them and bested all the men save Jimmy and Chuck, he'd not done any of them enough harm to prevent them from retrieving Hank.

Even with this line of logic salving his guilt, Fletcher knew that whichever way anyone looked at it, he would always feel partly responsible for Hank's demise.

When he set off for the Blackett house, the raccoons moved back towards their feast. Fletcher paid no attention to them. He had Quadrado to rescue, as well as Lila, and Mary-Lou, Deputy White and Hank to avenge. He'd never been one to believe in death or glory, yet he knew that until he'd dealt with the Blacketts, rescued Quadrado and found out what had happened to Lila, he'd do whatever needed to be done.

CHAPTER FIFTY-NINE

Fletcher checked both his pistols and the shotgun before scaling the gates of the Blackett house. He only had a single extra magazine for one of the pistols, yet that didn't worry him. He was confident he'd either be able to scavenge more from dropped weapons or he'd run out of enemies.

For all he was carrying two pistols, a shotgun and a hunting knife as well as a murderous rage in his heart, Fletcher had no intention to kill unless it was necessary. As the law stood, he was in the wrong by being on the Blacketts' land, and the fact he carried so many weapons would enable a first-year law student to get the Blacketts acquitted for shooting him. All the same, he wasn't going to use deadly force unless his hand was forced.

As soon as his feet touched the gravel of the drive, Fletcher pulled the shotgun from his shoulder and aimed it towards the house. Rather than go for subtlety and try to sneak past the various defenses, his plan was to engage the Blacketts with a direct assault.

Upon seeing no one, Fletcher changed his plan as he crossed to the nearest corner of the house. By standing a foot from the corner and looking along both walls Fletcher could observe two separate routes of attack for the Blacketts while keeping himself hidden from anyone inside the house. It was possible a security camera was detailing his position, but unless he'd missed someone leaving the house, he was confident that anyone who might offer a threat would come from either his left or right flank.

Fletcher waited at the corner for ten minutes. Nothing happened. There was no movement at either flank. He'd seen shadows moving across the windows of the rooms occupied by the older Blacketts, so he knew that they were up. They didn't show though. Nobody came.

In his head, Fletcher counted out the timeline from the point his crossing the gate would have triggered the alarms.

Minute one would have seen the Blacketts check monitors covering any CCTV feeds they had. He hadn't seen any obvious cameras, but that didn't mean there weren't hidden ones he'd missed. Minutes two and three would be spent grabbing weapons ready to defend their position, and dispatching someone upstairs to rouse or muster the other family members. Four to seven would see the Blacketts either fortify their position ready for an assault or come bursting out of the house with weapons in hand. With nobody having exited the house and him not having made their assault, Fletcher reasoned that calmer heads had taken over and minutes eight to ten would be spent wondering why the expected assault hadn't arrived. The Blacketts would then regain their confidence. The arrogance with which they lived their lives would return around minute fourteen or fifteen. After that, they'd decide the threat was manageable and they'd move to strike back. As always with them, it would be the younger members of the family who'd come first. As Hank had proven, they were the most disposable.

Rather than drop his eyes to his watch, Fletcher raised his arm so he could see the dial. Twelve minutes had passed since he'd started climbing the gate.

It was probable his timeline was out by as much as two or three minutes and he was aware there was a door at the rear of the house he couldn't observe, so it was possible the Blacketts had snuck out the back door and were approaching him unseen along the two walls he couldn't monitor. Their plan would be to burst round both corners at once and destroy him with crossfire. That was how he'd do things in their position.

Minute fifteen came and went, as did sixteen, seventeen and eighteen. When twenty came around, Fletcher made a decision, abandoned his position and moved along the wall to his left.

His thinking was simple, if the Blacketts tried the crossfire tactic, he'd be ready to deal with only one group of them rather than getting caught in the crossfire. A side bonus was that by shortening the distance, he was making the shotgun more effective.

Fletcher moved quickly, his eyes fixed on the corner. If anyone burst round the corner, their body would be two to three feet from the corner, their aim concentrated on the point where Fletcher had been standing. They'd take a moment or two to adjust their aim. Fletcher wouldn't need those moments; he'd be able to drop them where they stood.

The problem with rounding a corner as an assault force is that the first guy will always end up in the way of those who follow him. Either the first guy has to go wide or the guys following him do. The first guy sees threats before his buddies, which means the buddies have to also react to the first guy's reaction. All of these calculations were built into Fletcher's brain as he approached the corner.

His own shotgun was aimed low as he planned to shoot the legs out from under his opponents. Although he was looking to deliver non-fatal gunshots, he was sure the Blacketts would have a different idea. Whether they'd yet learned about him having escaped the kiln or not, they were out to kill him and as such their guns would be aimed at his center mass. Four foot was the usual point. Shots fired from hip or shoulder height only needed a little readjustment up or down and they'd strike the target. Center mass was the sensible point to aim for. It was only in the movies that shots nicked an ear on purpose; in real life, it was all about percentages: when your life was on the line, you went with the highest percentage you could.

While not playing for the highest percentage himself, Fletcher was confident the spread of the shotgun would level the odds for him.

Fletcher stopped a foot from the corner. If he was the one to round the corner first, he'd be the one at the disadvantage, but this was something he'd known from the moment he'd left his original spot at the other corner. His goal in moving was to take the fight to the Blacketts rather than have them surround and decimate him.

Where he was along one wall meant he could soon have enemies both in front of and in behind him. Again, this was something he'd known and planned for.

To remove himself from the area where any Blackett guns may be aimed, Fletcher dropped to his knees, darted his head past the corner and pulled it back again a fraction of a second after his eyes had grabbed a snapshot of the area.

It was devoid of human life, so Fletcher ducked round the corner and contemplated his next move. He now had to choose between two courses of action: he could try storming the house or he could cross to the garage and wait to ambush the Blacketts in a way that'd give him the advantage he'd lack by storming the house. If the Blacketts were holed up waiting for him, as seemed likely given the lack of threat he'd experienced since crossing the gates, they'd pick him off before he got a door open enough to pass through.

As much as Fletcher's heart wanted to engage in battle with the Blacketts as soon as possible, his head knew it would be a mistake, so he crossed the ten yards to the garage in a full-on sprint.

Once in the garage he ducked behind a pickup and assessed the possible hiding places. The garage wasn't a normal one filled with household overflow. There was a ride-on mower and a few spades, shovels and brushes in one corner, but for the most part the garage was equipped as an auto-repair shop. There were cabinets of Snap-on tools, jacks, grinders and the kind of portable hoist that could be used to lift an engine from a vehicle. Beneath the Mercedes, there was a row of timbers three feet long resting flush with the concrete of the garage floor. Fletcher had seen the same thing in many auto-repair shops and figured it was an inspection pit for looking at and working on the underside of vehicles.

As a hiding place it was out of the question. While it'd make a great place to hide, it would be a terrible place to launch an attack from. He could easily lift a couple of the timbers that were behind the Mercedes and drop into the inspection pit, but he'd never be able to get back out without putting himself at great risk of discovery.

At the far side of the garage, behind an unopened door, a pair of dirt bikes and an ATV quad were parked. Because neither of the trials bikes would have anywhere for Quadrado to sit when he found her, Fletcher put the keys for both of them in his pocket. She'd have to ride her own if that was how they escaped. His next move was to steal the key from the quad's ignition and toss it under one of the workbenches to prevent any of the Blacketts pursuing him should he need to make a rapid escape through the woods.

With all his preparation done, Fletcher climbed onto the workbench and up into the rafters of the garage's roof. Sheets of floor boarding had been used to create a storage area which held a number of paint cans and other oddments, but there was plenty of room for Fletcher to stash himself away until he could ambush the Blacketts. Sooner or later they'd hear about his escape from the kiln. They would want to investigate. At the very least Chuck or Jimmy would want to take a look at the damage he'd done to the kiln's door.

It didn't matter to Fletcher which one of the brothers he ambushed, just so long as it was one them. Hank's fate had outlined the disposability of the younger Blacketts. With one of the brothers at his mercy, he'd be in a much better position to learn what he needed to and, should he need a hostage, he could at least feel confident the hostage wouldn't be sacrificed.

Fletcher heard the slamming of a door and hunkered down out of sight ready to spring his ambush.

CHAPTER SIXTY

Fletcher could feel the desire to lay his head on the boards beneath him and grab some sleep growing with every passing minute. As a soldier he'd long ago learned to eat and sleep whenever he got the chance, but after four hours sleep in the last sixty, he was running on his last reserves.

To combat the encroaching stiffness he felt, Fletcher had taken care to make slow movements to keep himself supple. To stay alert he ran song lyrics through his head.

Just when he was beginning to think the Blacketts weren't coming he heard voices. Low at first but getting louder as the family came to towards their vehicles. The primary voices he could hear were those of the younger members of the family. He recognized Tall Boy and Cocky's voices first. Rather than being wary, they were chattering away as if unconcerned.

Fletcher's first thought was that it was a ruse to lure him into a mistake, but a harsh comment from one of the older men soon knocked the early-morning exuberance from the younger Blacketts.

The next sentence he heard was one which gave Fletcher hope his plan would work.

"You three go take some more pictures of that spic bitch. If she don't play ball, give her a little dip in the well insteada using that prod. Told you before it makes 'em shake too much. The pictures you got last night ain't no use to nobody. An' when you's at it, make sure and clean the damn blood off'n her face before you start snappin'. When you done that, feed the others."

Three young Blacketts came into view, followed by Chuck. As much as Fletcher wanted to spring his ambush, the four men were spread out and Chuck wasn't near enough to capture and use as a hostage. Plus, if what he'd observed about their garage habits was routine, Jimmy and Miss Constance would be sure to be outside waiting for Chuck to bring the Mercedes to them, as it was an old woman's voice he'd heard giving the young Blacketts their orders.

Sure enough, Chuck climbed into the Mercedes and drove it out the garage only to stop it a few yards out. Two car doors thunked closed and Fletcher heard the scrunch of tires on gravel as the Mercedes pulled away.

Fletcher watched the three young members of the Blackett family. He expected to see them clamber into a pickup, but they just looked at each other until Muscles gave a sigh and started lifting the timbers covering what Fletcher had presumed was an inspection pit.

One by one he set them aside until there were eight of the twelve by four timbers lying on the concrete beside the pit. Tall Boy chided Muscles and got nothing but a dirty look for his comments.

The removal of the timbers allowed Fletcher to see there was a set of concrete steps leading down into the pit. That was standard for such things, yet had Fletcher not heard the instruction from Miss Constance he might not have thought too much about it. The clincher that there was something down there was the way Muscles had left the timbers beside the pit. If they were going to use it as an inspection pit, the timbers would have been placed well out of the way so a vehicle could drive over the opening.

Muscles went down the steps first and, after another word from Tall Boy, he removed two more timbers before disappearing out of sight. Cocky went next with Tall Boy bringing up the rear.

All of this gave Fletcher a bunch of information. Quadrado was down there. But so were others. This gave him a glimmer of hope Lila would still be alive. Who the others were Miss Constance had mentioned was a mystery, but he guessed they'd be the most recent people to have gone missing. He also noted that far from being unaware of what her family were up to, Miss Constance was in charge of the operation.

Once again Fletcher had a decision to make. Should he go after the boys and effect a rescue, or now that he knew where the Blacketts were stashing people, make his own escape and bring help so things could be done legally and aboveboard? With the two main threats away with Miss Constance, he'd never get a better opportunity to rescue the hostages.

He deliberated for the best part of a minute before coming to the conclusion Chuck's instruction for the boys to use the well didn't bode well for Quadrado. Whether they planned to frighten her into compliance or full-on drown her was immaterial, there was no telling what may go wrong if he allowed them to try and frighten her. She was already injured; the comments about the blood on her face had told him that.

Fletcher clambered down using a series of slow, soundless movements and hung from a rafter until his feet were only four feet above the ground before dropping to the floor, his boots making no more sound than a tiny slap.

Foot by foot, he crossed to the pit, his eyes flicking between the driveway and the pit itself in case anyone appeared. Seeing nobody in the grounds or on the drive, Fletcher gave the pit his full attention.

The interior of the pit came into view over the sights of the shotgun. It was empty. Just a series of steps leading down to a chamber. Although the pit was gloomy, Fletcher could see enough to make out a doorway at the far end.

Fletcher entered the pit and approached the door with a series of noiseless steps. The door was metal and had three solid steel bolts to keep it fastened. The foul smell of raw sewage emanated from the doorway.

A metal handle protruded from the door. Before he took a grip of it, Fletcher swapped the shotgun for a pistol. Because the door opened towards him, a pistol would be a far easier weapon to control with one hand.

At times like this, hesitation was the enemy of success, so Fletcher whipped the door open and entered the next room, with first his eyes and then a millisecond later his pistol scanning every part of the room.

CHAPTER SIXTY-ONE

The room was empty on account of it being nothing more than a corridor. Its walls were aged concrete which had the first signs of crumble about it. The corridor was lit by a pair of bulbs that hung from twisted wires.

Nothing about the corridor suggested care or luxury. The space was sparse and functional rather than homely. Ahead of him there were two doors on either side of the walls.

Dust rose from the floor as Fletcher made his way along the corridor. All four of the doors were closed which meant that he couldn't gauge where the Blackett youths might be.

Foot by foot he closed the gap until he was at the first pair of doors. Rather than take any chances, Fletcher stooped down and checked the dusty floor. Scuffed boot prints were in front of the door on the left, but not the one on the right. There were also boot prints traveling further along the corridor, but there was no way Fletcher was progressing forward until he knew that there would be nobody who could ambush him from behind.

The door on the left swung open with only the slightest hint of a squeal. Over the sights of his pistol, Fletcher surveyed the room. It was kitted out to resemble a posh bedroom on one side. The other held various different recording devices, a collection of sex toys including restraints and what Fletcher guessed was a bondage chair.

It took Fletcher less than two seconds to scan the room and take all this in. What mattered more than the contents of the room was the absence of Blacketts and FBI agents.

Fletcher eased himself out of the room and checked the door on the other side of the corridor. It was locked and fit so snug in its frame there wasn't the slightest movement when he tried the handle.

Step by step he followed the footsteps in the dust until he came to the next pair of doors. Another examination showed him that someone had entered both doors.

Since left had been a bust last time, he tried the door on the right first. Like the other door on its side of the corridor, it didn't open. It was just there, all solid oak and no give.

Fletcher grasped the handle of the left door and prepared himself for what he might find as the fingers of his other hand gripped the pistol.

This door opened. It swung back its hinges as Fletcher was still going with shock-and-awe tactics and was bursting into the room, his eyes following the sights of his pistol. Unlike the door of the first room he'd entered, this one didn't open with the merest of noises. It creaked, groaned and protested every one of the ninety degrees Fletcher pushed it through.

The noise of the door made four pairs of eyes turn its way, as natural instinct took over and the three Blacketts and Quadrado looked to see what had caused the sudden noise.

What Fletcher saw wasn't good. Quadrado was tied up and she was standing beside a pit in the floor that he could only assume was the well Miss Constance had mentioned earlier. A rope was strung through a hoop fixed into the ceiling above the well, and it was tied off on the ropes which bound Quadrado's wrists together.

Muscles held the other end of the rope.

At first none of the Blacketts moved. Each was frozen in surprise at Fletcher's sudden entrance.

Fletcher acted before anyone else did.

"Don't move." He aimed the gun at the two men on his left: Cocky and Tall Boy.

True to his instruction, they didn't move.

Muscles did, though. Or rather, he fell to the floor. It would have been comical to see a man with his build take the tumble had he not retained his grip on the rope attached to Quadrado.

His superior weight and strength were enough to haul the FBI agent off her feet until she swung out above the hole in the floor. Quadrado's legs kicked and she writhed her body, but all she achieved was a spinning motion to add to the pendulum sway that Muscles's sudden haul on the rope had created.

Fletcher's pistol snapped onto Muscles, the sights lined up center mass. He didn't pull the trigger. Couldn't fire off the round that would end Muscles's life. Not when he was holding the rope by which Quadrado hung.

Muscles knew it too. "You shoot me, she drops. Lotta deep water and rats down there."

Quadrado screamed, the sound loud and shrill in the confined space. Fletcher didn't let himself be distracted and kept both his focus and aim on Muscles. From the corner of his eye he could see Tall Boy getting ready to rush him.

"Don't even think about it." Fletcher lowered his aim, so his pistol was pointing at Muscles's crotch. "I can still shoot without killing him."

Muscles released his grip on the rope for a fraction of a second and then clamped his fingers closed again. Quadrado dropped a foot, her terrified scream replaced with a pained yelp when the rope jerked taught and pulled at her shoulders.

If there was one thing Fletcher hated it was these kinds of standoffs. He daren't act against Muscles as Quadrado would be dropped into the hole. Likewise, Muscles wouldn't dare let Quadrado go as Fletcher had the superior weapon.

Fletcher considered taking the shot. He could put a bullet into each of the three Blacketts in as many seconds and then he'd be able to grab the rope to haul Quadrado up. She'd be gasping and choking, yet he reckoned he could have her head out of the water no more than ten seconds after she was dropped. The problem with that idea was that while Muscles had intimated there was deep water below, Fletcher didn't know how far the drop was. A glance at the end of the rope showed there was plenty of length beyond where Muscles had taken a hold of it. If Quadrado fell badly, she could receive a serious injury. Plus, for all Muscles had suggested there was deep water in the hole, it could have been a bluff.

It wasn't a chance he was willing to take.

As Fletcher stepped forward intent on keeping Muscles still until he could get one of his own hands onto the rope, he felt a thudding blow on the side of his ear.

He turned to face the threat and saw Tall Boy charging his way. Behind Tall Boy, Cocky stood, his right arm still extended from a throwing action. Fletcher heard the clatter of metal hitting the ground at the same moment Tall Boy's shoulder collided with his ribs.

As he was driven backwards, Fletcher was working out Cocky must have misjudged the throw and hit his ear with the knife's handle rather than the blade. The realization fueled his next action. The Blackett boys were playing for the highest stakes and that was fine by him.

Instead of resisting Tall Boy's charge, he went with it and let Tall Boy drive him against the far wall. The pistol had flown from his grasp at the first contact, yet Fletcher wasn't too worried. He'd beaten these boys once in hand-to-hand combat, a second time wouldn't be too hard.

Rather than allow Tall Boy to gain a position of superiority over him, Fletcher planted a foot against the wall and used it to propel himself across the room, dragging Tall Boy with him in a headlock. Upon nearing the hole, Fletcher released Tall Boy and gave him a shove to propel him to the yawning blackness in the floor.

Tall Boy tried to sidestep the hole and failed. As he fell forward his hands grasped at the rim of the hole, but they didn't find enough purchase to support him.

Fletcher heard a splash as he rounded on Cocky. The lad was backing away, but he'd picked up his knife and was flashing it in front of him to deter Fletcher's advance. Fletcher was aware of Muscles scrabbling to get up. Before he could worry about Muscles, he had to deal with Cocky.

Muscles was shouting and swearing, urging Cocky to kill Fletcher. Fletcher paid the exhortations no heed as he focused on disarming Cocky.

He feinted a grab. Cocky slashed the knife from right to left.

Fletcher danced back, the knife not getting within a foot of his body.

In that one movement, Fletcher was able to assess just how poor a knifeman Cocky was. Instead of making an attempt to cut Fletcher, Cocky had put all his strength into the swing and exposed his flank to Fletcher when his body twisted after not hitting his target and being slowed by its resistance.

Fletcher grabbed Cocky by the wrist of his knife-wielding arm, twisted the wrist outwards until the arm was extended in an armbar and drove his elbow down onto Cocky's.

Fletcher's elbow survived the impact. Cocky's didn't fare so well. So far as Fletcher was concerned the pain would be a vital lesson to Cocky. Fletcher shoved him away and prepared to face Muscles. In a flash he saw that rather than drop Quadrado on top of Tall Boy, Muscles had tied off the rope on a cleat and was now reaching for the pistol Fletcher had dropped earlier. Quadrado was still hanging, the lower half of her body out of sight in the hole.

Muscles's hand was an inch from the pistol meaning there was no time for Fletcher to retrieve another gun and bring it to bear before Muscles could take aim. Instead he flung himself forward, his boot lashing out and connecting with Muscles's meaty forearm.

The pistol clattered from Muscles's hand as Fletcher threw punch after punch at the younger, stronger man. Each punch sapped Muscles's strength a little, but this was a fight for life, and he reared upwards, his bloody face butting forward as he tried to circle his arms around Fletcher.

To counter the headbutt, Fletcher dropped his own chin onto his chest and let Muscles's blow miss its intended target. Because he'd expected the numbing clash of heads, Fletcher was the quickest to recover. He rammed a hard gut punch just under Muscles's ribs and grabbed the man's head between both his hands.

One twist would break his neck and Fletcher's hands were placed in the exact positions to exert the necessary force.

Fletcher tensed ready to deliver the coup de grace, then his arms went loose and refused to work.

In an abstract way, Fletcher felt Muscles's blows slamming into his body. He didn't react. Didn't try to counter them.

Not a week went past without him waking up covered in sweat after reliving the nightmarish events that had last caused him to break a neck.

But that time it had been a neck he'd snuggled against. Kissed tenderly when making love. That neck had belonged to the love of his life. To Rachel. Wendy's mother.

His wife. Whose head he had caressed, right before breaking her neck.

CHAPTER SIXTY-TWO

Consciousness returned to Fletcher in a series of slow and gradual steps. Piece by piece his brain patched together the necessary connections between what had happened and how he felt. Compared to now, his awakening in the kiln had been a cakewalk.

There wasn't a part of his body that didn't ache, sting or throb, yet it was his conscience that hurt the most. He'd failed Quadrado and all the other victims. Had he been able to defeat the Blackett boys, he'd have had a chance to save lives. Once he'd frozen, that opportunity had been denied him, and their fate had been sealed. As always when coming to, he reached for the locket at his throat. It was missing, which meant he'd also failed his own girls.

More than anything, he was surprised to still be alive. Cocky had twice tried to use a knife on him before he'd snapped his elbow, and he'd dumped Tall Boy down the hole. It stood to reason that one of them would have slit his throat or rammed a knife under his ribs. He'd made his murder easier for them by bringing a pair of pistols and a shotgun into the room. While the Blacketts hadn't killed him, they'd made damn sure that he got his ass well and truly handed to him. Muscles had aimed more than one fierce kick at his groin in revenge for what Fletcher had done to him in town.

The fact he'd been allowed to live was puzzling him, and while he was certain the Blacketts would kill him soon, he was more afraid of the method than the end result.

Fletcher had to raise a hand and rub the dried blood from his eyes before he could open them. Each movement ignited a new source of agony that had to be endured. Fletcher bore the agonies with bad grace as he mentally cursed every member of the Blackett family, wishing plagues and diseases upon them, yet he never let a single moan or curse escape his lips.

"Fletcher. Can you hear me? Are you okay?"

It was Quadrado's voice. She sounded far away and distorted as if she was speaking through an echo chamber.

Fletcher curled his hand into a fist and gave Quadrado a thumbs up and then tilted his fist sideways and gave it a little waggle. The pains around his body were so many and so intense he didn't know if he was okay or not. This wasn't a situation he was happy with. The Blacketts would soon be coming for him and he was damned if he was going to make anything easy for them.

For all his bravado, he knew he'd have to assess his battered body and work out if he had any broken bones. Inch by painful inch, he straightened his limbs then drew them back into his body. All four protested at the movement but they each complied with his desire for assessment. They hurt like hell, but they were mobile, and the pain was bearable. Next he pressed his hands against his chest and explored his ribs. They were tender to the touch and there were at least three of them he was sure were cracked. That didn't matter, cracked ribs might hurt, but so long as you could fight past the pain, they didn't slow you down.

Fletcher's next check wasn't one he was looking forward to. It took him a full minute to rise to his feet, but he made it. Step by tentative step, Fletcher moved himself around the small tight cell where he'd been dumped. It was a trip of purgatorial masochism, yet it was necessary. Not only was Fletcher assessing his own mobility, he was checking out the place where he'd been left after his beating.

Instead of the room with the hole in the floor, he'd been moved to another room. His pupils peered through the mailbox slots his eyes had become and picked out the different cells that the room held. There were people in most of the other cells and he was able to recognize Quadrado was in the one adjacent to his.

The young woman in the furthest cell caught his attention. "Lila. Are you okay?"

Her voice was groggy, but he knew it was her. "Uncle Grant? Is that you?"

"Yeah. It's me." He wanted to tell her that he would save her. That he'd get her back to her father. He couldn't say the words because at this moment in time he didn't believe them.

He took hold of one of the steel squares dividing the room and shook it. The timber framing held it firm. He tried again, putting more force into his efforts. All that happened was that his body moved rather than the steel grid. Fletcher had seen this type of mesh before; it was a standard mesh that was used to reinforce concrete slabs and flooring. The bars might only be a half inch thick, but they formed eight-inch squares that possessed a far greater collective strength than any individual bar might have had.

Fletcher moved round the cell's three mesh walls and tried various points to test their strength. None gave as much as a hint of movement. He would have slammed a fist or boot against them such was his frustration, but he had enough presence of mind not to add to his list of injuries. Instead of raging at what he couldn't change, he slumped against the back wall of the cell and turned his head towards Quadrado.

The FBI agent looked fraught. Her hair was bedraggled, her nose swollen and bulbous, yet it was the look in her eyes which bothered him the most. Unlike the defeat on her face, Quadrado's eyes held nothing but pity.

"That was some beating you took. I'm amazed you survived it."

Fletcher pulled his mouth into a semblance of a smile as his tongue wobbled a loosened tooth. "Doesn't feel like I did."

"You did, though." A gesture at their cells. "Any ideas on how to get out of here?"

"None at the moment, but I'm not done thinking."

Quadrado's face softened. "What happened to you back there? You just froze. You were winning and you just locked up."

This was the question he'd known would come and had been dreading. His freezing would cost him his life, Fletcher could accept that. Wendy was with her grandparents, and while he'd never see her grow into a woman or get to walk her down an aisle, he knew she'd be cared for and looked after. It wouldn't be good for her to lose her father as well as her mother, yet she was a good kid and Rachel's parents weren't the kind of people who'd fail her. The one positive of his death would be that the payout from his life insurance would mean she'd be able to go to an Ivy League university.

Unfortunately, it wasn't just him who'd suffer. Quadrado and the other prisoners wouldn't be rescued by anyone else. They all deserved to know why he'd failed.

Fletcher leaned his head against the wall, closed his eyes and began to confess to an FBI agent how he'd murdered his wife.

CHAPTER SIXTY-THREE

As he spoke everything about Rachel's death came back him with its usual crystalline clarity. Every time he relived the circumstances, he went right back to the moment and experienced everything in real time once more.

*

They are traveling home from Salt Lake City. Rachel driving, him in back keeping Wendy amused. She is in the terrible twos and has become a real daddy's girl, otherwise he'd have been behind the wheel, or at least riding up front.

Rain is lashing everything in sight and Rachel is driving according to the conditions. She's a good driver and Fletcher has no fears.

An SUV overtakes, drenching them in spray and then suddenly swerving back to their side of the road to avoid a truck heading in the opposite direction. Rachel jukes their station wagon towards the shoulder, but not soon enough to avoid the fender being clipped by the tail of the SUV.

Rachel is fighting to control the car. It slips and slides one way then the other as she wrestles with the wheel. The slope they're traveling down combats the braking effect of Rachel's stomp until a wheel digs into the verge and spins the car.

In back Wendy is giggling as the car spins off the road and down an incline. Rachel screams as she fights to bring the car to a halt. Nothing she does is working.

Fletcher is doing all he can to shield Wendy with his body for the impact he knows is coming.

A glance down the slope gives him a snapshot of what's to come. There's a river in flood at the bottom of the incline. Its waters brown and swirling with debris. A series of large trees adorn the banks of the river.

"Hold on."

Rachel's instruction is unnecessary. He's braced to protect Wendy whose giggles are now petrified wails.

Fletcher knows Rachel will be aiming for the trees. Not only will a crash into them be safer than plunging into a raging river, but he knows everything about his wife—that her biggest fear is drowning.

When the impact comes it jars him, pressing his body against the back of the seat in front. He doesn't care about the bruises he'll have, his only concerns are for his wife and daughter. Wendy is bawling her eyes out. Fletcher releases her from the straps holding her in her car seat. He isn't worried about Wendy. Her tears are of shock and terror, yet he's thankful there is no hint of the cry she gives whenever she hurts herself.

Rachel is a different story. Her fearful screams have devolved into low moans. He casts a look at her. Doesn't like what he sees.

The car shifts to the left as its weight fights against the grip the car's twisted fender has on the tree. Fletcher whips the door open, scoops Wendy in his arms, and gets her out of the car.

"You stay here, sweetie. I'm going back for Mommy."

As he repeats the words to Quadrado, Fletcher doesn't stop reliving the moment.

Rachel's door is jammed shut. His attempts to haul it open are a waste of time. He runs round to the passenger side. Wendy looks forlorn as she stands in the rain clutching Mr. Bunny, the soft toy she takes everywhere.

The passenger door opens, but when Fletcher climbs in the car slips another foot towards the river. The vehicle is rotating, slipping past the obstacle formed by the tree. It's at twenty degrees when Fletcher focuses on Rachel. Her face ashen and streaked by tear-ruined make-up.

"Help me, Fletch. I can't move my legs. Can't even feel them."

Fletcher glances down. Sees the way the car's engine has been directed by the tree until it's pinning Rachel. He knows at once that she'll have to be cut out. Either remove the car from around her, or amputate her legs.

The car shifts another few degrees. He knows that when it passes a certain point it won't stop moving until it slips into the raging brown waters.

"Fletch, speak to me. How bad is it?" As always, Rachel can read his face like it's a neon sign.

"Not good. Gotta stop the car from going into the river."

Fletcher darts back out of the car and looks for anything he can use to stop the car from sliding any further. There's nothing. Not a branch, a stone. Nothing.

He glances at the wheel leading the slide. It's six inches from a part of the incline that steepens. This isn't about degrees anymore, it's about inches.

In a desperate attempt to prevent the inevitable, he throws his shoulder against the car and tries to push it back up the slope. Every muscle in his body strains to the point where he thinks something will burst. It doesn't work. Even as he's pushing, the car slides another three inches.

"Fletch. Get your ass in here."

Fletcher obeys his wife and gets back in the car. Her face is resolute.

"I'm not going to make it, am I?"

"Yes, you are. You're gonna make it like no one's ever made it before."

His words sound as hollow today as they had back then.

"Fletch. I'm not. You have to face facts. I am likely paralyzed. I'm also stuck in this car and this car is headed to the bottom of that river in the next few minutes. I don't want to drown, Fletch! That can't... That can't be the way I die. I need you to make it easy for me. I'm begging you—"

"God, Rachel. You're not serious, are you?" He knows in his heart of hearts she's serious, knows she's petrified. He feels the same way about the idea of losing her. He'd swap places with her without a second's hesitation if he could, but that's not an option.

He gets a wan smile. "Deadly. Remember Helmand? The promise we made each other?"

Of course Fletcher remembers Helmand. How they'd promised each other that if either of them ended up in a vegetative state with no hope of recovery, the other would make sure their wishes were carried out and the machines keeping them alive were switched off. It was an abstract idea at the time, and Fletcher had been imbued with the dual invincibility of youth and love when he'd made the promise.

"No."

"Yes. Kiss me, do what you've got to do and then get your ass back to Wendy before this damn car pulls us both into the river."

Fletcher knows she is right. He cradles her head in his hands and delivers a tender kiss onto trembling lips, before putting his lips to her ear. "Wendy and I love you."

Rachel doesn't reply. As soon as he spoke he had twisted her head and snapped her neck, severing her spinal cord and killing her. It wasn't much, but he wanted the last thing she knew to be the love of her daughter and husband.

Had it not been for Wendy standing on the bank, he would never have climbed out of the car. As it was, he had to jump clear of the station wagon as it moved enough to send itself sliding down towards the river.

*

With his story told, Fletcher returned to the present. When he looked up and met Quadrado's eyes he saw that her cheeks were wet. Strange, his own felt that way too. This was the first time he'd told anyone this story, and the first time he'd shed a tear since the day Rachel's body was laid to rest.

Whenever the guilt at what he'd done threatened to overwhelm him, he'd always pressed his thoughts towards his chosen method. By snapping Rachel's neck when delivering a last message, he'd been able to look into her eyes one final time. As brutal as the execution was, he'd given her a quick clean death. She hadn't seen a knife or gun coming her way. Or worse, drowned slowly in an icy river. Her survival instincts hadn't kicked in while he was throttling her. He'd done all he could to save her and failed, so the least he could do was make her passing as peaceful for her as he possibly could.

All these rationalizations made logical sense. If their places were reversed, he'd want her to do the same for him. To hell with logic though, no matter how he tried to soothe his guilty conscience, he'd never forgive himself for killing the woman he loved.

Now she was growing up, Wendy was morphing into a younger version of her mother. It wasn't like the universe was replacing Rachel in his life, more that it was reminding him of what he'd done. He loved Wendy with all of his heart and would lay down his life for her without a second's thought. She was Rachel's legacy and he'd told her everything about her mother. The only thing he'd lied about to his daughter was the crash and how her mother's neck had come to be broken.

That was a conversation which had to be had one day, provided he was still around to tell his daughter the truth.

If he was honest with himself, Fletcher was more scared of that conversation with Wendy than whatever ideas the Blacketts had in store for him.

CHAPTER SIXTY-FOUR

Fletcher's head snapped up when he heard the door to the room opening. The scuff of boots was punctuated by the tapping of a cane on concrete as Miss Constance, Jimmy and Chuck walked along the narrow corridor between the two rows of cells.

Miss Constance rattled her cane round a mesh square as if she was the cook in a sixties western announcing dinnertime.

"You done caused us a lot of trouble, mister." A globule of spittle ran down her chin. "You gonna suffer for it. Suffer real bad until you's begging for death."

Fletcher climbed to his feet. His movements weren't as sprightly as he would have liked, although he was able to mask the pain he was in.

Up close Miss Constance was more formidable than he'd imagined. Until he'd heard her dishing out orders to Tall Boy and the others, he'd pegged her as a kindly old woman subjugated by the behavior of her sons, but now he could take a look at her, he saw the emptiness of her eyes. She wasn't in thrall to her sons; she was at least an equal partner in their crimes.

Miss Constance was of middling height; her body was broad and stout. For all she was a wealthy woman, she'd had no obvious cosmetic surgery. Her face was a railroad junction of lines and her chin bore two white-hair-sprouting moles. If a smile had kissed her face she might have been called wizened. To Fletcher's mind hewn was a better word.

"Ain't you got nuthin to say, mister?" Miss Constance's mouth pulled back into her right cheek as she spoke. "Thought you woulda been all smartass."

Fletcher kept his mouth shut. Instead of making one of the many wiseass remarks he could have, he was waiting to see if the Blacketts would open the cell and come for him. Two against one in his current state wasn't the fight he wanted, yet he doubted he'd get better odds any time soon.

They didn't come. They just assessed him. Three pairs of reptilian eyes and a foul smell from Jimmy's cigar.

As they were turning to leave, Fletcher gave up on waiting and progressed to goading. "Your boys couldn't fight their way out of a wet grocery bag. You should have heard the cries when I broke the cocky one's arm. He squealed like a pig. As for the lanky one, he was no better than a little girl."

All three of the Blacketts stopped and turned to look at him. Each of their faces was twisted into a grimace as they digested his words.

Miss Constance cleared her throat with a rasp that spoke of forty a day for a lifetime and spat the clearings into the nearest cell. "You's forgetting something, mister, you're the one who got his ass kicked the hardest. You mighta gotten yourself a couple of victories, but you done lost the war you egg-sucking dawg."

Egg-sucking dawg wasn't a term Fletcher was familiar with, yet he felt safe to assume it was an insult. Miss Constance had made a very good point; so far Fletcher *had* lost the war. However, he'd neither surrendered nor been killed, only captured, so as far as he was concerned, the war wasn't over.

CHAPTER SIXTY-FIVE

Quadrado had listened to the exchange between Miss Constance and Fletcher with a sense of dread for the man. Yet there was also reason to admire him. He'd faced down the threats with seeming unconcern and hadn't shown a flicker of fear.

Then again, she reasoned, he'd been a soldier. A Royal Marine, in fact. He'd been in Afghanistan and had probably faced death on more than one occasion. As a soldier he'd be better suited to managing the fear of death than a regular civilian.

Most of all, though, she thought about his confession. The jumbled way he told her the story of how he'd met his wife and fallen in love. Of how he'd killed his wife in a deliberate act. Whichever way she looked at it, Grant Fletcher had admitted to first-degree homicide, even with the extenuating circumstances. The sentence for which was life. As it happened in the state of Utah, there was a chance he could end up on death row.

After detailing the events surrounding his wife's death, Fletcher had gone on to say how he'd raised Wendy as a single parent. He'd never remarried or sought anyone to replace Rachel. Wendy was his world and he was content with that as she was her mother's double in every way that mattered, and so long as he had Wendy in his life, he still had Rachel.

Quadrado couldn't begin to imagine the pain of having to live with what he'd done. He'd been about to break the neck of a muscle-bound Blackett boy and had frozen, his face a mask of unseeing horror. Fletcher had admitted he had flashbacks in his dreams and that when the moment came when he was about to break another neck, all of a sudden he was in the car sliding towards a river and saying goodbye to his wife. Fat tears had rolled unnoticed down his cheeks as he'd relived the moment.

His freezing might well cost Quadrado her own life, yet after hearing his story, she couldn't assign one iota of blame to him for failing to kill someone else with the same method he'd used on his wife.

CHAPTER SIXTY-SIX

Fletcher eased himself upright. The time for self-pity and confession was long past. Now it was time for action. As cathartic as it had been to finally tell someone the truth about what had happened on that rainy night all those years ago, he was now cursing the moment of weakness that had made him bare his soul to Quadrado. Not just Quadrado. Lila, who he'd known since she was five, and the other captives of the Blacketts.

Never before had he been of a mindset where he'd given up hope, and now that he'd shared his guiltiest secret once, he was determined to share it one more time. Yes, if he got out of here alive, he could be looking at some serious jail time for taking Rachel's life. But he owed it to Wendy to look her in the eye and tell her the truth about her mother's death. She would no doubt hate him for it at first, that was to be expected; he already hated himself and had done for years.

First though, he had to find a way out of this cell. If he could save the lives of Quadrado, Lila and the other people imprisoned in the makeshift cells, he could accept his own fate, whatever that might entail.

Fletcher's initial move was to examine the construction of the cell. Not the mesh, or the lumber framing holding it in place, but the way the mesh was fixed to the lumber. At every point where a horizontal bar crossed a vertical part of the framing, a staple had been driven in. Rather than only being knocked so far in, as a fencer would do so they could easily remove the staple, each of the ones securing the mesh had been driven in until their necks were pressing the mesh's bars tight against the lumber framing.

Given a crowbar, Fletcher could have levered the bars off one by one until he could escape the cell. He didn't have a crowbar though, nor a hammer, nor a tool of any kind.

Next he turned his focus to the mesh door which held him in the cell. It was secured on both sides by tie wire. He'd seen and used tie wire before. It was thin, less than a sixteenth of an inch in width, but it was strong. Without tools he couldn't hope to break or cut it.

It did have a flaw though. It got its holding strength from being looped around two objects, usually the reinforcing bars in structures that were about to be clad in concrete, and twisted until it locked the bars into place. On a concrete pour, the twisted ends would be snipped off. The Blacketts had followed suit. Fletcher's groping fingertips felt the sharp ends where the tie wire had been cut. It would have been nice to have found unsnipped tails he could have used to untwist the tie wire, but he knew the Blacketts wouldn't be so lax.

With the construction of the cell understood, Fletcher started to put his focus on what he'd need to unpick the twists of stainless-steel wire. As with the staples holding the mesh to the lumber, he would need a tool of some description to deal with the wire.

Fletcher remembered the keys he'd filched from the trials bikes and patted his pockets only to find them empty; the Blacketts must have turned them out when they'd done beating up on him, so he looked to his wrist. His watch glinted the faint light of the cell back at him. The face smashed and the hands unmoving. The time wasn't important to him. The hour of the day bore no consequence as his escape needed to be made before the Blacketts returned, and that was an unknown, so he'd have to assume it could happen at any time.

What did matter about the watch was its leather strap. The metal fastening was the usual rectangular shape with a tongue which poked through a hole in the leather.

Fletcher unfastened his watch and pulled the part of the strap with the fastener away from the body of the watch. His next move was to thread a hand through a gap in the mesh and gently assess the way the tie wire had been twisted.

With that done he took the fastening's tongue and teased it against the end of the tie wire's twist. It took him a few minutes to tease it between the twisted wires and unpick a section large enough to feed the bladed end of the fastener between the wires, but once he'd got to that point, it only took him seconds to unwind the rest of the wire knot with the fastener acting as a twist key.

Ten minutes later he was working on the last piece of wire he needed to untie to escape from the cell. His fingertips were raw and bleeding from the times he'd caught them on the sharp ends of the wire, yet Fletcher wasn't worried about the pain, or the fact he was leaking yet more blood as his entire focus was on getting this last knot unpicked.

Although his fingers were slick with blood, he could feel the fastening of the watch beginning to fail. He'd twice had to straighten the tongue and the bladed end was bending out of shape. This last knot had been snipped off further from the mesh than the others which made it a longer job to unpick. The parts he'd already unwound were catching at his fingers and hampering his efforts.

Disaster struck. The fastener snapped. Such was the strain Fletcher had put on it, reversing it back and forth to counteract the bending, its metallic integrity had become compromised and it failed him.

Rather than accept defeat, Fletcher used his unscratched pinkie to assess how much of the knot was left intact. His best guest was one and a half twists. Two at most.

This knot was near the ground. Maybe six inches above the floor.

Fletcher stood with his back to the mesh and delivered a series of mule kicks at the mesh door. It stood firm against his assault, so he crossed to the furthest part of the cell from the door, bent low and after a couple of paces to gather momentum threw himself feet first at the part of the mesh closest to the remaining knot. His action was that of a baseball star sliding towards a base, except his feet hit the mesh a fraction of a second before his body landed on the hard concrete floor.

Spikes of agony flashed through Fletcher, piercing every part of his body as the twin jarring impacts rattled already bruised areas.

When Fletcher picked himself up, the door to the cell was a lot closer to being open.

He gave the mesh another two mule kicks and the door swung open.

Fletcher stepped through the door certain of only two things. The first was that he didn't dare leave the others locked in their cells as the Blacketts would surely leave no witnesses if he managed to escape.

The second point was that he wouldn't fail Quadrado and the others a second time. There would be no mercy shown to the Blacketts. No threats made at gun point, just the promise of death from whatever weapon he could lay his hands on.

CHAPTER SIXTY-SEVEN

Fletcher told Quadrado that he'd be back soon and set off for the door. When he reached the corridor he crossed to the room with the hole in the floor. His weapons had been in here when last he'd seen them, but the Blacketts had policed the area and removed not just his weapons but also the rope they'd used to hang Quadrado over the hole. He cast his eyes across the floor and found his locket. The chain was broken so rather than scooping it around his neck, he kissed both sides of it and slid it into his pants pocket for safe keeping.

Beyond the rotten stench the room was empty, so Fletcher made his way to the faux bedroom. Its door was still open, so he entered the room, ever cautious in case one of the Blacketts was lying in wait for him. They weren't.

Fletcher ignored the bedroom side of the space and made for the part with the bench laden with recording equipment. He'd spied a small toolbox among the cameras and other paraphernalia.

The toolbox held pairs of pliers. Not just the ordinary pliers most people had in their toolkits, there was also a set of the special pliers construction workers used to lash reinforcing bars together with tie wire.

Fletcher ran down the corridor and freed Quadrado. As he snipped the ties holding her in the cell, he was explaining to her that he was going to look for weapons and she had to free the other prisoners then come find him.

"Got it."

He liked that she was brief with her words and on point with him giving orders. She'd encouraged him as he was breaking out of the cell and rather than wasting time arguing about superiority, she was taking his instructions without complaint. Whether that would change when she had a weapon remained to be seen. He didn't think so. Of all the captives she was the one he expected to be the most use when things got down and dirty with the Blacketts.

As she set to her task, Fletcher dashed back to the bedroom and started looking for a weapon. A shotgun would be ideal for what he had in mind, a pistol more than good enough and a knife or club adequate at best.

He found none of these weapons. The nearest he could find to a real weapon was a craft knife with only a half inch of blade. When he thumbed the blade the rasp his skin made brought a rueful wince to his face. The knife was only sharp by Stone Age standards. If he managed to get someone in the right hold, he would be able to press it hard enough to nick a vein or artery. All things considered, though, he'd do better with his bare hands than the knife.

The toolbox yielded a few screwdrivers and nothing more. Screwdrivers made for a good stabbing weapon, but you needed a decent amount of force behind the blow to puncture skin and pass through muscle far enough to do significant damage to an organ.

He slid the screwdrivers into his back pocket along with the other set of pliers. From along the corridor he could hear sudden chatter that was at once hushed by Quadrado's voice.

Trailing six others out of the makeshift prison wasn't going to be easy, and Fletcher wasn't naïve enough to think he'd be able to do it without encountering the Blacketts at some point. The more of the prisoners he could arm with a weapon of some description the better their collective chances of escape.

"We're out."

Again, Quadrado wasn't using a syllable more than necessary.

"Good. Let's go."

Fletcher led them to the exit door at the end of the corridor. When he got to the door he stopped and looked back at the faces of the prisoners. Apart from Quadrado, they each had the stupefied look of someone who'd just worked their way through a joint or six.

He guessed they'd been drugged to keep them compliant. That they were drugged would be a good thing in the short term. They'd do as he said and not question his authority. If he was to get them out of here in one piece, he'd need them to obey his every command.

"Okay, guys. We're going to get out of here in a minute. When we do, I need you all to do two things. Number one: Be silent. No talking, no questioning me and no careless feet kicking things that will make a noise. Number two: You must, I repeat, *must*, do as I say when I say it without question. Got that?"

Five heads nodded his way with varying levels of comprehension, while Quadrado gave a single terse downward jerk of her head.

Fletcher turned to the door, placed a hand on it and gave a gentle push. It didn't move. Not even a fraction. He pushed harder and then as he was about to put his full weight against the door, he remembered the hefty bolt he'd seen on the door. If it had been slid home there was no way they were getting through the door.

"Change of plan."

Right now, Fletcher didn't have a clue what the new plan was. Yet he knew that he'd have to come up with something rapidly as the Blacketts could arrive back at any moment.

CHAPTER SIXTY-EIGHT

Fletcher looked around the bedroom at the faces assembled before him and wondered how he could turn them into fighters. The man Quadrado had introduced as Pierre might be useful; he had the physique of a gym bunny gone to seed, which Fletcher guessed was due to his time being held by the Blacketts, but there was still enough muscle mass to make him a threat. However, of the five prisoners, his eyes were the glassiest, therefore he would be the slowest to react and would in all probability be sluggish and undetermined in any attacks he made.

Of the females who were captives, Frances was trim and lithe, Lila looked to be the most alert, and following her was the older woman, Melissa. The fourth and final woman, Kiera, appeared to be the least doped up of the others, but she was in a state of shock and cowered behind Melissa whenever possible. She was young, still a teenager, and as such, she didn't seem able to handle the stress of the situation.

Over and over in Fletcher's mind, the same questions kept asking themselves. Would this ragtag force be any use against the Blacketts? How could he not just arm them but equip them for a fight to the death? Would Quadrado step up at some point and insist there had to be no killing? And if she did, how would he deal with her?

A touch on his arm and a head jerk informed him that Quadrado wanted to speak to him somewhere they wouldn't be overheard.

He followed her out of the bedroom into the corridor. His brain already working out answers to the points he expected her to make.

She turned, tucking a loose hair behind her ear as she looked up at him. "They're coming back, and if we want to survive we're going to have to fight them, aren't we?"

Fletcher liked this directness about Quadrado. It meant she understood the way things were, not the way they ought to be.

"We are. And there can't be any half measures. They're going to have guns and there will be at least four of them who are fit to fight. Apart from you and me, the others all look drugged up. They'll be slow and uncertain. You and I must be fast and decisive." He looked Quadrado in the eye. "We can't take any prisoners."

Quadrado pursed her lips, a plea filling her eyes, only to disappear as she gave a terse nod and fingered the crucifix hanging at her throat. "Lord forgive me for saying this, but you're right. If we are to save ourselves and the others, we're going to have to make sure that anyone we take down stays down."

"Agreed." Fletcher returned her nod. "I don't want to kill for killing's sake, but if necessary I won't hesitate to use lethal force. Are you cool with that?"

Quadrado's head shook. "No. I'm not cool with it, because you're a civilian. However, you're the best fighter we have, and as I can't see another way, I'm going to have to learn to accept it." Quadrado leaned back against a wall. "Do you have a plan? Some weapons I don't know about?"

Fletcher noticed Quadrado's acceptance of fact and the body language she employed. He needed her at her best; she was downbeat at the moment, although it'd be unfair to say she was pessimistic. She was out of her depth in this situation, and Fletcher was hoping against hope the same couldn't be said of him. Somehow he had to come up with a plan as he was their only fighter trained to military standards; Quadrado and the others needed him to foster belief before the first shoots of fatalism sprouted.

"Gather up everything you can find in the other rooms and bring it to the bedroom so I can see what we've got."

Weapons could be made from lots of everyday items. They might not be effective at any distance against guns, but the basis of the plan that was forming in Fletcher's head was one that would put a gun in his hand at the earliest possible opportunity.

With all of the items collected from the three rooms laid out on the bed, Fletcher assessed their usefulness as instruments of war. There were the two pairs of pliers, four screwdrivers, six bottles of water from the cells and the photographic equipment. The camera had a strap that was fastened to its body by a couple of clasps. The wide nylon strap could be used as a garrote, yet Fletcher preferred to keep the strap attached to the camera. With the right timing, a swing could cause the bulky camera to crash into a limb or head with enough force to at least numb the person it hit. If they got lucky, the blow might be heavy enough to crack bone. A bottle of perfume and a can of deodorant lay side by side and the final item was the toolbox itself.

The camera was given to Pierre. Gym-honed or not, his muscles swinging the camera would create a far greater impact than any of the other hostages might achieve. Frances, Melissa and Kiera were given a screwdriver apiece while Fletcher and Quadrado got a pair of pliers each.

"What about me?" Lila's voice was strong with resentment at being left out when the weapons were shared out. "What do I get?"

"You get the best weapons." Fletcher handed Lila the perfume and deodorant. "Think of these as pepper sprays. If you get close enough, aim for the eyes." Fletcher pointed at the light bulbs, video camera and hairbrush that lay on the table. "Your dad never stopped saying how you won medals for javelin when you were in college. Think you can pitch some of that stuff at the bad guys?"

A weak smile caressed Lila's mouth, yet her tone was grim. "Damn straight I can."

Fletcher returned the smile before raising his voice so the whole group could hear him.

"Right then. I guess you're all wondering how we're going to fight with the stuff I've given you. Don't worry, I'm going to give you a crash course." He cast a look Quadrado's way and gestured to the middle of the room.

For five minutes, Fletcher used the FBI agent as a dummy, pointing out where those armed with screwdrivers should aim their blows. Considering the screwdrivers were all dull weapons, he instructed them to aim for soft tissue areas like the throat, stomach, and lower back. He took care to also show them how to hold the screwdrivers dagger style, with their thumb on the top of the handle to prevent them being knocked from their grip when striking.

Areas such as the head, upper chest and legs were parts of the body he told them not to attack. When at his best, Pierre, whom Fletcher had chosen not to give a screwdriver, might have the strength to drive a screwdriver through someone's skull or through thick denim pants, but he wasn't at his best and the Blacketts would be doing all they could to defend against the attack Fletcher planned to spring. It was possible that a lucky strike to the chest would slip neatly between a pair of ribs and puncture the heart or lungs. It was just as likely the screwdriver would collide with a rib, or not penetrate the powerful chest muscles of Jimmy or Muscles deep enough to do any meaningful damage.

Lila had her throwing weapons, plus the makeshift pepper sprays. Fletcher would have given a small fortune for something that would generate a flame so the deodorant could be used as a flamethrower.

The last piece of training Fletcher gave was showing Quadrado how to use the pliers he'd given her as a Kubotan. She was familiar with the concept, but hadn't used one beyond her training. Neither had Fletcher, yet he was confident that he'd made the best choices for everyone when passing out the weapons. Basically the pliers were held in a way that allowed the head and the legs to protrude from either side of the hand. Forehand and backhand strikes could then be delivered to drive the metal of the pliers into sensitive areas of the body. A real Kubotan would be a lot more dangerous than the pliers, but they had to make the best of the weapons at their disposal.

With all the training complete, Fletcher led everyone back to the room where they'd been imprisoned and laid out his plan to them. It wasn't a plan he had massive faith in as he was relying on the element of surprise as well as untrained, drugged allies.

Along with Quadrado he'd prevented any of the others drinking more water as they were convinced that was how the drugs were being administered, yet he was aware of the dryness in his own mouth. His first thought had been that they should remove temptation by throwing the water bottles down the well hole, but he'd changed his mind when he realized that if it was a long time before the Blacketts returned, they might need that water. Better to be a little drugged than dead from dehydration.

With all of the prisoners positioned and armed, he settled in for what might be a long wait. He hoped the Blacketts' arrival would be soon. The longer they had to wait the more time his new recruits would have for doubts and fears to grow. A plus side of the wait would mean that the drugs would wear off making them more alert and physically adept. The lack of drugs would also allow their minds to turn to fear. It would give muscles time to cramp and his leadership to be questioned by the stronger characters.

The worst thing about a delay would be the wearying effect of starvation. They'd all scoured the rooms for anything that might be described as a foodstuff. All of them had found the same nothing.

Fletcher hoped against hope the Blacketts would come back soon and tried not to think about what would happen if they never returned.

CHAPTER SIXTY-NINE

Quadrado eased herself from foot to foot in an effort to combat the stiffness encroaching her body. Hunger pangs were gnawing at her stomach, and her throat and mouth were parched. She'd not once complained about the discomforts because that was all they were. Compared to the beatings Fletcher had endured, she was in great condition.

Now that she was alone—Fletcher had put her on guard duty beside the door into the underground prison—she had time to think. Her thoughts were centered on two key points: the surety that she'd die if their attempt to attack the Blacketts and escape failed, and the fact that as an FBI officer, she had not just ceded control of this situation to a civilian, she'd agreed to his plan of vigilante action and the possibility that lethal force would be necessary.

The thought of dying at the hands of the Blacketts was enough to weaken her knees and put a shake into her hands. There was no knowing exactly what the Blacketts had in store for their victims, yet she'd had enough time to join the dots together. She knew they planned to sell her, and the pictures they'd taken of her in her underwear didn't need a genius to work out how they planned to market her, or for what purpose she'd be bought.

They *must* prevail against the Blacketts as the alternatives were unthinkable. A life of sexual slavery wasn't something Quadrado had ever envisioned for herself and she was damned if she was going to accept it. She planned to fight with everything she had regardless of the risk to her own life. She'd rather die trying to save the others than face whatever fate the Blacketts had in store for her. The fact they had their own slave in Elena spoke to their thoughts on slavery.

With this resolution firm in her mind, Quadrado still felt the tremor in her limbs and the heightened throb of her pulse. It was easier to control these things when she was with the others. There truly was a collective strength in numbers. The fact that Fletcher oozed confidence and determination didn't hurt. For all he was a troubled man, he was good at what he did. In time she would have collected the same weapons he had. However, she wouldn't have thought to train the other prisoners in how to use them, or to have the screwdrivers scratched across the concrete floor to sharpen their points. Nor would she have come up with the same plan Fletcher had. Her own ideas about retaliation had centered on trying to hide out somewhere and then ambushing the Blacketts. Fletcher was more proactive with his plan. He wanted to draw the Blacketts into a trap rather than face the worry of discovery before the ambush could take place. With the lack of hiding places available, Fletcher's plan made more sense.

With every passing minute, Quadrado ran over the plan and her part in it. She was envisioning her role, the challenges and risks associated with it and the way Fletcher had coached her to minimize the risks.

To counteract the worst of her worries, Quadrado let her mind run free. Despite her fears for the immediate and long-term future of herself and the other prisoners, she couldn't help but wonder what was behind the fourth door in the corridor. It was locked tight and when Fletcher and Pierre had tried to shoulder it down, it had repelled their efforts as if they had the weight and power of fleas.

Another recurring thought of Quadrado's was how things would pan out if they did manage to escape. At first, she and Fletcher would be feted as heroes for the rescue. And then the investigation into her actions would begin. Question after unanswerable question would be put to her until all her decisions had been picked apart and found wanting. She'd let Fletcher turn her head with ideas of glory for solving a case, yet the reality had been that she'd allowed herself to be captured and then had to rely on a civilian to save her life. If by some miracle they managed to get out without killing any of the Blacketts, things would be a little easier. Whichever way she looked at it, if she managed to not be kicked out of the FBI for her failures to follow procedure, she would see her career stalled. She'd be the failure-tarnished agent sent out to investigate all the hopeless cases in all the most inhospitable areas. This trip to Georgia would seem like spring break compared to the assignments she might get in future.

She set her jaw and tried not to think of the future in such bleak terms. If she was fired, she'd still be alive. She could retrain, take on a new career and rejoice in the fact that she'd survived.

Quadrado's head snapped up as her ears picked out a sound. It was the sound of something heavy being dropped onto a solid surface. From what Fletcher had told her about the entrance to this dungeon she figured it was the Blacketts uncovering the inspection pit.

They were here. The Blacketts were back.

Every step Quadrado took back towards where Fletcher and the others were waiting saw apprehension tighten its grip around her stomach.

As she reached them she could see the fearful anticipation in their eyes.

Except Fletcher. His eyes were clear and held nothing but determination.

CHAPTER SEVENTY

Fletcher's first instinct was to tense when he heard Quadrado's footsteps come padding along the corridor. He forced himself to relax and bite down on the fear that his plan wouldn't work and would spell doom for himself and all these good people.

Quadrado looked his way as she slipped into position. Only because he'd gotten to know her a little could Fletcher see his own fears reflected on her face. He gave her a tight smile and turned to the others as he pushed the door closed. "Showtime."

He'd put as much positivity into the single word as he could. It had sounded hollow to him, like a person on their deathbed talking about the future for the sake of their loved ones.

Everyone around him was tense and he could hear deep breaths being inhaled as they psyched themselves up and prepared to enter a fight they might not survive.

Fletcher pointed a finger at Melissa, then swirled it upwards.

Melissa led the chorus of exhortations, with all save Quadrado joining in. Their shouts were encouraging him to break free of his cell. Telling him he was almost there. Saying he was nearly there and other such phrases.

Fletcher's thinking was them saying such things would raise alarm in the Blacketts. That by suggesting Fletcher had almost broken free, they'd come running to stop him while he was still held captive in the cell.

Heavy boots thudded along the corridor. The plan was working. Fletcher gave Pierre a wink and tightened his grip on the mesh door he'd removed from the nearest cell.

Tall Boy and Chuck burst through the door as a pair. Each had a pistol in one hand and there was a cattle prod in Tall Boy's other hand.

Fletcher lunged forward, the mesh door held vertical in a "landscape" position. As he lunged, Fletcher thrust the mesh barricade towards Tall Boy's and Chuck's outstretched hands. Just as Fletcher had planned, the mesh caught their gun hands and redirected them away from where all the prisoners were standing.

With his full weight behind the mesh, Fletcher was able to drive the two Blacketts against the far wall. A pistol shot was squeezed off, a panicked reaction Fletcher guessed, before both men were trapped. The others flew into action.

Now it was all about timing. If there were only these two Blacketts, timing didn't matter, yet if there were others, Fletcher and his ragtag bunch of troops would have three seconds at most to assert the advantage afforded them by the surprise attack.

Pierre's camera swung fast and hard into Chuck's wrist. Chuck dropped his pistol with a yelp. Fletcher bent to catch it before it could hit the ground.

To his right, Melissa and Frances were stabbing at Tall Boy's hand until he too dropped his pistol. A second swing from Pierre saw the camera smash into Tall Boy's head. Tall Boy went wobbly, but Fletcher paid him no heed.

With the gun in his hand, Fletcher wrapped his arm around Chuck's neck and ground the barrel into his ear. A scoosh from Lila sent a mist of perfume into Chuck's eyes causing him to curse and writhe.

Fletcher leaned back; Chuck was taller than him so he couldn't get his opponent onto his tiptoes as he would have preferred. At least he had control of him, though.

"Freeze."

Jimmy had appeared in the doorway. A shotgun held waist high was in his hands and confusion written over his face.

Fletcher had made a point of blocking the doorway with Chuck's body. He'd prepared for the whole of the Blackett force and hadn't expected all of them to crash through the doorway at once.

By isolating Chuck he'd gotten one of the key members of the family as his hostage. Hank might well have been deemed expendable, but from what he'd learned and worked out, Chuck was the technical brain of the business. As well as being a senior family member, he was too valuable an asset to be sacrificed. Nabbing either Chuck or Jimmy was key to his plan and he'd gotten the one he felt he could best control.

"Drop it, or your brother dies."

Jimmy hesitated, but didn't release the weapon. If he was applying Blackett logic and morality to the situation, he'd expect Fletcher to shoot them all the second he laid down his weapon.

Behind Jimmy, Muscles glared at them. His hands—unseen behind his father's back—suggested a threat, but what he didn't see was Quadrado creeping from the room with the well in its floor. Her movements were silent, and there was a balletic grace about her as she swung her makeshift Kubotan at Muscles's temple.

Miss Constance's voice boomed out from along the corridor, thick with southern accent and fury. "Behind ya."

Muscles started to turn. He wasn't quick enough to avoid Quadrado's blow, but he'd turned enough that it landed on his forehead instead of his temple.

The bones of a human temple are thin and easily damaged with a weapon such as a Kubotan whereas a forehead has a greater thickness and strength to it. Quadrado's blow split the skin and left Muscles visibly dazed. He flung up an arm in reflex as Quadrado wound up her arm for another strike.

Instead of striking with the Kubotan a second time, Quadrado swung her empty hand in a roundhouse punch. Muscles went to counter and Quadrado's other arm shot toward his head.

There was the kind of thwack that can be both satisfying and sickening.

Muscles went down.

Miss Constance came into view, cane first. It caught Quadrado on the top of her head, causing her to slump from Fletcher's view.

Now it was about two men with guns and the man between them without.

With a pistol or a rifle, someone in Jimmy's position might fancy their chances of squeezing off a shot at a part of Fletcher that wasn't covered by Chuck. Because he carried a shotgun, Jimmy didn't have that option. A superb marksman who could calculate the spread of shot might be able to work out how far to aim wide so Chuck was unharmed, but calculating the spread of shot was an inexact science at the best of times. First off, distance would have to be calculated with a high degree of accuracy. Second, there would be a need to combat the fear of getting it wrong. Due to their proximity, there was no room for error. A single ball of shot would inflict terrible damage to Chuck at this range. The lack of confidence in Jimmy's eyes suggested that he didn't trust himself to make the shot.

The shotgun was snatched from Jimmy and leveled at Chuck so quickly Fletcher had no time to fire a shot her way. There was no uncertainty in her eyes. Only determination and sadness.

"Say hello to your poppa for me."

CHAPTER SEVENTY-ONE

As soon as he realized Miss Constance's intent, Fletcher began to release Chuck. He couldn't spare any brain power on the subject of how a mother could shoot a son. Not now, anyway. For the moment his entire being was on getting himself out of the way of that shotgun.

Fletcher's arm was uncoiling from Chuck's neck and moving upwards as the shotgun boomed. He was also throwing himself sideways lest any shot travel clean through Chuck. As he was moving away from Chuck, he managed to snap off a shot in Miss Constance's general direction.

With no soft furnishings to absorb the noise, the shotgun firing in the confined space sounded more like a cannon or naval gun.

Chuck's body jerked backwards as a hole was driven through his midriff, pellets from the shotgun exploding blood and tissue across the room.

In anticipation of shots being fired, Fletcher had impressed upon the others the need to keep to the sides of the door so there was less chance of them being hit.

Fletcher snapped off another shot at the doorway without aiming.

When he looked he saw the corridor was empty save for a prone Muscles, and Quadrado who was crawling back to the well room.

He could hear retreating footsteps and Jimmy berating his mother.

"Goddammit, why'n you have to shoot Chuck?"

"Shut yer yap. I did what had to be done. If you were a real man, you would have done it yo'self."

Their conversation didn't matter. All that mattered was the fact they were retreating. If Jimmy and Miss Constance made it to the door, they'd be able to lock it behind them.

Miss Constance had already sacrificed one son rather than concede defeat. She'd be more than likely to seal up the inspection pit and leave them all to die of dehydration if she could get out alive.

He had to stop her doing that and the only way to achieve that aim was to take her down. The problem with taking her down was that he had two pistols. He'd not had a chance to check their clips to see how many shots they held so he might have twenty shots or two.

All the same, he had to do something and do it soon.

Fletcher stayed in the room where he was and squeezed off a couple of rounds along the corridor. He wasn't trying to be accurate; he was just seeing what reaction he'd get.

The shotgun boomed again, but it was aimed down the corridor, so it did no damage to anyone.

This was bad news. There had been only the tiniest delay between his shots and hers; therefore she was backing away, her focus on the threat from him rather than her direction of travel.

For an average person, a shotgun is a weapon that requires two hands to operate. The kickback can break a wrist if the stock isn't braced against the shooter's shoulder.

Miss Constance walked with a cane, which made her movements slow at the best of times. Backing up without her cane would be tough for her. She would be slow, cumbersome, and ever vigilant for threats from him.

Fletcher couldn't enter the corridor without being shot, so he had to devise a new plan. Six pairs of expectant eyes were on him as he lifted the second pistol.

He didn't have a plan as such, but he did have an idea. The narrow corridor would be his ally, a secret weapon she wouldn't expect him to use. He spent a moment lifting Tall Boy's pistol from the floor and checking it for a safety catch. It was a Glock, so its safety was incorporated into its trigger.

Trench's comment about shooting around corners came back to Fletcher as he positioned himself to the right of the door and loosed off ten shots. Each shot was a little over four feet above the ground and every time he pulled a trigger he moved his aim along the wall by six inches.

The corridor's walls were solid concrete. They wouldn't absorb water, sound, or bullets fired at an oblique angle. Fletcher was gambling the bullets he'd fired would ricochet off the concrete walls at roughly the same angle as he'd fired them. By aiming where he did, he was creating a field of fire that would spread along the corridor around four feet high. Right where the center mass was.

He heard a pair of wet thwacks and a woman cry out. He'd hit Miss Constance. Fletcher didn't like the idea of shooting at a woman. To him it seemed wrong with all the decency and respect for women that his adoptive parents had instilled in him. Yet he was in a fight for his life, so he figured it was sexist *not* to shoot a woman when he would have shot a man in the woman's position.

The best thing he heard was the clatter of the shotgun being dropped. He charged out of the room and along the corridor, his pistol held out in front of him ready to shoot Jimmy if he went for the shotgun.

Jimmy was beside his mother, five paces from the iron door at the end of the corridor. He saw Fletcher coming and made a decision.

Fletcher could almost see the flash of Jimmy's thought processes as his body was filled with fight-or-flight instincts. A fight would give him revenge for the family members that were littering the floor. It might also see him die in the attempt. With Miss

Constance down and Chuck dead, the Blackett empire would fall solely into his hands. Flight could offer him a wealthy life, without the influence of his mother, whereas fight would offer either vengeance or death.

Jimmy turned and ran for the door. Fletcher set off after him, his feet pounding on the stone floor, his eyes flicking down to Miss Constance as he passed her. She had a pair of blossoming red patches merging together on the top of her right shoulder. The rounds might have broken bones, but he judged it not to be a fatal wound.

As he ran he tried to put a bullet into Jimmy's back. The two rounds he fired before the gun clicked on an empty chamber went into the floor and the ceiling respectively.

Fletcher dropped the gun and pumped arms and legs as hard as he could. Jimmy was a pace from the door and four ahead of him when he roared for Quadrado to get the shotgun. He didn't want the old woman retrieving the weapon and holding anyone hostage.

Jimmy barged through the door and Fletcher saw Jimmy going to close it behind him. As the door was an inch from being closed, Fletcher threw his body at it shoulder first.

The door juddered and swung open a few inches. Before Jimmy could recover and set himself for a battle of strength, Fletcher forced the door open far enough that he could slide his body through the gap.

The door flew back against the inspection pit as Jimmy released his grip on it and threw a pair of punches at Fletcher. The first slammed into his gut, driving every last morsel of air from his body. The second connected with Fletcher's jaw hard enough to fill his vision with a thousand pinpricks of starry light.

Fletcher was gasping for air and trying to clear his befuddled mind while also anticipating another hammer blow from Jimmy when he heard footsteps on concrete. Focus came back to his eyes and he saw Jimmy running up the steps of the inspection pit.

As he stumbled up the stairs himself, Fletcher heard the nasal revving of a trials bike. Why Jimmy had chosen the bike over the pickups or the Mercedes was beyond Fletcher.

By the time he'd gotten up the stairs, Jimmy was scorching a trail towards the already open gate. Fletcher ran to the workbench he'd tossed the quad's key under and retrieved it. With the key grasped between his fingers he leapt onto the quad and gunned the engine. No way was he going to allow Jimmy to put whatever contingency plan he'd put together into action.

CHAPTER SEVENTY-TWO

At Fletcher's shout, Quadrado ran out from her hiding place and looked along the corridor. Miss Constance was alone on the floor. The old woman had guts, Quadrado would give her that. She was trying to scrabble for the shotgun despite the obvious bullet wounds to her shoulder.

Quadrado dashed along the corridor and kicked the shotgun from Miss Constance's reach just as grasping fingers got a tentative grip of the weapon's stock.

"Come on, guys." With the shotgun safely out of Miss Constance's reach, Quadrado bent to pick the weapon up.

One by one the five captives emerged from the room with the cells and walked along the corridor. They all looked to be in a state of shock at the events of the last few minutes with Kiera appearing to be on the verge of being catatonic.

Quadrado rounded the door at the end of the cell and crept up the stairs at the end. The shotgun was aimed wherever she looked. Her eyes searching for threats and finding none.

Once all the hostages were clear of the cellar door, Quadrado shot the bolt home and laid a row of the inspection pit timbers from the bottom step to the metal door. It was overkill with the bolts being in place, yet it made her feel like she'd done everything she could to block the three live Blacketts into their own prison. She toyed with the idea of driving one of the pick-ups or the Mercedes, so its wheels fell into the pit. In the end, she reasoned that would be a step too far.

With the hostages trailing behind her, Quadrado ran across to the house, the shotgun in her hands and fury in her heart. No way were any remaining Blacketts going to stop her from raising the alarm and summoning help.

The house's rear door was unlocked when Quadrado tried the handle. She entered the house and stormed through room after room until she found two women being served drinks by a maid she presumed was Elena.

"Don't move. FBI."

The Blackett women threw disgusted looks at her then exchanged uncertain glances. Elena's hands shot into the air as tears sprang from her eyes. "Please not send me back. I work hard."

"Here." Quadrado handed the shotgun to Pierre. "Cover these two. You have my permission to shoot them if they move."

Quadrado plucked a phone from its cradle and dialed a number she knew by heart. As she related the brief facts and summoned both FBI and EMT support, the Blackett women's faces turned ashen as she detailed the injuries the EMTs would have to deal with.

Once the call was over, Quadrado started to question the Blackett women about where she might find more weapons in the house, what the family had been doing with the prisoners and who else might be in the house or likely to return.

The two women looked at each other and remained mute. They'd no doubt be hoping a family member would rescue them before the FBI arrived. The contrast between the two women, dressed in designer clothes and living a life of luxury, and those townsfolk who'd had their lives suppressed and controlled infuriated Quadrado. She didn't dare think of how these women had been waited on by someone who was little more than a slave, while less than a hundred yards away, below the ground, men and women had been imprisoned and subjected to Lord alone knew what grisly fate. She'd tried asking the hostages what they knew. None had known anything beyond the fact that a prisoner would be taken out of the cell not to return. They all assumed the prisoners who were taken had died as they'd heard muffled screaming. Kiera had shed uncontrollable tears when she recounted how sometimes the screaming lasted for hours.

Quadrado froze when she heard the unmistakable sound of a gun being cocked.

"Put the gun down. Now."

It was the mouthy Blackett kid who had been the one to capture her. One arm was in a cast, but it was the other arm which interested Quadrado. The hand held a huge pistol. At first glance it looked to be a Desert Eagle. It was a serious pistol, semi-automatic and one of the most powerful handguns on the planet. Such weapons didn't belong in the hands of a callow youth. They ought to be handled by special forces soldiers who knew when to pull the trigger and when the pistol's threat would be enough.

"Don't just stand there, boy. Shoot him."

That was all Quadrado needed, the Blackett women inciting the lad to kill. The barrel of the pistol wavered and wobbled as he straightened his arm and took aim at Pierre as he covered the two women.

With a pistol as heavy as a Desert Eagle, most shooters would adopt a two-handed stance to both brace the weapon for accuracy, and better deal with the savage kickback. The way Cocky was holding it spelled disaster as the tip of the barrel was rotating as he tried to manage the pistol's aim while also fighting to keep his arm extended with the heavy pistol pulling it downwards.

The knuckles of the hand whitened as he closed the gap between him and Pierre to increase his chances of an accurate shot.

Quadrado had to act. She couldn't let a civilian get shot because she'd given him a gun. She had to save Pierre before the lad fired off a shot. Her legs propelled her forward as a curse sprang from her lips.

One, two, three steps she covered before he reacted. The pistol was swinging her way as she barged into him. Her left arm driving his gun arm upwards while her right encircled his body. Her legs pumping as she forced him backwards.

There was a huge boom above her head and then a pained yelp. It took Quadrado a moment to realize it was the Blackett boy who had yelped and not one of the room's other occupants. A quick leg sweep dropped him on his back.

'My wrist. My wrist.'

One of the Blackett women rose to her feet, took four paces until she was above the prone boy and sneered down at him. "Quit your whining. You tried running with the big dogs and you was found wantin'. You shoulda never crawled out from under the porch. You ain't half the man your daddy is."

Frances stepped into the room, a length of rope in her hands. It took her a few minutes, but she bound all three of the Blacketts to Quadrado's satisfaction.

Now it was just a question of waiting for the FBI and EMTs to arrive. They would bring salvation, medical care for the injured and the end of her career as she knew it.

CHAPTER SEVENTY-THREE

Fletcher thumbed the throttle lever forward as far as it would go. He had no idea whether the quad could match the trials bike for speed in a straight line. The one consolation he had was the quad was more a sports version than utility and had separately sprung wheels as well as a peppy engine whose exhaust was giving a whining roar.

Jimmy was going down the track when Fletcher passed through the wrought iron gates of the Blackett house.

A change of gear and another violent press on the throttle lever saw Fletcher's speed increase. His vision wasn't back to normal, and his breaths were still ragged. Having taken all that into account, Fletcher was just glad he still had Jimmy in his sights.

As Fletcher kicked the quad into top gear, he saw Jimmy peel off from the track and head into the woods. Fletcher felt a strong temptation to cut the corner, yet common sense prevailed. If Jimmy hadn't cut the corner, there would be a good reason. Perhaps a ditch or stream, something that would impede or block mechanized travel.

Fletcher swung after Jimmy at the same point and braced himself for the challenges of traveling at high speed through the woods. There was a narrow trail to follow and it was rutted with regular use by the trials bike. While Fletcher suspected the trials bike was used more by the younger Blacketts, Jimmy was adept at riding it and seemed to anticipate each turn and bend far better than he could.

The quad jerked and bucked beneath Fletcher as he thundered after Jimmy. As good as the suspension might be, the speed he was traveling along the undulating track was putting the kind of demands on it that its manufactures hadn't envisioned. A pro-racer would have been able to shift his weight around the quad in a way that would help the vehicle travel over the bumps in a safer and faster way. Fletcher wasn't a pro-racer and had no such advantages, yet he was gaining on Jimmy. He put it down to the quad being faster and him being lighter. The quad's bucking was aggravating his various injuries. The ribs he was sure were broken screamed with every jolt, as did the bruises on his arms and legs. Fletcher paid them no heed as he did everything he could to close in on Jimmy.

Jimmy tossed a backward glance over his shoulder to see where his pursuer was. Fletcher was close enough to see the surprise in Jimmy's eyes. Determination washed the surprise away as he twisted his head back to the direction he was traveling in.

A second later, Jimmy threw his bike into a tight turn and made straight for a steep bank. Fletcher followed, twisting the handlebars to weave between trees as the ground beneath his wheels grew ever steeper. Ahead of him, the back wheel of the trials bike was kicking up a rooster tail of woodland mulch as it fought for grip on the slope.

Jimmy crested the ridge and roared off as Fletcher was fighting to keep his front wheels on the slope while also doing his best to keep his weight over the back wheels to give them as much traction as possible. When he reached the top of the slope, he had to ease off the throttle, so he didn't flip the quad.

A quick glance located Jimmy roaring off across level ground. Fletcher gunned his engine and set off after him. The slope had given Jimmy his lead back, and now Fletcher had to wind a way through trees as well as manage the quad on rough ground. Fallen branches and protruding roots added to his problems, and as he chased after Jimmy he had to balance speed with his ability to not lose control of the quad.

The more Fletcher followed Jimmy, the more he found himself pushing both the quad and his own body to the outer edge of their limits. He'd learned from the early part of the chase which maneuvers would bleed speed from the quad and give him the roughest ride, so he used his newfound knowledge and understanding of the vehicle's quirks and behavior to wring the best possible pace from the machine.

The gap between Fletcher and Jimmy was closing. Not as fast as Fletcher would have liked it to, yet he was still gaining on the trials bike and the man riding it. A new worry came into Fletcher's head. How much gas was in the quad's tank? Would it last out until he'd caught up with Jimmy? Or would the vehicle splutter to an undignified halt, allowing Jimmy to make good on his escape?

When Fletcher had closed within twenty yards of Jimmy, the man and his bike dropped from view. One minute he was there and the next he wasn't.

Fletcher had just enough time to realize Jimmy had lifted the front wheel of the bike as he'd gone over the edge of a steep bank when he saw the ground just dropped away. He had two choices: slow down and risk giving up the ground he'd fought to make up on Jimmy, or trust the man he was chasing knew these woods well enough to not have made a fatal error. His mind flashed back to the last second of Jimmy before the jump. Jimmy had come this way on purpose and hadn't shown any sign of slowing before the jump or letting go of the bike as if he'd realized he'd make a mistake.

Fletcher's thumbnail went white has he pressed the throttle lever forward with every piece of strength he could muster and aimed for the spot where Jimmy had gone over the edge.

The quad went airborne.

Trees flashing past him as the ground fell away was enough to stir all kinds of remembered pain in Fletcher, none of it physical.

CHAPTER SEVENTY-FOUR

Fletcher had time to see that he was above a steep slope that was around fifty feet in height. A hefty branch lay on the slope. It was more than thick enough to have the stopping ability of a brick wall if he hit it.

With his front wheels threatening to rise to the point of flipping due to most of his weight being at the back of the quad, Fletcher had to lean forward to keep the vehicle something approaching level.

The slope was racing up at him, the branch waiting to halt his progress. With every fraction of a second that passed, the ground was nearer and the branch larger.

Somehow he cleared the branch. The quad's back wheels landed first pitching him forward until the front ones made contact. Fletcher slammed into the seat as the rear wheels squirted the quad down the slope only to find himself thrown upwards as each set of suspension did its job. The quad became a bucking bronco, desperate to rid itself of the pesky human on its back. Fletcher had to ease off the throttle until he'd regained full mastery of the machine.

A glance ahead told Fletcher Jimmy had gotten down the slope and cut a hard left. Again, Fletcher's thumbnail turned white as he wrung every drop of speed from the quad.

Fletcher had gotten back to within thirty yards of the trials bike when a rope appeared across the path in front of Jimmy. There was no time for Jimmy to stop or take evasive action. He tried all the same, dropping the trials bike into a low skidding turn.

Jimmy couldn't get low enough to pass under the rope. It caught his shoulder and pulled him to the ground. Fletcher eased his thumb back on the throttle and redirected his quad to where Jimmy was trying to scramble to his feet.

As he got closer, he prepared himself and launched off the quad in a brutal diving tackle using the quad's speed to add a further twenty miles an hour to his momentum.

Fletcher's shoulder speared into Jimmy's solar plexus, doubling him over and driving him backwards into a heap. Jimmy grunted at the blow, gasping to replace the air Fletcher had just knocked out of him. With his opponent down, Fletcher wasted no time in scrambling atop Jimmy and raining a series of heavy blows onto his head.

With each punch he landed, Fletcher could feel his strength waning. The wild chase through the woods, two brutal beatings and hardly any sleep for the last four nights had robbed him of a lot of his natural energy and power. But adrenaline kept him punching. Jimmy's face might be a bloody mess. But until Fletcher landed a knockout blow, Jimmy wasn't done.

Rather than try to cover his unprotected head and face, Jimmy was using his superior strength against Fletcher. Because he was flat on his back, he couldn't get any real power into his punches, yet he could still land some telling ones. The first counterpunch Jimmy threw by raising his left arm above his head and swinging it down like he was chopping wood.

Fletcher had time to see the punch coming and he ducked back, allowing the blow to land on his chest. Another of Fletcher's punches landed on Jimmy's face, his knuckles crushing an already broken nose.

Jimmy landed his next punch. Rather than try the same failing tactic again, he'd swung this punch from the outside of his body, where he could put the full power of his muscles into the blow. His fist crashed into Fletcher's side, the top knuckles hitting ribs that were already damaged; the bottom knuckles driving into the soft tissue and muscles that protected internal organs.

The punch was enough to rock Fletcher. Jimmy went to repeat the move, but Fletcher saw it coming and blocked the punch with his forearm. Instead of opening himself up to more of Jimmy's hammering punches, Fletcher tried a different tactic.

Their foreheads collided with a crump. Jimmy came off worst, his eyes went glassy, so Fletcher coiled back and thrust his head a second time.

He got the same connection as before. Jimmy's eyes remained glassy. He wasn't finished though; his arms snaked around Fletcher's chest and then constricted.

Fletcher's damaged ribs screamed a silent protest that grew ever louder in his ears as Jimmy's powerful arms squeezed. Breaths were getting harder with every passing second.

Jimmy had made a mistake though; he'd circled his arms below Fletcher's meaning Fletcher could still fight back.

Fletcher thudded fist after fist into Jimmy's face without success. The man's greater power was working to his advantage. With every exhaled breath, Fletcher's chest was being constricted that little bit tighter. His blows were growing weaker and because he was chest to chest with Jimmy, he couldn't get as much force into his punches as before.

Regardless of the damage Fletcher was doing to his face, Jimmy's grip around his chest hadn't lessened. His breaths were becoming ever more shallow, the edges of his vision was fading, and he knew that before long he'd pass out or that one of the broken ribs that were screaming inside his constricted chest would pierce a lung. He'd be done for if that happened.

There was only one thing left Fletcher could do, one way he could stop Jimmy from crushing the life out of him. He laid one hand on Jimmy's chin and the other at the back of his head.

Jimmy must have grasped what was about to happen; his neck muscles tensed as he tried to twist against Fletcher's hands.

Fletcher didn't hesitate. Didn't think of Rachel. Just of Wendy. By snapping Jimmy's neck he'd get to see his daughter again.

A last gasp heave. A familiar crunk and Jimmy's grip on Fletcher's chest went slack.

Fletcher rolled onto his back and sucked in beautiful lungfuls of woodland air. In other circumstances, the air might have seemed earthy or laden with the scents of rotting leaves. At this moment in time, it was the sweetest thing Fletcher had ever tasted.

Once he had his breathing under control, Fletcher picked himself up and looked round to see where the quad had ended up.

It was some ten yards away. Beside it stood Trench with a coiled rope in his left hand.

Trench gave Fletcher a brief nod and then raised his right hand in a military salute. Instinct and reflex made Fletcher's right arm snap upwards, the long-ago-learned mantra about how to deliver a salute still fresh in his ears. Long way up, short way down.

Fletcher walked to the quad as Trench stepped behind a tree and disappeared back to his own life without a word.

The salute had been enough for Fletcher. As had the way Trench had downed Jimmy and allowed Fletcher to catch him.

Fletcher gunned the quad and set off back towards the Blackett house. Such had been his focus on preventing Jimmy from escaping, he had no idea if Quadrado had been able to get the others out of the cellar. There was also the fact that he'd have to face the music for his actions.

CHAPTER SEVENTY-FIVE

Fletcher eased himself off the hard bed and began another round of exercises. Push-ups, squats and sit-ups wouldn't stop the thoughts whirling around his brain. On the other hand, they'd give his body some exercise.

Any kind of movement still caused his various injuries to make themselves known to him. Fletcher wasn't prepared to let such minor things as aches and pains stop him trying to distract himself from the boredom of being locked in a police cell for two straight days. He'd asked for a lawyer and been given one. The guy had been competent, if disinterested. All the same, the FBI had his fingerprints all over the quad and Jimmy's clothes. His and Jimmy's blood had been found in each other's clothes and he'd made no bones about pursuing Jimmy with the intention of bringing him to Quadrado so she could arrest him. Fletcher had known all along the forensic evidence would be against him.

All he had going for him in terms of acquitting evidence would be the testimonies of Quadrado and the other prisoners. In retrospect, he should have let Jimmy escape and trusted in the police to apprehend him. That wasn't how he was built though. When he was involved in the start of something, he stayed involved until it was finished.

There was no escaping one simple fact though. He'd killed a man, and the FBI had more than enough evidence to prove it. For all his efforts to save the prisoners' lives had earned him credit, the deficit from taking a life would outweigh his honorable actions.

The FBI agents who'd grilled him had shown him courtesy and respect, although they'd pulled wry faces at each other when he'd tried to pass off Jimmy's broken neck as a by-product of their fight rather than his reason for chasing after the man.

For all the quiet respect the agents had shown him, there was only one way they allowed information to flow. Time after time, Fletcher had tried to get answers to the questions that were plaguing his mind. Not once was he successful in finding out why the prisoners had been taken or what was behind the mysterious fourth door in the cellar.

Fletcher heard the rattle of keys and figured the guard was coming to get him. That could mean anything. Either he was in for another round of questioning, or Rachel's father had arrived with Wendy. As much as he wanted to see his daughter, he was also dreading her reaction to seeing his battered and bruised face. Wendy had never believed in violence as a solution to anything, and she despaired at the news on a daily basis whenever it reported on conflicts around the world or a local person who'd been attacked for the usual lack of good reason. Perhaps it was because both her parents had joined up that made her anti-war, or maybe losing her mother at an early age had made her more worried about anything which might deprive her of her father. Whichever it was, Fletcher knew he'd let her down by getting himself into situations that had ended up putting him in this cell.

The crisp tread of the custody officer's boots was accompanied by the pock of heels.

Quadrado came into view. Her hands were empty and there was a business-like air about her. When he scanned over her body, Fletcher saw no weapons protruding from the waistband of her pants. Nor was there anything tucked under her shirt.

It stood to reason that she was unarmed. Quadrado might be an FBI agent, but in the eyes of the custody sergeant, she'd just be someone else not to be trusted not to put a weapon into a prisoner's hands, be the action deliberate or after being attacked by a prisoner.

"Fletcher."

"Special Agent Quadrado." If she was prepared to dance around the subject before getting to the point, he'd not show her his worry by getting to the point.

"How are your injuries?"

Fletcher gave a low shrug. "I try to think of them as discomforts rather than injuries. The word injury suggests that I might not be able to continue moving as normal. I have no injuries that prevent me moving." He gave a tight grin to rob his words of any offense she might imagine. "On the other hand, my discomforts mean moving is a damn sight more painful than it ought to be."

Fletcher's grin was returned with enough interest for the bottom of Quadrado's teeth to show. "So you're still playing the tough guy?"

"Tried playing the smart guy once. Made a hash of it so I reverted to my genetic type."

"You're smarter than you think." The smile had gone as Quadrado prepared to get to her point. "I can think of at least three questions that have been bugging you ever since you were arrested."

"Only three?"

Fletcher knew that playing dumb wouldn't work with Quadrado, yet he couldn't help goading her a little. There were actually several questions he was desperate for answers to, and the way she was drawing things out was starting to needle him.

"There are more, but there's three you keep coming back to. The first is obvious, you want to know if you're going to stand trial for the murder of Jimmy Blackett, or whether the charges will be dropped in light of how you saved us all. I can't answer that. I've very much been kept out of that side of the investigation as, technically, I'm a witness like you."

Fletcher sat down on his bunk and looked at Quadrado through the bars of his cell. "The next question?"

"Why were the prisoners taken?" Fletcher gave a nod to show it was on his list. Quadrado's face took on a different look. Part sorrow, part grief, accompanied by a lot of righteous fury. "It seems the Blacketts were selling them on the dark web. When their electronic communication equipment was searched, we found the advertisements." A look of intense disgust covered Quadrado's face. "We also found videos of the prisoners' fates. They'd be auctioned on the dark web and then their purchaser would visit the cellar. If they'd been bought for sexual purposes, they'd be in the bedroom you saw."

"What other purposes were the hostages being bought for?"

"The sickest snuff movies you can imagine. The room we couldn't get into. That was a full-on dungeon, complete with torture instruments. The hostages who went into that room were beaten, scalded, whipped and a dozen other horrible things before they died. Every one of them died horribly. Most of the movies featured female victims, but I was told two men had also been filmed being tortured to death." Quadrado's voice wavered, threatening to crack as she imparted this information.

Fletcher didn't say anything. What was there to say? The horrors in his mind were already playing out the deaths in that room. He knew a bit about the dark web, how it was the part of the internet that was the least traceable and the most disgusting. It was where people went to look at child pornography, snuff movies, hire assassins and a dozen other things no decent human being would contemplate.

Finally his brain rid itself of the horrors long enough to question the Blacketts' motives for doing such horrific things. "Why? Surely they didn't need the money, the lumber mill would be making them a nice sum."

"Actually, they did. It was Duke Jackson who laid it all out for us. Apparently the Blacketts had been screwing the IRS for years with the help of their accountant and their attorney."

Fletcher could join the rest of the dots for himself. "Let me guess: either the attorney or accountant extorted the Blacketts, who started this new line as a way of making sure their lifestyle wasn't affected."

"It was the attorney. According to Duke, he was getting greedier and greedier. Hence the escalation from the Blacketts in terms of the number of victims they took. Duke also told us the Blacketts would have killed the attorney, except he had a file in a safety deposit box as insurance should anything nasty happen to him or his family."

"Sounds like the attorney had it all sewn up."

"He did." Quadrado raised her eyes to the ceiling. "He's been arrested, but from what I hear about his health, he'll not live long enough to stand trial."

Other questions were begging to be asked. "What about the folks who bought the hostages? Have you been able to trace them? And what about the accountants, can you get them as well?" In Fletcher's mind, the purchasers were as bad as the Blacketts. They were the ones who bought human beings for the sole purpose of acting out their depraved fantasies.

"We've gotten one or two of the purchasers already and are doing everything we can to get the others. We'll get them. It may take years, but we'll get them. As I understand it, the attorney and accountant are currently pleading the fifth, but there are a whole bunch of forensic accountants examining their books, so we're sure to get them in the end, although it might not be a quick process."

"And my third question? What do you think that is?"

Puzzlement crossed Quadrado's eyes. "I had the mystery room as your third question."

"It was, but there are more. Are the folks we got out okay? And other than the snuff movies, did you find any trace of the previous missing persons you were looking for?"

"The short answer is they are and we did." A huffed breath. "The survivors will probably be seeing therapists for years, but other than being malnourished, they were physically unharmed when they were put into ambulances. As for the others, we found them in the well. The water was ten feet below the cellar floor and at least thirty deep." An involuntary shudder jostled Quadrado's shoulders. "When we sent a diver in, he found two rotting corpses and a whole lot of skeletons that were all tangled up with each other."

Fletcher closed his eyes and offered up an entreaty for the victims of the Blacketts. It would take time before their remains could be released to their families. Yet there would come a point when all the bones had been identified and the case against the Blacketts was over. Then, and only then, would the families who'd been affected be able to lay their loved ones to rest and say their final goodbyes.

"What about the Blacketts?"

"They are all in custody. Jimmy and Chuck are dead, of course, and Miss Constance is under guard in a hospital bed. She'll survive and will stand trial once we've got all the evidence compiled. So far only Duke is talking, but we've got enough on them to proceed without getting confessions from them all."

"That's good. Did you find out anything about Trench? Without him, I might never have caught up with Jimmy Blackett."

Quadrado nodded. "Trench is in the clear. When Duke spilled his guts, he told how it was Trench's father who'd killed the teacher. Other than a minor charge of causing injury to Jimmy, there's nothing against him and there's no intention to pursue him for that."

A set of keys being rattled made Quadrado look over her shoulder.

"Looks like you better go."

"Yeah." A hesitant pause. "Thank you, Fletcher. I'd have ended up in that well without you. Please know that I'm doing everything I can to make sure that your charges are dropped." A first step away was followed by another pause. "One last thing. Your friend Lila, she's back with her father and her boyfriend. From what Duke told us, taking her was a mistake. The Blackett boys were supposed to snatch another woman, but she left before they arrived, and they mistakenly thought Lila was their target. She was the only person they'd snatched who was traveling with someone else. Apparently either Duke or Agnes at the diner would select the victims and summon the Blackett boys who'd do the snatch. I also learned the Blacketts had spread rumors around Daversville that the girls were going to Trench as a way of getting him to leave the townsfolk alone."

Fletcher nodded his thanks as there was no need for words. It was good to know Lila was back in the bosom of her family. It was the only place he wanted to be. Quadrado would fight for him, he was sure of that. Or she would until her inner FBI agent kicked in and she factored into her calculations that Jimmy Blackett's neck had been the second he'd broken as a civilian.

He settled down, opened his locket and thought of his daughter as he looked at her picture; while she wouldn't suffer any physical harm, it looked very much like she would still be a victim of the whole sorry mess, as she'd lose her father for an as yet undetermined number of years.

CHAPTER SEVENTY-SIX

Geoffrey Elliott looked around the table. The assembled men and women were among the most powerful intelligence operatives in the United States. There were the directors of the CIA, Homeland Security, NSA and one or two other shadowy agencies. Elliott was director of the FBI and he'd called the meeting.

While the agencies were often rivals when it came to funding and other administrative issues, he'd been able to nurture relationships with his opposite numbers so that when the agencies had to cooperate, it was done with respect and civility rather than the backstabbing ways of their predecessors.

It was Elliott who'd assembled all the directors and chosen the discreet meeting place, and his team who'd swept the room for listening devices.

Every one of the directors had surrendered their phones, tablets and any other electronic devices they might be carrying. They'd all been checked for wires. None had objected; mistrust was a common thing and while Elliott had only intimated at his reason for calling the meeting, the others carried the same concerns he did; therefore any measures he felt protected him would also protect them.

Elliott wasn't a natural orator, his rise to the FBI directorship hadn't been earned by fancy speeches that undermined his political opponents. He'd gotten the job because he was a good, honest man who worked hard and put others before himself. His way was to say what he thought needed said, then deal with questions from those he'd spoken to.

"Thanks for coming, everyone. I've called this meeting for a very specific reason. There's a subject we've all talked about. Often jokingly, but I think we all know it isn't a joke. Well, I believe I may have solved our problems and found a solution. It's one with the right level of plausible deniability and the right skill set to get the job done."

"Let me get this right so there's no misunderstanding." The CIA director was a tough woman who liked everything spelled out with a crystalline clarity. "You're talking about an expendable operative to deal with problems where we can't be seen to get involved for political, security or legal reasons?"

"That's right." Elliott looked at the faces studying his own. They were listening with keen intent. "I take it you're all aware of that business down in Georgia?" Every head nodded. "One of my agents was involved and the guy she ended up working with is our man. He's resourceful, tough and not afraid to kill if necessary. He's a Brit who has US citizenship. An ex-Royal Marine, in fact."

The NSA director gave Elliott a look that was asking permission to speak. "I trust you've had him researched. Who is he? What about his family? What makes you think he'll do what we ask of him?"

Elliott smiled, showing expensive dental work. "His name is Grant Fletcher. His wife died in an automobile accident fourteen years ago. He has a daughter who'll be looking to go to college in a couple of years. He's raised her himself and his social media feeds don't suggest he's dated since his wife's death. The daughter is college smart, but not quite smart enough to get a scholarship. Fletcher's finances, and those of his immediate family, aren't strong enough to put her through college. We, of course, can make that happen for him. Yale, Harvard, Princeton. With our connections, whichever one she chooses, we can get her in."

"So he's got a daughter who he'll want to do the best for, but why does that mean he'll risk his life for us? Surely he'll want to be around to see her grow up and live the life she's meant to?" The CIA director had allowed scorn to creep into her voice.

"Of course he will. However, he's currently sitting in a cell in an Atlanta police station with a charge of first-degree homicide hanging over his head. For those who can't recall whether or not Georgia has the death penalty, it does. I have also looked into his discharge from the Royal Marines. All classified, of course, but I got enough info to see the bigger picture. A mission in Helmand went south and Fletcher and six others had to fight their way out from behind enemy lines. They were there for six days with no food and only the weapons they'd carried in with them and no support. Fletcher was the only one to come back and it was a miracle he survived. In the normal course of things he'd have been hailed as a hero were it not for his reaction when he got back to camp. I was told it took eight men to pull him off the colonel whose mistakes led to Fletcher and the others being left behind. Reading between the lines, he was cashiered out to save everyone the embarrassment of a court martial. He's what we're looking for, and with the layers of separation we'll create, there's no way he'll ever know who's pulling his strings. The FBI agent who was sent to Georgia will be his handler. She's young, ambitious, and very keen to not have the Georgia fiasco hinder her upward trajectory. Naturally, this all plays into our hands." Elliott held each pair of eyes in the room until he felt confident they were on board with what he was proposing. "I think I have covered everything, so I suggest we take a vote. If we *all* agree, then we'll have the expendable asset we've been looking for with the necessary levels of plausibly deniability."

When Elliott raised his own hand to indicate his vote, every hand in the room lifted, sealing Fletcher's fate as a blunt instrument for whichever agency didn't want to risk their own people.

A LETTER FROM JOHN

Thank you, dear reader, for getting this far. If you enjoyed *First Shot*, and want to keep up to date with all my latest releases, just sign up at the following link. Your email address will never be shared, and you can unsubscribe at any time.

www.bookouture.com/john-ryder

I had an absolute ball creating and writing about Fletcher and Quadrado's first outing. For me the world is a better place for having characters like Fletcher in it as he's someone who's not afraid to do the things that terrify the rest of us.

I chose the setting of Georgia as I wanted to set this story somewhere it was plausible a town could be held in a time warp. This is no slight on the good people of Georgia, but merely a reflection of the isolation of some Georgian towns.

I do hope those readers who were horrified at Fletcher's backstory can forgive him for what he did for Wendy. It really was an act of love, and, as he can't forgive himself, he's going to need your help.

While I believe Quadrado's presence brings a subtle balance to Fletcher's escapades, I do feel that this is only the beginning for the two of them, and hope you'll join me in observing their future now Fletcher is under the control of Geoffrey Elliott.

I hope you loved *First Shot*, and if you did I would be very grateful if you could write a review. I'd love to hear what you think, and it makes such a difference helping new readers to discover one of my books for the first time.

I always enjoy hearing from my readers—you can get in touch on my Facebook page, Twitter, Goodreads or my website.

Thanks,
John

JohnRyderAuthor

@JohnRyder101

johnryderauthor.com

ACKNOWLEDGMENTS

My thanks as always go to my family and friends for their constant support of my writing.

To Isobel Akenhead, my editor, for showing great faith in me and for making my stories better every time she picks up her red pen. I'd also like to thank the whole publicity and marketing team at Bookouture for the sterling work they've done getting my book noticed.

To Tom Cain, whose Samuel Carver novel, *Revenger*, inspired Fletcher's backstory. Tom was gracious in accepting my desire to pick up the baton he'd carried so ably. I'm damned lucky to have Tom as a friend as well as a source of inspiration. Such is my gratitude to him, his name will be on the first copy I sign.

A special thanks goes to my beta readers and the bloggers who take time out of their busy lives to support me and my writing. Words cannot express how grateful I am.

Thanks go to the whole crime writing community for their generosity in accepting me among their ranks and their continued support. A special mention to the Crime and Publishment gang, without whom I might never have come this far.

A final word of thanks goes to you, dear reader, as without readers I'd be a lonely typist who's not very good at typing.